SNARE OF SERPENTS

VICTORIA HOLT

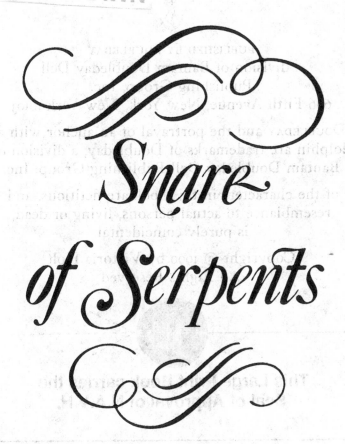

Snare

of Serpents

LARGE PRINT BOOK CLUB EDITION

DOUBLEDAY

New York • London • Toronto • Sydney • Auckland

PUBLISHED BY DOUBLEDAY
a division of Bantam Doubleday Dell
Publishing Group, Inc.
666 Fifth Avenue, New York, New York 10103

DOUBLEDAY and the portrayal of an anchor with a
dolphin are trademarks of Doubleday, a division of
Bantam Doubleday Dell Publishing Group, Inc.

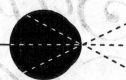

**This Large Print Book carries the
Seal of Approval of N.A.V.H.**

Printed in the United States of America

Quality Printing and Binding by:
Berryville Graphics
P.O. Box 272
Berryville, VA 22611 U.S.A.

Edinburgh

A Thief in the House

I HAD NEVER SEEN ANYONE look less like a governess. I was watching from a window when she arrived. She stood for a moment looking up at the house and I saw her face clearly. Her reddish hair—Titian, I think it was called—was visible under a black hat with a green feather. That air of genteel poverty which her predecessor, Lilias Milne, had had in common with most of her kind was completely lacking. There was a flamboyant quality about this woman. She looked as if she were about to join some theatrical group instead of coming to teach the daughter of one of Edinburgh's most respected citizens.

Moreover Hamish Vosper, son of the coachman, had been ordered to take the carriage to the station to meet her. It was too long ago for me to remember the arrival of Lilias Milne, but I was sure she had not been brought here by the family carriage. Hamish helped her out of the vehicle as though she were an important guest; then he collected her baggage—of which there was a considerable amount—and brought her to the front door.

At that point I went down to the hall. Mrs. Kirkwell, the housekeeper, was already there.

"It's the new governess," she said to me.

The governess was standing in the hall. She had very green eyes, their colour no doubt accentuated by the green feather in her hat and the silk scarf at her throat; but what made her face so startling were the dark brows and eyelashes which contrasted vividly with the colour of her hair; she had a short rather pert nose with a long upper lip which gave her a playful kittenish look. The full red lips made another contrast; they revealed slightly prominent teeth which suggested an eagerness, a greediness for what—I was only just sixteen— I was not quite sure.

She was looking straight at me and I felt I was being closely scrutinised.

"You must be Davina," she said.

"Yes, I am," I answered.

The green eyes were speculative. "We're going to get along," she said, in a coy voice which did not quite match the look she gave me.

I knew she was not Scottish.

My father had spoken of her only briefly. He had said: "There will be a new governess. I myself engaged her so I am sure she will give satisfaction."

I had been dismayed. I did not want another governess. I should be seventeen soon and I thought it was time I finished with governesses. Moreover I was still very upset by what had happened to Lilias Milne. She had been with me for eight years and we had become good friends. I could not believe that she was guilty of what they had accused her.

Mrs. Kirkwell was saying: "Perhaps you'd like to show Miss . . . er . . ."

"Grey," said the governess. "Zillah Grey."

Zillah! What a strange name for a governess! And why did she tell us? Why not say just Miss Grey? It had been a long time before I discovered that Miss Milne was Lilias.

I took her to her room and she stood beside

me looking round, studying it intently as a few moments before she had studied me.

"Very nice," she said. She turned her luminous eyes on me. "I think I am going to be very happy here."

THE EVENTS which had led up to the arrival of Miss Zillah Grey had been dramatic and the fact that they had burst so unexpectedly into our peaceful existence made them more so.

It began that morning when I went into my mother's bedroom and found her dead. After that, a sinister influence began to creep into the house—vaguely, insidiously at first until it culminated in the tragedy which threatened to ruin my life.

I had risen that morning as usual and was coming down to breakfast when I met Kitty McLeod, our parlourmaid, on the stairs.

"I cannot get an answer from Mrs. Glentyre," she said. "I've knocked two or three times. I dinna like to go in without her saying so."

"I'll come with you," I said.

We went up the stairs to the master bedroom which for the last year or so my mother had occupied alone, for she had not been in good health and my father sometimes was away on business until late and, not wanting to disturb her, he occupied the room next to hers. There were even nights when he could not get home at all.

I knocked. There was no answer so I went into the room. It was a very pleasant one. There was a large double bed with highly polished brass knobs and flounces which matched the curtains. It had tall windows from which one could look out onto the grey stone, dignified houses on the other side of the wide street.

I went to the bed and there lay my mother —white and very still—with a look of tranquility on her face.

I knew that she was dead.

I turned to Kitty who was standing beside me and said: "Get Mr. Kirkwell at once."

Kirkwell the butler was there almost immediately with Mrs. Kirkwell beside him.

"We'll send for the doctor," he said.

We were shocked and stunned, but we could only wait for the arrival of the doctor.

When he came he told us that she had died in her sleep. "It was very peaceful," he said, "and not unexpected."

We could not send for my father because we

did not know where he was. We believed he was on a business trip to Glasgow, but that was too vague. He returned later that day.

I had never seen such horror in any face as I saw in his when he heard the news. Strangely enough I had just a fleeting fancy that I detected a look of guilt.

It would be because he had not been at home when it happened, of course. But could he blame himself for that?

THEN THE CHANGE set in.

I had lived the sixteen years of my life in an orderly fashion and could never have suspected that it would change so drastically. I learned that peace, security, happiness, when we have them, are taken for granted and we do not value them highly enough until we have lost them.

Looking back, there is so much to remember: a roomy comfortable house where warm fires appeared as soon as the cold winds of autumn reminded us that winter was on the way. I had no need to fear the cold. I enjoyed the stimulation of going out walking in warm gaiters, coat tipped with fur at the neck and sleeves, woollen muffler, gloves and a fur muff for added protection. There was the knowledge that I was a member of one of the most highly respected families in Edinburgh.

My father was head of a bank in Princes Street, and I always felt a glow of pride when I walked past it. When I was very young I thought that all the money which went into the bank was his. It was a wonderful thing to be a Glentyre—member of such an illustrious family. My father was David Ross Glentyre and I have been named Davina which was the nearest they could get to David. If I had been a boy, which I supposed they would have preferred, I should have been called David. But there was never a boy; my mother had been too delicate to risk a second childbirth.

Such memories there were for me in that house which had become one of mourning.

Until a year or so before her death my mother and I had often ridden out in the carriage to the shops or to visit friends. Much homage was shown to her in all the big shops. Men in black coats came hurrying forward rubbing their hands in unctuous delight because she had deigned to visit them. "When would you like this sent, Mrs. Glentyre? Of course, of course, we can get it to the house today. And Miss Davina . . . quite the young lady now." It was all very gratifying.

We would visit friends—people as comfortably situated as ourselves, living in similar houses. We would take tea, bannocks and Dundee cake and I would sit and listen docilely to the accounts of the trials and triumphs of our neighbours; and sometimes there would be hints—although only hints because of my presence, with pursed lips seeming to hold back words which threatened to escape and so sully my ears—that there were fascinating details to come at a more suitable time.

How I loved driving along the Royal Mile from the castle on the rock to that most delightful of all palaces, Holyrood House. Once I had been inside the palace. I had stood in the room where Rizzio had been murdered at the feet of Queen Mary; I had shivered and dreamed of it for months afterwards. It was all so frighteningly wonderful.

Every Sunday I went to church with my mother and with my father if he was not away. In that case my mother and I went alone and after the service we would pause outside the church to chat with friends before we got into the carriage which Vosper, the coachman, would have waiting for us. Then we would drive through the streets with their Sunday quietness to the house and Sunday lunch.

That would have been a solemn occasion but for my mother; she laughed a good deal and could be a trifle irreverent about the sermon; when she talked about people she had a way of imitating them so accurately that it was as though they themselves were speaking. She did this affectionately rather than maliciously; and we were very amused. Even my father allowed his lips to twitch and Kirkwell would put his hand discreetly to his lips to hide a smile; Kitty would smirk and my father would look with mild reproach at my mother who only laughed.

My father was a very solemn man, very religious and anxious that everyone in the house should be the same. He conducted prayers every morning in the library when he was at home, and all must attend, except my mother. She had been told by the doctor that she needed rest, so she did not rise until ten o'clock.

After church Sunday lunches would be going on in all those tall granite houses. Most of them would have the requisite number of servants, similar to ours. We had Mr. and Mrs. Kirkwell, Kitty, Bess and the tweeny. Then there were the Vospers. They did not live in the house but had their own quarters in the mews where the horses and carriage were kept. There were Mr. and Mrs. Vosper and Hamish their son. Hamish was about twenty. He helped his father and if old Vosper was not able to drive the carriage, Hamish did.

There was something about Hamish which puzzled me. He was very dark-haired with eyes which were almost black. Mrs. Kirkwell said: "There's more than a touch of insolence about young Hamish. He seems to have a notion he's a cut above the rest of us."

He certainly swaggered. He was tallish and broad; he towered above his father and Mr. Kirkwell, and had a habit of lifting one eyebrow and the side of his mouth at the same time as he surveyed people. It made him appear supercilious, as though he were looking down on us because he knew so much more than we did.

My father seemed to like him. He said he had a way with horses, and he rather preferred the younger Vosper to the elder when it came to driving the carriage.

I loved those sessions when my mother and I were alone and we talked. She was fascinated by what she called the olden days and talked of them constantly. Her eyes would glow with excitement when she discussed the conflicts with our enemy below the border. She grew passionate about the great William Wallace who had stood against the mighty Edward when he had wreaked such harm on our country that he was known in history as the Hammer of the Scots.

"Great Wallace was captured." Her eyes would glow with anger and then with bitter sorrow. "They hanged and quartered him at Smithfield . . . like a common traitor."

Then there was Bonnie Prince Charlie and the tragedy of Culloden; there was the triumph of Bannockburn; and, of course, the ill-fated and ever romantic Mary Queen of Scots.

Enchanted afternoons they were and I could not bear to think that they had gone forever.

How I loved our grey city—so austere and so beautiful when the sun shone on the grey stone buildings. Such a comfortable, cosy life that was. The affairs of the household ran smoothly, or if they did not it never reached our ears but was sorted out by the excellent

Kirkwells. Meals were always on time. Prayers when my father was in residence, with everyone except my mother and the Vospers attending. The Vospers were excused, of course, because they did not live in the house. I was sure no prayer ritual was conducted in the mews rooms.

Until I was fourteen I had taken my meals with Miss Milne. After that I joined my parents. It was as I was beginning to grow up that I became such good friends with Lilias Milne. I learned a great deal about her, and it was through her that I understood something of the precarious and often humiliating life these ladies were forced to live. I was glad Lilias had come to us. So was she.

"Your mother is a lady in every sense of the word," she said on one occasion. "She has never made me feel that I am a sort of servant. When I first came here she asked me questions about my family and I could see at once that she understood and cared. She took an interest in other people; she saw what their lives were like and could put herself in their places. She always tried not to hurt people in any way. That's what I call a lady."

"Oh, I am so glad you came, Lilias," I said.

I was calling her Lilias then when we were alone. I reserved Miss Milne for when we were not. I was sure Mrs. Kirkwell would have objected to my use of the governess's Christian name—my father, too. My mother would not have cared.

Lilias told me about her family who lived in England in the county of Devon.

"I was one of six," she said. "All girls. It would have been better if some of us had been boys, although, of course, they would have had to be expensively educated. We were really very poor. We had the big house to keep up. It was always cold and draughty. How I love these warm fires here. You need them up here, of course, where it is so much colder. But in the house I'm warm. That's what I like."

"Tell me about the vicarage."

"Big . . . draughty . . . right close to the church. The church is ancient, as so many of them are, and there is always something going wrong. Deathwatch beetle, woodworm and leaking roof. We have it all. It's beautiful though. It's in the heart of Lakemere, which is one of our English villages, with the old church, the cottages and the manor house. You don't have them up here. You notice the difference as soon as you cross the border. I love the English villages."

"And the draughty old vicarage? You must admit it's warmer in our house."

"I do. I do. I appreciate it. Then I say to myself, how long? That's something I have to face, Davina. How much longer will you be needing a governess? I've been wondering that for a long time. They will send you away to school, I suppose."

"They won't now. Perhaps I'll get married and you can be governess to my children."

"That's a little way ahead," she said wryly.

She was ten years older than I and I had been eight when she came to us. I was her first pupil.

She told me about life before she came.

"Six girls," she said. "We always knew we should have to earn a living if we did not get married. We couldn't all stay at home. The two eldest, Grace and Emma, did marry. Grace to a clergyman and Emma to a solicitor. I was next and then there were Alice, Mary and Jane. Mary became a missionary. She's out in Africa somewhere. Alice and Jane stayed at home to help keep house, for my mother had died."

"And you came here. I'm glad you did, Lilias."

Our friendship was growing closer. I, too, was afraid that one day my father would decide that I was no longer in need of a governess. When would that be? When I was seventeen? That was not far-off.

Lilias had come near to marriage once. She talked of it sadly, nostalgically. But her lover had "never spoken."

"I suppose it was all implication," I said. "How did you know he might . . . speak?"

"He was fond of me. He was the son of the squire of Lakemere, the younger son. It would have been a good match for the vicar's daughter. He had a fall when he was riding. It crippled him very badly. He lost the use of his legs."

"Didn't you go to him? Didn't you tell him that you would look after him forevermore?"

She was silent, looking back into the past. "He hadn't spoken. Nobody knew how it was, you see. There would have been opposition, I daresay. What could I do?"

"I would have gone to him. I would have done the speaking."

She smiled at me indulgently. "A woman cannot do that."

"Why not?" I demanded.

"Because . . . she has to wait to be asked. He wouldn't ask me, would he . . . when he was in that state? It couldn't be. It was ordained."

"By whom?"

"By God. By Fate. By Destiny . . . whatever you like to call it."

"I wouldn't have allowed it. I would have gone to him and told him I would marry him."

"You have much to learn, Davina," she said, and I retorted: "Then teach me."

"There are some things," she said, "which people have to learn through experience."

I thought a good deal about Lilias and I sometimes wondered whether it was the idea of being married, of not having to be a governess, always wondering when she would be looking for another post in a strange household, that she had been in love with . . . rather than with the man.

I was growing very fond of her, and I knew she was of me and, during those weeks before my mother died, her fear of what the future held drew her close to me—and after my mother's death we were more friendly than ever.

But I was growing up. I was facing facts and I knew that Lilias would not be in the house much longer.

Nanny Grant had left only a short time before. She had gone to live with a cousin in the country. Her departure had saddened me deeply. She had been my mother's nurse and had stayed with her until her marriage and then she had come to this house and eventually nannied me. We had been very close in those early days. She was the one who had comforted me when I had my nightmares and fell and hurt myself. There would always be memories of those days. When the snow came she would take me out into the garden at the back between the mews and the house, patiently sitting on a seat while I made a snowman. I remembered her suddenly picking me up and crying: "That'll do. Do you want to turn your old nanny into a snowman? Look at you now. Your eyes are dancing at the thought. Ye're a wee villain, that's what ye are."

I remember those rainy days when we sat at

the window waiting for it to clear up so that we could go out. We would sing together:

> *Rainy rainy rattle stanes*
> *Dinna rain on me*
> *Rain on John o' Groaties' hoose*
> *Far across the sea.*

And now Nanny Grant had gone, leaving those wonderful memories—all part of a life over which a shutter was drawn on that tragic day I had gone into my mother's room and found her dead.

"MOURNING FOR A DAUGHTER is a year," announced Mrs. Kirkwell. "For us I reckon it should be from three to six months. Six for Mr. Kirkwell and me. Three months will be enough for the maids."

How I hated my black clothes. Every time I put them on I was reminded of my mother lying dead in her bed.

Nothing was the same. Sometimes I had a feeling that we were waiting for something to happen, waiting to emerge from our mourning. Lilias, I knew, was waiting for the summons to my father's presence to be told that as

I was growing up her services would no longer be needed.

As for my father, he was away more than ever. I was glad of this. I dreaded meals with him. We were both too conscious of that empty chair.

Not that he had ever been communicative. He had always seemed encased in a demeanour of formality. My mother, though, had been able to break through it. I thought of how his lips twitched when he felt amusement which he tried hard to suppress. I guessed he had cared for her deeply, which was strange because she was so different from him. She would have thrust aside the conventions to which he adhered so strongly. I remembered his gently reproaching voice when she said something which he considered rather outrageous. "My dear . . . my dear . . ." I had heard him murmur, smiling in spite of himself. If it had been left to her, our household would have been a merry one.

Once my mother said: "Your father is a man of high principles, a good man. He tries so hard to live up to his high standards. Some- times I think it is more comfortable to set them slightly lower, so that one does not have to disappoint oneself."

I did not quite understand what she meant and when I asked her to explain she just laughed and said: "My mind's wandering. It's nothing . . ." Then she shrugged her shoulders and murmured: "Poor David."

I wondered why she should be pitying my father. But she would say no more on the subject.

Some three weeks after my mother's death my father's sister, Aunt Roberta, came to stay with us. She had been ill at the time of the funeral and unable to attend, but at this time she had recovered her good health.

She was quite unlike my father. He was a reserved man who kept aloof from us. Not so Aunt Roberta. Her voice could be heard all over the house, high-pitched and authoritative. She surveyed us all with the utmost disapproval.

She was unmarried. Mrs. Kirkwell, who greatly resented her presence in the house, said she was not surprised that Miss Glentyre had not been able to find a man bold enough to take her on.

Aunt Roberta announced that she had come

to us because my father, having lost his wife, would need a woman to supervise his household. As my mother had never supervised anything this was unacceptable from the start. Moreover it sent shivers of apprehension through the house, for it implied that Aunt Roberta intended to make her stay a permanent one.

From the moment she arrived she began to disrupt the household. Resentment was brewing, and it occurred to me that the servants might soon be looking for new places.

"It's a good thing that Mr. Kirkwell is a patient man," Mrs. Kirkwell told Lilias, who imparted the information to me. Lilias added: "I really think that, comfortable as they have all been here, this might be too much for them."

How I wished she would go.

My father, fortunately, was less patient than Mr. Kirkwell. There was an acid conversation between them one evening at dinner.

The conversation was about me.

"You should remember, David, that you have a daughter," began Roberta, helping herself from the dish of parsnips which Kitty was offering.

"It is something I am not likely to forget," retorted my father.

"She is growing up . . . fast."

"At the same rate, I have always thought, as others of her age."

"She needs looking after."

"She has a perfectly adequate governess. That, I believe, will suffice for a while."

"Governess!" snorted Aunt Roberta. "What do they know about launching a girl?"

"Launching?" I cried in dismay.

"I was not talking to you, Davina."

I felt angry that she should consider I was still at the stage of being seen but not heard, yet not too young for launching.

"You were talking about me," I retorted sharply.

"Oh dear me. What is the world coming to?"

"Roberta," said my father calmly. "You are welcome to stay here, but I cannot have you attempting to rule my household. It has always been efficiently managed, and I do not care to have it changed."

"I cannot understand you, David," said Aunt Roberta. "I think you forget . . ."

"It is you who forget that you are no longer

the elder sister. I know that you are two years older than I, and that may have had some significance when you were eight and I was six. But at this stage I do not need you to look after my household."

She was taken aback. She shrugged her shoulders philosophically with an air of resignation, murmuring: "The ingratitude of some people is beyond all understanding."

I thought she might have left the house then, but she seemed to persuade herself that, unappreciated as she was, it was her duty to steer us away from disaster.

Then something happened which shocked me deeply—as it did all of us—and made her decision for her.

Hamish was driving my father almost all the time now. The position in the mews had been reversed. It was not Hamish who now stood in when his father was otherwise engaged, but the father who was called when Hamish was not available. Hamish was swaggering more than ever. He made a habit of coming into the kitchen. He would sit in a chair at the table watching everyone . . . even me if I happened to be there. It was clear that Kitty, Bess and the tweeny found his

presence exciting; and he indulged in conde-
scending flirtation with them.

I could not understand why they liked him
so much. I thought his hairy arms were revolt-
ing. He seemed to find great pleasure in displaying them, and his sleeves were invariably
rolled up to the elbow so that he could stroke
his arms caressingly.

Mrs. Kirkwell regarded him with suspicion.
He had tried to be jolly with her, but without
success. He had a habit of laying his hands on
the girls which they seemed to like; but the
charm he exerted so easily over them did not
extend to Mrs. Kirkwell.

Once he touched her shoulder as she passed
and murmured: "You must have been a bonny
wench in your day, Mrs. K. A bit of a wee
handful, if you asked me . . . but perhaps
not so wee, eh?"

She replied with the utmost dignity: "I'd
thank you to remember who you are talking
to, Hamish Vosper."

At which he made cooing noises and said:
"So it's like that, is it? I've got to mind me
pints and quarts here, I can see."

"And I can't have you lying around in this
kitchen either," retorted Mrs. Kirkwell.

"Oh aye. But I'm waiting for the master, you see."

"Well, the sooner he sends for you the better in my opinion."

Lilias Milne came into the kitchen at that moment, I remember. She wanted to speak to Bess to ask her if she had seen a packet of pins on her table that morning. She had left them there and now they were gone. She thought Bess might have put them in with the rubbish.

I noticed that Hamish was watching her with a look of speculation—not as he looked at the young girls, but intently . . . differently.

IT WAS A FEW DAYS LATER when the trouble arose.

It began when I met Aunt Roberta on the stairs. It was after luncheon and I knew she had a rest in the afternoon. It was the one time when the house settled down to a peaceful quietness.

Aunt Roberta had been a little subdued since her altercation with my father, but she still supervised all that went on in the house and her eagle eye constantly alighted with disapproval on most things around her.

I was on the point of hastily returning to my room when she saw me.

"Oh, it's you, is it, Davina? You are dressed for going out?"

"Yes. Miss Milne and I often take a walk at this time of day."

She was about to pass some comment when she stopped suddenly, listening.

"Is anything wrong?" I asked.

She put her fingers to her lips and I went quietly to stand beside her.

"Listen," she whispered.

I heard the sound of a stifled laugh and strange noises. They were coming from behind one of the closed doors.

Aunt Roberta strode to that door and threw it open. I was standing beside her and I saw a sight which astonished me. The tangled bodies of Kitty and Hamish were on the bed and both of them were in a state of seminudity.

They started up. Kitty's face was scarlet and even Hamish looked a little taken aback.

I heard Aunt Roberta's quick intake of breath. Her first thoughts were for me. "Leave us, Davina," she cried.

But I could not move. I could only stare in fascination at the two on the bed.

Aunt Roberta advanced into the room.

"Disgusting . . . I never saw . . . you depraved . . ." She was spluttering, for once unable to find the words she needed.

Hamish had risen from the bed and began struggling into his clothes. He assumed an air of truculent bravado. He grinned at Aunt Roberta. "Well," he said, "it's only human nature, after all."

"You disgusting creature," she said. "Get out of this house. As for you . . ." She could not bring herself to say Kitty's name. "You . . . you slut. You'll pack your bags immediately and get out . . . get out, both of you."

Hamish shrugged his shoulders, but Kitty looked stunned. Her face, which had been as red as holly berries, was now as white as paper.

Aunt Roberta turned and almost fell on me.

"Davina! What is the world coming to? I told you to go. It is quite . . . disgusting. I knew something was going on in this house. As soon as your father comes in . . ."

I turned and fled. I shut myself in my room. I, too, was shocked. I felt nauseated. "Human nature," Hamish had said. I had never been so close to that sort of human nature before.

• • • •

THERE WAS SILENCE in the house. The servants had congregated in the kitchen. I pictured them sitting round the table whispering. Lilias came to my room.

"There is going to be trouble," she said. "And you were there."

I nodded.

"What did you see?"

"I saw the two of them . . . on the bed."

Lilias shivered.

"It was so repulsive," I said. "Hamish's legs are hairy . . . just like his arms."

"I suppose a man like that would have some sort of attraction for a girl like Kitty."

"What sort of attraction?"

"I don't know exactly, but I can see that he is . . . virile. He could be quite overpowering to a young girl. They'll dismiss her, of course. They'll dismiss both of them. I wonder where Kitty will go. And what will they do with him? He lives there . . . in the mews. There's going to be great trouble over this when your father comes home."

I could not forget Kitty's face. There had been such terrible fear there. She had been

with us for four years and had been fourteen
when she had come to us from the country.

"Where will she go?" I asked. Lilias shook
her head.

I knew that when my father came home
Aunt Roberta would insist that Kitty left. I
could not get out of my mind a picture of her
standing on the pavement surrounded by her
few possessions.

I went up to the room she shared with Bess
and Jenny the tweeny. She was there alone,
sent there by Aunt Roberta. She was sitting on
the bed looking desperately afraid.

I went in and sat beside her. She seemed like
a different person in her skirt and blouse from
that half-nude creature on the bed.

"Oh, Miss Davina, you shouldn't be here,"
she said. Then: "Is the master home?"

I shook my head. "Not yet."

"Her?" she asked.

"You mean my aunt? My father has made it
clear that she does not run the household."

"I'll have to go when he comes."

"How could you . . . do that?" I demanded. And added: "With him?"

She looked at me and shook her head. "You

don't understand, Miss Davina. It's natural like . . . with him."

"Human nature," I said, quoting him. "But it seems so . . ."

"Well, there's something about him."

"All that hair," I said with a shiver. "On his legs as well as his arms."

"Maybe . . ."

"Kitty, what will you do?"

She shook her head and started to cry.

"If they send you away . . . where will you go?"

"I just don't know, Miss."

"Could you go to your home?"

"It's miles away . . . near to John o' Groats. I came down because there's nothing for me up there. There's only me old dad now. He couldna keep me up there. There's nothing. I canna go back and tell him why."

"Then where, Kitty?"

"Perhaps the master will give me another chance," she said hopefully, but I could see she thought there was little chance of that.

I thought of his reading the Bible . . . all the little bits about the vengeance of the Lord, and it occurred to me that he would consider Kitty's sin too great for forgiveness. I had always liked Kitty. She had been jolly and merry. I wanted to help her. I had a money box in which I put the odd coin saved from my weekly pocket money. She could have what I had there. It was not much, and the problem was where could she go?

"You must go somewhere," I said.

She shook her head in despair.

What happened to girls who had sinned as Kitty had? They were driven out into the falling snow. There was no snow at this time, but that was small consolation.

I had heard of a nun being walled up for a similar offence. It appeared to be one of the greatest sins. Because of it some girls had babies and were shamed forever.

I did my best to comfort Kitty. I hoped my father would not come home that night, which would give her a little respite—time to think of some solution.

I went to Lilias and told her that I had been with Kitty and what a state of desolation she was in.

"She's a fool," said Lilias, "to behave so . . . and particularly with a man like Hamish. She can't be quite right in the head."

"She really is desperate, Lilias. She has nowhere to go."

"Poor girl."

"What will she do? She might kill herself. Lilias, what if she did? I should never forget that I hadn't helped her."

"What could you do?"

"I could give her the little money I have."

"I doubt that would last long."

"I went to talk to her about having to go. *You* could go back to your vicarage. *You* do have a home. It's different for Kitty. She has nowhere to go. They wouldn't be so cruel, would they, to turn her out when she has nowhere to go?"

"She's committed the cardinal sin, it seems. They stoned people like that, according to the Bible. I think some people would do the same today."

"What can we do for her?"

"You say she has nowhere to go."

"That's what she says. If they turn her out she will just wander about the streets. Lilias, I can't bear it. She was so happy here. I can't forget the way she laughed when he looked at her and joked . . . and it has all led to this."

Lilias was thoughtful. She said suddenly: "I

feel as you do about Kitty. She's got caught up with that man. He's a rake and she . . . well, she's a silly flighty girl. He overwhelmed her . . . and she gave way. It's easy to understand. And for that her life will be ruined, while he goes merrily on his way."

"If my father dismisses Kitty he'll have to dismiss Hamish, so Hamish will have to go away."

"How can he dismiss the whole family? I've thought of something: I'll send Kitty to my home."

"To your home? What could they do?"

"My father is vicar of Lakemere. He is a real Christian. By that I mean he practises what he preaches. Few do, you know. He is truly a good man. We're poor . . . but he wouldn't refuse Kitty shelter. He might be able to find a place for her. It wouldn't be the first time he's helped a girl in trouble. I'll write and tell him about it."

"Would he take her in . . . after what she's done?"

"If I wrote to him he would understand."

"Oh, Lilias, wouldn't that be wonderful!"

"It's a hope anyway," said Lilias.

I threw my arms round her neck. "Will you

write that letter? Will you tell her where she can go? I'll see how much money I've got. If we could get her fare."

"I daresay she will be given the wages which are due to her and with what we can muster . . ."

"I'm going to tell her. I must. I couldn't bear to see that awful lost look on her face."

I went and told Kitty what we were planning and I had the pleasure of seeing her abject despair turn to hope.

IT WAS LATE THAT NIGHT when my father returned. Lying in bed, I heard him come in. The storm would not break that night.

The next morning Kitty was sent for. Pale, shame-faced, but not so desperate as she had been, she went to his study. I was waiting on the stairs for her when she emerged. She looked at me and nodded.

I went with her to her room where Lilias joined us.

"I'm to pack my box and leave. I've already packed."

"At once?" I asked.

She nodded. "He said I was a disgrace to

the house and he had a young daughter to think of."

"Oh, Kitty," I said. "I'm sorry you're going like this."

"You've been an angel, Miss Davina, you and Miss Milne." Her voice broke. "I don't know what I'd have done without your help."

"Here's the letter," said Lilias. "Take that. And here's some money."

"I've got my wages due to me."

"Then you'll have a little. It'll get you to Lakemere. My father is a good man. He would never turn anyone in distress away. He will pray a lot, but it won't be all prayers. He'll do his best to help you. He's done it for people in trouble before."

Kitty broke into tears and embraced us both.

"I'll never forget you two," she sobbed. "What I'd have done without . . ."

A cab had been ordered to take her to the station and solemnity reigned over the house. Kitty had been dismissed in disgrace. A lesson to foolish girls. And now it was the turn of Hamish.

He was to go to see the master. He swaggered into the house, hands in pockets. There was no sign of repentance.

He went to my father's study and the door was shut on them.

Lilias came to my room. "What will happen?" she asked. "It's going to be very awkward . . . his family living in the mews."

"He'll be dismissed, of course. He won't be able to come into the house. Well, we shall see."

The whole house was waiting for what would happen next. The interview was long. No one heard any raised voices coming from the study, and finally Hamish emerged and walked calmly out of the house.

It was not until the following day that we realised that Hamish was to drive my father just as usual, and that the punishment meted out to his partner-in-crime was not to be inflicted on him.

THERE WAS BEWILDERMENT. Hamish went about nonchalant as ever, whistling "Ye Banks and Braes" or "Loch Lomond" just as though nothing had happened. We could not understand it.

Aunt Roberta was not of a nature to allow the matter to rest there.

She raised it at dinner that evening.

"The girl has gone," she said. "What about him?"

My father pretended to misunderstand. He raised his eyebrows and assumed that cold manner which intimidated most of us. But not Aunt Roberta.

"You know to what I am referring, David, so please don't pretend you don't."

"Perhaps," he said, "you would be good enough to elucidate."

"Surely incidents such as that which has recently taken place in this household are not lightly passed over."

"I understand," he said, "that you are referring to the maid's dismissal."

"She wasn't the only culprit."

"The man is one of the best coachmen I ever had. I don't propose to dispense with his services . . . . if that is what you mean."

Aunt Roberta forgot her dignity and screamed: "What?"

My father looked pained. "I have dealt with the matter," he said coldly, "and it is closed."

Aunt Roberta could only stare at him.

"I cannot believe I am hearing aright. I tell you I saw them. They were caught in the act."

My father continued to look at her coldly and then gave a significant glance in my direction, meaning that they could not discuss such a matter when I was present on account of my youth and innocence.

Aunt Roberta shut her lips tightly and glared at him.

The rest of the meal was conducted in near silence. But afterwards she followed him into his study. She was there for quite a long time and when she came out she went straight to her room.

The very next morning she left, with the air of the righteous leaving Sodom and Gomorrah before disaster descended.

She could not stay another night in a house where sin was condoned because one of the sinners was "a good coachman."

THE MATTER was discussed at length below-stairs—not in my presence, but much of what was said was imparted to me by Lilias.

She said: "It's very strange. No one understands it. Your father sent for Hamish and we thought he was going to be dismissed as Kitty had been. But Hamish came out of that room, even more sure of himself, it seemed. What was said no one knows. But he is just carrying on as usual. And to think that poor Kitty was turned out as she was! It doesn't make sense. But then they always blame the woman in cases like this, and the men get off, scot-free."

"I can't understand it," I said. "Perhaps it's because he doesn't live in the house."

"He comes into the house. He corrupts the servants."

"I wonder why . . . I wish I knew."

"Your father is not a man to be easily understood."

"But he is so religious and Hamish . . ."

"Is a rogue. It didn't take this to tell me that. We could all see what he was. A pity Kitty was such a little idiot as to be tempted by him. I admit there is something about him. She must have found him irresistible."

"I know one who thinks he is wonderful."

"Who?"

"Himself."

"That's true enough. If ever a man was in love with himself that man is Hamish Vosper. But the servants don't like it, you know. Kitty was a good worker . . . and she was well thought of."

"I do hope she will be all right."

"I know she won't be turned away. My father will do what he can. As I told you, he's a real Christian."

"My father is supposed to be one and he turned her out."

"Your father is good at saying prayers and looking like a Christian. My father is good at being one. There is a difference."

"I hope so, for Kitty's sake."

"He'll write to me and tell me what happened."

"I am so pleased you are here to help, Lilias."

That caused a frown to appear on her brow. For how long? she would be wondering. My father had ruthlessly dismissed Kitty, and Lilias would have to go when her services were no longer required. She was right. My father was very good at showing a Christian demeanour to the world, but he had his own creed of right and wrong. Lilias had summed up his attitude; and I had seen what had happened to Kitty.

But what was the true reason why Hamish

had been forgiven? Because he was a good coachman? Because he was a man?

AFTER A WHILE the affair ceased to be talked of continuously. A new parlourmaid was employed to replace Kitty. She was Ellen Farley, a woman of about thirty. My father said she had been personally recommended to him.

Mr. and Mrs. Kirkwell were somewhat put out. The engaging of staff was their province and they did not like members of it to be introduced over their heads, as Mrs. Kirkwell put it. It was a reflection on her and Mr. Kirkwell that Kitty had been their choice. But the main culprit in that affair, if you asked Mrs. Kirkwell, was Hamish Vosper, and why he was allowed to stay on she would like to know.

However, Ellen came. She was quite different from Kitty—quiet, efficient and, said Mrs. Kirkwell, kept herself to herself.

Hamish still came into the kitchen and sat at the table, seemingly amused because Mrs. Kirkwell pretended that he was not there. He had an eye for Bess and Jenny but, remembering Kitty, they were wary.

Hamish's opinion seemed to be that he was unassailable; he could act in whatever way he pleased because it was natural that he should. It was human nature, as he had once said. A man such as he was, irresistible to the female sex, could not be expected to behave in any way but that which came naturally to him. But I fancied he would have to look elsewhere for his conquests because he would not find them in our house. The example set by Kitty was very fresh in everyone's mind.

In due course there was a letter from Lakemere vicarage. Lilias took it to her bedroom and I went with her that we might read it together.

Kitty had arrived and the vicar had behaved in exactly the way that Lilias had said he would.

"She is so grateful," he wrote. "She cannot say enough in praise of you, Lilias, and your charge Davina. I am proud of you. The poor child, for she is little more, was in acute distress. She has been useful to Alice and Jane in the kitchen and about the house. Mrs. Ellington up at Lakemere House needs someone in the kitchen. You remember Mrs. Ellington, a very forceful lady but with a kind heart. I went to see her and told her the story, which of course I had to do. She promised to give

Kitty a chance and I am sure the poor child will not slip up again. It seems that one of her maids is leaving in a few weeks to get married so there will be a vacant place. While she is waiting, Kitty can stay and help Alice and Jane. Lilias, I am so glad you did what you did. What would have happened to poor Kitty otherwise I cannot imagine . . ."

I gazed at Lilias and I felt the tears in my eyes.

"Oh, Lilias," I said, "your father is a wonderful man."

"I agree with you," she replied.

But the response of the vicar of Lakemere set me thinking about my own father. I had always regarded him as an upright and honourable man. But to have dismissed Kitty as he had and inflict no punishment on Hamish, except perhaps a verbal reprimand, had made me change my image of him. He had always seemed so remote, but now he was less so. In the old days I had thought he was too noble to be considered as one of us; now my feelings towards him had begun to change. How could he have cared so little as to what would become of another human being and send Kitty out into a harsh world, while he kept her part-

ner-in-crime because he was a good coachman? He was acting not out of righteousness
but for his own comfort. The image of the
good and noble man was fading.

If my mother had been there I could have
talked with her. But it would not have happened if she had been with us. She would
never have allowed Kitty to be sent away having nowhere to go.

I felt bewildered and apprehensive.

My father sent for me one day and when I
arrived in his study he looked at me quizzically. "You're growing up," he said. "Nearly
seventeen, is it not?"

I agreed that it was, terrified that this was a
prelude to the departure of Lilias whose services would no longer be required so that she
would be as cursorily dismissed as Kitty had
been.

However, it was not to be just then, for he
turned to a casket which was on the table. I
knew it well. It contained my mother's jewellery. She had shown it to me on more than one
occasion, taking out each piece and talking to
me about it.

There was the pearl necklace which her father had given her on her wedding day. There

was the ruby ring which had been her mother's. There were the bracelet set with turquoise, a turquoise necklace to match, two gold brooches and a silver one.

"You shall have them all when you are grown up," she had told me, "and you'll be able to give them to your daughter. It's rather pleasant to think of these trinkets going on through the generations, don't you think?"

I did.

My father picked up the pearl necklace and held it in his hands. My mother had told me that there were sixty pearls in it and the clasp was a real diamond surrounded by seed pearls. I had seen her wear it on several occasions, as I had most of the jewellery in the box.

My father said: "Your mother wished you to have these. I think you are too young for the jewellery as yet, but the necklace is different. You could have that now. They say that if pearls are not worn they lose their lustre."

I took it from him and my first thought was one of relief. He considered me too young to wear jewellery; therefore I would not yet be ready to dispense with Lilias. But I was pleased to have the pearl necklace.

I put it round my neck and when I thought

of my mother I was overwhelmed with sadness.

When I joined Lilias, she noticed the necklace at once.

"It's beautiful," she cried. "It really is."

"It was my mother's. There are several brooches and things. They are for me, but my father doesn't think I am old enough to wear them yet. But it's not good for pearls if they are not worn."

"I've heard that," she said. She touched the pearls lovingly and I took them off and handed them to her.

"The clasp is lovely," she said. "That in itself would be worth a good deal."

"Oh . . . I shouldn't want to sell them."

"Of course not. But I was just thinking . . . they'd be a nice little nest egg."

"You mean if I fell on hard times."

"Well, it's a comfort to have such things."

I saw that sad, rather faraway look in her eyes. She was looking into a future where a nest egg would be a great comfort to her, I guessed.

I went down to the kitchen to find out whether my father had said he would not be in for dinner that evening. He usually left a mes-

sage for Mrs. Kirkwell. There was that uneasy
atmosphere down there because Hamish was
sitting at the table, sleeves rolled up, pulling
idly at the hairs on his arms.

I went over to Mrs. Kirkwell who was stir-
ring something in a basin. She noticed the
pearls at once.

"My word," she cried. "They do look fine."

"Yes. They are mine now. They were my
mother's. I have to wear them because they
get dull if they are shut away too long."

"Do they now?" said Mrs. Kirkwell.

"That's what my father said."

"Well, he would know, would he not?"

"I think I have heard it before."

"Well, they look very nice. They suit you,
Miss Davina."

"The clasp is valuable, too," I said. "It's a
diamond with little pearls round it."

"There now."

"Miss Milne said it would be a nest egg
. . . if ever I was in need."

Mrs. Kirkwell laughed. "Oh, not you, Miss
Davina. But she would think of that, wouldn't
she? Poor wee soul. Governesses . . . well,
I've always said I wouldna be one."

"Has my father said whether he would be in to dinner tonight?"

Before she could answer Hamish looked up and said: "Nay, he'll nae be in. I know. I'm driving him."

Mrs. Kirkwell answered as though he had not spoken.

"He left a message that he would not be in."

And soon after that, I left.

THE NEXT DAY there was consternation. My necklace was missing. I had kept it in its blue case in the drawer of my dressing table and I could not believe it when I discovered that the case was there but not the necklace. Frantically I searched through all the drawers, but they revealed nothing. The necklace had disappeared. It was a mystery because I would not have dreamed of not putting it away in its case.

Everyone was shocked. When a valuable article like the necklace disappeared, said Mrs. Kirkwell, it was not very nice for those close by.

She was right. The necklace had been in my room. Now it was no longer there. Where was it? "Necklaces don't walk," said Mrs. Kirkwell. Therefore the inference must be that someone had taken it. Who? No one could feel entirely free from suspicion.

My father had not returned until late that night, driven home by Hamish, and as the household had retired he had not heard of the missing necklace until the next morning.

I don't suppose I was the only one in the house who had a sleepless night. We had a thief in the house and my suspicions naturally turned to Hamish. If he were capable of that other thing, might he not believe that it was "human nature" to take a necklace from someone who did not need it and give it to someone who did—himself in this case?

But Hamish did not go beyond the kitchen. Since he was discovered in one of the bedrooms with Kitty it had been a tacit agreement that the upper floors were out of bounds to him unless he was summoned there by my father. Of course, there was always a possibility that he had not kept to the rule; but I had never seen him anywhere except in the kitchen since that affair. Yet it was not impossible that he might have crept up to my room and taken the necklace. If he had been caught there I was sure he would have had a ready explanation for his presence.

During the night when I was trying to sleep I went over what had happened since I last put the necklace on and I was sure I had put it back in the case when I last took it off.

My father was naturally horrified. He ordered that my room be thoroughly searched. He fired questions at me. Did I remember taking off the necklace? Did I remember putting it into the case? Who had been in my room since then? Only the maid to clean and Miss Milne, of course. She came to discuss something with me. I forgot what.

He said that everyone should assemble in the library.

"This is a grievous matter," he said to the company. "A valuable piece of jewellery is missing. Someone in this house knows where it is. I am going to give that person a chance to hand it over now. If this is done, I will consider the matter. But if it is not brought to me this day I shall inform the police. Is everyone here?"

"Where is Ellen?" asked Mrs. Kirkwell.

"I don't know," said Bess. "She was giving me a hand with the rooms. I called out to her when we had the order to come to the library."

"Someone should be sent to tell her," said Mrs. Kirkwell. "I'll go myself."

Mrs. Kirkwell did not have to go for just at that moment Ellen appeared. In her hand she held the pearl necklace.

"Ellen!" cried Mrs. Kirkwell.

"I heard Bess calling that we were to come here," said Ellen. "But . . . I was finding this. I couldn't shut the drawer . . . it looked untidy . . . half open. I thought something in the drawer below might have caught up somehow. So I opened the lower drawer. It was a petticoat. I pulled it out and as I did this fell out. Is it the one that's been lost?"

"In what drawer did you find this?" demanded my father.

"It was in Miss Milne's room, sir."

I looked at Lilias. Her face had turned scarlet; and then it was deathly pale. It was as though a voice was clanging in my head. "A nest egg . . . a nest egg . . ."

It could not be Lilias.

Everyone was looking at her.

My father said: "Miss Milne, can you explain how the necklace came to be in your drawer?"

"In . . . my drawer . . . it couldn't have been."

"But Ellen has just told us it was. And here it is. Come, Miss Milne, an explanation is needed."

"I . . . I didn't put it there. I . . . can't understand."

My father was looking at her severely. "It won't do, Miss Milne, I want an explanation."

I heard myself say in a high-pitched hysterical voice: "There must be some reason . . ."

"Of course, there is a reason," said my father impatiently. "Miss Milne will give it to us. You took the necklace, did you not, Miss Milne? Unfortunately for you, you did not shut the drawer properly so Ellen saw that something was wrong. That was fortunate for us . . . but not for you."

I have never seen such horror in any face as I saw in Lilias' then.

How could you? I thought. I would always have helped you. Why did you take the necklace? And my father knows! My father is the sort of man who will not tolerate any sin—and stealing is a great sin. "Thou shalt not steal."

It is one of the commandments. Think of Kitty. Hamish, of course, was all right, but then he was a good coachman.

I wanted this nightmare to be over. The silence was terrible. It was broken by my father. "I am waiting for an explanation, Miss Milne."

"I . . . I do not know how it came to be there. I did not know it was there . . ."

My father laughed softly but derisively.

"It will not do, Miss Milne. You have been discovered. I could, of course, hand you over to the police."

She caught her breath. I thought she was going to faint. I had to restrain myself from going to her and putting my arms around her and telling her that whatever she had done she was my friend.

She raised her eyes and looked at me . . . pleadingly . . . asking me to believe her. And in that moment I did. I could not believe that Lilias would ever have stolen my necklace even though she so longed to have some bulwark against a needy future . . . a nest egg. I marvelled that I could ever have doubted her innocence and loathed myself for having done so.

"This is a crime," went on my father. "All these years you have been in my household and I have been harbouring a thief. It is very distressing to me."

"I did not," cried Lilias. "I did not. Someone put it there."

"Indeed someone put it there," retorted my father grimly. "You, Miss Milne. You are the daughter of a vicar. You must have had a religious upbringing. That makes the matter so much worse."

"You are condemning me without question." Lilias' eyes flashed. It was the spirit of desperation. Who could have put the necklace in her room? What was the point of it? If someone had taken it, of what use would it be to steal it and give it up . . . just to accuse Lilias?

"I have asked you for an explanation," went on my father, "but you have none."

"I can only say I did not take the necklace."

"Then explain how it came to be in your room."

"I can only say that I did not put it there."

"Miss Milne, as I said, I could prosecute you. You could then give your explanations in a court of law. But because of your family and the fact that you have been in this house for so many years during which time no thefts have been discovered against you, I am taking a lenient view. I will say that you were overcome by a sudden temptation . . . and you submitted to it. So . . . I am going to ask you to pack your bags and leave this house at once. Mrs. Kirkwell will accompany you and make sure that you take nothing with you which does not belong to you."

She looked at him with hatred. "How can you? How can you judge me so unfairly? I will not be treated like a criminal."

"You would prefer to have your case judged in court?"

She covered her face with her hands, and then, without another word, turned and went out of the room.

My father said: "This is regrettable but the matter is closed."

Closed? With Lilias dismissed for theft! Her reputation was tarnished. She would live her life in fear of the fact that she had been accused of stealing would be brought to light.

I went to her room. She was sitting on her bed staring gloomily before her. I ran to her and put my arms about her.

"Oh, Lilias . . . Lilias," I cried. "This is awful. *I* believe you."

"Thank you, Davina," she said. "Who could have done this to me? What could be the point?"

"I don't know. First poor Kitty and now you. It's as though there is some horrible curse on this house. It's ever since my mother died."

"I shall have to go home and tell them. How can I do that?"

"Your father will understand. He will believe you. He is a Christian."

"I shall be a burden to them. I shall never be able to get another post."

"Why not?"

"Because they will want to know where I have been . . . why I left."

"Couldn't you say I was getting old. It's true."

"They would get into touch with your father."

"Perhaps he would say nothing."

She laughed mirthlessly. "Of course he would say something. He would consider it unrighteous not to. He is so holy that he cannot give a woman a chance to defend herself. People like him love to find sin in others. They are so eager to find it that they see it where it does not exist. It makes them feel even more good . . . thanking God they are not like other men."

"Oh, Lilias, it is going to be so miserable without you. I wish I had never seen that necklace."

"I should have stood up for myself. I should never have allowed myself to be accused of something of which I am completely innocent. I should have dared him to prove it."

"Oh, Lilias, why didn't you?"

"It could have been even worse. He didn't believe me. Perhaps others wouldn't. If he had called in the police . . . people would have known. The disgrace would have been terrible . . . for my father. I could see that I had to get away . . ."

"You must write to me, Lilias. Give me your address. You did tell me, but I want it written down. I'm going to find out who took the necklace out of my room and put it in yours. I know someone did. Perhaps it was Hamish."

"Why? Just because he was caught with Kitty? This isn't the same thing. I could understand his stealing the necklace, but if he had done so he would want to sell it right away. There isn't any reason why he should try to incriminate me."

"Perhaps he wanted revenge. Had you done something he didn't like?"

"I hardly know him. He never even looks at me."

"Someone must have done it. What about Ellen?"

"Why? What would be the point?"

"Whichever way you look at it, there seems to be no reason."

"Thank you, Davina, for your trust. I shall never forget it."

"Oh, Lilias. It's what I've dreaded . . . your going away. Though . . . I never thought it would be like this."

"Write to me and I'll write to you. I'll let you know what happens."

"At least you have your family to go to. They'll be kind and understanding."

"They will believe in my innocence. They will never believe that I could be a thief."

Mrs. Kirkwell came in. She looked grim and resolute.

"Miss Davina!" she said reprovingly, surprised, I supposed, to find me there.

"I think this is a great mistake," I said.

Mrs. Kirkwell ignored that and said: "What about this packing? I see you haven't begun yet."

I went back to my room. I thought of all that had happened in a short time: my mother's death, Kitty's misdemeanour which had resulted in her dismissal—and now Lilias.

HOW DREARY the house was without her. She had been my special friend for so long, and I had known that I would miss her; what I had not realised was how much. I felt very melancholy.

A few days after Lilias had left, my father sent for me. He was in his study, unsmiling and forbidding.

"I wanted to speak to you, Davina," he said. "It is about a governess."

I stared at him. For the moment I thought he had discovered the real thief and let myself fancy that Lilias was coming back.

"You are not yet fully educated," he went on. "I had considered the idea of sending you away to a finishing school, but I have decided against that. So there will be a governess."

"A new governess, but . . ."

He looked at me with faint exasperation.

"A new one, of course. I myself will make sure that this time I engage someone who is reliable and is not going to shock us all by stealing our property."

I flushed and began: "I do not believe . . ."

He went on as though I had not spoken: "This one will be able to teach a great deal you should know. Deportment, good manners. It will not be so much a schoolroom governess as someone who will be able to equip you with social graces."

I was not listening. How foolish of me to think even for a moment that he was going to say that Lilias was coming back.

"Miss Grey will be arriving at the end of the week."

"Miss Grey . . ."

The irritation showed again. "I am sure that Miss Grey will give every satisfaction."

I came out of the study, dazed and very sad.

I knew I was not going to like Miss Grey. How should I stop comparing her with Lilias?

And a few days later Miss Zillah Grey arrived.

The Governess

THE HOUSEHOLD was in a state of disbelief. Miss Zillah Grey astonished them all; and what was most amazing was that my father had engaged her.

She was the sort of person whom people would turn to look at when they passed her in the street. She had what I can only call a flaunting manner. Her clothes, her gestures, everything about her seemed to be saying "Look at me."

She was definitely not what Mrs. Kirkwell would call "ladylike" but she was very affable to everyone and within a short time of our acquaintance she was calling me "dear." I had thought I should hate Lilias' successor, but I could not hate Zillah Grey. I could only marvel at her.

She had brought a great many clothes with her . . . all of them quite unsuitable, I should have thought.

When I had taken her to her room on her arrival she had looked round and said she knew she was going to be happy. Then she had taken off her hat and removed the pins from her hair; she shook it out so that it fell in seductive waves about her shoulders like a reddish cloak.

"That's better," she said. "You see I'm making myself at home."

I was amazed by the pots and bottles which were soon arrayed on the dressing table. I had thought there might have been some books in her baggage, but there was no sign of even one. She hung up her clothes and asked for more coat hangers.

Bess was amazed. I could imagine what she was telling them in the kitchen.

When my father came in he asked if Miss Grey had arrived and when he was told that she had, he said he would see her in his study at once.

I saw her going down the stairs. She had piled her hair high on her head, which made her look very tall, and I noticed that she had reddened her lips.

I was certain that he would decide she was most unsuitable. I was sorry in a way for, although I deeply regretted Lilias' departure, I felt it would be more interesting to have a governess like Miss Grey than the normal kind.

I wondered what the servants were thinking. Lilias was no longer there to tell me what they said. But I was sure there would be marked disapproval from the Kirkwells.

The interview with my father lasted over an hour. I was surprised, expecting it to be brief. When it was over my father sent for me.

He was looking rather pleased, I thought, and I wondered what that meant.

"So," he said. "Your new governess is here. She has met you, she says."

"Yes. I took her to her room and we talked a little."

"Good. I am sure she will be of great benefit to you."

I was astonished. How could he think that?

He said to me: "She will dine with us. It seems to me the most suitable arrangement."

"You . . . er . . . approve of her?"

He looked pained. "I am of the opinion that she will teach you a great many things you should know."

It was extraordinary. Was it because I was comparing her with the really rather conventional Lilias that I found her so strange? My father, obviously, did not.

She appeared at dinner that night in a black dress which fitted her figure rather closely. She had what Lilias had referred to as "an hour-glass figure." Her red hair was wound round her head in what was meant to be a severe fashion—but somehow it was quite the reverse on her.

My father was gracious. It was more like having a guest to dinner than a governess.

He said: "Of course, you have not yet had an opportunity to assess Davina's capabilities, but when you have you will be able to decide what is best for her."

"Davina and I are going to get along wonderfully," she replied, smiling at him.

"Her governess left in rather a hurry. I fancy she was not entirely competent."

I could not resist cutting in. "Miss Milne was a very good governess, Papa. She made learning interesting."

"And that is what it should be, of course," said Miss Grey. "And that is how I intend to make it."

"I suppose my daughter will be having some sort of season. But that, of course, is a little way ahead. We can wait until after her seventeenth birthday before we need to consider that."

"I am sure you are right."

The conversation went along on conventional lines. I gathered Miss Grey had recently come to Edinburgh. Her home had been in London.

"And what do you think of our Scottish ways?" my father asked almost playfully.

"I think they are divine," she answered.

I glanced at him, wondering whether he would think this blasphemous in some way. It was a strange word to use. But she lowered her eyes so that the fanlike black lashes lay demurely against her skin; the full red lips smiled and the little nose and long upper lip looked more kittenish than ever. My father's look was indulgent. His lips twitched a little as they used to when my mother said something which amused him and at the same time shocked him a little.

"I hope," he said, "that you will continue to do so."

I left them together over coffee in the drawing room.

It was an extraordinary evening. Everything seemed so different now . . . even my father.

DURING THE NEXT WEEKS, although I spent a good deal of time with Zillah Grey, I felt I did not really learn a great deal about her. She seemed like two different people . . . no, more than two. She appeared to be able to slip into different personalities with the greatest of ease. With my father she played the ladylike person who is suddenly confronted with the need to earn a living. That was characteristic of most governesses; but with her it was different. They were usually quietly retiring, very much aware of their reduced circumstances, unsure where they belonged, poised between upstairs and down. Zillah Grey, although she had a habit of lowering her eyes, did not strike me as modest. I suspected she did it because it was an excellent way of calling attention to those long thick eyelashes. She was certainly not without guile. She knew exactly how to behave with my father and he approved of her wholeheartedly.

With me her attitude was more volatile. Sometimes she threw off all pretence. She would laugh uproariously and I noticed her accent changed a little—her words became more racy.

It soon became clear that there were to be no set lessons.

"What I have to do is prepare you for society, so your father tells me," she announced.

I was amazed. I could not imagine her being a great success in Edinburgh society, or even being accepted into it. What was she going to teach me?

I asked her what I needed to know.

"Clothes for one thing," she said. "You have to make the best of yourself. You could be quite good-looking."

"Could be?" I said. "Surely one either is or one isn't?"

She winked at me. She had a habit of doing that when she was in certain moods. "That's one of the things I'm going to teach you. Oh, we're going to have a lot of fun together."

She said I ought to learn to dance. "Ballroom dancing, of course," she added. "Is there anyone here who can play the piano?"

"I don't think so. I've had lessons. Miss Milne, my last governess, played well."

"Well, you can't play and dance at the same time, can you? I'll have to see what we can do about that. I can knock out a bit of a tune myself. I wonder if there's someone who could partner you."

"You mean one of the maids?"

"We'll see about that. I'll teach you how to walk."

"To walk?"

"Gracefully. How to make the best of yourself."

"What about lessons . . . books and all that?"

She wrinkled her kitten's nose and laughed. "We'll see about that, shall we?"

She made her own rules. Often she went out and stayed out for several hours. I had no idea where she went.

"It's a funny way of going on, if you ask me," said Mrs. Kirkwell. "I mentioned it to the master and got a flea in my ear for my pains. I don't know what the world's coming to."

It was certainly a strange situation.

Only a week after she arrived she asked that the carriage should take her somewhere one afternoon. Hamish arrived at the door just as though she were a member of the family.

The Kirkwells were watching from one of the windows when I came upon them.

"What's all this about?" she was demanding of her husband, unaware of my presence.

"It's a wee bit fishy to me," he replied.

Then they saw me.

"That Miss Grey's gone off in the carriage," said Mrs. Kirkwell.

"Yes, I know."

"Seems to think she owns the place. I wonder what the master will have to say about this."

She need not have wondered, for nothing was said.

During the carriage drive she must have decided that Hamish would make a dancing partner for me.

When she sent for him I was horrified. I had always found Hamish repulsive and the intimacy of the dance would be most unpleasant. I could not shut out the image of him with Kitty on the bed.

Miss Grey demonstrated the dance, first with me and then with Hamish. She sang as she danced and I had to admit that she did it with the utmost grace. She floated by herself . . . her arms outstretched, muttering: "See.

One two, one two three . . . the lady turns . . . the gentleman guides her . . . there. Let me try it with you, Hamish, while Davina watches. Then I'll take Davina while you watch . . . then you two can do it together. Oh dear, I wish we had someone who could play the piano."

She turned to me and held me loosely. She smelt of musk and attar of roses. I could see her white teeth and greedy lips closely—but it was wonderful to dance with her. It was much less so with Hamish.

He grinned at me. I believe he understood my feelings and they amused him.

I could have enjoyed the dancing lessons but for Hamish.

Mrs. Kirkwell was shocked when she heard that he was my partner in these lessons—so much so that she bearded my father in his study to tell him what was going on.

She was so bemused and indignant when she emerged that she forgot my youth for once and while I was present told Bess what had taken place.

"I said to him, 'There he was . . . dancing with Miss Davina . . . that man who was as much to blame as Kitty for what happened.'

And what do you think he said to me? He said, very cold like, 'I wish to hear no more of the matter, Mrs. Kirkwell.' I spoke up bold as brass because I knew it were the right and proper thing to do. I said to him, 'Well, sir, to see that man holding Miss Davina . . . as they have to do in this dance . . . well, it's more than flesh and blood can stand after . . .' He wouldn't let me finish. He said: 'I trust Miss Grey to do what is best for my daughter. She needs a dancing partner for the practise apparently and he is the only young man available. That is an end to the matter.' He was as cold as a fish. Well, there's nothing more I can do. But I've made my feelings known and I reckon I've done my duty."

And Hamish continued to practise with me.

There were a great many demonstrations, though, and Miss Grey danced more often with Hamish than I did.

I had a letter from Lilias.

My dear Davina,

I am very unhappy. I feel I have brought a blight on my family. Sometimes I cannot believe this has happened and I am filled with hatred towards that person who played that trick on me—for I am sure it was a trick. Someone must have hated me almost as much as I hate that person now, although I don't know whom I am hating.

My father has been wonderful. He makes me pray with him. He says I must forgive this enemy, but I cannot, Davina. I feel this wicked person has ruined my life.

I know you believe me and that gives me great comfort. But I am home now and I shall never be able to take another post. This terrible stigma will hang over me for ever.

I am helping Alice and Jane at the moment and Alice is going to take a post as governess . . . so I shall step into her shoes. I shall remain at the vicarage. Although my family believe in me, I am very unhappy. I should be grateful for their trust, I know, and I am, but I suffer still from this malicious accusation.

I saw Kitty the other day. She is settling in at Lakemere House, which is one of the two big houses here—the other being the Manor. Kitty seemed to be getting along quite well. We are the two disgraced ones, but I think she will be better able to get over her shameful humiliation, even though guilty, than I, innocent, ever shall be.

My dear Davina, I shall always remember

you. Write to me and tell me how you are getting on. Perhaps we shall be able to meet one day.

All happiness to you and my love,

LILIAS

I wrote back.

Dear Lilias,

Thank you for your letter which I was delighted to receive. I think of you a great deal. I am going to try and find out who did that terrible thing. You know where my suspicions are, but I can't think of a reason.

I loathe him. He has been brought in by my new governess to partner me. I am learning dancing and need a partner. There isn't anyone else, Miss Grey says. I could enjoy dancing lessons but for that.

Miss Grey is the new governess. She came very soon after you left. It is hard to describe her because she is more than one person. She is beautiful in a way that makes people look at her. She has reddish hair and green eyes. My father seems to approve of her. That surprised me because we don't do lessons in the ordinary way. She tells me what to wear . . . how I should walk . . . and, of course, I am learning to dance. I think it is a sort of preparation for launching me into society. I'm getting old, I suppose.

Oh, Lilias, how I miss you! I wish you could come back.

My love as ever,

DAVINA

MISS GREY said I was not to wear black any-more.

"It doesn't become your colouring, Davina," she said. "You are too dark. Dark hair and blue eyes . . . an attractive combi-nation, but not for black. I can wear it, though it is not my favourite colour. It's too sombre. I'm fair skinned, you see. There is hardly any skin fairer than redheads. So I can get away with black . . . but it is not for you."

"Mrs. Kirkwell said I should wear it for a year."

She held up her hands in mock horror. "But I say no black . . . and no black there shall be."

I was not displeased. I hated the black clothes. I did not need them to remind me of my mother.

Of course, the Kirkwells were very shocked, but my father raised no objection.

I discovered that Miss Grey was very interested in the family. She wanted to hear about my mother and all the relations I had. There was little family except Aunt Roberta, I told her. I found myself talking quite frankly, for she had a way of drawing me out. I was soon telling her how Aunt Roberta had descended upon us after my mother's death and how she had discovered Hamish and Kitty together in one of the bedrooms. I thought that might make her realise that Hamish was not a fit person to be my dancing partner.

She was thoughtful. "The young devil," she said at length.

"Yes. It was very shocking. Aunt Roberta and I were together at the time. She opened the door . . . and there they were."

"Caught in the act! And you a witness. Oh, Davina, what a sight for you!" She laughed and went on laughing, the greedy mouth open, the green eyes full of tears, so great was her mirth. "And little Kitty was given her marching orders, eh? 'Don't darken these doors again.'"

"It was not very funny for Kitty."

"No. I suppose not."

"Lilias . . . Miss Milne . . . has a father who is a vicar. He took Kitty in."

"God's good man, eh?"

"He was good to Kitty. He found her a post in a house near him."

"Let's hope there aren't any good-looking young men around like Hamish."

"Do you call him good-looking?"

"He's got something. There's no doubt about that. I don't suppose Kitty was the only one who couldn't say no."

I did not want to talk about Hamish. I felt I should say too much and that I suspected him of stealing the necklace and putting it in Lilias' drawer. I must not tell anyone of my suspicions as I had no proof.

She asked a lot of questions about what had happened when my mother was alive. I told her how we used to go shopping and visiting friends.

"It was not so long ago," she said.

I discovered that she kept a flask of brandy in her room. It was in a cupboard which she kept locked. She let me into the secret once. She had been out to luncheon on that day. I did not know with whom, but she did now and then make these mysterious excursions and on this occasion she came back rather flushed and extremely talkative. Her speech seemed different and she was more affectionate than ever.

I went to her room on some pretext—I forget what—and found her lying fully dressed on her bed, propped up by pillows.

"Hello, Davina," she said. "Come and sit down and talk to me."

I sat down and she told me she had had a very good luncheon . . . too good in fact . . . with a very great friend.

"I feel sleepy," she said. "I could do with a little tonic. Here. Take the key in that drawer and open that little cupboard. There's a bottle in there and a glass. Just pour out a little, will you? It's just what I need."

I could smell that the tonic was brandy.

I poured it out and took it to her.

She drank it quickly.

"That's better," she said. "Leave the glass, dear. I'll wash it later. Put the key back in the drawer. Now sit down. There. Let's talk. I've had a lovely meal . . . and the wine was delicious. I like people who know how to choose a good wine. It's one of the things I'll have to teach you, Davina."

"I didn't think I had to learn things like that. I know absolutely nothing about wines."

"When you're in a big house with a nice husband and he brings his guests home . . . you'll have to know how to entertain them."

"So that's what I have to learn as well!"

"Well, it's as good a reason as any . . ."

"What do you mean, 'as good a reason as any'?"

She hesitated. I could see how sleepy she was. She seemed to rouse herself.

"I'm just babbling on. I like to talk to you, Davina. I think we've become friends . . . and that's nice. That's how I wanted it. You're a nice girl . . . a nice *innocent* girl, and that's how young girls should be, shouldn't they?"

"I suppose so."

She went on: "What a nice cosy time you must have had, Davina, my dear. Living all your life in this house . . . with kind Mama and stern Papa, the worthy banker, pillar of society in a great city." She laughed. "You ought to see London."

"I'd like to."

"We've got our grand houses, you know. Grander than this even. But we've got some which are not so grand."

"That is so here. I suppose it is like that everywhere."

"In big cities the contrasts are greater."

"This is a big city."

"I was thinking of London."

"It's your home, is it?" I asked. "Why did you come up here?"

"I came for a little while and decided to stay . . . awhile at least."

She sounded as though she would soon be asleep.

"Were you a governess before?" I asked.

She laughed. "Governess, me? Do I look like a governess?"

I shook my head.

"I was on the boards," she said.

"Boards?"

She was laughing again. "Music hall," she said in a slurred voice. "Song and dance act. It went down well for a time . . . as that sort of act goes. Quite a long time really."

"You mean you were on the stage?"

She nodded dreamily. "Those were the days . . ."

"Why did you come here then?"

She shrugged her shoulders. "I like a change. Besides . . . well, never mind. I was in Glasgow with the Jolly Red Heads. Three of us there were . . . all red-haired. That was what gave us the idea. We'd come on stage with our hair flying loose. Brought the house down . . . to start with. People get tired. That's the trouble. Fickle, that's what they are. We toured the provinces and then we came to Glasgow. Did quite well there. It's a hard grind, though. There comes a time when you feel like settling . . ."

"And are you going to settle, Miss Grey?"

"Yes," she murmured.

"I'll leave you, then you can sleep."

"No, don't go. I like to hear you talking. You're a nice girl, Davina. I like you."

"Thank you. I had no idea you were on the stage."

"Didn't you, dear? That's because you're a nice little innocent."

She was changing again, but her voice was getting fainter. I was sure she was almost asleep.

I said: "When I first saw you, I thought I had never seen anyone less like a governess."

"Thank you, dear. That's a compliment. How am I doing then?"

"What do you mean?"

"Governessing," she said.

"You are a very strange governess."

"Hm," she murmured.

"You are quite different from Miss Milne."

"The one who stole the necklace?"

"She didn't steal it. It was put in her drawer . . . by someone."

She opened her eyes and some of the sleepiness dropped from her. "You mean, someone planted it?"

"I mean that someone did it deliberately to make trouble for her."

"Who told you that?"

"Nobody told me. I just knew."

"How could you know?"

"Because Miss Milne couldn't possibly have stolen anything."

"Is that the only reason you know?"

I nodded. "I wish I could find out the truth."

"You never know people, dear. They do the oddest things. You never know what's going on inside people. They go on and on . . . in the same old way and then suddenly they break out and do something you couldn't have believed they ever would."

She was growing dreamy again.

"You don't seem to be interested in the usual things," I said.

"Like what, dear?"

"Mathematics, geography, English, history. Miss Milne was ever so keen on history. My mother was, too. She knew a lot about what happened in the past and she used to talk to me about it. It was very exciting. Once I went to Holyrood House."

"What's that?"

I was astounded.

"Surely you know. It's the old palace. Mary Queen of Scots was there, Rizzio was murdered there. And then there's the castle where King James was born . . . the Sixth of Scotland and the First of England. His mother was Mary Queen of Scots."

She was almost asleep. Then suddenly she began to sing:

Wasn't it pitiful what they did to Mary Queen of Scots?
Of her emulsion I have taken lots and lots and lots.
They locked her up in Fotheringay,
Fotheringay was not so gay,

Mary, Mary, Hanover Squarey, Mary Queen of Scots.

I listened in amazement. Then I thought: she is drunk.

HOW COULD MY FATHER, who was so stern and so conventional, allow such a woman to remain in the house, and moreover to have brought her in in the first place?

Of course, he had never seen her lying on her bed singing "Mary Queen of Scots." She changed her personality when he was there. She wore the black dress often. It seemed to me that she could adjust herself to fit the occasion.

She did refer to that afternoon.

"I don't know what I said, dear. You see, I had been to lunch with a dear friend. She'd been in trouble . . . it was a love affair and suddenly everything came right. I was so happy for her. She wanted to drink. She told me what had happened . . . how it had nearly gone wrong and then come right. And there was champagne . . . to celebrate, you see. She made me drink with her. Well, I'm afraid I'm not used to it."

I thought of the brandy in the locked cupboard and she must have guessed my thoughts for she went on quickly: "I just keep a little something in case I'm off-colour. I know I look robust, but I have my little weakness. Internal, dear. I get quickly upset if something doesn't agree with me and a spoonful always puts me right. I had to drink with her. It would have been sort of unkind not to. You understand?"

"Oh, yes," I reassured her.

"I must have said a lot of silly things, did I?"

"You sang a song about Mary Queen of Scots."

"It was . . . awful?"

"Well, it was joking about Fotheringay, which was very sad really, and something I didn't understand about 'hanover squarey.' I didn't know what that meant."

"It's a well-known place in London. Hanover Square, actually Squarey, to rhyme with Mary. That's why that's there. It was silly. An old music hall song. Was that all? Did I say anything else?"

"Only that you used to be with the Jolly Red Heads."

She looked a little grave. "People talk a lot of nonsense when they have been so foolish as to be persuaded to drink too much. I'm sorry, Davina, my dear. Forget it, will you?"

I nodded again and she swept me into her perfumed embrace.

"I'm getting very fond of you, Davina," she said.

I felt a sense of uneasiness and a desperate longing came to me for the old days with Lilias.

Soon after that we were in Princes Street shopping and she said to me: "It's beautiful, isn't it? Doesn't the castle look grand? You must tell me about all that history sometime. I'd love to hear."

Certainly she was the most unusual governess any girl ever had.

She bought a dress that afternoon. It was green with the tightly fitting bodice which she favoured and the skirt billowing out from the nipped-in waist. It was piped with ruby velvet.

She tried it on and paraded before the shop girl and me.

"Madam is . . . entrancing," cried the girl ecstatically.

I had to admit that she looked startlingly attractive.

Before we went down to dinner that night she came into my room wearing the dress.

"How do I look?" she asked.

"You look beautiful."

"Do you think it's suitable for dinner tonight? What do you think your father will say?"

"I don't suppose he will say anything. I don't think he notices one's clothes."

She kissed me suddenly. "Davina, you are a little darling."

A few nights later she wore the dress again and during dinner I noticed that she was wearing a very fine ruby ring.

I could not stop looking at it because I was sure I had seen it before. It was exactly like one my mother had worn.

The next day I mentioned it to her.

I said: "I noticed that lovely ring you were wearing last night."

"Oh?" she said. "My ruby."

"It's a beautiful ring. My mother had one just like it. It's going to be mine one day. My father just didn't think I was old enough to wear it yet."

"Yes . . . I see what he means."

"I don't suppose it's exactly the same. But it is very like it."

"I suppose one ring can look like another. There are fashions in rings, you know."

"Are there?"

"They were probably made about the same period."

"It is lovely anyway. May I see it?"

"But of course."

She went to a drawer and took out a case.

"The case is like my mother's, too," I said.

"Well, aren't all those cases rather alike?"

I slipped the ring on my finger. It was too big for me. I remembered there was one time when my mother had been wearing her ruby ring. I had admired it and she had taken it from her finger and slipped it on mine. "It will be yours one day," she had said. "Your fingers will be a little fatter perhaps by that time."

Miss Grey took it from me and put it back in the case.

I said: "The ruby matched the piping on your new dress."

"Yes," she said. "I thought that. It was the reason why I wore it."

She shut the drawer and smiled at me. "I

think we should practise our dancing," she said.

The next time she wore the dress I noticed that she did not put on the ruby ring.

THERE WERE TIMES when I felt that I had been thrust into an entirely different world. Everything had changed so much since my mother's death. The servants were different; they were aloof and disapproving. When my mother was alive it had seemed as though life went on just as it had been doing for generations. Now it was all changed.

Lilias' departure had helped to change it. Lilias had been what one expected a governess to be. She and I had had a close friendship, but that did not mean that our lives had not been conducted in a strictly conventional way. When I thought of the old days . . . Sunday church . . . Sunday lunch . . . prayers . . . the amiable but regulated relationship between the upper and lower sections of the house . . . it was all so natural and orderly . . . just as it must have been for generations.

Now it was as though a whirlwind had struck the house and left the old order in ruins.

There were prayers every morning; the whole household attended, Miss Grey, discreet and demure, praying with the rest of us. But it was different. My father went to church on Sundays and I went with him, Miss Grey—as Lilias used to—accompanying us. But there was no chatting outside the church, only the occasional "How do you do" from my father and myself.

There was smouldering resentment in the kitchen, often openly displayed by the Kirkwells. They did not understand, any more than I did, why Miss Grey was allowed to remain in the house, or why she was chosen in the first place. She was a disruptive influence, not so much because of the manner in which she behaved—indeed she seemed to want to be on good terms with all of us—but because she was so different and people are suspicious of anything that does not conform to the rules.

It was at this time about nine months after my mother's death. I felt bewildered. How often I wished that Lilias was with me so that I could have talked frankly to someone. I was caught up in the general uneasiness which pervaded the house; and then suddenly I stumbled on a clue which explained a great deal to me. It was like finding a key which opened a door to . . . knowledge.

It was night. I was in bed. I could not sleep and lay tossing and turning when suddenly I heard a faint noise. I sat up in bed listening. I was sure I heard light footsteps going along the corridor past my room.

I got out of bed and opened my door very slightly. I was in time to see a figure on the stairs. I tiptoed to the banisters and saw quite clearly that it was Miss Grey. She was in her night attire—very different from mine which buttoned up to the neck. Hers was diaphanous, pale green with lace and ribbons. Her hair was loose about her shoulders.

What was she doing? Walking in her sleep? I must be careful not to wake her. I had heard somewhere that this could be dangerous to sleepwalkers. Very quietly I started to follow her.

She had descended the staircase and was walking along the corridor. She paused at the door of the master bedroom. It was where my father slept.

She opened the door and went in. I stood still, staring after her. What was she doing?

What would happen now? She would awaken my father.

I waited in trepidation. Nothing happened. I stood there staring at the door. He must be awake by now.

I waited. My bare feet were cold. Nothing happened.

I mounted the stairs and stood at the top looking down. Minutes passed . . . and still she was there.

Then I knew, of course, why she had come here . . . why she was unlike any other governess. The truth came to me in a flash of understanding.

She was no governess. She was my father's mistress.

I LAY IN MY BED thinking of what this meant. But he was so religious! He had been so outraged by Kitty's conduct. How could he when he was acting in a similar way himself? How could anybody be so hypocritical? I felt sick with disgust.

So he had brought her here for this. She went to his room at night. He had given her my mother's ruby ring which was to have been mine. And this was my father—the worthy citizen, whom the people of this city so respected. Already he was putting Miss Grey in the place of my mother.

I did not know how I should act. I wanted to go to that room and burst in on them . . . as Aunt Roberta had on Kitty and Hamish. I wanted to tell them what I thought of them. Not so much for what they were doing—that was something I knew nothing about—but because it was despicable to stand in judgement against people who did the same.

What could I do? My impulse was to leave the house. How foolish! Where should I go? To Lilias? Again foolish. The Lakemere vicarage was not a home for all those in trouble. In any case, what I suffered from was not that sort of trouble.

I had a home, plenty to eat, comfort, and I felt I could never look my father in the face again.

And Miss Grey. What of her? I did not mind so much about her. She was not a lady. I knew that. That she was exceptionally beautiful and attractive I had to admit. I supposed she would be considered quite fascinating. But my father . . . how could he?

What should I do? What should I say when

I met them? Say nothing, was the wise answer. Certainly not yet . . . not until I had thought how I must act.

If only Lilias were here how different it would be. But Lilias had gone. If she had not, Miss Grey would not be here.

My father had wanted Miss Grey to come to the house. It was fortuitous that Lilias had been dismissed for a crime of which I was certain she was innocent.

I was getting entangled in the maze of my thoughts. I felt lost, bewildered, completely shaken by this sudden understanding.

I WISHED that I could get away . . . out of this house. I was writing to Lilias but, of course, I could not mention in a letter what was in my mind. It would have been different if I could have talked to her.

My father did not notice the change in my attitude. It was different with Miss Grey. She noticed at once.

"Is anything troubling you, Davina?" she asked.

"No," I lied.

"You seem . . ."

"How do I seem?"

She hesitated for a moment. "Different . . . as though you have something on your mind."

I looked at her and I could not stop myself seeing her and my father on that bed as I had seen Kitty and Hamish. I felt sick.

"Do you feel all right?"

"Yes."

"I think you might be sickening for something."

Yes, I thought. I feel sick when I think about you and my father.

I hated him more than I did her. I thought: that is her way of life. She wasn't really so shocked about Kitty and Hamish and didn't pretend to be. She would say with Hamish: it's human nature. Human nature for people like her and Hamish . . . and it seemed my father. He only held up his hands in horror when girls like Kitty succumbed to it. He went to church and prayed and thanked God that he was not as other men.

Then I started to think about Lilias. How strange that she should have been dismissed just when he wanted to bring another governess into the house. But Zillah Grey was not a governess. She was a Jolly Red Head. She was really a loose woman. That was what they called them. She was one of those and my father was by no means the good man he pretended to be.

My mind kept going back to Lilias. Who had put the necklace in her room? The more I thought of it the more strange it seemed. Could it be that my father had wanted Lilias out of the house so that he could conveniently bring Zillah Grey in . . . so that she could share his bed at night with the greatest ease?

He himself had selected her. He had said that. And it would have been impossible for her to masquerade as an educated woman, a proper governess, one of those genteel ladies who had fallen on hard times. So she had come to teach me the social graces. That was really amusing. I felt waves of bitterness sweeping over me.

What had this done to Lilias? She would have to go through life with that stigma upon her. People would say she had been dismissed for theft because a missing necklace was found in her room. I had always believed that someone had put it there. Now it seemed that someone might have had a reason for it, and I had a burning desire to find out who.

I could not imagine my father's stealing into

my room, taking the necklace and putting it
into a drawer in Lilias' room. That was beyond my imagination. But a short while ago
should I have been able to visualise my father
in positions which I could not get out of my
mind?

I often found Miss Grey looking at me
speculatively. I was betraying myself. I was
not as skilled at subterfuge as they were.

I wondered whether Zillah Grey had
guessed that I had discovered the truth about
her relationship with my father. She was
clearly a little anxious and I was not subtle
enough to hide my feelings.

One afternoon my father arrived home early
and very soon afterwards Miss Grey came to
my room.

She said: "Your father wants you to go to
his study. He has something to say to you."

I looked surprised. I fancied he had been
avoiding me lately. When we dined he seemed
determined not to meet my eyes, but as he
rarely addressed a remark to me it was not
really necessary to do so.

She came with me to the study and shut the
door behind us.

My father was standing leaning against his desk. She went and stood beside him.

"Sit down, Davina," he said. "I want to tell you that Miss Grey has promised to become my wife."

I stared at them both in astonishment.

Miss Grey came to me and kissed me.

"Dear Davina," she said. "We have always got on so well. It is going to be wonderful." She turned to my father. "Wonderful for us all," she added.

She held out her hand and he took it. He was looking at me rather anxiously I thought.

"The wedding will not take place for another three months," said my father. "We must wait the full year . . . and a little more, I think."

I wanted to laugh at him. I wanted to cry out: "But you did not wait. This is a pretence. It's all a pretence. There is sham everywhere."

But "I see" was all I could manage to say.

"I am sure," he went on, "that you will realise this is the best thing possible. You need a mother."

And I thought, you need someone . . . as Hamish did.

It was disturbing how I heard myself speaking inwardly . . . saying things which I would never have dared say aloud, things which I would never have believed possible a year ago.

How I hated them standing there, pretending . . . both of them. But I hated him more than I did her.

"There will be a wedding," I heard myself say stupidly; and that other voice within me said, of course there will be a wedding. A quiet one . . . all very right and proper . . . just as it should be . . . and no one will know.

"A quiet one naturally," said my father.

"Naturally," I repeated and wondered whether they noticed the sarcasm.

"Are you going to congratulate us?" asked Miss Grey archly.

I did not answer.

"It is something of a surprise, I have no doubt," said my father. "But it will be the best thing possible . . . for us all. You will have a mother . . ."

I looked at Zillah Grey. She grimaced and somehow I liked her for that. She was not the hypocrite he was, whatever else she might be; and I think at that time it was the hypocrisy which was the greatest sin in my eyes.

"Well then," said my father. "I want us to drink to the future."

He opened a cupboard and took out three glasses and a bottle of champagne.

There was a little for me, less than half a glass. I kept thinking of Miss Grey lying on her bed singing "Mary Queen of Scots"; and I began to laugh.

My father smiled quite benignly, not understanding. When had he ever? I asked myself. But I think Miss Grey was aware of my feelings.

AT FIRST the news was received with dismay throughout the household, but after a few days they all seemed to accept it.

Mrs. Kirkwell had a little talk with me.

She said: "A lot has happened in this house lately, Miss Davina. Mr. Kirkwell and I were beginning to look on you as the mistress of the house. Of course, you are young as yet. We had thought that Mr. Glentyre might marry again, but we hadn't thought it would be so soon."

"It will be a year since my mother died when they marry."

"Oh yes. Well, they couldna very well do it

before. That wouldn't have been right and Mr. Glentyre, he's one who'll always do what's right. It's soon . . . but it will be the full year. And we shall have a new lady of the house." Mrs. Kirkwell wrinkled her brows. I knew she was thinking that it would be difficult to imagine Zillah Grey as the mistress of a staid Edinburgh residence.

"There'll be changes," she went on. "I'm sure of that. Well, we must take them as they come, I suppose. A man needs a wife . . . even a gentleman like Mr. Glentyre, and having a daughter to bring up."

"I think I am brought up by now, don't you, Mrs. Kirkwell?"

"Well, there'll be things to arrange and a woman's best for that even if . . . ."

"I am glad you and Mr. Kirkwell are not too upset by all these changes."

She shook her head sadly and I guessed she was thinking of the days when my mother was alive. I wondered if she were aware of Miss Grey's nightly excursions. Mrs. Kirkwell was shrewd and she had always liked to be aware of what was going on in the house.

I imagined she and Mr. Kirkwell might have decided that when there were certain "goings-on" in a respectable house—men be-ing what they were—it was as well to have them legalised.

And so the house settled down to a mood of greater serenity than it had enjoyed since my mother died.

Later I heard Mrs. Kirkwell's comments on the mistress-of-the-house-to-be. "She's not the interfering sort. That's the kind neither Mr. Kirkwell nor me would work for."

So, unsuitable as the match might seem to outsiders, it was—if somewhat grudgingly—accepted in the house, largely because it was recognised that a man needed a wife and the chosen one in this case was "not the interfer-ing sort."

THE WEDDING was, as had been decided, quiet—just a simple ceremony performed by the Reverend Charles Stocks who had been a friend of the family all my life.

There were few guests, chiefly friends of my father. Aunt Roberta did not appear, for the feud between her and my father continued. There were no friends of Zillah Grey present. The reception at the house was brief and very soon my father, with his bride, left for Italy.

I went at once to my room to write to Lilias. "I have a stepmother now. It seems incongruous. So much has happened in the last year. Sometimes I wonder what is going to happen next . . . ."

Jamie

WHEN THEY HAD GONE the house seemed very quiet and the strangeness of everything that had happened struck me afresh. I could not get out of my mind the fact that just over a year ago my mother had been alive and Lilias had been with me.

I had reached my seventeenth birthday in September and had left my childhood behind me—not only because of my age. I had learned so much—chiefly that people were not what they seemed to be. I had learned that a man like my father—outwardly a pillar of virtue—was capable of urges as powerful as those which had lured Kitty to abandon herself recklessly to disaster. They had carried my father so far that he had not only brought a woman like Zillah Grey into the house but had actually married her. So there was no doubt that I had grown up.

A sense of aloneness came over me. I had

lost my best friends. There was no one now. Perhaps that was why I was so ready to welcome Jamie into my life.

I found a great pleasure in walking. In the old days I should not have been going out alone, but now there was no one who could stop me. In the absence of my stepmother I was the mistress of the house. I was on the way to becoming eighteen years old . . . an age, I supposed, when one could, in some circumstances, take charge. Mrs. Kirkwell had made it clear that she would rather take orders from me than from the new Mrs. Glentyre.

It will be different when they return, I reminded myself.

There was comfort in exploring the city, and the more I saw of it, the more captivated I became by its inimitable charm.

I was struck by the Gothic buildings which had been infiltrated with a touch of the classic Greek which gave an added dignity. In the first place, the situation was impressive. From one point it was possible to overlook the estuary of the Forth flowing into the ocean, and away to the west were the mountains. Such a superb position must be paid for, and the toll demanded was the bitter east wind and the snow from the mountains. But we had grown accustomed to that and it made our warm houses the more luxurious.

The coming of spring was particularly welcome and it was during that delightful season when I was able to indulge in my explorations. How beautiful it was then, with the sun shining on the tall grey buildings lighting them to silver. Sometimes I would sit in the gardens looking up to the castle or along Princes Street; and at others I would wander into the old town and listen for the bell of the university which rang out every hour.

It was a revelation to discover what a great divide there was in our city between the comfortably situated and the wretchedly poor. I suppose it is so in all big cities, but in ours it seemed more marked, I think, because the two were so close together. A few minutes' walk could take one from the affluent to the needy. One could be in Princes Street where the carriages rolled by carrying the well-dressed and well-fed, and very soon be in the wynds, where dwellings huddled together, where many lived in one small room, where the lines of pitiful garments hung out to dry and bare-footed, ragged children played in the gutters.

It was called the old town; and that was where I met Jamie.

Of course, if I had been wise I should not have been there. A well-dressed young woman could only be visiting such a neighbourhood out of curiosity. But I had become fascinated by my discoveries, and, contemplating on what I saw, I forgot my own dilemma, for my discoveries broke into my brooding on what the future might bring.

When I went out on my walks I carried a small purse with a chain handle which hung on my arm. In it I carried a little money. Since I had visited the poorer parts of the city I liked to have something with me to give to people. There were quite a number of beggars to be encountered and I was very moved to see children in such circumstances.

I knew that I should not venture deep into these streets. For one thing, there was such a maze of them that it was easy to lose one's way.

I had come to a street which was full of people. There was a man with a barrow selling old clothes, children squatting on the pavement and several people standing at their doors gossiping.

I turned away and started to go back as I thought the way I had come, but I soon realised how unwise I had been to enter these streets. I came to a small alley. At the end of it was a young man; he was just about to turn the corner. He looked respectable, out of place in these streets and I thought I might ask him the way back to Princes Street.

I started after him and just at that moment two young boys darted out of a side alley and approached me. They barred my way. They were poorly clad and obviously undernourished and they said something in an accent so broad that I could not understand them, but I knew they were asking me for money. I took the purse from my arm and opened it. One of them immediately snatched it and ran towards the young man who was about to turn the corner.

"Come back," I called. The young man turned. He must have guessed what had happened. No doubt it was a common occurrence. He caught the boy with the purse. His companion darted away and disappeared.

The young man came towards me, dragging the boy with him.

He smiled at me. He was young . . . not

much older than I, I guessed. He had light blue eyes and fair hair with a reddish tint; he looked clean and healthy, which struck me as it was such a contrast to the boy he was dragging with him. He smiled; he had very white teeth.

"He has taken your purse, I believe," he said.

"Yes. I was going to give him some money."

The boy let out a stream of words, some of which I understood. He was terrified.

"Give the lady her purse," commanded the young man.

Meekly the boy did so.

"Why did you do it?" I said. "I would have given you something."

He did not answer.

"Poor little devil," said the young man.

"Yes," I said. And to the boy: "You shouldn't steal, you know. You'll get into trouble. My mother gave me this purse. It would have hurt me to lose it and it wouldn't have been worth much to you."

The boy stared at me. He was beginning to realise that I was not going to be harsh. I saw hope flicker in his eyes. Poor child, I thought.

I said: "You're hungry, are you?"

He nodded.

I took all the money in the purse and gave it to him. "Don't steal again," I said. "You could get caught and someone might not let you go. You know what that would mean, don't you?"

He nodded again.

"Let him go," I said to the young man.

He lifted his shoulders and smiled at me. Then he released the boy, who darted off.

"So," said the young man. "You've let a thief loose among the people of Edinburgh. It's only just postponed his stay in jail, you know."

"At least I shall not be responsible for it."

"Does it matter who is? He'll be there, sure enough."

"Perhaps he's learned his lesson. He was hungry, poor child. I felt so desperately sorry for them."

"But . . . . may I ask what a young lady like you is doing in this part of the city?"

"Exploring. I've lived in Edinburgh all my life and I have never seen this part before."

"Perhaps we should introduce ourselves. I'm James North . . . known as Jamie."

"I'm Davina Glentyre."

"Should I escort you back to a more salubrious part of the town?"

"I wish you would. I'm lost."

"May I make a suggestion?"

"Please do."

"If I were you I would not venture into these parts alone again."

"I shall certainly be more careful in future."

"Then our young vagrant has done some good in his criminal life."

"Do you live in Edinburgh?"

"I have rooms. I'm at the University."

"A student?"

"Yes."

"How interesting. What do you study?"

"Law. But at the moment I'm doing a thesis on this city. I find it the most fascinating project I have ever undertaken."

"Were you researching in the wynds when you rescued me?"

"Yes. I want to see all aspects of the city— its glories and its horrors. This place reeks of history. You can feel it everywhere you go."

"Is that why it is called Old Reekie?"

He laughed.

"Why did they?" I asked.

"I am not sure. Perhaps it is because it is set

on a hill. It may have started when someone saw the city from a distance with the smoke from chimneys rising over the buildings. That's the sort of thing I probe for. I want to recreate not only the city as it is today but as it was throughout its history."

"That must be exciting work. I'm only just starting to know it."

"Yet you say you have lived here all your life."

We had come to the end of the narrow streets.

"You know where you are now," he said.

I was disappointed because I thought he was implying that now he had safely delivered me, he was going to say goodbye.

"It was very kind of you to come to my rescue," I said.

"Oh aye," he replied with a laugh. "I did not exactly have to face a fire-breathing dragon, you know. You could hardly call it a rescue."

"I should have hated to lose my purse."

"Because your mother gave it to you. And she is dead now?"

"Yes."

"I'm sorry."

We had come to the gardens. "If you are not in a hurry . . ." he began.

"I'm not in a hurry," I replied eagerly.

"Shall we sit down for a while?"

"I'd like that."

So we sat and talked and an hour slipped by. It was the most stimulating hour I had spent for a long time.

I learned that his father was a minister and he had lived all his life in the manse north of Edinburgh—a small place which I had never heard of before—Everloch. Great sacrifices had been made to send him to the University and he was determined to make a success and repay his parents for all they had done for him.

I liked him more every moment. It was so pleasant to talk to someone near one's own age. I told him about my mother's death and what a shock it had been. "I had had a governess who was a great friend of mine, but she . . . left. And now my father has married again."

"And you are not happy about that?"

"I don't know. It all happened so quickly."

"And your stepmother . . ."

"She is rather . . . different. As a matter of fact she came as my governess."

"I see. And your father fell in love with her. I expect he was lonely after your mother died."

"I don't know. There are some people one doesn't understand very well. Whereas this morning I hadn't met you and now I feel I know quite a lot about you . . . much more than I do about Zillah Grey."

"Zillah Grey?"

"She is the governess . . . my stepmother now."

He said: "I suppose it all happened so quickly that you are not used to it yet. I think it can be quite a shock when a parent remarries . . . particularly if you have been close to the one who has departed."

"Yes, that is so. You see, if my old governess were there . . ."

"The one who left. Why did she go?"

I stammered: "She . . . er . . . she just had to."

"I see . . . her family or something, I suppose . . ."

I was silent and he went on: "Well, it is not

as though you are a child. You'll make your own life."

"They are going to be away for three weeks," I said. "One of them has already gone."

"I expect it will work out all right. These things usually do."

"Do they?"

"Yes, if you let them."

"That's a comforting philosophy. I'm glad we talked."

"Yes, so am I."

"Do you have a lot of spare time?"

"For a week or so, yes. It's a break now. I could go home, but it's cheaper to stay here. I'm just exploring . . . making notes, you see . . . and writing it all up in the evenings."

"What an interesting life you must have."

"It has its moments." He smiled and added, "Like today." He turned to me suddenly. "You've got an interest in the city . . . exploring the wynds, seeing parts you have never seen before. I'm doing the same. Is it possible . . . ?"

I looked at him eagerly, questioningly.

"Well," he went on, "if you have no objection . . . and when it fits in with your arrangements . . . I don't see why we shouldn't do a little exploring together."

"Oh," I cried, "I should love that."

"Well then. It's settled. When is your best time?"

"This, I think."

"Of course, there are some places to which I should hesitate to take you."

"It would be better for two to go to those places than one."

"Well, for all those that are not safe there are dozens that are."

"Let's go to those places together."

"It's a promise."

"Where shall we meet?"

"Here on this seat."

"Tomorrow morning?"

"Ten o'clock. Is that too early?"

"That would suit me very well."

"Well, that's settled."

I thought it better if he did not escort me right to the house. It would be difficult to explain who he was if I were seen by the Kirkwells or any of the servants and, of course, they would start to speculate.

It had been a pleasant morning, the most enjoyable for a long time. I wondered what my

father would think if he knew I had talked
with a stranger and, moreover, arranged to
meet him the following day.

I simply do not care, I told myself.

GETTING TO KNOW JAMIE—we had become
Jamie and Davina to each other very quickly
—was a wonderful and stimulating experience.
The morning after our first meeting we met
again and it became a custom.

There was so much to talk about. He had
made me see the manse and his younger
brother Alex, who was going into the ministry,
his father and mother, the aunts and cousins
all living close by, the family reunions. It
seemed a very jolly life, quite different from
mine.

And then there was Edinburgh which came
to mean something special to me, probably because of Jamie.

He loved every stone of the place, and memories of those days when we explored the place
together will always be with me. I lived
through them with an intensity, for I knew
they could not last. When my father returned
with Zillah there would be enquiries. They
could hardly be shocked because I had strayed

a little from conventional behaviour. I felt that
if this were suggested I should not be able to
restrain my anger and I might let him know
that I was aware that he had not always kept
rigorously to the paths of virtue. But then, of
course, I was not facing him.

I shall never forget the banner floating over
the castle . . . the wonderful view we had of
the Pentland Hills when the air was clear. I
shall always remember strolling along the
Royal Mile from the castle to Holyrood
House. The cathedral, the house where John
Knox had lived. How I hated that man! I
could grow angry to think of his thundering
abuse at the Queen. Was he such a good man?
I wondered. What secret vice had he? I was
suspicious of all men who boasted of their virtues. Jamie was amused by the way in which I
fulminated against John Knox.

Jamie was entranced by the past. He knew
so much more about it than I did. It was wonderful to have my eyes opened by such an exciting companion.

He made me see Bonnie Dundee with his
dragoons riding behind him; Queen Mary
fresh from the splendour of the French court
coming to dour Scotland; those Covenanters

who had died there in the Grass Market for
what they believed; he told me stories of the
fabulous thief Deacon Brodie and Burke and
Hare, the body snatchers.

Then my father, with Zillah, returned from
Italy. They looked sleek and satisfied. They
were affable to everyone. Zillah was excited in
a rather childlike way, but I felt in my heart
that there was really nothing childlike about
her. My father was indulgent, as besotted by
her as ever.

She had brought presents for everyone: a
blouse from Paris for Mrs. Kirkwell, for they
had stopped there on the way home, a statu-
ette for Mr. Kirkwell and embroidered handkerchiefs for the others. They were all delighted and I thought, she certainly knows
how to please people.

For me there were clothes. "My dear, dear
Davina, I know your size and exactly what
suits you. I spent hours choosing, didn't I,
dear?"

My father nodded with an expression of
mock exasperation which made her laugh.

"We're going to try them on at once," she
announced. "I can't wait."

And there we were in my room while she

fitted the dress on me, the coat, the skirt, the blouses—one frilly, the other plainish but stylish. She stood back admiring.

"They do something for you, Davina. They really do. You're quite good-looking, you know."

I said: "It *was* good of you to remember everyone. The servants are delighted."

She grimaced. "A little bit of bribery. I sensed disapproval before." She laughed and the pretence dropped from her. "Governess marries the master of the house! I mean to say . . . a little bit of a disturbance in the servants' quarters, eh?"

I found myself laughing with her.

Perhaps, I thought, it is going to be all right after all.

I was right when I thought the gifts from Paris would have a good effect. The servants were almost reconciled now.

I heard Mrs. Kirkwell remark: "Like a pair of turtledoves, they are. Well, there's no harm in that and she's not the interfering sort."

My thoughts were, of course, with Jamie. It was difficult now to slip out of the house without saying where I was going. We had to get messages to each other which was not easy.

I was always afraid that a note from him might come to me at an awkward moment, when my father was present. Fate was perverse and it could happen. I could imagine Kirkwell coming in with it on one of the silver salvers. "A young man left this for you, Miss Davina." A young man! Suspicions would be aroused. It was easier for me to drop a note into Jamie's lodgings.

However, we did manage to meet, though it was not the same as it had been in those idyllic weeks.

It was always a joy to see his face light up when I arrived. He would get up and run towards me, taking my hands and looking into my face. And I felt a great exhilaration.

We talked endlessly during those mornings, but I always had to watch the time, which I was sure passed more quickly than it had before.

I believe Zillah was aware that I harboured some secret. I called her Zillah now. She had been Miss Grey in my thoughts, but I could not call her that now. In any case, she was no longer Miss Grey.

"You must call me Zillah," she said. "I refuse to be called Stepmama." She appealed to my father. "That would be quite ridiculous, wouldn't it, darling?"

"Quite ridiculous," he agreed.

And so she had become Zillah.

She was given to those coy moods, especially when my father was present; but I was always aware of the sharpness beneath them. She was as shrewd and watchful as she had been on the day of her arrival.

I knew there was something not quite natural about her; she had been an actress—well, a kind of actress, if one could call the Jolly Red Heads that. In any case, she would know how to play a part. It seemed to me that she was playing a part now.

She fussed over my father, giving the impression that she was worried about his health.

"Now you must not overtire yourself, dearest. That journey was quite exhausting."

He shrugged off her cosseting, but he liked it. She continued to play the ingenue when I was certain that a very mature woman lurked beneath.

One day Jamie and I arranged to meet on our seat in the gardens. When he saw me he came hurrying towards me as usual, his face alight with pleasure.

He took my hands. "I was afraid you wouldn't come . . . that something might prevent it."

"Of course I'd come."

"Well, I'm never sure nowadays. I wish . . . it weren't like this. I can tell you're uneasy. They were wonderful days we had."

"Yes," I sighed and we sat down.

He said seriously: "I think we have to do something, Davina."

"What do you suggest?"

"Your people don't know you are meeting me."

"Good heavens, no. My father would think it was quite improper to pick up an acquaintance in the street."

"Well, what are we going to do about it? I want to call at your house. I don't like this hole-and-corner business."

"I don't like it either. I agree with you. They could discover sooner or later. So far we have kept our meetings secret . . . but one of the servants might see us . . . and there would be talk. They would all be wondering who you are and why you don't call at the house."

"Davina, do you think it is possible to fall in love in a short time?"

"I think I do," I answered.

He turned to me and took my hands. We laughed together happily.

"I'd have to pass exams and get out of the University before we could marry," he said.

"Of course."

"So would you . . . will you?"

"I think it would be wonderful," I said. "But do you know me well enough?"

"I know all I want to know about you. Haven't we talked and talked . . . as much in these few weeks as people do in years?"

"Yes, we have."

"And isn't that enough?"

"It's enough for me. I was wondering about you."

He kissed me then. I withdrew, embarrassed. It was not the kind of behaviour expected on a seat in public gardens in midmorning.

"People will be shocked!" I said.

"Who cares?"

"Not us," I said recklessly.

"Then we're engaged?"

A voice broke in on us. "Davina!"

Zillah was coming towards us. She stood there, her green eyes glowing, her reddish hair bright under a black hat. She looked very elegant in her black coat with the green scarf at her neck.

She was smiling at Jamie. "Please introduce us."

"This is James North and . . . er . . . this is my stepmother."

She put her face close to his and whispered: "But we don't usually mention that. I am conceited enough to think I don't look the part."

"No . . . no," stammered Jamie. "Of course you don't."

"May I sit down?"

"Please do," said Jamie.

She was between us. "You two seem to be good friends."

"We met while you were away," I said. "I wandered into the old town and got lost in the wynds. Mr. North rescued me and showed me the way to go home."

"How interesting! And you became friends."

"We were both enormously interested in the city," said Jamie.

"I'm not surprised. It's fascinating . . . historically and otherwise."

I was surprised. She cared nothing about the city. "Mary Mary, Hanover Squarey." I could hear her singing.

"Well," she went on. "So you are good friends . . . apparently. That's very nice." She smiled beguilingly at Jamie. "I daresay my stepdaughter has told you all about me."

"All?" I said.

"Well, I daresay she has mentioned that I have lately come into the family."

"She did mention it," said Jamie. "I know you have recently come from your honeymoon in Venice and Paris."

"Venice! What an enchanting place. Those fascinating canals. The Rialto. Full of wonderful treasures. Paris, too . . . the Louvre and all that history . . . Davina, why do you not invite Mr. North to come to the house?"

"Well, I didn't think . . . I didn't know . . ."

"Oh, you foolish girl! I'm very cross, Mr. North, that I have not met you earlier. Davina has been keeping you to herself. You must meet my husband. He will be delighted to meet you. What about tomorrow evening?

Come to dinner. Are you free? Oh . . . good. It won't be a big party. Just the four of us. Do say you'll come."

Jamie said: "I should like that very much."

"Wonderful!"

She sat back on the seat and I saw she intended to stay until I left. She talked a great deal with animation and much laughter. Jamie joined in. I was longing to ask him what he thought of her.

Moreover I was a little dismayed to have been so discovered, and also faintly annoyed. She had broken into a moment when we desperately wanted to talk about ourselves.

IT WAS AN UNEASY MEAL. Jamie was clearly a little overwhelmed by the formality. I imagined meals were very different in the manse. My father's dignified appearance and cool manner did not help.

He was polite. He thanked Jamie for rescuing me when I was lost and asked a great many questions about his studies and his home.

"You must find Edinburgh quite different from your little country village."

Jamie admitted that he did and that he was quite fascinated by the city.

"Mr. North is doing a thesis on the city," I said. "It means delving into history."

"Very interesting," said my father. "And you were brought up in the manse and your parents are still there?" he went on.

Jamie confirmed this. It was all very stiff and stilted.

Zillah, of course, introduced a light note into the evening and I was glad of her help.

She talked about Venice and Paris, to neither of which places Jamie or I had ever been; but she was so pleasant to him and did her best to make him feel that he was a welcome guest, which softened the ordeal to which my father appeared to be subjecting him.

I knew it was more serious than it appeared to be and that my father was very disapproving of the acquaintance.

He would be thinking that it was very remiss of me to talk to a stranger in the street. I suppose if one had lost one's way there might be some excuse for doing so; but the proper procedure after that would have been for the rescuer to have taken me back to my home and called the next day to enquire how I was.

Then it would have been for my family to decide whether he was worthy to be invited to the house to resume his acquaintance with me.

Jamie was clearly pleased when the ordeal was over and when I asked him what he thought about the meeting he replied: "I don't think your father approves of me. He doesn't know, of course, that we are engaged and what his reaction to that will be I can well imagine."

"I don't care what he says."

"Well . . . I think it would be better for us to say nothing as yet. I am sure he has not reckoned on having the penniless son of a manse as his son-in-law."

"It is something to which he will have to grow accustomed."

"He is the sort of man who would want everything according to convention."

Inwardly I laughed. I thought of Zillah, selected by him, creeping along to his bedroom. I said nothing. But I would remember it if he ever reproached me for unconventional behaviour.

"So," went on Jamie, "for the moment we'd better plan in secret."

I knew he was right and we had a wonderful time talking about the future.

He did say during the course of that conversation: "That stepmother of yours . . . she's quite different, isn't she?"

"Different from what?"

"From your father. She's jolly. Good fun. I don't think she would be cluttered by conventions. Do you know, I had a feeling that she would be on our side."

"I never know with her. I have a feeling she is not all she seems."

"Who of us is?"

We parted with a promise to meet in two days' time.

Before I saw him again, Mr. Alastair McCrae, who had been a widower for five years, came to dine.

He was between thirty-five and forty, tall, upright and quite good-looking. He was a colleague of my father; and I knew he was wealthy for he had a private income and there was a family estate not far from Aberdeen.

I had seen him once some years before when he had come to the house to dine. I, of course, had not been present at the dinner party, but I had taken a peep through the banisters and seen him arrive with his wife who had been alive at that time.

My mother had mentioned him to me. "Your father has a high respect for Mr. Mc-Crae. He comes of a very good family and I believe the estate he owns is very large."

I was interested to see the gentleman with the large estate and I must have been quite unimpressed because all thought of the gentleman went out of my mind until the recent mention of his name.

Zillah said: "This is going to be a rather special dinner party. You know that dress I bought for you in Paris? It's most becoming. Your father has asked me to make sure you are presentable."

"Why should he be interested in what *I* look like?"

"Well, you are his daughter and he wants you to grace the dinner party with me." She grimaced. "Between us, my dear, we'll open this fine gentleman's eyes."

There were two other guests, my father's solicitor and his wife; and rather to my surprise I was seated next to Alastair McCrae at dinner. He was quite attentive and we talked pleasantly together. He told me about his estate near Aberdeen and how he liked to escape to it whenever possible.

"It sounds delightful," I said.

He then told me how much land he owned and it seemed considerable. The house itself was quite ancient. "It needs propping up from time to time," he said, "but what ancient house doesn't? The McCraes have been there for four centuries."

"How exciting!"

"I should like to show it to you one day. Perhaps we could arrange something."

My father was smiling quite benignly at me.

"Davina is very interested in the past," he said. "History has always fascinated her."

"There is plenty of that here," said Alastair McCrae.

"There's plenty of it everywhere," I said.

Zillah laughed loudly and everyone joined in. My father was very affable, smiling at me as well as at Zillah. It was very different from that other evening when Jamie had been our guest.

I found Alastair McCrae quite a pleasant man and I was glad to see my father in such a mellow mood. I would ask Zillah if Jamie could come to tea. It would be more friendly than dinner as my father would not be there to assess him.

I asked her the next day.

She looked at me and laughed. "I don't think your father would approve of that."

"Why not?"

"Well, dear, we have to face facts, don't we? You're what they call of a marriageable age."

"Well?"

"Young men . . . particularly young men who meet you in romantic places . . ."

"In those squalid wynds! You call them romantic?"

"Romance springs up everywhere, dear child. Those streets may not have been romantic, but the rescue was. And then seeing each other every day . . . looking at each other in such a charming way . . . well, that tells a good deal . . . especially to an old warhorse like me."

"Oh, Zillah, you are very funny."

"I'm glad I amuse you. To be able to amuse people is one of the gifts from the gods."

I thought how she changed. I wondered if my father ever saw Zillah as the woman she was now.

"So," I said, "you want me to ask my father if he can come to tea? This is my home. Surely I can have my friends here?"

"Of course you can and of course you shall. I was merely commenting that your father wouldn't like it. Let us ask the young man to tea. We won't worry your father with telling him. That's all."

I looked at her in astonishment. She smiled at me.

"I understand, dear. I want to help you. After all, I am your stepmother—only don't call me that, will you?"

"Of course I won't."

I wondered what my father would have said if he had known she was in league with me to keep Jamie's visit to the house a secret.

Jamie came. It was a very happy time. There was a great deal of laughter and I could see that Jamie enjoyed Zillah's company.

I saw him the next day. It was easier to arrange our meetings now that Zillah knew and clearly wanted to make things easy for us. He told me how kind he thought her and it was wonderful that she was so helpful.

As for Zillah, she said he was a charming young man.

"He dotes on you," she said. "He's clever, too. I am sure he is going to pass all those exams and become a judge or something. You are a lucky girl, Davina."

"My father doesn't know we're meeting," I reminded her. "I don't think he will approve of Jamie . . . not for Jamie himself, but because he isn't rich like . . . like . . ."

"Like Alastair McCrae. Now, there is a fine man and, as we used to say, 'well padded,' which in the vernacular of the halls, my dear, means that he has a nice little fortune stacked away. I have to admit that your father would approve of him . . . most heartily."

I looked at her in horror. "You don't think . . . ?"

She lifted her shoulders. "Fond parents will plan for their daughters, you know. Your future is very important to him."

"Oh, Zillah," I said. "He mustn't. Jamie and I . . ."

"Oh, he has spoken, has he?"

"Well, it's all very much in the future."

She nodded gravely and then a smile curved her lips.

"If my father objected," I said fiercely, "I wouldn't let that stand in the way."

"No, of course you wouldn't. But don't you

worry. It'll all come right in the end. Don't forget you've got me to help you."

Alastair McCrae came to dinner with other friends of my father. He was seated next to me as before and he and I chatted in a very friendly way. He was quite interesting and less dignified than my father and he seemed to want to hear all about me.

The day after he called he asked us to spend the weekend at his country house.

Zillah told me that my father had agreed that it would be an excellent idea to accept.

It was a very pleasant weekend we spent at Castle Gleeson. I was rather taken with the place. It was small as castles go, but because it was of ancient grey stone and had a battlemented tower I thought it worthy of the name. It faced the sea and the views were spectacular. There was a sizeable estate and Alastair was quite proud of it. That was made clear when we drove through it in the carriage which took us from the station to the castle.

He was frankly delighted that we were paying this visit. It was the first time my father had been there in all the years of their friendship. That was significant, of course.

I enjoyed being shown the castle and listening to the history of the place and the part the family had played in the conflicts between Regent Moray and his sister Mary, of the troubles with the English enemy. I was fascinated by the hardy Highland cattle I saw in the fields. The country was grand, majestic and awe-inspiring.

But everything was particularly cosy within the castle. I had a room in a turret and there was a fire in the grate in spite of the fact that it was summer.

"The nights can get cold," the housekeeper told me. I learned that she had been born in the castle; her parents had been servants to the McCraes; now her son worked in the stables, her daughter in the house. There was an air of serenity about the place. I was not surprised that Alastair was proud of it.

Dinner was served in a dining room which led from a hall which must have been the same as it had been for centuries, with stone flagged floor, whitewashed walls on which ancient weapons hung. It was darkish, for the windows were small and set in embrasures.

"When we are a large company we eat in the hall," Alastair explained, "but this dining room is more comfortable for small parties."

"What a pity," I said, "that you are not here more often. I suppose the greater part of your time is spent in Edinburgh."

"That has been the case. Business, you know. But I escape on every opportunity."

"I can understand that."

He looked at me intently. "I'm so glad you like the old place. I enjoy playing the laird when I can, but mostly the affairs of the estate have to be left to my manager."

"You have the best of both worlds," said my father. "It's a very pleasant house of yours in Edinburgh."

"But I always think of this as my home."

Over dinner he asked me if I rode.

I said I greatly regretted that I did not. "There would not be much opportunity in Edinburgh."

"One needs a horse in the country."

"It must be wonderful to ride," I said. "Galloping over moors and along by the sea."

He smiled and leaned towards me. "Would you like me to teach you?"

"Well, I think that would be most exciting, but I couldn't learn in one lesson."

"One can learn the rudiments. It takes practice, of course, before you are able to handle a horse properly. But somehow I think you would be a receptive pupil."

I laughed. "Well, one lesson will not take me very far."

"It would be a beginning."

"What are you two concocting?" demanded Zillah.

"Miss Davina and I are arranging a lesson in riding."

"What a wonderful idea! An excellent opportunity for you, Davina dear."

"Miss Davina is protesting that she cannot get very far in one lesson."

"You never know," said Zillah slyly, "there might be more."

The next morning I was in the paddock, seated on a small horse on a leading rein, chosen for its gentleness, with Alastair beside me. He looked very distinguished in his riding coat. The housekeeper had found a riding habit for me. It belonged to Alastair's sister, who visited the castle occasionally but hadn't worn it for some time.

"She used to ride all the time," the housekeeper told me. "The family has always been one for the horses. But since she had her children she doesn't ride so much. I'm sure she'd be glad for you to use her old habit."

The fit was not too bad. It was a little large for me, but it served its purpose and I was equipped for the exercise.

I must say I enjoyed it. Round the paddock we went. Zillah and my father walked in the gardens and came to watch us for a few minutes. They seemed very pleased.

At the end of the lesson, Alastair said: "You're a wonderful pupil. We must have another lesson tomorrow."

"I think we are leaving tomorrow."

"I'm hoping to persuade your father to stay another day. Why not? We can travel back together on Tuesday."

And so it was arranged and the next morning I spent in the paddock with Alastair.

At luncheon Alastair said to my father: "Your daughter will soon be a champion rider."

I laughed. "You exaggerate. Besides, I shall not have the opportunity for all the practise I should need."

"You must come again . . . soon, before you forget what I have taught you. We'll arrange something."

"That is most hospitable of you," began my father.

Alastair raised a hand. "Please . . . the pleasure is all mine. What about the weekend after next?"

My father hesitated. Zillah gave him a sideways glance. He turned to her and said: "What do you say, my dear?"

"It seems delightful," she answered.

"Well, Alastair, if you are sure we shall not be encroaching . . ."

"Encroaching, my dear fellow! As I have told you, the pleasure is all mine."

"Not *all* surely," said Zillah with a little laugh. "David dear, you know we should love to come. The week after next, is it?"

"That is settled then," said Alastair.

We travelled back to Edinburgh on the Tuesday.

When I was unpacking Zillah came into my room. She sat on the bed regarding me slightly sardonically.

She said: "The McCrae affair progresses with speed. What a charming gentleman he is. Is he beginning to wean you from the impecunious but oh so charming Jamie?"

"What do you mean?"

"Oh, just is it going to be Papa's choice or yours?"

I was alarmed. It was obvious, of course, but I had refused to think of it too seriously.

Alastair McCrae would be a suitable husband. He had wealth and standing in the city. Jamie was a humble student. He had his way to make and there was the question as to whether he would make it.

I had been stupid, while I was enjoying my riding lessons under the benevolent eyes of my father, not to accept the fact that this was part of a well-laid scheme.

How incredibly innocent I was! My father disapproved of Jamie, whose existence had brought home the fact that it was time I married and settled in life out of the path of penniless students who in his view were in all probability grasping adventurers.

There would be no questioning that with Alastair McCrae; he was probably more wealthy than my father.

Zillah was watching me through half-closed eyes. There was a smile about her lips.

I should be grateful to her. She was making me see life through her somewhat cynical but highly sophisticated eyes.

. . . .

IT WAS SOON AFTER OUR RETURN that my father was taken ill. It happened during the night, but I did not hear about it until the morning.

Zillah said he had awakened her at about three o'clock feeling very sick. She had been up with him half the night. She had given him a powder to settle his stomach, she said. It was a well-known recipe for that sort of trouble. It had not been effective immediately, but after a while he had felt better; and now he was sleeping peacefully.

"Shall I send for the doctor, Madam?" asked Kirkwell.

"I think we might wait awhile," said Zillah. "You know how he hates the thought of the doctor coming. He kept saying he didn't want him. He'd be better soon. I'll watch him carefully. And if there is a return of the symptoms . . . yes, certainly we'll get the doctor. It's just that he hates a fuss and we don't want to upset him. It's something he's eaten most likely, so . . . let's wait awhile."

She kept him in bed all day.

I heard Mrs. Kirkwell mutter something about old men's marrying young wives. Sometimes it was too much for them. "A man's as old as his years and it's not going to do him much good to fancy he's a young one . . . when he is not. He's going to pay for it . . . sooner or later."

I think everyone was surprised by how assiduously Zillah played the nurse; and he had recovered the next day, except that he felt a little weak, which was natural.

"You were wonderful, my dear," he told Zillah. "I'd never thought of you as a nurse, but you played the part perfectly."

"I'm good at playing parts," she replied lightly. "There's a lot you have to discover about me, my dear husband."

The next day I met Jamie.

He was working hard, he said. He had had to forget the thesis for a while. He had to think of passing his exams with honours and setting out on his career as soon as possible.

He asked about the weekend and I told him of the riding lessons.

He was somewhat gloomy.

"What castle was this?"

"It belongs to Alastair McCrae, a friend of my father."

He wanted to know about Alastair; and I

told him we should be going to the castle again the weekend after next.

"If my father is well, of course," I added. "He has been ill."

"He'll recover in time for this visit, I daresay. What is the man like?"

"Alastair McCrae? Oh, he's quite pleasant. He's old, of course."

"Your father's age?"

"Oh . . . not quite. Late thirties, I imagine."

"Oh," said Jamie with relief. "Some twenty years older than you."

"About that, I imagine."

That seemed to satisfy him. I did not tell him of Zillah's hints and what was becoming more and more obvious to me.

He asked after Zillah. She had clearly made a great impression on him.

I told him how she had looked after my father when he was ill . . . not seriously ill, of course, only mildly so, but it had left him a little weak. It seemed she had been very efficient in the sickroom.

"There's something very nice about her," he said.

"Yes, I'm beginning to think so. I resented

her, of course, when she first came. It was because I was so fond of Lilias . . ."

And then I was telling him about Lilias' departure.

He listened intently. "Do you really think that someone put the necklace in her room to incriminate her . . . deliberately?"

"I have to think that because I know Lilias would never have stolen anything. She had been brought up in a religious way. Similar to your upbringing, I should say. She came from an English vicarage . . . you from a Scottish manse. People like Lilias don't steal, do they?"

"People do strange things . . . unexpected things. You can never be sure what anyone will do."

"Well . . . she did say something about the necklace's being a nest egg for me. I keep remembering that. What she wanted desperately was a nest egg for herself, for she was always worried about the future."

"Most people whose future is insecure worry about it. You mean that perhaps in a moment of temptation she took it? It had not all that material value to you. Sentimental, of course, because it had belonged to your mother. But you were not in need of a nest egg."

"All that has occurred to me, but nothing will make me believe that Lilias stole the necklace."

"If she did not, the implication must be that there was someone in the house who did this terrible thing. Ruined her life to a large extent, you could say. Who could have done that?"

"Why should anyone? There seemed to be no reason."

"Reasons can often be obscure."

"I can think of nothing. But at the same time I am convinced that Lilias did not take the necklace."

"It has to be one thing or the other. Either she took it or someone put it there."

"Oh, Jamie, I can't bear to think of it. I can't get anywhere . . . Don't let's talk of it. One just goes over and over the same ground. But I had to tell you. I don't want there to be any secrets between us."

"I wish that I were two years older," said Jamie.

"They say it is foolish to wish your life away."

"Well, I can't help wishing the next two

years away. If they were over I should be in a different position. I wish we could be at least officially engaged."

"You mean announce it?"

"I do not think your father would approve. I think he would try to stop us."

"Zillah is on our side."

"She knows?"

"She guessed. She'll help us."

"I daresay she has a great deal of influence with your father."

"He dotes on her. I have never seen him with anyone as he is with her. What of your family?"

"I've written to tell them."

"And what do they say?"

"My father has sent me a long letter. He wishes me all that is good. They want to meet you, of course. I am sure you will like them. The manse is a bit shabby."

I turned to him indignantly. "You think I would care about that?"

"Well, your home is rather grand . . . and you visit castles . . ."

"There was only one castle, and that was quite a small one. But tell me about your father."

"They are all delighted. I told them about our meeting and they enjoyed hearing about that. I said that I had dined at your house. I may have given the impression that I have been accepted by your family."

"Zillah thinks it better if we don't say anything just yet."

"She's probably right. Oh, how I wish everything was settled. You see now why I wish I were two years older."

"Are you working very hard, Jamie?"

"Yes, burning the midnight oil. Trying not to think too much of you because that is very distracting."

"Isn't it wonderful that we have met? If I hadn't happened to be in the wynds that day . . . lost . . . you would have gone on with your walk and we should not have known each other."

"You haven't any regrets?"

"What a foolish question! Everything is going to work out well for us, Jamie. I believe that, don't you?"

"Yes, I believe it. I'm sure of it . . . because we are going to do everything to make it come right. And because of that we can't fail."

· · · ·

We went to Castle Gleeson for another weekend as we had arranged and the second visit was as successful as the first. I had some riding lessons and Alastair said that during our next weekend he would take me out hacking. If he were with me I should have nothing to fear.

I must say that I did enjoy being in the saddle. He was a wonderful teacher and it gave me a sense of security to have him riding beside me.

"You're doing amazingly well," he told me. "You must come down again very soon so that we can continue."

My father smiled indulgently when he heard this. He said he could think of no way of spending a weekend more agreeably than at Castle Gleeson.

And, of course, when we were in Edinburgh Alastair was frequently asked to dine with us.

Zillah watched it all with an amusement which bordered on the cynical.

"We are working up to an interesting situation," she said. "I have no doubt of the worthy Alastair's intentions, have you?"

I was afraid she was right.

"Do you think I ought to let him know that I am secretly engaged to Jamie?" I asked.

"Oh no. That would be most unmaidenly. It would suggest you knew to what he was leading. Society's rules demand that you, an innocent young girl, know nothing of what is in his mind. Remember the approved surprise of the well brought up young lady when she is confronted with a proposal of marriage. 'La, sir, but this is so sudden.' "

She could always make me laugh.

"Perhaps I should not accept invitations . . ."

"My dear, it is for your papa to accept invitations. We all know they are offered because of you, but modesty forbids you to betray you know."

"What am I going to do?"

"That is for you to decide. Do you want to be the wife of a doting older husband with a castle in the north of this land and comfortable house in this city? Or do you want to be the wife of a young man who is not yet a struggling lawyer, hungry for briefs which might not come his way with great speed, even when he first sets out for a career at the bar? It lies in your hands."

"You know I am going to marry Jamie."

"And renounce the bawbees?"

"Of course. I love Jamie. It's love that is important, isn't it?"

"Providing you have the roof over your head to cover you and food to sustain you that you may enjoy it."

"If there is any difficulty . . . you'll help me, won't you, Zillah?"

She put her hand on my shoulder and, drawing me towards her, kissed my cheek.

"That's what I want to do, my dear," she said.

EVER SINCE Zillah had discovered Jamie's existence she and I had grown closer together. I was getting more and more worried. It was clear now that my father looked upon Alastair McCrae as a suitable husband for me and was delighted that Alastair was paying such attention to me in accordance with the accepted custom. I was sure Alastair would conform as rigorously as my father to the rules and this could only mean that a proposal of marriage was imminent.

My father knew of my friendship with Jamie. Had he not been invited to the house?

And after that . . . nothing. Did my father
think the friendship had ceased because I, as a
dutiful daughter, recognised his wishes for
me? In his opinion we were now waiting for
Alastair to make his proposal . . . and then
we should go on from there.

It would all seem so predictable and so suitable to my father. He would dispose of his
daughter to a man in a position similar to his
own; and she could be expected to continue in
that state to which she had been accustomed.
What more could any father do or any daughter ask? It was all natural, convenient and
traditional.

So I was pleased to have Zillah in the house
because she understood my feelings, laughed
at the conventions and could advise me what
to do.

She often came to my room to talk to me
and would sit where she could see herself in
the mirror, finding, I was sure, her image of
immense interest. I would watch her as she
talked.

I said to her one day: "You are very beautiful, Zillah. I am not surprised that you like to
see yourself reflected there."

She laughed. "I am really just looking to

make sure everything is all right. You could say that I am conscious of my appearance and not confident about it—that is why I have to keep looking to check up."

"I don't believe that. I think you like to look."

"Well, a little bit of both, I daresay."

"I think you are the most beautiful person I have ever seen."

She patted her hair complacently. "I work hard at it," she said.

"What do you mean?"

"Well, you don't think all this is quite what Nature bestowed on me, do you?"

"Well, yes. How else . . . ?"

She raised her eyebrows. "Mind you, I will say that Nature was *kind* to me. I came into the world rather well endowed in that respect. But when you have been given special gifts you have to cherish them . . . cultivate them."

"Well, naturally. But your hair is a glorious colour."

"There are means, you know, of keeping it so."

"Means?"

"My dear, a little something out of a bottle when it is washed."

"You mean it's not naturally that colour?"

"It's not far-off. Inclined more to the ginger. I keep it up to standard, you might say."

"Oh, I see. And your skin . . . it is so white and beautiful. What are you laughing at?"

"You are an adorable little innocent, Davina. But I do have a wonderful secret to keep my skin clear and beautiful. It's daring, but it works."

"What do you mean . . . daring?"

"You won't believe it, but it's due to arsenic."

"Arsenic? Is that a poison?"

"In large doses it kills people . . . but a lot of things if taken to excess are dangerous. In small doses it is beneficial."

"Where do you get it? Don't you have to go to a chemist?"

"Well, yes . . . but there's a bit of fuss about buying it over a counter. I resort to other methods. Ellen is wonderful at that sort of thing. She gets it from flypapers."

"Flypapers? Those sticky things you hang up to trap the flies?"

"The very things. She soaks them in boiling water. The result is a liquid which looks a little like weak tea."

"And you drink that?"

"Only in very small quantities."

I was looking at her in horror.

She said: "You see what people will do for beauty. But beauty is a weapon. If you're beautiful people do things for you. It's a gift, like being born wealthy. You see what I mean?"

"I do. But I believe that without the arsenic and that stuff which makes your hair brighter, you'd still be beautiful."

"Do you know, I rather imagine I would . . . but slightly less so."

"And you think it worth it?"

"If God gives you a gift, He expects you to make the most of it. Isn't there a parable of the talents or something?"

"Yes," I said. "I see what you mean."

"Don't you start trying things," she cautioned. "I shouldn't want you to start soaking flypapers and drinking the solution. It could be dangerous."

"Perhaps for you, too."

"I'm wise. I know what I'm about. Ellen's a

bit of an old witch. She knows a lot about this and she's become an ally of mine. They don't like her very much belowstairs . . . and in a way that makes two of us. I know they tolerate me because I don't bother them, but your father did step out of line when he married the governess. Now you've got a nice skin as it is. Yours is untouched . . . perfect. It won't need any attention for some time."

"I'm glad you let me into the secret."

"Well, didn't you let me into yours? How is Jamie? Don't you dare tell him about my aids to beauty. I shouldn't have confessed to you, but we're such good friends, aren't we?"

"Yes, good friends. Jamie's all right. He's getting impatient. He doesn't like those weekends at Castle Gleeson."

"I'm not surprised. Oh, Davina, I hope it will all come right for you and Jamie."

"If you were in my place you would marry Alastair McCrae if he asked you."

"Why should you think that?"

"You would think it was wise."

"I'm a romantic at heart, dear. That's why I'd do anything I could for you and Jamie."

"I think you would have a lot of influence with my father."

"In some ways, yes. I'm not sure about this matter. He's a stickler for conventions, you know."

"Not always," I said.

She laughed again. "Well, hardly anyone is . . . always. Sometimes it suits them not to be and then they forget how important they've always thought them. But never mind. Trust me. I'll do my best for you and Jamie."

SHORTLY AFTER THAT my father was ill again. This time Zillah had a mild form of the illness. She recovered first and gave herself up to the task of looking after my father with my help.

"It must have been something we ate," said Zillah.

Mrs. Kirkwell was indignant.

"Does she mean something which came out of my kitchen?" she demanded.

I reminded her that they had both dined at the home of one of my father's business colleagues on the night when they had been taken ill. "It couldn't have been here," I added, "because I dined at home on that night and I was all right."

That mollified her. She said: "I think Mr.

Glentyre ought to see a doctor. This is not the first time he's been taken ill in a little while."

"I'll suggest it," I told her.

When I did, Zillah said: "It might not be a bad idea, although I'm sure it was something we'd eaten, and that sort of thing soon passes. Moreover, I was ill, too. Admittedly I was not *very* ill, but I eat a good deal less than your father. I think it was the veal we had at the Kenningtons. Veal, I've heard, can be a little tricky. I'll see what he says about seeing a doctor."

He was firm in his refusal at first, but she managed to persuade him.

When Dr. Dorrington called my father was back to normal. The doctor came at about eleven-thirty and was asked to stay to luncheon. He had been a friend of the family for years. He must have been quite sixty and we had been wondering for the last year when he would retire. There was a young nephew in the offing who was just passing through the last stages of his training and was at the time working in one of the hospitals in Glasgow. It was an understanding that in due course he would take over his uncle's practise.

I heard my father greeting the doctor in the hall.

"Oh, come on in, Edwin. This is all very unnecessary. But I've at last given in to my wife . . . for the sake of peace."

"Well, it can't do any harm to have a little check."

They went upstairs to the bedroom.

When I went down to lunch, the doctor greeted me warmly. He had, as he was fond of saying and did so almost every time we met, brought me into the world. This seemed to give him a kind of proprietary interest in me. He had attended my mother through her illness and had been very upset when she died.

I could see that he was a little fascinated by Zillah.

"Is everything all right?" I asked.

The doctor replied: "Oh yes . . . yes." But he did not sound altogether convincing.

However, it was a very pleasant luncheon. Zillah was in good spirits and made much of the doctor. She flirted with him mildly, which he seemed to like, and my father looked on with amusement.

Afterwards I talked to her.

"Is anything wrong with him?" I asked.

"Well, he's not a young man, is he? But there's nothing to worry about."

"You don't seem very certain."

"Well, I made old Dorrington tell me the truth . . . the absolute truth. I made sure he knew that this was the second attack your father had had. It must have been the food the second time . . . because I had it, too. He said your father should take care. There could be a weakness . . . an internal weakness. His heart's all right, but the doctor kept stressing his age."

"He's not so very old."

"He's not so very young either. People have to be careful as they advance in years." She laid a hand on my shoulder. "Never mind. I'll look after him. I'm discovering a hidden talent. Do you think I'm rather a good nurse?"

"My father seems to think so."

"Oh, he'd think anything I did was good."

"That's nice for you."

"Indeed it is, and I intend to keep it so."

MATTERS CAME TO A HEAD soon after that when Alastair McCrae came to the house to see my father.

He was taken to the study and was there

some time. He left without staying to lunch or seeing anyone else.

My father sent for me and when I arrived in his study he smiled at me benignly.

"Shut the door, Davina. I want to talk to you."

I did so.

"Sit down."

When I was seated he went to the fireplace and stood, his hands in his pockets, rocking on his heels as though he were about to address a meeting.

He said: "I have some very good news for you. Alastair has been to see me. He has asked my permission to marry you."

I stood up. "It's impossible."

"Impossible! What do you mean?"

"I'm engaged to someone else."

"Engaged!" He was staring at me in horror, words on his lips which he was too shocked to utter. "Engaged," he said at length, "to . . . to . . ."

"Yes," I said. "James North."

"That . . . that . . . student!"

"Yes," I said. "You met him."

"But . . . you are a fool . . ."

"Maybe." I was feeling bold. I was not going to be intimidated. I loved Jamie. I was going to marry him. I was not going to allow my father to rule my life. How dared he, who had brought Zillah into the house . . . who had kept her here in the pretence that she was a governess to me? I thought of her creeping into his bedroom. It gave me courage.

"You will forget this nonsense," he said.

"It is not nonsense. It is the best thing that has ever happened to me."

He raised his eyes to the ceiling as though speaking to someone up there. "My daughter is an idiot," he said.

"No, Father. I am not. This is my life and I will live it as I want to. You have done what you want and I shall do the same."

"Of all the ingratitude . . ."

"Gratitude for what?"

"All these years . . . I have looked after you . . . made your welfare my chief concern . . ."

"Your chief concern?" I said.

I thought he was going to strike me. He came towards me and then stopped abruptly.

"You've been meeting this young man?"

"Yes."

"And what else?"

"We have discussed our future."

"And what else?" he repeated.

I was suddenly angry. I said: "I don't know what you are suggesting. James has always behaved to me with the utmost courtesy and in a gentlemanly fashion."

He laughed derisively.

"You must not judge everyone by yourself, Father," I said.

"What?"

"It is no use playing the virtuous citizen with me. I know you brought your mistress into this house. I know she visited your bedroom before you were married. As a matter of fact, I saw her going to your room."

He stared at me, his face scarlet.

"You, you . . . brazen . . ."

I felt I was in command. I said: "Not I, Father. You are the brazen one. You are the one who poses as virtuous, self-righteous. You have your secrets, do you not? I think you should be the last one to criticise my behaviour and that of my fiancé."

He was aghast. I could see he was deeply embarrassed. I had unmasked him and he knew that I must have known this of him for some time.

His anger burst out suddenly. There was hatred in the look he gave me. I had cracked the veneer. I had exposed him as an ordinary sinful man; the aura he had always tried to create about himself had been destroyed by those few words of mine.

"You are an ungrateful girl," he said. "You forget I am your father."

"I find it impossible to do that. I am sorry I shall have to refuse Alastair's offer, but I shall tell him that I am already engaged to Jamie."

I opened the door and was about to go. He had lost control. He shouted: "Don't let that student think he is going to live in luxury for the rest of his life. If you marry him, you'll not get a penny of my money."

I ran upstairs to my room and shut the door.

IT WAS ABOUT AN HOUR LATER when Zillah came to me. I was still in my room, shaken by the shock of the encounter and wondering what was going to happen next. I longed to see Jamie and tell him what had taken place between my father and me.

Zillah looked at me in horror.

"What have you done?" she asked. "Your

father is raving against you. He says he's going to cut you out of his will."

"Alastair McCrae is coming to ask me to marry him. He has asked my father if he might and, of course, my father has said yes. He has already given him his blessing and was prepared to do the same to me. Then I told him I was engaged to Jamie."

"Yes. I gathered that from him. Rather rash, wasn't it?"

"What else could I have done?"

"Nothing, I suppose. But what are you going to do now?"

"I shall not marry Alastair McCrae just because my father says I must."

"Of course you won't. Oh, Davina, what a mess! You'll have to talk this over with Jamie."

"I shall send a note to his lodgings and ask him to see me tomorrow."

"Give it to me and I'll send one of the servants over with it."

"Oh, thank you, Zillah."

"Don't fret. It will all come right."

"I don't think my father will ever forgive me."

"He will. He'll get used to it. These things happen in families."

"Oh, thank you, Zillah."

"You know I want to help, don't you? Besides, I'm a little anxious about your father's health. I know old Dorrington says there is nothing to worry about, but I don't want him too upset."

"Yes, yes, I know. I'm so glad you're here."

"Well, write that note and we'll get you and Jamie together. See what he has to say. He might suggest a runaway match at Gretna Green."

"Do you think he might?"

"It would be very romantic."

"But where should we go? Where should we live?"

"They say love conquers all."

"I feel I want to get away from my father, and I feel he'd want me to go."

"What he wants is a nice rich marriage for you with a man of solid worth like Alastair McCrae. After all, that's what all fathers would want for their daughters."

"But if the daughter loved someone else . . ."

"Well, write that letter to Jamie. Tell him

what's happened, and if he suggests Gretna Green, I'll do all I can to help you get there."

"Thank you, Zillah. I am so glad you're here."

"So you said, dear, and so I am glad I'm here. You want someone to look after you."

I wrote the letter and it was despatched for me.

THE NEXT DAY Jamie was waiting for me at the seat in the gardens.

When I told him what had happened he was aghast.

"So this man is coming to ask you to marry him and he has your father's approval?"

"I shall explain to him at once that I am engaged to you."

"And your father?"

"I don't know what he'll do. He might turn me out of the house. He says he will cut me out of his will if I marry you."

"Good heavens! What a terrible thing to do!"

"He means it. He will never forgive me for what I said to him . . . even if I agreed to marry Alastair McCrae. Jamie, what are we going to do?"

"I can't see what we can do."

"Zillah said we might run away and get married at Gretna Green."

"Where would we go? You couldn't live in my lodgings. I've yet to go through those two years before I can take my exams. How could we live?"

"I don't know. I suppose some people manage."

"You've always lived in comfort. You don't know what it would be like."

"Perhaps your people would help."

"They are desperately poor, Davina. They couldn't help in that way."

"Well, what are we going to do?"

"I can't see what we can do."

I was dismayed. I had thought he would be so delighted that I had admitted to my father that we were engaged and that I had stated so firmly that I would not marry anyone but him. It seemed that romance was crumbling before the mediocre problem of how we were going to live.

"There is only one thing to do," he said gloomily at length. "We can't afford to marry. We've got to wait until I'm through. I'm taking help from my family now. I can't ask them to keep a wife as well."

"I can see that I shall be a burden."

"Of course you won't. But you see it simply isn't possible yet."

I was deflated. I realised I had been rash.

"What can I do then? I've told him now."

"You'll have to hold him off for a while. Wait until we can work something out."

"Zillah said she would help. I think she thought you would suggest our running away together."

"It's not practical, Davina. I wish it were. Oh, why did this have to happen now?"

"Things don't happen when we want them to. How can I go back and refuse Alastair Mc-Crae? My father is furious. He has decided that I shall marry him."

"Surely he'll allow you to have some say in the matter."

"My father never allows anyone—except Zillah—to have any say in any matter. His word is law and he expects everyone to accept that."

"We must think of something, Davina."

"But what?"

He was silent for a moment. Then he said:

"It's distasteful, and I hesitate to say it, but . . . I think you will have to play this fellow along."

"What do you mean?"

"Well, tell him that you can't give him an answer. You have to think about it. It's so unexpected and all that. Ask him to give you time to think. It will be giving us time really. I'll see what can be managed. Who knows, there might be something. We might live in rooms . . . find something cheap until I'm through. I don't know whether it's possible. I'd have to have time to work things out . . . I need time . . ."

"You think that you could work something out so that we could be married?"

"I can talk it over with my family. They might come up with something. But I must have time."

"We *must* work something out, Jamie."

"What sort of man is this Alastair McCrae?"

"He's a very good man, I am sure. He's pleasant. I quite like him. He's very courteous and gentlemanly. I think it would be possible . . . as you say, to hold him off. I don't like doing it. It seems dishonest because I know

I'm not going to marry him . . . and to pretend I might."

"I know, I know. But so much depends on this. I'll soon get us out of it. We'll be married . . . but in my position . . . I have to give a lot of thought to it."

"Of course. I wish Alastair McCrae would find someone else. I wish he would fall hopelessly in love with someone and forget all about me."

"We can always hope," said Jamie.

ZILLAH WANTED TO KNOW what had been said. I told her.

"He's hardly the reckless knight, is he?" she said. "I thought he'd dash you off to Gretna Green right away."

"It wouldn't make sense, Zillah. Where should we live?"

"He has lodgings in the town, hasn't he?"

"There's only room for one."

"Love knows no boundaries, as well as laughing at locksmiths."

"Oh, Zillah, you must see his point of view."

"Of course I do. He's right to be practical.

But I thought he might have been carried away by the romance of it."

"I am sure *you* would always be most practical."

"In such circumstances?" she said, as though questioning herself.

"In all circumstances," I insisted, and I told her what Jamie had said about not giving Alastair McCrae a positive answer.

"It's a wise plan," she said. "Alastair will understand. He'll say he'll wait. Your father will be mildly placated. He'll think you're coming to heel and want to save your pride by taking a little time over it. I'll drop a little whisper of this into his ear. And in the meantime we'll go on as normal, hoping something will turn up."

"I suppose I shall have to see what I can do," I said.

"You will," she told me.

And when the time came I did.

Alastair was charming, and I hated deceiving him. He proposed marriage in a dignified manner.

He began by saying: "I have been a widower for over six years, Davina, and never thought to marry again, but when I saw you at

Gleeson, I said to myself, 'It is time I took another wife.' And I knew that there she was. Will you marry me?"

It was difficult. I drew away and he looked at me tenderly. He went on: "You think I have spoken too soon."

"We have not really seen a great deal of each other."

"For me it is enough."

"I hadn't thought that you . . . felt like this," I forced myself to say untruthfully.

"No, of course not. My dear Davina, forgive me for speaking too soon, but I wanted you to know in what esteem I held you. What do you say?"

What could I say? It was hard enough not to shout out the truth. I shall never marry you. I am engaged to Jamie and as soon as he is able to marry me he will. But I must not say that. There was so much at stake. Jamie needed time and my father in his rage might turn me out. I must prevent that at all costs.

I steeled myself to say: "I can't . . . not yet . . . please."

"Of course I understand. This has been thrust on you. You need time to consider. My dear Davina, of course you shall have time.

And while you are thinking I shall be patient. I shall try to persuade you what a blessing it would be for us both . . . to marry."

"You are very kind and understanding, Mr. McCrae."

"Oh, Alastair, please—and kind and understanding is what I intend to be for the rest of our lives."

It had been easier than I imagined although I could not help despising myself for what I was doing.

Alastair went up to my father's study and as I made my way to my room I heard his first words before the door shut on them.

"Davina was a little taken aback. I'm afraid I have been rather hasty. It's going to be all right. She just needs time."

I could imagine the look of satisfaction on my father's face.

I soon discovered that he was not displeased. It was not out of place for a young girl to show a certain amount of hesitancy; and although I must have proved to him that I was not quite the docile innocent daughter he had previously imagined me to be, he did regard me with a little more favour.

My outburst and the fact that I had caught

him in a compromising situation could not be forgotten and it would always be there between us; but if I gave in to his wishes and married Alastair McCrae, he would be mollified to a certain extent.

ZILLAH INSISTED that he rest. She made a great show of forbidding him to go out when she considered he was not fit to do so. He protested but obviously liked her attentions.

"You're making an invalid of me," he grumbled in mock irritation.

"No. No. I'm nursing you back to the strong man you really are. Give it a little longer. Don't be impatient like some naughty little boy and I tell you you will soon be quite well again."

It was extraordinary to hear someone talk to him like that, but he enjoyed it . . . from Zillah.

She took to going out more frequently, sometimes with me and sometimes in the carriage driven by Hamish. She talked vaguely about shopping or just going for a drive round the wonderful old city. She said she thought Hamish was rather amusing.

One day I went to the kitchen on some pretext. Mrs. Kirkwell was there talking to Ellen when Hamish came in.

He said: "Rats."

"What's that?" demanded Mrs. Kirkwell.

"Rats in the mews. I saw one . . . black it was and nigh on as big as a cat."

"Get away with ye," said Mrs. Kirkwell, sitting down and looking shocked.

"Running round the stables," said Hamish, "having a rare old time. Bold as brass. Saw me and just looked at me . . . brazen like. I threw a stone at it and it just glared at me."

"I don't like the sound of that," said Mrs. Kirkwell. "I hope they don't start coming into my kitchen."

"Dinna fash yeself, Mrs. K. I know how to get rid of the little beggars."

"How will you do that?" I asked.

"Arsenic, Miss."

"Arsenic!" cried Mrs. Kirkwell. "That's poison."

"You don't say! Well, that's what I'm giving to the rats. I'm going to poison the lot of them. That's what."

I said: "Where will you get the arsenic?"

He grinned at me and winked. "I can get it from Henniker's."

"Will they sell it over the counter?" I asked.

"Yes. You tell them what you want and put your name in a book. That's it."

"You can get it from flypapers," I said unguardedly.

"Flypapers!" cried Mrs. Kirkwell. "Oh, yes. I remember that case. Forgotten who it was. Woman murdered her husband. Soaked flypapers or something like that. It was what gave her away. She said she soaked the flypapers to get stuff for her complexion."

"Yes, that's right," I said. "Some ladies do that."

"I'm surprised you know about such things, Miss Davina. As for you, Hamish Vosper, you get those things away from me. Rats indeed! I wouldn't want to see the likes of them in my kitchen, I can tell you."

"I heard," said Hamish, touching his forehead. "You leave the rats to me."

ALASTAIR MCCRAE came to dine with us and we went to dine with him. He had a fine town house in a quiet square similar to our own. It was very comfortable, tastefully furnished and contained the requisite number of servants.

My father was pleased and, I think, becoming a little reconciled to the fact that I knew something of his private life, though of course he would much rather have kept it secret. He believed that I was, as he would say, "coming to my senses."

The same thoughts were in Zillah's mind, I guessed from the looks she gave me. I felt ashamed of myself for continuing with this farce. I felt I was betraying myself, Jamie, Alastair . . . everyone.

I kept reminding myself that I had to do so. Jamie had suggested it. I had to think of our future together. That was more important than anything.

Jamie had changed. Some of the joy had gone out of our relationship. He was thoughtful, a little melancholy. He told me that he hated to think of my meetings with Alastair McCrae and the subterfuge I was forced to practise.

"But what can we do?" he demanded. "It's this wretched poverty. If only I were as rich as Alastair McCrae."

"Perhaps you will be one day, Jamie, and we shall laugh at all this."

"Yes, we will, won't we? But this happens to be *now*, when I am as poor as the mice in my father's kirk. Does he talk to you . . . about marriage?"

"No. He is very kind really. He thinks that in time I shall agree to marry him. He thinks of my being young . . . younger than I really am. He wants to wait until I am ready. He is sure that in time I will agree. He's trying to tell me how good he will be to me. I feel terrible really. It's all such deceit. How I wish I could get away. I don't want to stay in the house anymore. I don't know what it is, but . . ."

"You get on very well with Zillah, don't you?"

"Yes. She is a comfort in a way, but . . . I don't always feel that I know her very well. I think she's an actress at heart, and I never quite know when she is acting."

"She's a good sort."

"My father dotes on her."

"I'm not surprised."

"Oh, Jamie, what are we going to do?"

"Just wait. Something will happen. We'll think of something."

We tried to cheer ourselves by talking of what we would do as soon as we were able, but the joy had gone and had been replaced by a deep apprehension; and we could not shake it off, however much we pretended to.

THE NEXT DAY I was on my way to see Jamie and as I came into the hall I met Ellen.

She said: "Oh, I'm glad I've seen you, Miss Davina. Are you going out? I don't like to ask you, but I wonder if . . . ." She hesitated, frowning.

"What is it, Ellen?"

"I'd go myself, but I can't get out just now, and I don't want Mrs. Kirkwell to know. It will upset her. She'll be in a real panic. I did ask Hamish . . . but he's run out of it and he asked me to get it. He'll show me how to use it, he said."

"What is it you want, Ellen?"

"Well, this morning when I went to the dustbin which you know is just outside the kitchen door, I lifted the lid and a rat jumped out."

"Oh dear!"

"Yes. I'm glad I was the one who saw it . . . not Mrs. Kirkwell. I told Hamish and he said he can't get to the shop today. Mr. Glentyre wants him on duty. But he said it ought to be seen to right away. He's killed two or three in the mews already and he thinks they are trying elsewhere. He said rats are clever things."

"Mrs. Kirkwell will be horrified."

"Yes, Hamish said you have to take prompt action; otherwise they'll be in the house and they multiply quickly. I thought . . . as you are going out . . . you might drop in at Henniker's and get some of that arsenic."

"Is that what you ask for? Arsenic . . . just like that?"

"Yes. Sixpennyworth of arsenic. They'll ask you what it's for and you can tell them it's for the rats. Lots of people use it for that. Then you have to sign a book, I think. That's what Hamish said."

"Of course I'll get it."

"Oh thanks. Don't tell anyone. People get so panicky about rats and if it got to Mrs. Kirkwell's ears she'd be hysterical."

"All right. Don't worry. I'll get it and say nothing."

"And as soon as you come back, I'll put it in the dustbin. Thanks so much, Miss Davina."

I went straight to the drug shop. There was

a young man behind the counter. He smiled at me.

"I want sixpennyworth of arsenic," I said.

He looked at me, faintly surprised. "Oh . . . er . . . Miss, I have to ask you what you want it for. It's a sort of rule . . . if you know what I mean."

"Of course. We have rats in the garden. They have been round the mews quarters and seem now to have come closer to the house."

"It will do the trick," he said. "But as it's poison, I have to ask you to sign the book."

"I understand that."

He went to a drawer and brought out a book with a red cover. A label had been stuck on it which stated: "Henniker's Sale of Poisons Registration Book."

"Do you sell a lot of arsenic?" I asked.

"No, Miss. But people use it for vermin and things like that. It's very effective. One lick and that's the end of them. They do say it does something for the complexion and that ladies use it for that. I couldn't say. Men take it, too." He looked at me slyly. "They say it has powers."

"Powers?"

"When they are not so young, you know."

He opened the book, and wrote the date and my name and address which I spelt out for him. "Sixpennyworth of arsenic for vermin in garden. Now you sign here, Miss."

I did and came out of the shop with a small packet in the pocket of my skirt.

I found Jamie waiting for me, and we talked as usual and I felt frustrated, for I knew it would be a long time before he could take me out of this difficult situation.

When I came back to the house Ellen was waiting for me. Surreptitiously she took the packet.

"I haven't seen any more yet," she said. "I'll use this right away."

A FEW DAYS LATER when I saw Ellen she told me that it had worked beautifully, she was sure. She had not seen anything since and Mrs. Kirkwell had no idea that the rats had been so close. She impressed on me not to mention it to her.

It was later that afternoon. Zillah had gone out in the carriage as she often did. She enjoyed going to the shops and sometimes, she told me, Hamish took her for a tour of the town. Listening to my talk of it she had become interested and was finding it fascinating.

Usually she was home before five o'clock when she would change for dinner—by no means a short operation with her.

I fancied my father had been weaker since his last bout of illness. Zillah thought so, too. Sometimes when he came home he seemed very tired and needed little persuasion to have his meal in his own room. Zillah would, of course, take hers with him.

"It makes him feel less of an invalid and he likes me to be there," she said.

On this particular occasion it was getting late and Zillah had not returned.

I went over to the mews. The carriage was not there. Mr. and Mrs. Vosper were in. They told me that Hamish had taken Mrs. Glentyre out as he often did and they expected him to be back at any moment.

Mrs. Kirkwell was wondering whether to serve dinner. The master was having his in his room, but he would expect Mrs. Glentyre to have it with him there.

"He'll have to be told," said Mrs. Kirkwell. "You'd best tell him, Miss Davina."

I went to his room. He was dressed for dinner and was sitting in a chair.

"Is that you, my dear?" he said with relief.

"No," I replied. "It is I."

"What's wrong?"

"Zillah has not returned."

"Where is she?"

"I thought she went shopping."

"In the carriage?"

"Yes."

"She wouldn't be shopping at this hour surely?"

"No."

"Then where is she?"

He was clutching the sides of his chair and had half risen. I thought how ill he looked. He had lost weight and there were dark shadows under his eyes.

I remembered Mrs. Kirkwell's saying how he had changed and repeating her conviction that it was not good when old men married young women.

It was just at that moment when I heard the sound of carriage wheels. I rushed to the window.

"It's the carriage. She's here."

"Oh, thank God," said my father.

In a few moments Zillah rushed into the room.

"Oh, my dears, what an adventure! Were you wondering where I was? The carriage broke down. We had driven out to take a look at Arthur's Seat. I wanted to see it—hearing you talk about it, Davina . . ."

"Didn't Hamish know what was wrong?" asked my father.

"Oh yes. He tried to put it right. He discovered that he needed something . . . I don't know what. He said he would get a cab for me to come back . . . but it was so difficult right out there to get one. Anyway . . . he managed to fix it up . . . enough to get us home. But it made this terrible delay."

"I have been so worried," said my father.

"Oh, how sweet of you!"

"But of course I was worried."

"He's only just heard that you hadn't come back at the time," I said.

"I was wondering what could have happened to you," went on my father.

She ruffled his hair. "Well, here I am. And we are going to have our cosy little meal for the two of us. You'll excuse us, Davina . . . I think that's how it should be tonight."

"But of course," I said.

I left them together and went downstairs and ate a solitary meal.

THE NEXT AFTERNOON Miss Appleyard called. Zillah had not gone out. I thought she was a little shaken by the carriage incident of the previous day. She and I were in the drawing room together when Miss Appleyard was announced.

We knew her only slightly. In the old days my mother had exchanged a word or two with her after church. I had heard it said that she was a rather malicious gossip who thrived on scandal. My mother had once said that she was a person from whom one should keep one's distance.

Why should she come calling on us? I wondered.

Bess said: "She's asking for Mr. Glentyre. I was sure she said Mr."

"Doesn't she know he is at the bank at this hour?" said Zillah.

"I wouldn't know, Mrs. Glentyre. But that's what she said."

"I suppose you'd better show her in."

Miss Appleyard came into the drawing room and looked abashed when she saw us.

"I asked to see *Mr.* Glentyre," she said.

"Good afternoon, Miss Appleyard," I began.

She nodded in my direction and then looked rather venomously, I thought, at Zillah.

"I wanted to speak to Mr. Glentyre," she reiterated.

"Is it banking business? He's at the bank at this time, you know," said Zillah, regarding her coldly.

"Well, I know he's home quite a lot."

Now how did she know that? I wondered. But she was the sort of woman who would make other people's business hers.

"Can we help?" asked Zillah.

For a few moments Miss Appleyard stood biting her lips as though making a decision.

"I'll have a word with Mrs. Glentyre," she said, looking significantly at me.

I said: "I'll leave you."

Miss Appleyard nodded approvingly and I went out, wondering what this was all about.

Some ten minutes later I heard her leave the house and I went back to Zillah.

She was sitting in the sofa staring ahead of her. She looked troubled.

"What was that all about?" I asked.

"Oh, she was indignant about somebody's 'goings-on.' I didn't know what she was talking about half the time. Silly old fool!"

"She seems to have upset you."

"Oh no. I just can't stand that sort of person. They pry into other people's affairs and try to make trouble."

"Why did she want to see my father?"

"Oh, it was something about money . . . I don't know. Somebody at the bank. I'm glad he wasn't in. He wouldn't have much patience with that sort of thing."

"She evidently thought it was too shocking for my ears."

"Silly old gossip! What's the time? Your father will be home soon. I think I'll go up and have a bath and get ready. Would you tell them to send up some hot water?"

"Of course. You sure you're all right?"

"Certainly I'm all right." She sounded a little irritated, which was unlike her. I wondered why Miss Appleyard's visit had upset her so much.

I left her then and did not see her again

until we were at dinner, which we took together in the dining room that night.

My father was unctuous. His anxiety of the
previous evening over her late return to the
house had no doubt made him feel how very
important she was to him.

She remarked that he was looking tired and
if he were not better in the morning she was
going to insist that he spend a day in his room.

"Zillah!" he said.

"But I shall," she said firmly. "I shall keep
you here . . . and dance attendance on you
all through the day. It's no use protesting. I
shall insist."

He shrugged his shoulders and looked at
her with great tenderness.

I thought what a change she had wrought in
him. He was a different man with her.

TRUE TO HER WORD, she insisted on his staying home next day.

"He's all right," she said. "All he needs is
rest."

It was mid-morning when Ellen knocked at
the door of my room.

She said: "Miss Davina, I must speak to
you. I've bad news."

"Bad news?" I echoed.

She nodded. "From my cousin. She lives near my mother. My mother is very ill . . . as a matter of fact, not expected to live. I must go to her."

"But of course, Ellen."

"I'll leave today if I can, Miss. There's a train to London at two-thirty. If I could leave in that . . ."

"Can you be ready? It's such short notice."

"I must."

"Have you spoken to Mrs. Glentyre?"

"Well, she's up with the master. I wanted to have a word with her, of course, but I thought I'd tell you and see if it was all right."

"I'll go and tell her you want to see her. In the meantime you get on with your packing. Hamish can take you to the station."

"Oh, thank you, Miss Davina. That's a great weight off my mind."

I went to the master bedroom and knocked. Zillah came to the door. I glimpsed my father. He was sitting in his chair in his dressing gown.

I said: "Ellen's in trouble. Her mother is very ill. She has to leave today for London. She wants to see you."

"My goodness. Poor Ellen. I'll go to her right away. Where is she?"

"In her room packing."

I left and she turned to my father and said something to him.

Ellen left that afternoon.

THAT EVENING I dined with my father and Zillah. He was wearing his dressing gown, but Zillah had said she thought it would be better for him to come to the dining room.

"She treats me like a child," said my father, pouting like one.

Zillah talked with her usual animation throughout the meal, and it seemed that the day's rest had been good for my father.

"We shall do this more often," announced Zillah.

When we had finished eating my father was impatient for his glass of port which he always took at the end of the meal. Kirkwell was not there. After the last course had been served he would disappear and come back later to pour out the port. But on this occasion it seemed we had finished more quickly than usual.

I said: "I'll get your port wine, Father," and I went to the sideboard. There was very little left in the decanter. I poured out a glassful and as I did so Kirkwell came into the room.

"Ah," he said, "you are already at the port. I'm sorry. I noticed the decanter was almost empty, so in case there was not enough I went down to the cellar for another bottle. I have decanted it and here it is. Have you enough in that one, Miss Davina?"

"Oh yes," I said. "Would you like a glass, Zillah?"

"Not tonight," she said.

Kirkwell looked questioningly at me. I shook my head and said: "No thanks."

He set the full decanter down beside the empty one.

When my father had finished his port Zillah said: "We'll say goodnight, Davina. I don't want your father overtaxed."

Again that exasperated and loving look.

I said goodnight and went to my room.

IT MUST HAVE BEEN about two o'clock in the morning when there was a knock on my door.

I sprang out of bed and Zillah came in. She was in her nightdress, her hair loose about her shoulders, her feet bare.

"It's your father," she said. "He's very ill.

He's terribly sick and in pain. I wonder whether we ought to send for Dr. Dorrington."

"At this hour?"

I was seeking for my slippers and putting on my dressing gown.

"I don't know," she said. "I don't like the look of him."

I went to their bedroom with her. My father was lying on the bed, his face ashen; he was breathing with difficulty and his eyes were glassy. He seemed to be in some pain.

"It's one of his bad turns again," I said.

"It's worse than the others, I think. We must send for the doctor."

"I'll wake Kirkwell. He's very capable. He'll go for the doctor. We can hardly send one of the maids at this hour."

"Will you do that?"

I went to the Kirkwells' room, knocked and went straight in. Kirkwell was already getting out of bed.

"I'm sorry to wake you like this," I said, "but Mr. Glentyre seems very ill."

Kirkwell, slightly embarrassed at my seeing him in his nightshirt, was hastily reaching for his dressing gown.

As we went out Mrs. Kirkwell was hastily rising to follow us.

Kirkwell took one look at my father and said he would only stop to put on a few clothes and go for the doctor. He thought it was necessary.

Then Mrs. Kirkwell joined us. There was very little she—or any of us—could do.

It seemed a long time before we heard the sound of the brougham bringing Kirkwell with the doctor. But by that time my father was dead.

The Accused

THAT WAS THE BEGINNING of the nightmare. The weeks which followed seem now to have been quite unreal. I felt I had stepped into a mad world which was full of menace. And it had begun on that night.

The doctor had stayed with my father for a long time and when he finally came out he looked very grave. He did not speak to me. He walked straight past as though he did not see me. He seemed deeply shocked.

I soon realised why.

When he had gone Zillah came to my room. She was a little incoherent, unlike herself.

She stammered: "He . . . he thinks it could be some sort of poison."

"Poison?"

"Something he took . . . or . . ."

"Or what?"

"Was given to him."

"Poison given to my father?"

"He says there will be a postmortem. Then . . . an inquest."

"But . . . why . . . he'd been ill. It was not so unexpected."

She looked at me fearfully and shook her head. Then she said: "There is nothing for us to be afraid of." She looked at me intently and added: "Is there?"

"But," I cried, "it's horrible. Why . . . why?"

"They do when people die mysteriously."

"It's . . . horrible," I said.

She came to my room and lay on my bed with me.

We did not sleep all through that night and spoke little. I guessed she was as preoccupied with her horrified thoughts as I was.

The next day they came and took my father's body away.

THERE WERE the thick black headlines: "Mysterious Death of Edinburgh Banker. Postmortem on Body."

It was discussed everywhere. The house had become an object of interest in the town. From my window I glimpsed people passing—and a great many more than did usually—and they would pause and look up at the house staring at the windows. The servants whispered together. I felt they were all watching us furtively.

"It's horrible," said Zillah. "I wish they'd get on with it and let us know the worst. It's the suspense I can't bear."

The day of the inquest was fixed. The entire household must attend. Many of us would be called as witnesses.

They were all in a state of nervous tension, fearful yet half-revelling in the excitement of being at the centre of the drama but still dreading it.

Dr. Dorrington gave evidence first. He said he had suspected poison when he had visited Mr. Glentyre and found him dead. Then the doctors who had carried out the postmortem were questioned. Dr. Dorrington had been right. There was evidence of arsenic in Mr. Glentyre's body. They had found definite inflammation of the stomach and bowels due to an irritant poison. The liver and content of the stomach had been placed in sealed bottles for further investigation, but there was no doubt in the minds of both doctors that doses of arsenic had been taken—or perhaps administered

—probably in port wine, and this was the cause of death.

There was a hush in the court.

They had discovered a great deal. They knew that I had bought sixpennyworth of arsenic at Henniker's. The young man who had served me was there with his red-covered book, and there was my name and the date of the purchase.

He had previously sold sixpennyworth of arsenic to another member of the household, Hamish Vosper. First they wanted to know why Hamish had bought it. There were rats in the mews and Mrs. Vosper had seen them. She had also seen Hamish using the poison. She told the court that she did not like the idea of having poison around but she disliked the rats more. One of the boys who cleaned out the stables had also seen the rats and watched Hamish putting down the poison.

It was my turn. They wanted to know why I had bought the arsenic. I told them it was because there were rats just outside the kitchen. One had been seen in the dustbin. Who else had seen the rat? I told them I had not seen it. It was Ellen Farley who had seen it and asked me to buy the poison that day because she was unable to go out herself. This Ellen Farley was no longer employed at the house. Where had she gone? I did not know and I was muddled about which day it was. I thought it was the day before . . . or two days before my father had died.

I could see the looks of disbelief and sensed that the coroner was suspicious.

I was asked about a quarrel with my father. I was engaged to marry a student, was I? And at the same time a gentleman of Edinburgh was courting me?

"Well, er . . . not exactly. We were only secretly engaged . . ."

"But you liked having two strings to your bow?"

"It was not like that."

"Your father had threatened to disinherit you if you married your student?"

"Well . . ."

"Was that so?"

"I suppose so."

"Did he say in no uncertain terms that the relationship with the student must cease? Was there a scene between you?"

Of course they knew it all. They only asked the questions to trap me.

Hamish Vosper gave evidence. He said he did not know about rats being near the kitchen. They had had them in the mews and he had got rid of them with sixpennyworth of arsenic. Had he used all the arsenic on the rats? Yes, he had. You didn't get all that much for sixpence and they were quite big rats.

"And you never heard of them being near the house. Did you tell Ellen Farley to get arsenic for rats?"

He looked bewildered and shook his head.

"Did you talk about rats to Ellen Farley?"

"Not special to my recollection. I mentioned them in the kitchen once and Mrs. Kirkwell was all shook up."

"Was Miss Glentyre there when you mentioned them?"

"Yes . . . come to think of it, she was."

I felt they were all looking at me accusingly. Zillah, who was sitting next to me, took my hand and pressed it comfortingly.

She looked beautiful, rather pale and her reddish hair was plaited neatly. It was just visible under the black hat. She looked terribly sad—the tragic widow.

They asked her about the port wine. She said her husband usually took a glass after dinner. He kept some in his bedroom and if he did not feel tired he had a glass. He said it made him sleep.

"Did he take some on the night he died?"

"Not in the bedroom. He was very tired, he said. And then . . . he started to be ill."

"So the glass he had was at dinner."

"Yes."

"Was there anything special about the wine?"

"Special? I . . . er . . . don't understand. Oh . . . it was near the end of that in the decanter. I remember Mr. Kirkwell, the butler, came in with another . . . freshly decanted."

Kirkwell was called. He told how he had found there was very little in the decanter and had gone down to get another. When he came back I had poured out the wine and given it to my father.

"What about the rest of the wine in the decanter?"

"I threw it away. There was a little sediment and I thought they wouldn't want that."

"Where is the decanter?"

"In the cupboard. They are always washed

and put away when they are empty . . . till
we want them again next time."

The coroner's jury agreed unanimously that
my father had died from the administration of
arsenic and gave a verdict of murder against
some person or persons unknown.

AS WE DROVE BACK to the house in the carriage, sitting well back lest we should be seen
and recognised, both Zillah and I were limp
with shock. We did not speak. Our thoughts
were too horrifying to be put into words.

A small knot of people were gathered on the
other side of the road. When the carriage
stopped and we alighted they moved a little
closer.

As we went to the door I heard a voice say:
"Murderess." It was terrible.

We went to our separate rooms. I lay on my
bed and tried to recall all that had happened,
all that had been said in that dreadful courtroom.

How had this happened? Just a sequence of
events . . . which . . . when fitted together,
created a suspicion of guilt. My relationship
with Jamie. What was Jamie thinking now?
He would not doubt me, I was sure. My quar-

rel with my father . . . that outburst which had been heard by the servants. The simple act of pouring out a glass of port wine. And then, of course, the most damning of all—buying the arsenic. It seemed as if some evil spirit were at work, determined to destroy me, turning what had seemed the most insignificant acts into those of vital importance. And where was Ellen Farley, who could have told them that she had asked me to buy the arsenic? Indeed, I could believe some malevolent fate had made her mother ill so that she was spirited away when it was so necessary that she corroborate my story.

What had they implied? That I had bought arsenic that I might kill my father? And all because he had threatened to disinherit me if I married Jamie?

I felt sick and very frightened.

That night I wrote to Lilias. I had always found comfort in writing to her and receiving her letters. She was becoming reconciled to her fate now; she had settled down to village life; one of her sisters had become a governess and Lilias had stepped into her shoes.

Now there seemed a special bond between us. We were both wrongly accused, for there was no doubt in my mind that all in the court-room had made up their minds that I had murdered my father.

And murder was a far more serious matter than theft.

I was exaggerating, I told myself. They could not believe that of me.

I told Lilias the details, how I had quar-relled with my father, how he had threatened to cut me out of his will.

"I don't care about the money, Lilias. I re-ally don't. Nor does Jamie. We just want to be together and we shall be when he is a fully fledged lawyer. We'll set up in Edinburgh and have lots of children. That's what I want. But in the meantime there is this thing. People were waiting for us when we came home from the court. I can't tell you how upsetting it was. The worst thing is the matter of the arsenic. I did go to Henniker's. I did sign my name. They've got it all, Lilias. And Ellen isn't here to confirm what I tell them. If only she would come back. Perhaps she will . . ."

Yes, it was comforting to write to Lilias. It was like talking to her.

I sealed the letter and left it to be posted next day.

I went to bed, but sleep was impossible. Scenes from the courtroom kept flashing before my eyes. I could hear the voices droning on, the questions . . . the answers that seemed like betrayal.

Two days later, on the orders of the Procurator Fiscal, I was arrested on suspicion of having murdered my father.

OFTEN DURING THOSE DARK DAYS which followed, I told myself, if this had not happened I should never have met Ninian Grainger.

I was taken away by two men in a closed carriage. Several spectators saw me leave the house and I sensed the excitement among them. I wondered what the headlines in the papers would be now. I found I did not greatly care. I could not believe that I, hitherto insignificant, could be the subject of headlines in the newspapers. I could not believe that I was not only involved in a case of murder but at the heart of it. It seemed years since my mother and I had ridden out in the carriage together and taken conventional tea in the discreetly curtained rooms of neighbours as prosperous as ourselves. It even seemed a long time since Zillah had come to us. Could such things happen to ordinary people such as I was?

So many unusual events and the most unusual was that I, Davina Glentyre, daughter of a respected banker of Edinburgh, was in custody accused of his murder.

How could this have come about? It began when Zillah came to us—no, before that—when Lilias was dismissed. If Lilias had stayed, Zillah would never have come. My father would not have been married. I should have told Lilias that I had bought the arsenic. She would probably have come with me to the shop. Why hadn't I told someone? Zillah . . . Jamie . . . ?

I was put in a little room. I was glad to be alone, and it was there that Ninian Grainger came to see me.

Ninian Grainger was a tall, rather lean man, about twenty-eight, I should say. There was about him an air of authority and what I needed most at that time—confidence.

"I'm Ninian Grainger," he said. "Your stepmother has arranged for my firm to defend you. You are going to need someone to help you. I am that one."

He was pleasantly friendly from the start

and I was soon aware of the compassion he felt for a young girl accused of murder before she really knew a great deal about the world. He said that he had been convinced of my innocence from the moment he saw me. At that bewildering and horrifying time, this was what I needed more than anything and I shall never forget he gave it to me.

His approach was, I am sure, quite different from that of most advocates. From the beginning not only did he give me confidence but that fearful feeling of being alone in a hostile world began to disappear. I felt better even after our first encounter.

Oddly enough, he told me a little about himself so it was rather like a social meeting between two people who would become friends. His father was the senior partner in Grainger and Dudley. One day it would be Grainger, Dudley and Grainger and he would be the second Grainger.

"I have been in the business for five years . . . ever since I qualified. Do you remember the Orland Green case? No, I suppose you wouldn't. Things looked very black against Mrs. Orland Green, but I got her off, and that was a feather in my cap. I'm telling you all this so that you don't think my firm is sending you an inexperienced fellow."

"I wasn't thinking that."

"Well . . . let's get down to facts. You won't be allowed to go into the witness box. A pity. I'm sure you would have done well. No one looking at you could believe you guilty."

"That's because I am not guilty."

"I know that and you know it, but we have to convince other people of it. You'll have to make a Declaration. That's what I want to talk to you about. It's a pity you bought that arsenic and this Ellen Farley is not around to confirm your story. If we could find her, it would help enormously. It's too bad she's disappeared. Never mind. We'll find her. How long had she been with you?"

"I'm not sure whether she came before or after Zillah. Just before, I think."

"Zillah is your stepmother, Mrs. Glentyre."

"Yes. She came as my governess when the previous one left."

"And married your father. That was rather romantic, wasn't it? She does not look like a governess."

"That is what I have always told her."

"A most attractive lady. I am not sure what impression she will make in court."

"She will have to be there, I suppose."

"She'll be a major witness. She was with your father when he died. Oh yes, she will be very important. But we must try and find this Ellen Farley to confirm that she asked you to buy the arsenic for her. You bought it, you gave it to her, and that was the end of the matter as far as you were concerned."

"Yes, that's true."

"Then we must find her."

"I know she went to London. She caught the London train. Hamish Vosper took her to the station."

"London is a big place, but we must find her. It's imperative to your case that we do. Now tell me about the student."

"His name is James North. We met when I was lost in the wynds and we became friends."

"I see. And it went on from there. You met secretly."

"It was only my father who did not know of the meetings."

"Your stepmother knew?"

"Yes, she was very sympathetic. Jamie came to dine. I think she suggested it."

"And it was then that matters came to a head with your father who wanted you to marry Mr. McCrae?"

"Yes. Mr. McCrae had invited us to his house and was a fairly frequent visitor to ours."

"He came to see you?"

"Well, he had not come much before."

"He was the husband your father had chosen for you and he threatened to disinherit you if you married the student. You did not tell Mr. McCrae of your attachment to the student?"

"No . . . I was afraid of what my father would do and Jamie said we needed time."

"I see. And this was the state of affairs when your father died of arsenic poisoning?"

He was frowning. I knew he was thinking that the case was black against me.

"Well," he said, "we'll get to work on this Declaration. We'll marshall the facts . . . just as they really happened. We'll present them simply and go on from there. The important thing is to find Ellen Farley. I'll go and see your stepmother."

He rose, smiled at me and held out his

hand. I took it and said: "You do believe me, don't you?"

He looked at me earnestly and replied: "I do indeed, and I am going to bring you out of this. Never fear."

WHILE I WAS AWAITING my trial I saw Ninian Grainger frequently and he continued to be of more comfort to me than anyone. He had an air of buoyant confidence. Never once would he allow himself to visualise failure. It meant a great deal to me that he showed his belief in my innocence, though when I considered my declaration of what had led up to the tragedy there was so much which seemed to suggest my guilt.

But that had to be proved and I was awaiting the trial which was to take place two months after my arrest.

One cannot remain in a state of shock forever; and when I awoke in the morning it was no longer to unfamiliar surroundings. There was no longer that feeling of blankness as realisation of what had happened swept over me.

An ordeal lay before me and the passing of each day was a relief to me because it brought it nearer; and I longed for it to be over.

I had no idea what the outcome would be. Ninian Grainger was wonderful. He filled me with hope which I could not entirely believe in unless he was there. In his presence I had the utmost faith in him and myself.

I was allowed visitors, but I was never alone with them. There was a woman with sharp eyes and an alert manner sitting in a corner watching me all the time. She was not unkindly, just impersonal. I never knew whether she thought I was a murderess or an innocent victim of an evil fate.

She saw to my creature comforts to a certain extent, but there was no warmth in her. I began to regard her as an inanimate object, which was just as well in a way because it enabled me to talk more freely to my visitors when I had a chance to do so.

Zillah came. She was full of compassion. "This dreadful, dreadful business," she said. "But it must come out right, Davina. Your very nice barrister seems to think so. He's been to see me several times. He's very eager to find Ellen. I told him that she'd come from London and I thought her mother was there."

"And London's a big place," I said, echoing Ninian Grainger.

"Yes, I'm afraid so. Mr. Grainger did go to London. He's put a notice in the papers to see if he can trace her."

"Do you think he will?"

"I expect so. These people do a marvellous job, don't they? Oh, Davina . . . I do hope you'll soon be home."

"There's the trial first. And do you think they'll believe me?"

"I think that Ninian Grainger is very good. He's young and full of energy. It means a good deal to him to get you off."

"Yes, he's in his father's business. He hopes to be a partner and I suppose he wants to prove himself."

"He wants that, of course. But it's more than that. He really believes in you."

"He has been very good to me. I don't know what I should have done without him."

She was silent.

"Zillah," I said. "What's it like at home?"

"It's awful. They rush out and get the papers as soon as they hear the boys in the street. They're always hoping there'll be some news."

"And you're bearing it all!"

"*You*'re doing very well, Davina."

"I don't know. I feel it is all so strange. I

feel like another person. I keep going over it all. I keep thinking of everything that happened. Have you seen . . . Jamie?"

"He did come to the house. He seemed absolutely broken-hearted. He'll come to see you, I think. He didn't know whether he should . . . whether it would be right. He's just so shocked by the whole thing."

"Who is not?"

"I wish there were something I could do."

"They'll ask you a lot of questions, Zillah."

"I know. I'm dreading it."

"I'm longing for it. I think waiting is one of the worst things about it. I want to get it over . . . even if . . ."

"Don't say that," said Zillah. "I can't bear it."

We were seated at a table facing each other, which was according to the regulations, and the watchdog was seated in a corner, her eyes discreetly averted.

Zillah gripped my hands.

"I'm thinking of you all the time," she said. "It's got to come out right. It *must*. Everyone must see that you couldn't possibly do such a thing."

. . . .

JAMIE CAME. He looked like a different person. All the joy had gone out of him. He was pale and there were shadows under his eyes.

"Davina!" he said.

"Oh, Jamie, I'm so glad you came to see me."

"This is terrible."

"I know."

"What will be the outcome?"

"We have to wait and see. The advocate is very optimistic."

He put his hand to his forehead covering his eyes.

"Davina . . . they are saying the most terrible things."

"I know."

"You bought that arsenic. You signed for it. Your name is in that book with the date and everything . . . and soon after your father is dead . . . after you bought it."

"I know that, Jamie. I've explained it all."

"People are saying . . ."

"I can guess what they are saying, but Ninian Grainger is going to prove them wrong. He's going to make them see the truth."

"Can he?"

"He says he can, Jamie. And he must because it is the truth, Jamie. I believe you think . . . I did it."

He hesitated for too long before he protested that of course he did not believe that.

"Your family?" I said. "What are they thinking?"

He bit his lip and did not answer.

"I suppose," I went on, "it is not good for a minister to be caught up in this sort of thing . . . even if it is remotely."

"Oh," he said after a pause, "it is not good for anyone, is it?"

"I'm sorry, Jamie . . . so sorry to have involved you in this."

He said: "I shall be called to give evidence at the trial. Everyone is talking about it. My fellow students . . . they think I know something. It's horrible."

"Yes, horrible things have happened to us both. But Mr. Grainger is sure everything will come right."

"But . . . it will always be there, won't it? People will remember."

I stared at him in horror. I had not thought of that. I imagined that once Ninian Grainger had made the court agree with him that I was innocent, that would be an end of the matter. I would return home, marry Jamie and this would all become like a dream . . . not a recurring nightmare.

He had changed. He was remote. He was not the warm-hearted lover I had known. Whatever he said there was doubt in his heart. I recoiled from him.

He was aware of this, but there was nothing he could do to hide his true feelings. We had changed towards each other.

The doubt was in his mind. It hung like a cloud between us; and for me there was the knowledge that the love he had had for me was not strong enough to bear this strain.

Jamie's visit had not made me happier.

Alastair McCrae did not come to see me. I fancied he was congratulating himself that he was not sufficiently involved for the glare of publicity to alight on him; and he wanted to keep it like that.

MY TRIAL TOOK PLACE in the High Court of Justiciary. I felt dazed. The courtroom was crowded and it seemed that the object of everyone present was to scrutinise me. I had been prepared by Ninian Grainger for what I must expect. I should stand at the bar and the Crown would state the case against me when the Defense would endeavour to prove the accusation wrong.

My feelings were so tumultuous that it is impossible to describe them. They changed from moment to moment. Innocence is the greatest defence. It gives courage. If one tells the truth, surely that must prevail. That thought remains with one all the time. It is the greatest ally.

I looked at the members of the jury—those who would decide my fate; and they gave me confidence.

Even at this stage, after the weeks of waiting for this day, there was an element of unreality about it all. I . . . Davina Glentyre, the young girl who had gone to church with her mother, was now the prisoner at the bar in a court of law accused of murdering her father.

How could it have come about? It must be a wild mad dream.

There was silence through the court while the indictment against me was read.

"Davina Scott Glentyre, now or lately prisoner in the prison of Edinburgh, you are indicted and accused at the instance of Her

Majesty's Advocate for Her Majesty's interest: that albeit by the laws of this land and of every other well governed realm, the wickedly and felonious administering of arsenic, or other poisons, with intent to murder, is a crime of a heinous nature and severely punishable. Yet true it is that you, Davina Scott Glentyre, are guilty of the said crime . . ."

It went on detailing the evidence against me —most damning of which was, of course, my buying the arsenic at Henniker's shop, my signature in the poison book being an important piece of evidence.

Then came the witnesses.

Dr. Dorrington explained how Mr. Kirkwell, the butler, called him in the early hours of the morning. He was not surprised because Mr. Glentyre had, over a few months, suffered from bilious attacks. He had expected to find this just another, perhaps more severe than the previous ones, and he had felt it was unnecessary to call him out at such an hour. However, he had been shocked on arriving at the house to find Mr. Glentyre dead.

"Did you examine him?"

"Briefly. I saw at once that there was nothing I could do for him."

"Did you suspect poison?"

"I thought there was something unusual about his sudden death."

Other doctors followed. There was Dr. Camrose, professor of chemistry at the University. He had examined certain of the deceased's organs and had found undoubted traces of arsenic. Another doctor was called and confirmed this. He said there had been a final dose which had resulted in death and which had obviously been taken in port wine. But there were traces of arsenic in the body which suggested that it had been taken over some little time.

There followed a great many scientific references which I was sure none but the specialists understood; but the fact emerged that my father had died through arsenical poisoning and that he had been taking it in smaller quantities over some time.

The doctors were asked if it were a common practise to take arsenic.

"It is said to have rejuvenating powers," replied the doctor. He had known men take it for that reason. Women used it here and there, he believed, because it was thought to be good for the complexion. It was a dangerous practise.

At length it was time for the people I knew to take their places. I was alert, watchful of them. It seemed so strange to see them there, though stranger still for them, I supposed, to see me where I was.

On trial for murder! It was not the sort of thing one would think could ever happen to oneself. That sort of drama was for other people. And now here we all were . . . people who had known each other over the years . . . ordinary, simple people . . . all here in the centre of the stage, with the whole of Scotland . . . and perhaps beyond . . . watching us.

I could imagine the excitement which people were feeling. A young girl on trial for her life!

Mr. Kirkwell was questioned about being called by me in the early morning and dashing off to get the doctor.

"Did you go to the bedroom where Mr. Glentyre was dying?"

"Yes, sir."

"Did it occur to you that it was strange that he should be so ill?"

"Well, sir, he'd had one or two of these attacks. I thought it was just another . . . only worse."

Mrs. Kirkwell followed her husband into the witness box.

"Mrs. Kirkwell, you were worried about the rats which had appeared near the house, were you?"

"Yes, sir. They were in the mews. I never had them in the house, sir."

"Did you ever see any near the house?"

"Oh no. I couldn't have borne that. Rats near my kitchen! Horrible things. Dirty. Hamish told me they were in the mews . . . stables and all that. But he got some arsenic and finished them off."

"Was there any mention of getting arsenic because he had seen them near the kitchen door?"

"Never in my hearing, sir. I never knew they were in the dustbin. I would have been out of my mind, I can tell you, if I'd heard that."

"So you would undoubtedly remember. Now I want you to cast your mind back. A young man, a Mr. James North, had been invited to the house, had he not?"

"Yes. He came once or twice. He was sweet on Miss Davina."

"And Mr. Glentyre did not approve of the young man. Is that it?"

"I don't reckon he had anything against him, but he was poor and wasn't what Mr. Glentyre had in mind for her."

"And there was a scene."

"Well, sir. I just happened to be on the stairs with Bess . . . that's one of the maids. The door of the study opened. I heard them shouting and Miss Davina flounced out. He was going to cut her out of his will if she married Mr. North."

"And Miss Davina was upset, was she?"

"Oh terribly. She shouted back at him. She said he could cut her out if he wanted to. It wouldn't change her mind . . . or something like that."

Ninian rose and said: "Do you often listen to your employer's private conversation, Mrs. Kirkwell?"

"No, I do not, sir. I just happened . . ."

"Just happened to be conveniently placed when Miss Davina flounced—I think you said —out of the study and went to her room. When did you hear all this conversation? It must have lasted more than a few seconds. Yet in that time you hear that Mr. Glentyre is going to cut her out of his will and her saying that she did not care."

"Well, that's what I heard."

"I suggest that you heard voices and as time passed you imagined you heard those words spoken."

"No, I did not."

Ninian smiled and said: "That will be all."

Mrs. Kirkwell, flushed and indignant, left the witness box.

Hamish was next. He looked slightly less jaunty than usual.

"I am Hamish Vosper," he said, "coachman to the late Mr. Glentyre. At the beginning of this year I saw a rat in the stables. I bought sixpennyworth of arsenic at Henniker's drugstore and managed to get rid of three of them in a week."

"Did you mention this in the kitchen to the servants?"

"Yes, I did."

"To Mrs. Kirkwell and the maids? Was anyone else there when you talked of the efficiency of arsenic?"

He looked across at me and hesitated.

"Was Miss Davina Glentyre there?"

"Well, yes, she was."

"Did she express interest?"

"I . . . I don't remember."

"Did the maid Ellen Farley tell you she had seen a rat near the kitchen . . . in the dustbin?"

"No."

"Did Miss Farley ever speak to you about rats?"

"I don't think so. She didn't speak much to me. She wasn't the talking sort."

"Are you sure that she did not tell you she had seen a rat jump out of the dustbin?"

"If she did I can't recall it."

"That will do."

Ninian rose.

"Mr. Glentyre was pleased with your services as a coachman, was he not?"

Hamish preened himself. "Oh yes, he reckoned I was very good."

"So good that you took the place of your father?"

"Well . . . yes."

"Excellent," said Ninian. "And you were naturally proud of your skills?"

Hamish looked pleased. I could see he was enjoying this.

"You like to go out with your friends . . . in the evenings?" went on Ninian.

"What's wrong with that?"

"I ask the questions, remember, please. There is nothing wrong with it unless you decide to use the family carriage for these excursions . . . without your employer's permission."

Hamish flushed.

"Did you do this on several occasions?" persisted Ninian.

"I . . . I don't remember."

"You don't remember? Then I will assure you that you did and I can produce evidence to prove this. But your memory is not good. You forgot. Might it not be that you could also have forgotten that Ellen Farley mentioned to you that she had seen a rat in the dustbin and you recommended her to try the arsenic which had proved effective?"

"I . . . I . . ."

"No more questions."

I saw how successfully Ninian had planted doubts in the minds of the jury as to the reliability of Hamish's evidence; and he was, after all, a key witness.

Zillah made a good impression on the court, but I felt it was not the Zillah I knew who stood in the witness box.

She even looked different. She was all in black; her face was pale, her hair simply dressed under the small black hat with the veil. She gave the impression of being a young, beautiful and lonely widow, suddenly bereft of a loving husband, looking out in bewilderment on a cruel world which, with one stroke, had taken her husband and put her stepdaughter in the dock.

She was a superb actress and like all her kind enjoyed having an audience to perform to. On the other hand, so well did she play the part that she did not appear to be acting.

She had I supposed cared for my father. She had always behaved to him most lovingly; she had seemed genuinely concerned about his illness. She had made the last months of his life happy. Yet I wondered.

The Lord Justice Clerk was clearly impressed by her—as I think was the whole court. Her beauty seemed the more outstanding because of the simplicity of her dress and her quietly tragic manner.

"Mrs. Glentyre." The questioner spoke in a gentle voice. "Could you tell us what happened on that tragic night?"

She told them that her husband had not been well on the previous day and she had insisted on his remaining at home.

"Was he very ill?"

"Oh no. I just thought he should have a restful day."

"That night at dinner he took a glass of port wine?"

"Yes."

"The wine was in a decanter on the sideboard?"

"Yes."

"Your stepdaughter, Miss Davina Glentyre, offered to pour it out?"

"Yes. There was nothing unusual about that. Kirkwell, the butler, was not present."

"He was usually present, was he?"

"Er . . . yes, mostly. But he had been bringing up another decanter."

"You did not take a glass of wine on that occasion?"

"No."

"Nor your stepdaughter?"

"Neither of us did. We rarely did."

"So it was just Mr. Glentyre who had his glass from the decanter which was poured out by Miss Glentyre?"

"Yes."

"Did you know that there had been trouble between your husband and his daughter about her determination to marry a young man?"

"Yes . . . but I didn't think it was very serious."

"But he had threatened to cut her out of his will."

"I just thought it was one of those little upsets that would blow over."

"Did he talk to you about it?"

She shrugged her shoulders. "He may have mentioned it."

"Did he want her to marry someone else?"

"Parents do have plans for their children. I think it was all rather vague."

"And did your stepdaughter speak to you of this matter?"

"Oh yes. We were good friends. I tried to be a mother to her." She made a little gesture.

"More like a sister, I imagine," said the Justice Clerk smiling and allowing his admiration for her to show a little.

"And you talked to her about this matter? Did she mention how bitterly she felt against her father?"

"No. Not at all. I convinced her that it would come all right in the end. Parents often disapprove of their children's marriages."

It was Ninian's turn.

"You and your stepdaughter quickly became good friends?"

"Oh yes."

"You came as governess originally, I believe."

"That is so."

"And within a short time you married the master of the house."

I could see that the court was with her. It was charmingly romantic and the most natural thing in the world that the master of the house should be overcome by her charms. A happy ending for the governess—but, oh, how tragically her happiness had been cut short!

"We have heard that traces of arsenic were found in your husband's body. Can you give us any idea how they came to be there?"

"I can only say that he must have taken it himself."

"You have heard that it is a practise among some people to take arsenic for certain purposes. Do you think there is a possibility that your husband may have been one of these people?"

"Well . . . . there is a possibility."

"Why do you say that?"

"He once told me that some time ago he had taken small doses of arsenic."

There was tenseness in the court. Everyone was watching her. I felt myself caught up in it. My father . . . taking arsenic!

"What effect did he say this had on him?"

"It made him better, he said. Someone told him that it was dangerous . . . and he stopped taking it."

"Did he tell you where he got this arsenic?"

"I did not ask him and he did not say. He travelled sometimes abroad. He could have got it somewhere on the Continent. He was there on business some years ago. It may have been then."

"Did he say so?"

"No. I did not think to ask. I was just surprised that he had taken it."

"This could be important evidence. Why did you not mention it before?"

"I only remembered it when you asked."

"Did it not occur to you on your husband's death that the arsenic found in his body might have been taken voluntarily by himself?"

"No . . . only just now."

"And now you think that is a possibility?"

"Oh yes, I do."

There was a hushed silence over the court. I had the feeling that she was lying. I could not believe that my father would take arsenic. It was true that some years ago he had gone to the Continent on business. Could it possibly be that he had acquired the arsenic then? After all, what did I know of his secret life? Much had recently been revealed to me, but there must be so much of which I was ignorant.

I could sense Ninian's excitement.

The Prosecution wanted to question Zillah further.

"If your husband had a secret store of arsenic in the house, where would he keep it?"

"I don't know. He had a cabinet in which he kept certain medicines."

"Did you ever see arsenic there?"

"I hardly looked at it. I had no reason to go

there. I don't think it would have been labelled 'arsenic' if it had been there."

"Was not the bedroom searched at the time of Mr. Glentyre's death?"

"I think so."

"No arsenic was found then. If he were taking it, would it not be strange that there was no trace of it in the room?"

"I do not know."

The Prosecution was shaken; but I could see the dawning triumph in Ninian's attitude.

I should have been elated, for there was a possibility that my father had killed himself. But was this true? Was Zillah inventing this story in an attempt to save me?

The first day was over. I had an idea that there would be many more to come.

NINIAN CAME TO SEE ME that evening. He was elated.

"It's a breakthrough," he said. "This must be our line. If we can prove he has taken the stuff himself, we've got the answer. It's plausible. A man who is no longer young married to a beautiful young wife. Naturally he wants to improve his health. He wants to be young again . . . . so he resorts to this."

"I cannot believe that my father would ever have taken arsenic."

"You cannot be sure what people will do. If only we could find this Ellen Farley who would confirm that she asked you to buy the arsenic . . . we should be in the clear. We could romp home. I can't think what's happened to the woman. It's not easy to find people in London . . . particularly on such little information. If it had only been some country town . . . or village . . . we should have had her by now. They are still searching, of course. But I did think something would have come to light by now. Your stepmother was a wonderful witness. I have the idea that she desperately wants to help you."

"Yes, I think she does."

He took my hands and gripped them hard. "Bear up," he said. "We are going to get there."

I was thinking: Zillah is my friend, but I never feel I know what is in her mind. As for Jamie, I knew too well what was in his, and it meant that his love was not strong enough to bear this trial.

. . . . .

THE NEXT DAY Jamie went into the witness box.

"You and Miss Glentyre met by chance in the street?" he was asked.

"Yes. She was lost."

"I see, and she called on you for help?"

"Well . . . I saw that she was lost."

"You took her home and arranged to meet again?"

"Yes."

"And you became engaged to be married?"

"It was not official."

"Because you, as a student, were unable to support a wife?"

"Yes."

"What did Miss Glentyre tell you about her father?"

"That he had forbidden her to see me."

"Yet she continued to do so?"

"Yes."

"Do you think that was becoming conduct?"

"I was upset by it."

"You hated deceiving Mr. Glentyre?"

"Yes, I did."

"But Miss Glentyre insisted?"

Ninian was on his feet. "I protest at the

question," he said. "Miss Glentyre could not force the witness to the tryst. He must have gone willingly."

"A forceful young lady," said the Justice Clerk. "But this was a man in love. The court will realise he went to the meeting willingly as Mr. Grainger insists."

The questions were resumed. "What did you propose to do about the matter?"

"We were to wait until I had finished my training."

"That would be in two years' time at least?"

"Yes. Miss Glentyre suggested . . ."

"What did she suggest?"

"That we elope."

I paused. I could see the picture the Prosecution was trying to build up of a forceful woman who knew exactly what she wanted and was determined to get it even if it meant eloping with her lover against her father's wishes . . . or alternatively murdering her father.

"And you did not fall in with this suggestion?"

"I knew we could not do it."

"Because you had no money of your own. All you had came from your family and if

Miss Glentyre were cut off as her father had threatened she would have nothing either."

I felt sick, praying for him to stop. I knew that Jamie was regretting that we had ever met; and that was the most cruel realisation of all.

It was Ninian's turn.

"Had you discussed marriage with Miss Glentyre before you were aware of her father's disapproval of the match?"

"Yes."

"Do you think that because she was indifferent as to whether you would be poor or rich she wanted to show her loyalty by being prepared to endure a few years of hardship before you could become established in your profession?"

"Yes, I suppose so."

It was the best he could do with Jamie, and I wondered if we had lost the advantage won by Zillah's evidence.

Two more days dragged on. The coming and going of witnesses continued. There were more doctors and a great deal of scientific terms which I could not understand, but I knew that it was not going well for me.

There was no news of Ellen's whereabouts. I thought: there is only one consolation. It will soon be over.

Then something happened. Ninian visited me and I saw at once that he was excited.

He sat down opposite me and smiled.

"If this works out, we've done it," he said. "Thank God for the divine Zillah."

"What's happened?"

"You remember she told the court that her husband had once confessed to taking arsenic?"

"Yes."

"She has discovered a piece of paper, screwed up, she says, at the back of a drawer in which your father kept things like socks and handkerchiefs. A piece of white paper with the remains of a seal on it. She opened this paper. There was nothing on it . . . no writing to show what it might have contained, but she thought she detected a few grains of powder on it."

"Powder?" I echoed.

He grinned at me, nodding. "In her husband's drawer! She immediately thought . . . you know what she thought. Wise woman. She took it to the police. It is now being analysed."

"What does this mean?"

"That if the paper contained what we hope it did, there is a possibility . . . a great possibility . . . that the dose that killed your father could have been self-administered."

"When shall we know?"

"Very soon. Oh, Davina . . . Miss Glentyre . . . don't you see?"

I had rarely seen anyone as overjoyed as he was at that moment; and in the midst of all my muddled thoughts I wondered whether he brought such feeling to all his cases.

EVENTS MOVED QUICKLY from there.

Dr. Camrose was recalled. There was no doubt that the piece of paper had contained arsenic.

The court was astounded. Zillah was recalled.

"Can you explain why this piece of paper was not brought to light before?"

"It was right at the back of the drawer."

"Can you explain why it was not seen when the room was searched?"

"I suppose because the searchers were not careful enough."

There was a ripple of mirth throughout the court.

Zillah went on: "You know how things get caught up in chests of drawers? It was not actually lying in the drawer. It had got caught up and really was midway between the upper and lower drawers, if you know what I mean."

She smiled beguilingly at her questioner who grunted. But there was nothing he could do to spoil the impression she had made on the court.

Ninian said he had no questions to ask.

From that time the atmosphere changed and it was time for the speeches from the Prosecution and the Defense.

The Prosecution was first. The Lord Advocate spoke for a long time. He set out all the facts against me. First there was the disappearance of the elusive Ellen Farley which seemed highly suspicious. Then there was the fact that I wished to marry and my father had threatened to disinherit me if I did. There was motive for murder.

As I listened I thought how strange it was that so much that was innocent could be misconstrued.

When the day ended with this speech I felt that everything had turned against me.

Ninian came to see me.

"You look troubled," he said.

"Aren't you?"

"No. I am certain that you will soon be free."

"How can you be so certain?"

He leaned towards me. "Experience," he said.

"Tomorrow . . ." I began fearfully.

"Tomorrow is our turn. You shall see."

He took my hand and put it to his lips and we looked steadily at each other for a few moments.

"This means more to me than anything," he said.

"I know. There has been a great deal of notice given to the case. If you win you will have that partnership surely."

"Perhaps. But I wasn't meaning that."

Then he released my hand.

"Now you must have a good night's sleep," he said. "I've asked them to give you a mild sedative. Please take it. It's necessary. You have been through a trying ordeal and now we are nearing the end. But remember this: we are going to win."

"You are so certain."

"I am absolutely sure. We can't fail. Things looked black at the start, I admit. But it's working out now in our favour. A good night's rest . . . and I'll see you in court tomorrow. I promise you you won't be there much longer."

I fell asleep thinking of him.

He was magnificent. His eloquence carried the jury along with him. He was so confident.

"Members of the jury, can you convict this young woman who is so clearly innocent?" He went through it all. I had met a young man. Most young women meet young men at some time in their lives. I was carried along on the stream of young love. I had been prepared to elope and lose all chance of my inheritance. Was that the attitude of one who could plan cold-blooded murder?

He went on at length about my father. A man who had fallen violently in love with the beautiful woman who had come to the house as a governess. She was many years younger than he was. What would a man do in such circumstances? Who could blame him for trying to recapture his youth? And when he thought he had a chance of doing so, rather naturally he took it. He had admitted taking arsenic. It seems likely he obtained it when he was abroad. He had tried it and knew it was a dangerous practise so he stopped. But then he married a young woman. Let us say that he had a little of the poison stowed away somewhere. He found it and once more experimented. He had one or two bouts of illness which were obviously due to what he had been taking. This did not deter him, however, and on that fatal night he took the remains of that packet. It was more than he realised. In fact it was a very large dose. He screwed up the paper and put it in the drawer where it became caught up with the drawer above and was missed when the place was searched.

"You, members of the jury, will agree with me that that is a logical explanation of what happened that night.

"Members of the jury, you see before you a young girl. How many of you have daughters of your own? Those of you who have will understand. Think of your own daughter . . . or the daughter of a friend whom you love well. Think of her caught up in a chain of circumstances over which she has no control

. . . and suddenly finding herself—as this young girl did—in a court of law facing a charge of murder.

"You have heard the evidence. If you have the shadow of a doubt you cannot find this young girl guilty. She is not the perpetrator of crimes but a victim of peculiar circumstances.

"You are observant. You are shrewd and when you think over the evidence, when you consider all we have heard in this court, you will say to yourselves and each other: 'There is only one verdict we can give. That is Not Guilty.' "

There followed the summing up by the Justice Clerk. He went through the evidence very carefully.

I was young and that must influence them. But this was an indictment of murder. There was the mysterious Ellen Farley who, according to me, had asked me to buy the arsenic for her and this I had done. The signed book at Henniker's drug shop was evidence of that. But no one had heard Miss Farley ask me to buy arsenic; no one had seen the rat in the dustbin except—it might be—Ellen Farley. And Ellen Farley was unavailable. So that was a piece of evidence about which the jury would have to come to some conclusion. Did the mysterious Ellen Farley ask the accused to buy arsenic for the rats? Or did the accused buy the arsenic for the purpose of killing her father? She had reason. He was going to disinherit her if she married her lover.

On the other hand, the deceased had confessed to his wife that he had taken arsenic at some time and this he may have procured outside this country, which meant that it was impossible to trace the purchase. Did he find what was left in the packet, misjudge the amount, and so kill himself?

"That is what you have to decide, and only if you are convinced that this is not so and the arsenic was administered from the almost empty decanter by the accused who put it there—only then can you find the accused guilty."

It was a fair summing up and the Lord Justice Clerk had made the jury's duty clear to them.

They went out to consider their verdict.

I WAS TAKEN BELOW. How the time seemed to drag. An hour passed and there was no verdict.

What would happen to me? I wondered. Could this be the end? Would they condemn me to death? That was the penalty for murder. I wondered how many innocent people had been sent to their deaths.

I should be taken back to the courtroom. I should see Ninian . . . tense and waiting. And yet he had seemed so sure.

The Kirkwells would be there . . . Bess . . . Jenny . . . the whole household. Zillah would be waiting. If I were found Not Guilty I should owe my life to her. Jamie had shown me quite clearly that what he had felt for me was not true and lasting love.

I kept remembering incidents from my life, as they say people do when they are drowning. Well, I was—metaphorically—drowning.

I tried to look ahead. Suppose Ninian was right and I came through this? What would it be like? Nothing would be the same. Everywhere I went people would say: "That is Davina Glentyre. Do you really think she did it?"

No . . . nothing would ever be the same. Even if I walked free out of the courtroom, the memories of it would be with me forever . . . with others, too.

The jury was out for two hours. It had seemed like days.

As soon as I went up I was aware of a breathless tension in that room.

The jury had filed in. The Lord Justice Clerk asked them if they had reached a verdict and would they let the court know what it was.

I held my breath. There was a long pause. Then I heard a clear voice say: "Not Proven."

There was a hush in the court. I saw Ninian's face. For a moment an expression of anger touched it; then he turned to me, smiling.

The Lord Justice Clerk was talking to me, telling me I was dismissed from the bar.

I was free—free to carry with me as long as I lived the stigma of Not Proven.

At the Vicarage

I LAY IN MY OWN BED. The house seemed wrapped in an obtrusive silence—a silence broken only by whispering voices.

"They have let her go? But is she guilty? Her innocence was not proven."

Those words seemed to go on and on in my mind. I could hear the foreman of the jury. I had so desperately wanted him to say "Not Guilty" and he had said "Not Proven."

"The case is over. You are free." That was Zillah, exultant.

But I knew I should never be free. Not Proven. Those words would come back again and again over the years. People would remember.

"Davina Glentyre," they would say. "Haven't I heard that name somewhere? Oh yes . . . she was the girl who murdered her father. Or did she? It was Not Proven."

What a cruel verdict! A stigma to carry through one's life.

Zillah had said: "I am going to put you straight to bed and you are going to stay there for a while. You've been through a terrible ordeal. It's been a great shock. More than you realise. But you are going to be all right. I'm going to look after you."

I was not really listening. I was still in the courtroom. I could not escape from those pictures which kept crowding into my mind. I could hear Ninian Grainger's voice—vehement, tender, angry, sentimental, pleading to the jury's good sense and humanity. He had been magnificent and I believed I owed my life to him . . . to him and Zillah, of course. When it was over he had held my hand briefly while the triumph shone in his eyes.

Of course, I represented success to him, for if he had not gained the verdict he wanted, he was halfway there. The case had been black against me and at one stage a conviction of murder seemed almost certain, but he had averted that—with Zillah's help, and we must think ourselves fortunate that the verdict was Not Proven. I was a feather in his cap, a big step towards promotion; a case which had seemed hopeless and if it had not exactly been won, had been as successful as it possibly could have been in the circumstances.

I was glad to be alone. I did not want to have to face the rest of the household. They would be tactful, but I should read their thoughts.

"Did she do it?" they would be asking. "Who could be sure? But they let her go because it was Not Proven."

Not Proven! Not Proven! It was like the tolling of a funeral bell.

ZILLAH HAD BROUGHT ME HOME. She had had the carriage, with Hamish Vosper, waiting for us.

"I knew it was going to be all right," she said. "And I wanted to hustle you away from that place as soon as I could."

We sat side by side, close. She held my hand, every now and then pressing it reassuringly and murmuring soothing words. "It'll be all right. I'm here to look after you, dear."

Everything seemed strange and unreal. Even the street seemed different.

"Don't take the carriage to the front, Hamish," I heard Zillah say. "Go straight to the mews. There might be people hanging about in the street."

Yes, I thought. Come to see the peep show, to take a look at the young woman who might have been condemned to a murderer's death. Who was to say whether she deserved it? Her innocence was not proved; it was a murder which was Not Proven.

There would be people like that always. They would be there to stare at me. They would remember. It was not proved against me but . . .

"Right you are," said Hamish jauntily. "Mews it is."

Then I was getting out of the carriage and entering the house by the back door. Mr. and Mrs. Kirkwell were embarrassed. How do people greet a member of the household who has just been on trial for murder and has come home because the case was Not Proven?

Mrs. Kirkwell managed: "Nice to see you back, Miss Davina."

Mr. Kirkwell nodded and Jenny and Bess just stared at me. I was a different person to them all.

Zillah took charge.

"Now, dear, we're going to get you to your

room right away. I'll get something sent up.
You need to eat a bit . . . and you need rest.
You've got to get your strength back. I'm go-
ing to see you're all right."

In my room she shut the door and faced me.

"It's hard at first," she said and repeated
once more: "but it will be all right."

"They don't know what to say to me. They
think I did it, Zillah."

"Of course they don't. They just don't know
how to express their feelings. They're as
pleased as dogs with two tails, because you're
back and the miserable business is over."

How long those days seemed! I did not want
to emerge from my room. I could not face the
ordeal of seeing people and reading their
thoughts. Zillah was often with me. She
brought my food and sat and chatted while I
ate it.

"Talk about it if you like," she said. "It
might help. I always knew you were innocent.
I wish they'd given the proper verdict. Ought
to have been clear to that pompous old judge
and the stupid jury that you couldn't have
hurt a fly."

Zillah had changed subtly. I fancied she was
not keeping such a curb on herself. Her con-

versation was a little more racy, the red of her lips was brighter, her cheeks more coral-tinted. There was an air of something like triumph about her.

Occasionally she spoke of my father and when she did a mask of melancholy would slip over her face.

"He was such an old darling . . . always so good to me. He used to say he had never been so happy in his life as he was with me."

I could not help myself saying rather sharply: "He was very happy with my mother. He loved her."

"Of course he did, dear. That was different. And she'd gone and he was just reaching for a bit of comfort. He found me . . . and at his time of life. Oh well, I know men. It's just that he never expected to find all that again . . . and that something extra . . . if you know what I mean. It's a consolation to me that I was able to do so much for him. Not that he didn't do a lot for me."

"He seemed to change so much. He was quite different from what he had ever been before."

"He used to say I'd made him young again.

That was nice. But it was wanting to be young that made him take that horrible stuff."

I shivered.

"We won't talk of it, dear," she said. "But when I think of how I found that bit of screwed-up paper, I can't help saying 'What luck!' That did the trick. Got you off. Put you in the clear."

"Not Proven," I murmured.

"Never mind that. You're here. You're free. The case is over. They can't bring it up again."

But I thought: I shall never be free because the verdict was Not Proven.

I WENT SHOPPING with Zillah. Hamish Vosper drove us. I found him looking at me almost conspiratorially. He was jaunty and I fancied a little more familiar. I preferred the embarrassment of the other servants.

I wrote to Lilias. I could tell her more easily than anyone else how I was feeling. She had suffered a similar tragedy—not so serious, of course; but it had been momentous to her, and the case against her had been hastily judged and she had been branded Guilty.

I was comforted by a letter in reply to mine.

My dear, dear Davina,

I feel so much for you. I have read about the case in the papers, of course, and have been with you in spirit all through the trial. How I wish I could have been there in fact. When I heard the verdict I was overcome by relief. I wish it could have been more certain, but at least you are free now.

I have tried to picture what it must have been like in the house with your father's second wife. The papers imply that her evidence changed the course of the case. She seemed to be a kind person and very attractive—according to the press.

It is so long since we met. I can guess what a turmoil you must be in, and it has occurred to me that you might like to get away. You could come to stay here for a while . . . if that appealed to you. We should be able to talk and be together. The vicarage is roomy, so there would be no trouble on that score. But don't expect the same degree of comfort that you get at home. What I can offer you is the comfort of my love and sympathy . . . and belief in your innocence. Think about it. There's no hurry. Just when you are ready, write and tell me you will be coming.

You are always in my thoughts.

My love to you,

LILIAS

What a lovely letter! I wept a little over it and read it again and again.

I did think about her suggestion. To get away from this house where it had happened would be good for me. In the secluded atmosphere of the vicarage I could talk to Lilias of the future, for I was realising that I could not go on in this state forever. I had to go forward. I needed to talk with someone who knew me well. I wanted advice, and who better than Lilias to give me that?

I mentioned the invitation to Zillah.

"I think it is a good idea," she said. "You like Lilias, don't you? You get on well with her. Typical governess, your father said she was . . . until she was overcome by temptation."

"She never was tempted," I cried indignantly. "It was all a terrible mistake. She was innocent."

"I was just telling you what your father said. Poor girl. She might have been worried about money. They have a hard time of it, governesses. I can understand the temptation. After all, I've been a governess myself."

"Zillah, Lilias did not steal. She had nothing to do with the wretched pearls. I'm sure of it."

"Oh well, you'd know. You were here with her. But your father seemed to think . . ."

I felt exasperated and was about to make a further protestation, but Zillah held up her hand.

"All right. I'm sure you'd know best. After all, she was special for you, wasn't she? You're sweet and I love you—honest I do. There are some stepmothers who'd say you oughtn't to go to someone who's under suspicion . . ."

"I'm under suspicion, Zillah."

"Well then, there you are. I think it would be good for you to go." She put her arm round me. "I can see you really want to . . . and therefore I think you should. That's settled then. You write to her and tell her you'll go. I agree it would do you a world of good to get away from here for a bit."

"Zillah, I do assure you that Lilias is quite incapable of stealing anything."

"Of course. I don't doubt it for a moment. You go. It'll be nice for you and that's what

concerns me. By the way, there's something
I've got to tell you. I've been trying to say it
for some days. It's about your father and . . .
er . . . money. He was most anxious to pro-
vide for me and . . . he's left me everything
. . . almost. This house . . . bonds . . .
and things like that. Poor darling, he said he
was so grateful to me. He was going to cut you
right out. He said if you'd married Alastair
McCrae you would have been well taken care
of, and if you went to Jamie, well then . . .
he would certainly have cut you right out. I
told him that wasn't right. I said if he didn't
leave something to you I couldn't take it. I
worked on him and, well, I made him see my
point. He has left you something. The solicitor
reckons it would bring you in about four hundred pounds a year. I feel awful about it. All
the rest comes to me."

"I . . . I see."

She pressed my hand. "This is your home,
dear. Always will be as long as you want it. I
told him it would be like that. He said I was
too good. I said I was not. I said, 'I just love
the girl. I look on her as my daughter.' He was
ever so pleased really. Of course, I never

thought he'd go off like that. How was I to know he was taking that stuff?"

I was silent and she went on: "Four hundred a year! It's quite nice. It's not as though you will be penniless. And I'm always here. I want to share it all with you."

I don't think I was surprised. Of course, he had left everything to her. He had doted on her. I was not concerned with money just now and I had a little of my own that would suffice.

My thoughts were with the possibility of a visit to Lilias. There was one thing which made me hesitate. They would naturally have heard of the case in Lakemere. What would Lilias' father's parishioners think of their vicar's harbouring someone who might be a murderess? I knew he was a good man for he had taken Kitty in and found a post for her, but I must not allow him and his family to be made uncomfortable because of me.

"What is it?" asked Zillah anxiously.

"I can't go," I said. "People will have heard of me in Lakemere. It will be most uncomfortable for my hosts."

"Well," said Zillah, "why not change your name?"

"What?"

"You can't very well do that here where people know you. But you could when you went away."

"I . . . I suppose I could."

"No suppose about it. Why shouldn't you? Choose a name they won't connect with the case. It's simple." She warmed to the subject, her eyes glistening. "It's advisable to keep to your initials. You never know when they might turn up on something . . . and then there would be a bit of explaining to do. D.G. That's what we've got to look for."

"What a good idea!"

"It's being on the boards, dear. Lots of people there change their names. Have to sometimes for show business . . . if not for anything else. Now let's think. Davina. Well, that is the sort of name people would remember. What about Diana?"

"Oh yes. That starts with a *D.*"

"Diana. Now we want a *G.*"

"What about Grey? Diana Grey?"

"You're taking my name. I was Miss Grey before I became Mrs. Glentyre."

"It's short and it begins with a *G.*"

"I think it goes well. Diana Grey. Well, that's what you're going to be while you're

with the parson's family. It's better for them
and you."

"I'll write to Lilias at once."

I went straight to my room to begin the letter.

My very dear Lilias,

I want so much to come to you, but it would
be unfair to come as I am. I hope your father
won't think this deceitful, but I want to escape
from myself. I want to be a different person
. . . and I do not want to bring gossip to you.
I am sure people in your neighbourhood would
know of the case, so I have decided I shall
come as Diana Grey. I'll keep my own initials,
which Zillah says is very wise. I will come if
you agree to this deception. I don't think I
could face coming if there was a danger of
people's suddenly remembering.

I just want you to write and tell me that you
approve of this, and then I shall pack my bag
and come right away.

I hope to hear from you soon.

With my love,

DIANA

I sealed the letter and was surprised to find
my spirits had lifted considerably.

I would take it down to the hall and put it

on the silver salver where letters which were to
be posted were laid until, at a certain time,
Kirkwell would collect them and take them to
the post.

I laid it on the salver and as I stood in the
hall I was suddenly startled by the sound of a
door being loudly shut. It was followed by an
immediate clatter of footsteps. I was not anxious to come face-to-face with any of the servants, so I slipped into the sitting room and
half closed the door.

The footsteps were coming down the stairs.
I looked out and to my amazement saw Hamish Vosper. His face was scarlet and dis-
torted with rage. He rushed through the hall
and out by the back door.

What had he been doing in the upper part of
the house? I wondered. Had Zillah sent for
him because she wanted the carriage? Surely
not at this time.

It was very strange.

My thoughts however were centered on
Lilias. I wondered what she would have to say
about my changing my name.

It would only be for the visit, of course; but
the idea had occurred to me that I should get
right away . . . start a new life with a differ-

ent name. It would mean leaving Edinburgh. Where could I go? It was a wild dream really. But it would be something to discuss with Lilias.

I WAS IMPATIENTLY WAITING for a reply, but had started to pack for I was sure she would tell me to come soon. Then I had a caller.

Bess came to my room. "There's a gentleman to see you, Miss Davina."

"A gentleman!"

"Yes, Miss. I've put him in the drawing room."

Who was it? I asked myself. Jamie . . . come to tell me he loved me after all; he was ready to face anything with me? Alastair McCrae?

"Who is it?" I asked.

"A Mr. Grainger, Miss."

I felt a tremor of excitement. Could it really be? What could he want? The case was over as far as he was concerned.

Hastily I went down to the drawing room. He rose to greet me and took my hand, looking searchingly into my face as he did so.

"Miss Glentyre, how are you?"

"I'm all right, thank you. And you?"

"Well, thanks. It's . . . just a little difficult, is it?"

"Yes, but I'm thinking of going away for a while."

"Ah, that would be the best thing."

"I'm going to stay with my governess."

He looked surprised.

"Oh," I said. "I mean the governess I had years ago before . . ."

"I see there have been several governesses in your life."

"Only two."

"And both important to you. Tell me, where?"

"In England. Devonshire actually. A place called Lakemere."

"Devonshire is, I believe, a very attractive county."

"I'm going to stay at a vicarage. Miss Milne was a vicar's daughter."

"That sounds ideal."

The habit of confiding in him was still with me. When we had been fighting for my life he had let me know that I must hold nothing back, that every seemingly trivial detail might prove to be of the utmost importance. So now I found myself saying: "I'm . . . thinking of

changing my name because it might be uncomfortable for my hosts."

"It's often done in such circumstances."

"So you think it's a good idea?"

"I do really. You see, there was a great deal
of press coverage. It could be uncomfortable,
as you say."

"Yes, I was thinking mainly of my hosts."

"Well, they apparently invited you."

"I know, but I imagine Lilias' father is a
little unworldly."

"Oh?"

"He's such a good man . . . a saint almost."

"Do you think the saintly are unworldly?"

"Not exactly, but if he thought someone
needed help he would give it without considering whether it would be inconvenient to him."

"He sounds like a most unusual person."

"He is. Lilias—that's Miss Milne—says he
is a true Christian. So many talk like them and
are not. He was wonderful about Kitty
whereas others . . ."

I paused.

"Kitty?" he prompted.

"She was one of the maids. She was caught
in a compromising situation with one of the

grooms. She was promptly dismissed whereas the man . . . because he was a good coachman . . . was allowed to stay."

"That was in this household?"

"Yes. What I was saying was that Lilias' father took Kitty in when she had nowhere to go and he found a job for her. And, of course, he was wonderfully understanding when Lilias went."

"What happened about Lilias?"

I felt I was going too far. I was forgetting that he was no longer my legal adviser who had to learn everything about me. His profession made it second nature for him to extract information. Nonetheless I found myself telling him the story of Lilias and the necklace, to which he listened earnestly.

"So she was dismissed," he mused. "The parson's daughter."

"Yes, it was terrible. I can't think how it could have happened. There is only one thing I am certain about and that is that Lilias could not have stolen the necklace."

"It seems hardly likely. Did anyone have access to the house from outside?"

"No. There were only the servants. Why should any of them take and put it in her room? If they had taken it surely they would have wanted it for themselves? It's worth a considerable amount of money."

"It looks as though someone might have had a grudge against her."

"I can't think who. They did not have much to do with her, but none of them disliked her."

"Someone wanted her dismissed."

"Why should they?"

"That's the mystery."

"Well, it happened long ago and I don't suppose we shall ever know."

"And meanwhile poor Lilias has been unable to prove her innocence."

"Like . . ."

He touched my hand gently. "It seems clear that your father took the arsenic himself. The jury thought that."

"Then why?"

"Because there was a shadow of a doubt."

"And for the rest of my life, I . . ."

"You must not let it hurt you more than you can help. You must grow away from it. Go to this parsonage. Try it for a while. Your new name will help you to forget. Leave me your address. Perhaps we could keep in touch."

"But the case is over for you."

"A case such as this would never be over for me. I don't like the verdict. In my heart I know it should have been Not Guilty. I shall always hope that someday the truth will come to light."

"You do not think my father really killed himself?"

"It's the most likely possibility, but there remains that shadow of a doubt." He lifted his shoulders. "However, let me have that address."

I gave it to him and he put it into his wallet.

"So the governess was dismissed," he went on, "and the new one came: the beautiful Miss Zillah Grey whose surname you are going to use."

"Yes."

"And in a very short time she was married to your father. That's very interesting."

"I suppose it is. I believe governesses occasionally do marry the widowed fathers of their charges."

"It comes about in . . . a natural kind of way," he said slowly.

Then Zillah came into the room.

He rose and I said: "You remember my stepmother."

"But of course." He had taken her hand and was smiling warmly at her. "We met in court."

She returned the smile dazzlingly, and in spite of the fact that I was accustomed to her beauty it struck me forcibly. She seemed to blossom in the society of men—like a flower in the rain.

"You were wonderful," she said. "I can't thank you enough for what you did for . . ."

"I was grateful to you. Your evidence was vital to our case."

She sat opposite him, rather carefully, I thought, placing her back to the light as though she did not want to be seen too clearly. She was deferential, as though displaying admiration for him. He liked it obviously and did not appear to question the fact that it might be a little false.

She immediately engaged him in conversation.

"Has my stepdaughter been telling you her plans to go away for a while? Do tell me. Do *you* think it's a good idea?"

"I think it's an excellent idea. I was just saying so to Miss Glentyre."

"And did she tell you . . . ?" she began anxiously.

"About changing her name? Yes. I think that might be a good idea, too."

"I am so glad. It was my suggestion. I was a little worried. I do so want . . ."

"To do the best for Miss Glentyre, of course. Yes, I am sure it is a good idea, both to get away and to ensure a little anonymity."

"Then I shall feel happier about it now. Davina, my dear, did you offer our guest refreshment?"

"No, we were talking and . . ."

She looked at me with indulgent reproof.

"It's very kind of you," said Ninian quickly. "But I must be on my way. I just called in to see how Miss Glentyre was faring."

"How very good of you! So sympathetic and understanding. I often think how lucky Davina was to have you to defend her."

"I don't really deserve so much praise."

"You do!" She added almost archly: "And I shall insist on giving it to you."

I smiled. I felt he was very pleased that she had joined us. There was a little more chat— mostly between him and Zillah—then he rose to go.

I felt disappointed in him. He had been so obviously impressed by Zillah's charms. Of course, I had always known they were considerable, but I would not have thought that he would succumb to them so easily.

Zillah's mood changed abruptly when he had gone.

"Why on earth did he want to come here like that?" she demanded.

"He said he just wanted to know how I was getting on."

"Does he go round visiting all his ex-clients?"

"I think he regards this as a rather special case."

"*I* think he is rather inquisitive. He got you off . . . and that is where the case ends for him."

"He very much wanted a verdict of Not Guilty."

"Didn't we all?"

"Well, he seemed to get on well with you."

She allowed a self-satisfied smile to cross her face.

"Oh well, it's all over now, and what we have to do, dear, is forget about it."

As if I ever could!

· · · · ·

LILIAS' ANSWER had arrived.

I am expecting you. We understand about the name. So from the moment you arrive you will be Diana Grey. Don't worry. No one will know except my father, my sister Jane and myself. We all want to do what we can to help. Dear Davina—but I suppose I must start thinking of you as Diana—rest assured that I have convinced my family that you have been as wrongly suspected as I had. We are a closely knit family and trust one another absolutely.

It has occurred to me that it is a rather strange coincidence that we have both been wrongly accused. It is almost as though there is some malignant spirit in the house. That's nonsense, of course, but it does seem odd. Oh, what a lot we shall have to talk about! I am so looking forward to seeing you.

It's going to be a long journey for you. You'll have to come to London first and then take the train to the west country. We're about three miles from Tinton Crawley, but I'll be at the station with a dogcart to meet you.

I can't wait. With love,

LILIAS

P.S. I am enclosing instructions about the journey, together with the address of the

London hotel where I spent the night. It's small, quiet and near the station.

I started at once to make my preparations.

IT WAS WITH GREAT RELIEF that I set out and even as the train steamed out of the Edinburgh station I felt as though a great burden had dropped from me. I believed that I had, to some extent, made a gap between the present and the nightmarish past.

As we speeded to the Border I looked anxiously at my fellow passengers, for I had the sudden fear that one of them at least might know me. My picture had been in the papers; and there had been one in particular, an "artist's impression," which had horrified me. The sketch had been sufficiently like me to be recognisable, but the artist had managed to twist my features into a mask of cunning. At that time the world had made up its mind that I had murdered my father and the artist was fitting the face to what he believed were the facts.

There was a young couple opposite me, perhaps going on their honeymoon; they seemed entirely absorbed in each other and gave me no qualms; nor did the man intent on his newspaper. But there was a rather garrulous woman in the far corner who was determined to talk to someone, and as the others were obviously engrossed, she turned to me. She was going south to visit her married daughter and was longing for the reunion with her grandchildren. She asked me a few questions about my destination, but rather perfunctorily, I realised. Her thoughts were clearly for her coming visit, and I breathed more freely.

I need not have worried. My confidence returned. I was just nervous. I must stop imagining that people would recognise me. I was escaping to Lilias, that refuge to which she had returned, confident of love and understanding.

I spent a night in the London hotel near the station, just as Lilias had explained. It was not a very restful night, but I did not mind. I was on my way.

The following morning when I caught the train from Paddington Station the sense of relief was growing with every minute. Settling in a corner of the railway carriage, I looked out on the green countryside, noticing that the plants and trees were a little more advanced here than they were in the harsher north. My fellow passengers were agreeable, and there was a little general conversation. I knew that none of them had the faintest idea who I was, and that I had been oversensitive on that score.

The train steamed westwards; the country had grown even more verdantly lush. I caught a glimpse of the sea. I had seen little villages clustering round churches such as Lilias had often described to me in the old days; I saw the rich red soil of which she had talked, and I knew that we were in the county of Devonshire.

At last I had arrived. As we came into the station I saw Lilias on the platform and I was happier than I had ever been since the nightmare began.

We ran together and clung for some seconds. Then she held me at arm's length. "It's wonderful to see you. And you are looking better than I expected to see you. Oh, my dear, what a time! But it is over now. Come on. The dogcart is waiting. We'll get the luggage out."

The stationmaster was standing by, smiling at us.

"Oh, Jack," she said. "Could you get Jim to put the luggage into the dogcart?"

"Right you be, Miss Lilias. Jim, Jim! Hi, Jim! Luggage for Miss Lilias." He smiled at me. "And you be come to Lakemere, Miss. You be staying long?"

"I . . . er . . ."

"We're hoping Miss Grey will stay for a long time. There it is, Jim."

She took my arm.

"They are waiting impatiently at home," she said. "Longing to meet you."

Then we were gambolling along lanes so narrow that the hedges almost brushed against us as we passed.

"I'm so glad you came," she said.

"I feel so much better since I left Edinburgh."

"Of course. You wanted to get away. It's the right thing. It's the only thing. And we can talk. It will be just like the old days."

I was overwhelmed by emotion as I sat beside her. She talked animatedly, stressing every now and then how delighted she was that I had decided to come. It was a wonderful welcome.

"We shall soon be there," she said. "Oh, look down there! You can see the church tower. Our church is just about one of the oldest in the west country. More than seven hundred years old—a perfect example of Norman architecture, as it says in the guide books. Oh yes, we get visitors. There's some lovely stained glass, too. My father is very proud of it. I must make sure he doesn't bore you about it. Jane and I tell him he gets obsessions, and one of them is his dear old church."

As we drew nearer I saw the grey stone walls of the church, the graveyard with the old stones leaning a little askew in some places among the yews and the cypresses.

"Some of those trees have been here for centuries," Lilias told me. "They have seen many vicars come and go. Aren't the cypresses lovely? Someone told me they represent eternity and that is why they are so often planted in graveyards. Country lore! I'm preparing you. You'll get plenty of that from my father. And here we are . . . . the vicarage."

It was a largish house, grey stone like the church; before it was a well-kept lawn with flower beds surrounding it. And there at the door was a man whom I knew at once was Lilias' father—and with him a woman, clearly sister Jane.

They came towards us as Lilias brought the dogcart to a halt.

"Here we are," cried Lilias. "The train was on time, for once. This is . . . Diana."

My hands were clasped in a firm grip and I was looking into the smiling, benign face of the Reverend George Milne.

"Welcome, welcome, my dear," he said. "We are so pleased that you have come. Lilias has been so happy since you said you would."

"And this is Jane," said Lilias.

Jane was rather like Lilias and I knew I was going to like her for that reason alone.

Her greeting was as warm as that of her father had been. I said how glad I was to meet them and what a peaceful spot it was. The flowers were lovely.

"You've won Jane's heart," said Lilias. "She has an obsession with the garden."

"It's a good thing that I have," retorted Jane. "Someone has to do it. It would be like a wilderness left to you. Come along in. I expect you're hungry. Dinner's almost ready. We hoped the train wasn't going to be late and took a chance on that. So . . . in half an hour? Lilias can show you to your room and Daisy will bring up some hot water."

"Thank you. That would be lovely," I said. "One gets grimy travelling."

I felt at home immediately. I had slipped into a new role. I must get accustomed to my new name, and when I had I should be able to believe I really had stepped away from the past.

We went into a hall. I noticed the highly polished furniture; on a hall table was a large bowl of flowers, colours exquisitely blended and beautifully arranged.

Lilias noticed my glance. "That's Jane," she said. "She fills the house with flowers."

"They are so lovely," I said. "Oh, Lilias . . . I am going to be happy here."

"We are going to do our best to make you," replied Lilias.

I followed her up the staircase to a landing.

"We've put you on the first floor," said Lilias. "You have to mind your head when you enter some of these rooms. I think people must have been smaller at the time places like this were built." She opened the door of a room and I followed her in. It was large but rather dark and there was only one window and that was leaded. There was a bed in one corner, and a dressing table and a mirror and a wash hand stand. A large cupboard almost filled one wall.

"There you are," she said. "I'm afraid it's not like your home in Edinburgh, but . . ."

"It's lovely," I said, "and I can't tell you how happy I am to be here with you . . . and your family."

I went to the window. I was looking over the graveyard. I had a view of the tottering gravestones, the ancient yews and cypress trees. It was fascinating.

Lilias came and stood beside me. "I hope you don't think it's a little morbid? I chose this room for you because it is a little bigger than the other spares and the graveyard has a kind of friendly feeling when you get to know it. At least, that's what my sister Emma used to say. She's married now, you know. I have a niece and nephew through her and two nephews through Grace who married a clergyman. Emma used to say that if there were ghosts they were nice ones."

At that point the door was opened by a middle-aged woman who came in carrying a can of hot water. Lilias introduced her as Daisy.

"It's nice to see 'ee, Miss," she said to me. "I hope you'll enjoy your stay."

"We're going to make sure of that, Daisy," Lilias told her.

"That we be," said Daisy.

"Thank you," I murmured.

When she had gone Lilias said: "Daisy has been with us all our lives. She came when my father and mother were married and this is her home as it is ours. We just have a girl coming in some mornings to help with the cleaning. Jane is an excellent housekeeper though. Otherwise I don't know how we'd manage. I'm rather a poor replacement for Alice."

I remembered that Alice was the sister who had left the household to become a governess when Lilias had been forced to return home.

"No," went on Lilias, "I'm not much of a help in the house. My father calls Jane and me his Mary and Martha."

"I daresay you have your uses."

"I shop and help with the local good works . . . . bazaars and so on . . . . everything that goes with the routine of a country vicarage."

"Which is very important, I've no doubt."

"Well, I suppose I could say I am of some use."

"What strikes me so forcibly about the place is the peace of it."

"I'm glad you find it so. It's what you need."

"Oh, how I wish that I had come in different circumstances! But it's no use wishing you can change what's gone before."

"No good at all. But it is going to get better. We're going to put the past behind us. We both have to do that. We're just going to forget it all happened. It's the only way."

"But can we?"

"We can try. Now, I am going to leave you to wash and change if you want to. Can you find your way down?"

"I'm sure I can."

She was gone and I was alone. I washed and changed. I felt elated. I knew I had been right to come here.

AS THE DAYS PASSED I became more sure of this. I had slipped into a new identity and was no longer startled when I heard myself addressed as Diana. I was caught up in a new way of life. I was becoming very friendly with Jane who was quite different from Lilias. Jane was no dreamer; she was practical in the extreme which was very necessary in running the vicarage household on what I imagined was by no means a large stipend. I wanted to contribute to the household expenses, but my hints that I should do so were so firmly brushed aside that it was difficult to pursue the matter. Jane and Daisy put their heads together so skillfully that there was no sign of any deprivation. Meals were simple but wholesome. Daisy had taught Jane to cook long ago and she had taken to it, as Daisy said, like a fish to water.

Lilias lacked an interest in domestic affairs. She and Alice had been "the clever ones." Alice was now making use of her skills while alas Lilias, because of that unfortunate incident, was unable to do so.

The vicar was very much as I had expected him to be, due to Lilias' description. He was one of the most contented people I had ever met. He was completely unselfish and his life seemed to have been given over to the service of others. He was a little absent-minded, but between his daughters and Daisy he was taken good care of. He was greatly loved by all with whom he came into contact and his little foibles were looked upon with the greatest indulgence. He was indeed a very happy man. I thought how lucky Lilias was to be his daughter, which sent my thoughts back to my own father; I recalled his anger over my friendship with Jamie and his outraged dismissal of Kitty and how Zillah had crept into his bedroom at night.

But I must not think of my father—nor of Jamie. Jamie had failed me. His love had not been strong enough to stand up to trouble and at the first sign of it he had crept away.

That had hurt me deeply. But I supposed it was the terrible nature of what had followed which had helped to subdue the bitterness of that particular blow.

On my first day I heard that Major Jennings, who ran the riding stables, was a great friend of the vicarage family. He knew that Lilias liked to ride and could not afford to, so he had asked her if, as a favour to him, she would help with the exercising of his horses. Lilias had accepted the offer with the greatest alacrity. Therefore she rode a good deal.

"I go over to help with the grooming and clean out the stables," she said. "I enjoy being with horses. Sometimes, if they are hard-pressed I give people lessons. It's a wonderful opportunity. How would you like to ride?"

"I'm not a rider, but I did have a few lessons in Scotland, so I'm not exactly a novice."

"Well, here's your opportunity."

"What a good idea! I could pay for my lessons and you, Lilias, could teach me."

Lilias looked disturbed, so I explained hastily: "It's all right. My father left me some money. I have a small income so I am not exactly poor. The house and the bulk of his fortune went to Zillah."

Lilias was thoughtful: "It all happened so quickly. It seems odd. It's not so very long since I was there. She came . . . and almost immediately she married your father. It's almost as though it were arranged." She hesitated, staring into space. "I'm talking nonsense," she went on. "Let's go to the Jennings' this morning and see what can be arranged about the riding. You'll like them. Besides the major there are Mrs. Jennings and Florence, their daughter. They all work with the horses."

"Tell me about the other neighbours."

"Well, there's the manor."

"I remember your telling me about that. It's where the squire lives . . . and the young man you were going to marry."

"Yes. Charles . . . Charles Merrimen."

"Is he still there?"

"Oh yes, he's there. I go and see him quite often. He's in a wheelchair most of the time. He's such a fine man."

"Shall I meet him?"

"Of course. And then there are the Ellingtons at Lakemere House. They are the important family here. They are the rich ones, the benefactors of the village. It was to them that Kitty went. Oh! I'd forgotten Kitty. Just in case you meet her she'll have to be prepared, won't she? We don't want her blurting out . . ."

It was as though a cloud had settled about us. The euphoria was slipping away. Was it always going to be like that? Should I constantly be wondering whether someone was going to recognise me?

Nanny Grant's voice came back to me over the years:

Oh, what a tangled web we weave
When first we practise to deceive.

NEVERTHELESS the harmony of the vicarage was bringing back to me a sense of security. I would wake with a feeling of anticipation, wondering what the day would bring.

I would stand by the window looking out over the graveyard. Those ancient tombstones might have looked eerie in moonlight, but somehow they conveyed a sense of peace; the troubles of those who lay beneath them were over. Friendly ghosts indeed.

Lilias' company had a further healing effect. I could open my heart to her; and how good it was to share my troubled thoughts! I could tell her how hurt I had been by Jamie's desertion.

"It was just as well," was her verdict. "If he failed you when you most needed him, he would not have been the partner with whom you could have gone happily through life. He might have cared for you . . . . a little; but he cared more for himself. Better not to marry than marry the wrong one. You were young, inexperienced and lonely; you had lost your mother; you and I had parted; your father had remarried and you were not sure of your step-mother. I believe you were ready to fall in love. In love with love, as they say. And that's not so hard to get over as the real thing."

Yes, she was indeed comforting.

Then there was the riding. Major Jennings

was a hearty middle-aged man, bronzed through service in India; when he came home he had settled down to run his stables with the help of his wife and daughter. Both Mrs. and Miss Jennings were brisk and jolly people; they were surrounded by dogs—four at least, but they were large and intrusive and made their presence felt.

The first time I met the family we were taken into a comfortable but rather shabby room, on the walls of which hung several pictures of horses, and given tea by Mrs. Jennings. Miss Florence Jennings came in while we were having it. She was a tall young woman of about thirty, I imagine, with abundant reddish hair and a crop of freckles. She was in a riding habit. I was to discover that she spent most of her days garbed thus.

"This is Florence, my daughter," said Mrs. Jennings. "Horses are a passion with us, and Florence, if anything, is more besotted than the rest of us over the four-legged darlings, aren't you, Flo?"

Florence admitted that she was.

There were a great many brass and carved wooden ornaments in the room as well as two Benares tables—all obviously from India.

They seemed to have brought a flavour of that country into their home.

The dogs came in to inspect us, one fawning, one curious and the other two inclined to be suspicious.

"That's enough, Tiffin. You, too, Rajah. These are good friends."

The dogs immediately drew back at the sound of the voice of authority.

Both Mrs. Jennings and Florence were interested to hear that I intended to ride and so far had only had a few lessons.

"You'll soon be a rider," Florence assured me. "I sense it. Long practise, you know. Don't let your mount know you're nervous. That's when they play up. Let them know you're in charge . . . right from the start. Pet them a little, and they are yours."

Lilias said she thought it would be a good idea if she gave the lessons, at which Mrs. Jennings slapped her thigh and said that would be just the ticket.

The outcome was that I was instructed by Lilias and after three or four days of discomfort, I was well on the way to becoming a horsewoman.

Lilias took me to the manor and there I met

Charles Merrimen. I liked him from the beginning. There was something almost saintly in his acceptance of his disability and there was clearly a bond of deep affection between him and Lilias. His father, the squire, was a rather taciturn and dignified man and the family had lived in the manor for centuries. There were Charles' elder brother David, his wife and two sons, but it was Charles who was of special interest to me for he might so easily have married Lilias and then she and I would never have met. That made me ponder on the strangeness of chance.

I accompanied her on one or two occasions when she visited him, but I quickly began to feel that those meetings should be for the two of them alone. She told me that she was reading Gibbon's *Decline and Fall of the Roman Empire* aloud to him and he enjoyed it so much. So I excused myself and, as Lilias and I had always understood each other, she accepted my decision not to go with her.

Then came the invitation from Lakemere House.

"Mrs. Ellington regards herself as lady of the manor," Lilias explained. "I think she feels that the Merrimens are rather lax in carrying out their duties. Well, the squire is getting on, David is quite absorbed in his family and Charles, of course, can do nothing. Mrs. Ellington is very efficient, of course. She is one of those women who thinks she knows what is good for people better than they do themselves. The maddening thing is that she often does. We are invited to tea. If she approves of you you will be invited again. By the way, we shall have to do something about Kitty before we go there . . . just in case we run into her. I wonder if I could get her over here for some reason? Let's see. I'll ask Jane. She might have some ideas."

Jane did.

"I heard Father say that she has never been confirmed. She wants to be and, of course, Mrs. Ellington is all for it. Get her over here on the pretext of discussing that."

The message was sent and on the day before we were due to visit Lakemere House Kitty arrived. We arranged that I should keep out of sight until Lilias had talked to her.

I had a glimpse of her from my window as she arrived. She looked plumper and more contented. I thought: the life here suits her.

She had not been in the house long when

Daisy came to my room and told me that
Lilias thought I should now go down to the
drawing room.

When I arrived Kitty ran to me and threw
her arms about me. Then she withdrew—a little shocked, I think, at her temerity.

I kissed her cheek and said: "It's good to see
you, Kitty."

"Oh, Miss D . . . er, Miss er . . . It was
terrible . . . the things they said . . . ."

"It's over," I said. "We try to forget it."

She nodded. "But I'll never forget what you
done for me, Miss . . . you and Miss Milne. I
just don't know what I would have done without you."

"So you're happy at Lakemere House?"

"Oh yes. It's nice. I really like it there."

"I hope it will stay like that."

"You mustn't forget that it is Miss Diana
now," said Lilias. "Miss Diana Grey. It is important, Kitty, that you should not forget."

"Oh, I won't, Miss."

She told us how different from Edinburgh it
was living in Lakemere House. She had made
friends and Mrs. Ellington took an interest.
She knew she had done wrong, but she
couldn't think what had come over her. It was

just that . . . She blushed and we changed the subject.

Lilias hustled her off to the vicar that the subject of her confirmation might be broached. Lilias was a stickler for the truth and she wanted to adhere to it as much as possible.

I could not help feeling a little apprehensive when we drove over to Lakemere House in the dogcart, even though I tried to repress my fear and assure myself that I must not feel so nervous every time I was going to meet someone new.

Lilias was saying: "As she regards herself as the guardian of the village, Mrs. Ellington likes to know everything that is going on. She is especially interested in the church. I think she believes it is her duty to watch over my father. She respects his goodness, but deplores his unpractical way of going about life. She regards him with a mixture of affection and exasperation. She admires his Christian virtues and despairs of his unworldliness. I daresay she will try to get you to give a hand in village affairs while you are here."

"I shan't mind that. Is there a Mr. Ellington?"

"Oh yes. He's very rich. He goes back and

forth to Exeter and is often in London. He never interferes with Mrs. Ellington's affairs—he just supplies the comforts which enable her to continue with her good works. He is said to be a lion in business and a lamb in the domestic circle."

"So Mrs. Ellington is the resident lioness."

"That's about it. Then, of course, there is Miss Myra Ellington—the fruit of the marriage. She must be approaching thirty. She is unmarried."

"I'm surprised at that. I should have thought Mrs. Ellington would have found a suitable match for her daughter."

"There are some who say that Miss Myra is not the marrying kind. She is pleasant . . . but rather quiet, self-effacing almost, which seems strange in Mrs. Ellington's daughter. I believe that she is rather well off in her own right. Rumour says her grandfather left her money . . . the bulk of his fortune, they say. That would give her a certain independence, I suppose."

"I see. I suppose a great many people marry for security."

"A great many, I fear. Well, Miss Ellington doesn't have to think of that. Though I did hear through Kitty that she seems to be rather interested in a man who is visiting the house."

"I suppose in a village it is difficult to keep secrets, however much one tries . . ."

Lilias was looking at me severely. "You've got to stop thinking that everyone is obsessed by your case. It was just a nine days' wonder. People quickly forget what doesn't affect them."

She was right. But so many conversations seemed to lead back to the subject.

Lakemere House was an impressive building of eighteenth century elegance. Marble steps led up to a portico. On the lawn, which was bordered by flower beds, was a large pond, in the centre of which was a statue which could have been Aphrodite.

A maid took us up to the drawing room where Mrs. and Miss Ellington were waiting to receive us.

Mrs. Ellington, seated in an armchair which resembled a throne, held out a hand. "Oh, Lilias . . . how nice to see you."

Miss Ellington had risen and hovered beside her mother.

"This is Miss Diana Grey," said Lilias.

The hand was extended. I took it, feeling I

should curtsy, for there was something decisively regal about Mrs. Ellington.

"So nice. Welcome to Lakemere, Miss Grey. This is my daughter."

We shook hands.

"So pleased you could come," murmured Miss Ellington to which I replied that it was kind of Mrs. Ellington to invite me.

I studied the rich Miss Ellington. She was tallish and rather angular. There was an awkwardness about her and she had no real claim to beauty whereas her mother must have been a very pretty woman in her youth. But there was something appealing about Miss Ellington. It was due to a certain gentleness in her big brown rather spaniel-like eyes.

"I hear you have come to stay at the vicarage, Miss Grey," said Mrs. Ellington. "What do you think of our little village?"

"I haven't seen a great deal of it yet, but what I have seen I find charming."

"We're rather fond of it. So much is going on. It keeps us busy."

A maid came in, wheeling a trolly on which everything needed for tea was laid out, including thinly cut sandwiches and a fruitcake.

"Thank you, Emma," said Mrs. Ellington.

"You may go. We'll manage. Miss Grey, cream? Sugar?"

Miss Ellington took the cup and brought it to me.

A few minutes later the door opened and a man looked in. He stood in the doorway conveying surprise and penitence.

"Oh, I am so sorry. I had no idea you had guests. I'm interrupting."

"Come along in, Roger," said Mrs. Ellington warmly. "And indeed you are not interrupting. Mr. Lestrange is staying with us," she said to me. "Come in and meet our guests."

He was tall and powerfully built. I imagined he was in his late thirties. He was a very striking looking man—probably because of his physique. But it was something more than that. His complexion suggested he had been in a country with a warmer climate than ours; and he had intensely blue eyes which contrasted vividly with his almost black hair.

He advanced into the room, looking at me with interest.

"We have met," said Lilias.

"Of course, but . . . er . . ." He was smiling at me.

Miss Ellington said: "This is Miss Grey who is staying at the vicarage."

"How interesting!"

"Do sit down, Roger," said Mrs. Ellington. "Myra, my dear, take Roger his tea."

While the tea was being served Mrs. Ellington said to me: "Mr. Lestrange comes from South Africa. He is in England for only a short while, and he is spending a little time with us. He and my husband have business interests in common."

"I've been riding," he said, smiling at us all. "I find the countryside fascinating."

"A little different from where you've come from, I daresay," said Mrs. Ellington.

"Delightfully so. You are visiting, too, Miss Grey? From what part do you come?"

"From Scotland."

"A beautiful country. What part?"

"From . . . er . . . Edinburgh." I felt myself flush a little. I must control my fears. Since my ordeal I had felt so uneasy when anyone asked questions about myself.

"And what part of South Africa do you come from, Mr. Lestrange?" I asked quickly.

"A place called Kimberley. You may have heard of it."

"Who has not heard of Kimberley?" said Mrs. Ellington. "Your diamonds have made you famous."

"Perhaps notorious," he replied, smiling at her. "Oh yes. There is no doubt that diamonds have put us in the news."

"Mr. Lestrange is attached to one of the biggest diamond companies in the world," said Mrs. Ellington proudly.

"Oh come," he said with a laugh. "There are others."

"You are a very modest man, Roger," said Mrs. Ellington almost fondly.

"It must be very exciting when diamonds are discovered," I said.

"Yes, and it can create chaos. Diamonds . . . gold . . . we've had our share of both. People begin to think they are lying in the ground just waiting to be picked up."

"Once they are found there is a great deal of work to be done on them, I suppose," said Lilias. "When people talk of diamond discoveries I do believe they think of bracelets and rings just waiting to be worn."

"That's true. And for every find there are hundreds of disappointments. I'm glad to say I have been one of the lucky ones."

"Do you actually live *in* the town of Kimberley?" I asked.

"Yes. I have quite a large house . . . well, it's adequate. I must say that since my wife died I have thought of moving. But . . . well . . . I have had to travel a great deal and have just not got round to it."

There was a brief silence of respect for the death of his wife which he had spoken of with some feeling. He bit his lips and smiled brightly at us, and Miss Ellington said quickly: "It must be very interesting to be in a *new* country. Here, everything is so ancient."

"Well, I would hardly call Africa new," said Mr. Lestrange. "But here you have so much to remind you of a not-so-distant past. For instance your Norman churches and some of the houses."

"The climate must be very different from here," said Lilias.

"It is. But ours in Kimberley is healthy . . . so we are told."

"One only has to look at you to see that," said Mrs. Ellington.

"Are you staying long in England?" I asked.

"Until my business is completed. I am

tempted to make it last a long time. You've no idea how they spoil me here."

"We enjoy having you," said Mrs. Ellington, "don't we, Myra?"

Miss Ellington agreed, with real feeling, I thought.

"It makes a change in our simple life," went on Mrs. Ellington. "My husband's friends stay from time to time." She raised her eyes to the ceiling. "But on this occasion Myra and I are finding it most enjoyable and we shall do our best to make you extend your visit, Roger."

I could not help noticing Myra Ellington. She had changed since he came in. Her spaniel's eyes strayed often to him. She is attracted by him, I thought.

As for him, he was different from anyone I had ever known. I wondered about him. He came from South Africa. Had he been born there or was he one of the men who had gone out from home in search of diamonds? He was not what I would imagine an Afrikaner . . . which would mean that he was of Dutch origin. His name suggested he might be French. I believed that when the Dutch agriculturists who were Boers settled in South Africa, they were joined by some Huguenots who were in flight from France. But he did not look French either.

However, since his arrival the tea party was turning out to be more interesting than I had thought it would be. Instead of the expected conversation of village affairs we were given an interesting insight into a world of which hitherto I had known nothing.

Mrs. Ellington allowed Roger Lestrange to dominate the conversation, which surprised me; but she, like her daughter, was clearly very attracted by him.

He was a vivid talker and obviously enjoyed his attentive audience. He touched briefly on the beauty of the scenery, often rugged, majestic, awe-inspiring; he talked of the animals— lions, leopards, panthers, giraffes, buffalo, rhinoceros and hyenas; and as I listened I felt I was there in a new world, far away from all the fears and nightmares which seemed to be constantly with me.

"It sounds like paradise," said Myra Ellington.

"There is another side to it," he said ruefully. "You can see a lion descending on a beautiful deer—the poor creature's terror when it realises its fate. That is nature. Every animal must fend for itself. They go in fear of their lives. One moment they are running along, exulting in the joys of being alive and free. They do not see the powerful enemy waiting for the moment to spring. Suddenly they are powerless. Death is facing them."

"It sounds awful," said Myra, shivering.

"It's nature."

"Thank goodness we are not like the animals in the jungle," said Lilias.

"People find themselves facing dangers sometimes," I could not help saying.

Roger Lestrange was looking intently at me. "How right you are, Miss Grey. We are all in a jungle of sorts. Ours is different, of course . . . but the dangers are there."

"What a morbid conversation!" cried Mrs. Ellington. "Mr. Ellington will be returning home tomorrow. I am sure you will be pleased, Roger. Then you won't have to see so much of us tiresome females."

"They are far from tiresome! I promise I shall try to see more and more of their delightful company."

It was not long before the conversation turned back to Africa and I learned more about that country during that tea party than I had known before.

Roger Lestrange said he could see trouble coming. The Boers resented British rule in South Africa. There had been discontent since the British came in as far back as 1814. They were far too eager to give privileges to the black races since they had brought in emancipation of slavery. This had crippled the farmers for it deprived them of free labour.

He talked of Cecil Rhodes who had founded the state of Rhodesia and had wanted British rule all over Africa; of how he had shared that dream with a man called Leander Starr Jameson who, two years before, had been engaged in the famous raid which had ended in disaster for him.

We all remembered hearing of the Jameson Raid, but had either forgotten or never really known what it was all about.

"Jameson was a hothead," said Roger Lestrange. "That was surprising because he was a doctor. He was born in your city. You did say you came from Edinburgh? He studied medicine there and came out to practise in Kimberley where he became friendly with Cecil Rhodes. There was a good deal of trouble between the Uitlander party (those are the people settled there who are not Boers— mostly English) and the Boer government. The President was Stephanus Johannes Paulus Kruger, usually known as Paul Kruger. You must have heard of him."

"We have heard of him most certainly," said Mrs. Ellington grimly. "There was all that trouble about the letter sent by the German Kaiser congratulating him."

"Ah, yes, that was about the Jameson Raid. Rhodes and Jameson had planned together to surprise the Boers west of Johannesburg. Rhodes then decided that the plan could not succeed and called the whole thing off. But, as I said, Jameson was a hothead; he thought he could act alone and win—so he decided to carry on. When he arrived at Krugersdorp just west of Johannesburg he was surprised by a strong force of Boers, was overwhelmed and taken captive. The Jameson Raid was therefore a failure and responsibility for it was disowned by Rhodes and the British government. It was a complete disaster."

"And nearly resulted in war between us and Germany," said Mrs. Ellington. "Mr. Ellington was horrified at the prospect. It was a near thing. We felt we had to put that horrid Kaiser in his place."

"However," went on Roger Lestrange, "the British government decided that what was happening in South Africa was not worth a war with Germany and so allowed the trouble to blow over."

"I should have liked to teach those arrogant Germans a lesson," said Mrs. Ellington.

"The situation is explosive," went on Roger Lestrange. "Rhodes and Kruger are very watchful of each other. The Jameson Raid may not have succeeded in what it was meant to do, but it is not forgotten."

"I should like to see South Africa," said Myra Ellington.

Roger Lestrange smiled at her. "Perhaps one day you will."

Mrs. Ellington evidently felt that for too long the conversation had been out of her control and I could see she was determined to change it.

She talked about the village and the fête which was some weeks off but needed a lot of planning.

"I wonder if you will be with us then, Miss Grey," she said.

"Diana's plans are a little uncertain just now," Lilias told her.

"But of course. Well, if you are . . . I wondered if you would take over one of the stalls?"

"I am sure I should like that," I told her.

"And you will help, too, Roger?"

"I don't think I should make a very good stall holder."

"Oh, we'd find something for you to do."

"Is there a possibility of your being here?" asked Myra.

"I am not sure how long my business will take. But I must not continue to encroach on the hospitality I have received in this house."

"Oh, nonsense," cried Mrs. Ellington. "It's a pleasure to have you."

"So kind . . . but I am afraid sometimes that I am imposing."

"Nonsense. I would not hear of your leaving and going to some hotel. My husband would be most displeased . . . and so would I."

He smiled at Lilias and me. "You see what a wonderful hostess I have. I consider myself most fortunate to be here." He included us all in his smile.

Lilias was glancing at her watch. It was five-thirty, I saw from my own. I knew that visits with Mrs. Ellington were usually on village business and given a limited time.

And now it was clearly the time for us to depart.

We thanked Mrs. Ellington and said goodbye.

Mr. Lestrange, with Myra Ellington, accompanied us out to the dogcart.

As we turned out of the drive, Lilias said to me: "Well, what did you think of that?"

"Very interesting. I enjoyed hearing about South Africa. I think Myra Ellington is quite fond of him."

"Exactly my impression. It would be nice for her if he married her. I think she would like a husband."

"I wonder how she would feel about leaving home?"

"She was very eager to hear about Africa."

"Well, we shall see."

THE NEXT DAY I had a letter from Zillah. She had written once before. She really seemed to care and to understand my feelings.

My dear, dear Davina,

I hesitated whether I should call you Diana, but somehow it seemed going a bit too far. But perhaps I should have, in case this falls into someone else's hands. You will have to destroy it as soon as you have read it—which sounds rather dramatic.

How are you getting on? I think a great deal about you. But I'm sure you did right to go and become Diana. You're going to feel better . . . calmer and all that.

It seems very strange here without you. People are different. Well, I fancied those round here never much approved of me—so I don't miss them. I keep saying "I must tell Davina that" and then . . . you're not there.

Do let me know how things are.

By the way, your Ninian Grainger has called twice. Really, it is most extraordinary! And, I think, a little indiscreet!

I hinted this but he shrugged it off. He gets me to talk about myself. He's very inquisitive. I suppose he gets so used to asking questions that it's a habit with him. He's attentive. Perhaps I ought to ask him what his intentions are! Pretty obvious, I suppose. But I am rather surprised.

Well, it makes a diversion.

He took me out to dinner one evening. I am

sure he thought I was going to ask him in when he brought me home. There's men for you! I suppose I ought to send him about his business. Then I remember that he did get you off and I'm tremendously grateful to him for that.

I thought I might go to London for a little spell. I feel I want to get away.

Do write. I am thinking such a lot about you.

Lots and lots of love,

ZILLAH

I sat back, the letter in my hand. I was thinking of Ninian Grainger, and I was disappointed in him. I had thought he had some regard for me, but from the moment he had seen Zillah he had become bemused by her. I thought of those sessions together when we had talked so earnestly and the most important thing in the world to him seemed to be to prove me Not Guilty. I remembered that when the verdict had been given, he had held my hands and I had seen with emotion the joy in his face; and, smarting as I was from Jamie's desertion, I had felt uplifted by it. At that moment I had seen so clearly what Jamie's affection for me had really been. It had simply grown out of the meeting between two lonely people in the streets of Edinburgh; and so we had believed ourselves to be in love—but it was a love which had wafted away on the first harsh wind.

I had seen it then for what it was and I had allowed myself to believe that Ninian's care for me—I might say his dedication—was of a very different calibre.

I must remember, of course, that I had been in a hysterical state of mind. I had just stood on trial for my life. I should have realised that my relationship with Ninian was that between an advocate and his client in a case which, if he won, could greatly enhance his reputation. He had not had a clear win, but still he had triumphed to some extent.

That was all it was; and I had seen in it the beginnings of a deep friendship which might lead to something deeper. That was because I was naïve, completely unworldly. As soon as my attractive stepmother had appeared he had lost interest in me.

And now he was actually pursuing her! I felt dismayed and bitterly disappointed.

I could not get the thought of him and Zillah out of my mind. It had affected me more deeply than I had thought possible.

Lilias was aware of my depression and tried

hard to interest me in village affairs. I could now ride reasonably well and that provided a diversion. We went out often and I began to know some of the villagers quite well.

As the daughter of the vicarage, Lilias was expected to call on the inhabitants from time to time—especially those who were infirm. She explained to me that Jane was well occupied in the house and this task naturally fell to her, Lilias. She had developed quite an aptitude for it and took the burden off her father's shoulders.

"They're all interested to see you. Some of them are confined to their houses and a new face in the village creates a lot of interest."

That was how I came to be with her when she paid her periodical call on Mrs. Dalton.

She always explained to me a little about these people on the way to them so that I had some idea of what I was going to find.

As we rode along she said: "Mrs. Dalton is an interesting old lady. She must be all of eighty and has lived in this village all her life. She had six children—four girls and two boys. Two of them went abroad—one to America, one to New Zealand—and it is a sore point with her that she doesn't see those grandchildren as well as their parents. They keep in touch and it's a great day when she hears from them. The whole village soon learns the contents of the letter. She's an inveterate gossip and a purveyor of scandal. It's all she has to do. She can only just move about and she's in her chair most of the day . . . just sitting . . . looking out of the window. Two of the daughters and a daughter-in-law live nearby, and take it in turns to come in and look after her—so there is no worrying on that score. But she loves to have visitors and there is usually a stream of them going in and out. One of the grandchildren goes in to read the paper to her every day; then she relates what she has heard to her visitors. She's bright and uncomplaining as long as she can get plenty of people to talk to her."

"I'll be interested to see her. I like meeting them all. It's a different way of life here from what I have ever known before."

"Oh, you'll be amused by Eliza Dalton."

We walked across the green to the cottage. The door was on the latch, so Lilias knocked then opened it and walked in.

"Good morning, Mrs. Dalton. Is it all right if we come in?"

"Oh, it's you, Miss Lilias? Yes . . . yes . . . come in. I'm all alone."

"I've brought Miss Grey to see you. Remember, she is staying with us."

"So you're Miss Grey." She peered at me intently. "Nice to meet you. A friend of Miss Lilias. I've heard all about you."

I felt that uneasy qualm and immediately suppressed it.

"Bring up your chair close, so that I can see you."

"And how are you, Mrs. Dalton?" asked Lilias.

"Well, it's my rheumatics . . . come and go, they do. Some days worse than others. The weather don't help, I can tell you."

"No. I suppose not. Tell me about the family."

"Charley's doing well. Got his own bit of land. He had to go all the way to New Zealand to get it. He says he's got on quicker out there than he could here. And his daughter's getting married. My granddaughter and me not there to see her wed. What do 'ee think of that?"

"A great pity," said Lilias. "Still, you've got plenty of your family close and that's a good thing."

"I think of them that's far away."

"Well, you've got good daughters and a daughter-in-law to see to your comforts."

"I've nothing to complain of in them. Only Olive . . ." She turned to me. "That's my daughter-in-law . . . she's in and out like a flash. A good cleaner. But do you know what she says? 'There b'aint time to sit and chat, Ma. I've got things to see to at home.' "

"One can understand that," said Lilias soothingly. "But you do have lots of visitors."

"Oh yes . . . yes . . . they come and see me." She turned to me, her eyes in her wrinkled old face alight with curiosity. "It's nice of you to come and see me. Tell me, what do you think of our village, eh?"

"I'm finding it most interesting."

"Seen many of us?"

"Quite a number."

"And what part of the world do you come from? I can see you're not a Devon girl."

"No. I come from Scotland."

"Oh." She looked at me with some suspicion. "That's a long way."

"Well, it is not really so far by train."

"I've never been in one of them newfangled things."

Lilias laughed. "Oh, they have been going for a good many years, Mrs. Dalton."

"All these years . . . it's been the chair for me. You can't go about when the rheumatics strike. And before that there was the family to bring up."

"Well, you see the world . . . the world of Lakemere . . . from your cottage window."

"There was that murder case up in Edinburgh. Edinburgh, wasn't it?"

"Edinburgh . . . yes, that's the capital," said Lilias. "How is young Clare doing at school?"

"She's all right. There was a lot about it in the papers."

My heart had begun to beat so loudly that I thought they might hear. Lilias was looking at me anxiously. She said: "It was a good year for fruit, Mrs. Dalton."

"Do ye say? There was this terrible murder in Scotland. Edinburgh . . . that's where it was. The place you come from. They let her off."

"Has the doctor been today?" asked Lilias.

"Oh, he says there's not much he can do for me. Just got to live with it, he says. People of my age is bound to get something. He calls in when he feels like it . . . takes a look at me and says, 'Just rest. Do what you can.' It was as plain as the nose on your face. She had her reasons, didn't she? Going off buying that stuff. And her own father! That woman . . . beautiful, wasn't she? I reckon she was making it all up. Him taking arsenic to make himself more of a man! I never heard the like. What's the world coming to?"

"Well," said Lilias who was becoming quite agitated. "I really think we should be going. We have some more calls to make."

"You've not been here much more than five minutes. I wanted to tell you about Mrs. Mellish's lodger and that daughter of hers. Oh, and I'm forgetting the great news. It's not out yet. It will soon be all over the village. What do you think?"

"I've no idea," said Lilias coolly.

"It's them at the House. He's a very upstanding sort, don't 'ee think? It's all very nice and proper and I reckon Mrs. Ellington be pleased. As for Miss Myra, well, it's about time, I must say. She's getting a bit long in the tooth. Must have been thinking she was right and truly on the shelf. Then he comes . . . this rich and good-looking widower. Well, no wonder they're pleased up at the House. 'Tis going to be announced tonight."

"How do you know about this?" asked Lilias.

"Mrs. Eddy told me and her being housekeeper up there, she'd know. We're mates. I went to school with her oldest sister so if she couldn't give me a bit of news, who could? She popped in this morning. Hadn't gone more than a minute or two when you arrived. There's a dinner party tonight . . . so it's all cut and dried. It won't be long before there's a wedding up there. That Mr. Lestrange will be wanting to go back to Africa and taking his bride with him."

"I see," said Lilias.

"So, Miss Myra will be off to Africa." Mrs. Dalton grimaced. "Rather her than me. Wild horses wouldn't drag me to an outlandish place like that."

"Let us be thankful that those wild horses will not be needed," said Lilias. She had been deeply put out by Mrs. Dalton's references to my father's death and wishing, I knew, that we had not paid this call.

As we untied our horses, Lilias said: "That old gossip!"

"It's always going to be like that, Lilias," I reminded her. "I've got to face it. At least she didn't know who I was."

"No. What a good idea it was to change your name."

We did not speak much as we rode back. I thought it was just another incident . . . another warning that I should never be able to escape from the past.

Overseas Assignment

WHEN I RETURNED HOME there was a letter awaiting me. It was addressed to Miss Diana Grey. Eagerly I took it to my room and impatiently opened it. It was from Ninian Grainger.

Dear D,

Forgive me for addressing you thus, but you will know the reason. I have been thinking a great deal about you and wondering how you are getting on. I think you were very wise to get away and I do hope you are recovering from your ordeal. I have seen your stepmother on one or two occasions. She seems to have put all behind her remarkably well.

Do write to me and tell me how you are feeling. I assure you I am most concerned.

Sincerely,

NINIAN GRAINGER

It was a letter an advocate might send to a client whose case had been of especial interest to him. How foolish I had been to imagine that, because he had meant so much to me during that trying time, he held deeper feelings for me.

I was still so shocked by the encounter with Mrs. Dalton when I sat down to write to him.

Dear Mr. Grainger,

Thank you for your letter. It is kind of you to be concerned. I have heard from my stepmother that you have been meeting.

Everyone here is very kind to me and they are all trying to make me comfortable. But it would not be true to say that all is well.

I have to face the fact that taking a new name is not enough. I am uneasy every time anything leads to some disclosure from my past life, however trivial. When people ask me where I live and I tell them Edinburgh I am afraid they may connect me with the case. Miss Milne and I have just visited one of her father's parishioners who actually talked about it when she learned that I came from Edinburgh.

Do forgive my writing thus. It happened only today and I feel rather shaken.

The terrible truth is that it is always going to be so.

Thank you for your kind concern, but it is something I have to live with and it fills me with dread.

However, you did what you could for me and I shall always be grateful for that.

Sincerely,

D.G.

When I had posted the letter I wished that I had not. What would he think of such an hysterical outburst? I should not have been so outspoken. Nor should I if I had not so recently been shaken by Mrs. Dalton's comments.

I WAS SURPRISED by the promptness of his reply. It came within a few days.

Dear D,

I was distressed to read your letter. I do so understand your dilemma. It is no use telling you this sort of thing will not happen again, though, of course, it will become less likely as the years pass.

My father remembers a case in his youth. There was a young lady in a similar position. She went abroad. She married there and has had a very good life ever since. She has been able to put the past right behind her.

That is a way you might decide to take. Let us face the fact that the case did attract a great deal of attention; there was a wide coverage, but it is hardly likely that there would have been much interest outside the British Isles.

You might want to consider this—I mean to make a new life somewhere outside this country . . . as my father's client did, most successfully.

A friend of the family, a Mrs. Crown, works with a society which was formed some twenty-odd years ago. It is called the Female Middle Class Emigration Society. The object of the Society is to find posts abroad for those who are seeking them. This would be mainly in the Colonies . . . Australia, New Zealand, South Africa . . . and even in America. This is for ladies who, for some reason, wish to leave the country. It may be that they cannot find employment at home, or they wish to leave for some other reason.

This client of my father's went to America through this Society. My father still has the occasional letter from her. She said it was a great opportunity and gave her new interest in life. She took a post as a governess, which is the usual practise, although other occupations are dealt with.

The Society will lend money to an applicant who will pay it back by degrees when she is working, thus paying travel and living expenses until the applicant is settled in.

I am just sending you this idea for you to ponder on. It is not something you would be able to decide in a hurry.

If, however, you feel it would be a way out of your difficulties, and that it could release you from the perpetual fear that someone might know what happened, I could arrange for an interview with Mrs. Crown. The offices of the Society are in London and if you think there is something in this suggestion, just let me know.

In the meantime, my very best wishes to you.

Sincerely,

NINIAN GRAINGER

I read that letter several times. I was not sure what I thought about it. Leaving the country was something which had not occurred to me. It was running away, of course. And to a foreign country. Many women became governesses. It was a fate which had befallen Lilias and Zillah. True, they had stayed in their own country . . . or near enough.

They had both come from England, not Scotland, but that was not like going overseas.

Lilias saw how preoccupied I was and asked if something had happened.

I told her I had had a letter from Ninian Grainger.

She looked at me steadily and I guessed I had betrayed something of my resentment because he was so taken with Zillah.

"And it has given you food for thought," she said.

"He suggests I must go abroad."

"What?"

"I wrote to him. I was probably rather hysterical. I felt so awful after what Mrs. Dalton had said. I knew it was what people were saying everywhere and that it was going to happen again . . . perhaps as long as I live. I hate hearing people talk about it . . . . and they are saying it all over the country, that I should not have been freed . . . . I shall have to be on guard against it all my life."

"Oh no . . . . it won't go on. People forget. After all, it is really rather recent as yet. What is all this about going abroad?"

"Apparently there is some society he knows

of which arranges it. He could put me in touch
with it . . . if I thought about leaving."

She was speechless.

"I . . . I have never thought of that," she
said slowly.

"To go right away, Lilias . . . just think of
it. One might never come back."

She said nothing for a few seconds. Then:
"It would take a lot of thinking about."

"That's what Ninian Grainger says."

Lilias was silent, obviously deep in thought.

LOOKING BACK afterwards, I felt that Fate
was leading me to make my decision, and that
all around me events were falling into place to
make me go the way I did. It was like a jigsaw
puzzle when all the pieces fit into place and
the picture is complete.

The main topic of conversation was the
coming wedding of Myra Ellington and Roger
Lestrange. It would be a grand affair—none
the less so because preparations would have to
be hurried, in view of the bridegroom's need to
return to South Africa.

Mrs. Ellington could be trusted to overcome
difficulties.

Tradespeople were arriving at Lakemere

House every day. Excitement prevailed. It was a nine days' wonder. Most people had decided that Miss Myra would never make her journey to the altar, and now that she was about to achieve it, it was a matter of wonder and perhaps hope to those who felt themselves to be in a similar position to that of the bride-to-be.

Moreover the bridegroom was eminently suitable. He was good-looking and rich; and if he were a widower, which might just tarnish the romance a little, there was the fact that Miss Ellington was not so young herself and a mature man was just what she needed, even though it was rumoured that he had a child in South Africa. Well, Miss Myra could be a mother to him.

It was all very agreeable.

Kitty came over to see me one morning. She was as excited as everyone else about the wedding. She thought Mr. Lestrange was ever so nice. "There is no side about him, Miss, if you know what I mean. He's nice to us servants . . . just as though we were of importance. The family like him . . . from the mistress to the stable boys. I reckon Miss Myra's lucky."

Lilias and I often talked about Ninian Grainger's suggestion. There were times when

I thought it would suit me to follow the example of those young governesses; and there were others when I would swerve away from the notion. A terrible uncertainty would sweep over me. As Lilias had said, it was a step that should not be taken lightly.

While we were at breakfast one morning a message came from Lakemere House. Mrs. Ellington wished to see Lilias and me at eleven-thirty that morning. She could only spare a short time, but it was important and could we please be as punctual as possible?

Lilias grimaced at me. "The royal command. It's a nuisance. I promised old Mrs. Edge that I'd take her some of the wine that Jane makes. She says it puts new life into her."

"Couldn't we take it another day?"

"Well, she's so lonely. She'll be watching for us. There's time to take it and we can go straight from her to Lakemere."

That was agreed.

We delivered the wine and chattered for a while, Lilias keeping her eye on her watch.

Mrs. Edge was disappointed, but Lilias explained that Mrs. Ellington wished to see her and me as well—and we all knew how busy Mrs. Ellington was at this time.

Mrs. Edge wanted to talk about the wedding so we indulged her for another five minutes, telling her all we knew, and then we departed.

We put our horses in the Ellington stables and were taken to Mrs. Ellington's private sitting room. She was seated at her bureau with papers before her.

"Oh, Lilias," she said, "and you, Miss Grey. So good of you to come. I'm so frightfully busy . . . guests and so on. Some will have to stay in the house. I shall see you both at the reception, of course. But you've no idea. It's all so sudden. If only we had more time. But needs must."

"I am sure you are very happy about it, Mrs. Ellington," said Lilias.

"I should be if I could be sure everything will go well on the day."

"You couldn't fail to make it so," said Lilias perfunctorily.

"No, of course not. I did want to speak to you both about the stalls at the fête. That's why I asked you both to come. My big concern is the village drama meeting. As you know, they usually have it here, but I simply cannot have them. It's tomorrow . . . short notice, I know, but could you possibly have it at the vicarage? You've plenty of room there and . . ."

"But, of course, we can," said Lilias.

Mrs. Ellington beamed on her. "I knew you would, but I wanted you to call personally because there is the list of the cast for the Nativity play. It's early yet, but they need lots of rehearsal . . . and they'll be discussing it tomorrow. I wanted them to see my suggestions. They do need guidance; otherwise they select the most incongruous people . . . and then once it's done . . . it's awkward to change."

"I'll see that everyone knows it will be at the vicarage and I'll give Miss Crew the list. She's in charge of all that, isn't she?"

"Thank you so much. I hope I have not dragged you away from something, Miss Grey."

"Oh no, not at all."

"We'll talk about the fête later. Thank you so much for coming. Now . . . I have to get on."

"We should be going anyway," said Lilias.

"Thank you. Thank you for coming."

We were graciously ushered out and made our way to the stables.

"There was no need to summon us to the presence," said Lilias. "She could have sent a note with her cast of players."

"I think she enjoys being frantically busy."

Kitty was standing outside the stables chatting with one of the men. I was reminded of Hamish then and how she had fallen victim to his lust. I supposed some people never changed. Kitty had also reminded me of Zillah. They both seemed to sparkle in the admiration of men.

The man went into the stables when he saw us and brought out the horses. Just at that moment Roger Lestrange rode up.

"Oh, good morning, Miss Milne, Miss Grey. How nice to see you! Are you just coming to the house?"

"No," said Lilias. "We are just leaving. We've been to see Mrs. Ellington."

"Oh . . . what a pity!" He smiled at us warmly. He was a very attractive man. I could understand why people thought Myra lucky. Soon she would be going to a new country with this charming husband. I might be going away. But how different my departure would be.

"We must be getting on," said Lilias, mounting her horse.

I was not sure what happened next. I had my foot in the stirrup and was about to mount when suddenly my horse turned abruptly. The next thing I knew was that I was on the ground, my foot caught in the stirrup. The horse began to move away, fortunately at only a slow pace. Nevertheless I was dragged along the ground.

"Miss Davina!" It was Kitty's voice—shrill, loud, audible to all.

The incident was over in a few seconds. Roger Lestrange had seized my horse and brought it to a standstill. My foot was released and I stood up, unhurt.

He put an arm around me and looked at me steadily. "All right?"

I could not answer. All I could hear was that shattering cry of "Miss Davina!"

Lilias looked shaken. She was standing beside me and she took my arm.

"How are you feeling?" she asked. "What a nasty shock! What happened?"

"He just moved in the wrong direction, that's all," said Roger Lestrange. "You shouldn't have let him do that, you know."

"Miss Grey has only just learned to ride," said Lilias.

Roger Lestrange was looking at me intently, his eyes more blue than I remembered them. "You'll have to look on it as an experience, Miss Grey. It's lucky we were here and the horse didn't gallop off. That could have been . . . well . . . let's not think of it. You're not hurt . . . that's the important thing. It was just a bit of mischief on the part of the horse. He knew you weren't up to all the tricks he could play . . . so he tried one. They're like that sometimes, aren't they, John?"

"Aye, sir, they be that," said John. "You make sure when you mount him, Miss. Look, like this. He couldn't have done it then."

"All's well that ends well," said Roger Lestrange. "Do you feel like mounting again, Miss Grey?"

"I must."

"That's the spirit. Never give up. At least you won't do that again. Just give him a pat to show he's forgiven and he'll be friends again. That's so, isn't it, John?"

"Aye, sir, that be it."

Rather shakily I mounted the horse; but I was not thinking of the danger I might have been in but of the shrill penetrating cry of "Miss Davina!"

Lilias and I rode back to the vicarage in silence. We had no need for speech. Each of us knew what was in the other's mind.

I went straight to my room, and sat staring out at the graveyard.

"Davina," Ninian Grainger had said. "It's an unusual name." What if Roger Lestrange had noticed? What if he remembered that I came from Edinburgh?

There was a knock on the door and I knew it was Lilias. She came in and stood for a few seconds looking at me.

"He must have heard," I said.

"He probably didn't notice."

"It was so loud and clear."

"Only to us because we understood. I am sure Kitty was very upset about it. It came out involuntarily. It's understandable. She was worried about you. She looked so . . . penitent. She didn't mean any harm. That's the last thing. But she thought you were going to be hurt and it slipped out naturally. I don't think anyone noticed. We were too concerned about you."

I said suddenly: "I'm going to write to

Ninian Grainger to ask him to put me in touch with Mrs. Crown."

"Well . . . I suppose you might go and hear what she has to say. There's no commitment in that."

"I think I have made up my mind. It's what I'm going to do. I can't stay here . . . on edge, as it were . . . just waiting for something to come up . . . like this morning."

"I think you have been more upset by that than by the accident. If that horse had started to gallop you could have been very seriously hurt."

"I know. But it's showed me that when Kitty called out my name like that, it's the sort of thing that could happen at any time. I am going to explore this possibility."

Lilias said slowly: "I see."

She left me and I sat down and wrote a letter to Ninian Grainger.

Dear Mr. Grainger,

It has taken me some time to make up my mind, and I cannot be sure that I have done that yet, for this is such a big step I have to take. There was another incident today and this has decided me that at least I must see Mrs. Crown and discuss a few details with her.

It is so kind of you to take so much trouble to help me. I do appreciate that.

With grateful thanks,

Sincerely, D.

The letter was posted. I had taken the first step.

I was preparing for bed that night when there was a knock on my door. Lilias came in wearing a dressing gown and carrying a candle.

"I thought you might have been asleep," she said.

"I shan't sleep. I have too many things to think about."

"This is only the first step."

"Yes, but it's an important one."

"I've been thinking . . ."

"Yes?"

She paused for a moment and then she said quietly: "I might come with you."

Joy swept over me. This would change everything. That which I had contemplated with fearful apprehension could be planned with excitement. Two people together could face difficulties so much more easily than one alone; and if that person was the best friend one ever had . . .

"Lilias!" I cried. "Do you really mean that?"

"I have been considering it ever since I heard of it. The Society . . . it sounds interesting to me. You see, I feel this isn't what I want to do . . . visiting people like Mrs. Dalton, being directed by Mrs. Ellington. I suppose I get through . . . as anybody would, but it's not what I want. I want to be teaching. I really feel I have a vocation for that. I want to get back to it."

"Lilias . . . this is so unexpected. You didn't tell me . . ."

"No. Like you, I couldn't make up my mind . . . but I have been thinking more and more of it."

"If we went together . . . it would be so exciting. If I could believe you were coming with me, it would be so different."

"We both have something we don't want revealed."

"Oh, yours wasn't like . . ."

"No. My ordeal was not so horrific. Yours was carried out in the light of publicity. But I have a slur on my character. I'm in a quandary. I don't know whether it's the right thing or not . . . but if you go, I want to go with you."

"Oh, Lilias, I can't tell you how much I want that, too. Have you really thought about it . . . deeply?"

"From every angle. Alice could come back. She is much more useful at what I am trying to do. She doesn't like teaching in any case, though she pretends all is well. I know her, and I sense this is not entirely the case. If I went, she could come back."

"There's Charles Merrimen," I reminded her. "Have you thought of him?"

"I've thought a great deal about him. It's over really. It seems we were just trying to keep something alive . . . something which isn't really there. I go and read to him. Several people could do that for him. We talk about the books I read to him. We could go on like that till one of us dies. I am beginning to realise that if there had been deep love between us we should have married. It's rather like you and Jamie. There is something for a time . . . but it's a fragile plant."

"You were away from him all those years when you were with me."

"And when I come to think of it, those were the most rewarding years of my life so far. One has to be realistic. We have our lives to lead. I want to teach. I think I have a vocation for it. I do believe I want that more than anything. Also I want to get away from the past . . . just as you do. Yes, if you go, I am coming with you."

"Oh, Lilias, I feel so much better. I know I can face whatever there is to come if you are there."

We talked far into the night. We both knew that sleep was impossible; and for the next few days impatiently we awaited Ninian's reply.

At length it came. Mrs. Crown was writing to me and I should be hearing from her very soon.

And in due course the letter arrived. The heading was The Female Middle Class Emigration Society with an address in the City of London. Mrs. Crown would be pleased to see me round about three o'clock in the afternoon of the fifth of June.

This gave us a week to make our plans to go to London and this we did without delay.

· · · ·

WE HAD BOOKED into a small hotel recommended by Ninian which was not very far from the Society's premises; and at the appointed time were mounting the stairs to Mrs. Crown's office.

She came to the door to greet us—a fresh-faced middle-aged woman with a kindly smile.

"Miss Grey . . . Miss Milne . . . Mr. Grainger has written to me about you. Do sit down."

When we were seated she went on: "You want to emigrate and take posts as governesses, I understand. This is the usual profession ladies such as yourselves undertake. Our Society deals with all kinds of employment, but governesses are the most usual because so many of our people are ladies of education and small means. Let me tell you something about the Society. It was founded by a lady who believed that women should be given more chances of employment. The lower classes have been engaged in domestic service for centuries, but she felt that the educated woman should be brought more into public life. She discovered that such ladies were badly needed in the Colonies and she believed that women of strong character and high moral sense should take charge of the young. So she formed this Society to help people like yourselves who want to go abroad for some reason. So many people in these circumstances cannot afford the fare and they need something to enable them to support themselves until they get settled. The object of the Society is to help them over this difficult time. It is, you might say, a philanthropic association, kept going by voluntary subscriptions, and the object of our members is to be of assistance in helping the right people to start a new life in another country."

She then asked us for our qualifications. I could see she was impressed by Lilias' experience, but, as she said, I was a young lady of obvious education and she thought we should have no difficulty in finding employment.

"So many of our colonists deplore the fact that they cannot get a good education for their children. The Society does what it can to find that employment, but it is difficult being so far away, and many of our people go out and find employment for themselves. The most popular countries are Australia, America and New Zealand. South Africa, too."

"Mr. Grainger has given me some idea of the Society's methods," I said.

"Ah yes. Mr. Grainger, Senior, has a very high opinion of us; and has indeed been very benevolent towards us. I understand, Miss Grey, that you have a small private income."

"That is true."

"And you would not be needing financial help from us for your passage?"

"That is so. Does that mean . . . ?"

"It means that we will help in arranging your passage just the same. Now, Miss Milne . . ."

"I'm afraid I cannot afford to pay my passage," said Lilias.

"I want to help Miss Milne," I said. "But I fear I am not rich enough to pay for her passage as well as my own."

"That's perfectly easy. We will advance what is needed, Miss Milne, and you can pay us back gradually, when you are in employment."

"I don't care to be in debt," said Lilias.

"I know how you feel. But you will pay back when you can. We have always found that most of our clients in time meet their obligations. We have no fears . . . nor need you have. You have to decide to which country you wish to go."

"We heard that Australia is more like England," I ventured.

"In the towns maybe. It depends where you are employed. However, would you like to think about it? If you know someone who is connected with Australia . . . then that would be good. But of course there is the difficulty of finding employment when you arrive."

"That could be a little daunting," said Lilias.

"It is an undertaking, of course," agreed Mrs. Crown. "I will show you some of the letters we have received from people that will give you some idea of the difficulties and the rewards."

She took us into a small room, the walls of which were lined with files, and she gave us letters to read from people whom they had helped. The letters were from Australia, South Africa, New Zealand and the United States of America.

They were very revealing. The majority of the writers had found posts fairly easily, but some had not been so fortunate. There were very few who regretted their decision to leave England.

We spent more than half an hour reading those letters before Mrs. Crown came back to us.

"It gives you an idea of what you may find," she said. "How do you feel now?"

Lilias was more practical than I and therefore perhaps less certain. But perhaps she did not feel the same urgent need to escape as I did. I could not stop myself going over Mrs. Dalton's words and hearing that sudden cry of horror from Kitty when she used my real name. I was sure I had to get away.

There was another point. Lilias was not very happy about borrowing the money, even though it was lent by philanthropists. I wished that I could have afforded to pay her passage; but she would not hear of that. I consoled myself with the fact that my money would be a bulwark against absolute destitution.

It was Lilias who said: "May we have a little longer to think about this?"

"But of course. It is your decision."

"We shall have to think where we should go. It is very difficult to make up one's mind when one knows nothing, or very little, about such places."

"You are right to make absolutely sure that you want to go," said Mrs. Crown.

"We could make up our minds in say a week," said Lilias, appealing to me.

I said I thought we could do that and it was a good idea.

So we left the Society's offices and after another night in our hotel we went back to the vicarage.

WE HAD, of course, made no secret of our intentions. Lilias' father and sister had been informed right from the first. Jane understood absolutely why Lilias wanted to get away. She knew she had felt frustrated. I believed that Jane thought it was rather a reckless step to leave one's country, but she understood the need for it. So did the vicar. They were saddened at the thought of Lilias' departure but made no efforts to persuade her to stay. It was not quite the case with Daisy. She laboured under the assumption that heathens lived in foreign parts and the idea of Lilias' travelling to such places appalled her. She expressed her disapproval and, as she was something of a gossip, very soon the whole village was aware of our plans.

So there was great excitement in Lakemere that summer with two major events about to take place: the marriage of Myra Ellington to Roger Lestrange and the possible departure to foreign parts of the vicar's daughter.

The annual fête always took place in June and, since the Manor House was lax in its duties, the gardens of Lakemere House were thrown open for the occasion. This was posing some questions this year as the wedding was to take place about a week later.

Mrs. Ellington, however, was not one to shirk her duties and, awkward as it might be, she decided that the fête must go ahead.

We were all summoned to work for it. I was not sorry, because my thoughts were dominated—not so much as to whether we should go abroad as to where to. Lilias and I talked endlessly when we were alone; but it did seem to me that we covered the same ground again and again. Lilias' doubts centred on the fact that we should have to find posts when we arrived at whatever place we decided on. She feared we might not do so immediately and she would already be in debt—a state of affairs which she deplored.

In vain did I point out that I had a little money of my own which I would share with her. It was no use. I was afraid that she might decide she had been rash to agree to come with me and would change her mind.

They were uneasy days and that was why it was a help to be caught up with the fête.

I was in charge of what was called bric-a-brac, which mainly consisted of articles which had been given as presents, put away in a drawer and never used, to be brought out and presumably passed on to others who would do the same with them as their previous owners. However, it was all in a good cause; Norman churches needed constant bolstering up.

It was a warm sunny day which was a blessing, for the stalls could be set up on the lawns. Lilias had said it could be a nightmare if the weather was uncertain. At least if it were definitely raining they could be set up in the hall which was quite spacious.

I was presiding over my stall, attending to the occasional customer, when Roger Lestrange strolled up.

"Good afternoon, Miss Grey," he said. "How is business?"

He was smiling at me with that intent expression which made me feel a little uncomfortable. But that was only because I harboured secrets. It was something I had to live with while I stayed here.

"Hardly brisk."

"What do you suggest I should buy?"

"Here's a delightful little pig."

"Not my favourite animal."

"Look. There's a little slit in his back where you can save your pennies."

"How useful!"

"Here's a pillbox. Such a pretty picture on the lid."

"Enchanting," he said, looking at me.

"Here's a figurine. The *Venus de Milo*."

"Certainly more attractive than the pig and I have not much use for pillboxes. Let me have Venus."

I handed it to him and our hands touched. He was smiling. "I have been hearing news of you. You're leaving this country."

"Oh yes."

"What a decision for a young lady to make!" Again that quizzical look. I was afraid

I was going to blush. I took a firm grip of myself. I must overcome this terrible suspicion that everyone knew who I really was. It would be different when I was away, I consoled myself.

"It's rather an exciting project," I said.

"Indeed it must be. Miss Milne is going with you, I gather. I don't remember hearing where."

"We haven't decided yet."

"Oh?" He looked surprised.

"We have been making enquiries. There are several possibilities. Australia . . . America . . . somewhere like that."

"And what did you propose to do when you get there?"

"There is only one thing women in our position can do. Take a post."

"The ubiquitous governess?" he said. "Well, if that's the case, why not here?"

"We like the idea of travel."

He nodded. "It has its appeal . . . to the adventurous. But you say you haven't decided. Does that mean you have no posts in view?"

"It's something we have to arrange when we get there."

He raised his eyebrows. "Yes," he said

slowly. "I would say you are adventurous. Why don't you try South Africa? It's a beautiful country. And I'm sure there is a shortage of the right sort of governesses—which you and Miss Milne would undoubtedly be. As a matter of fact there is a school in Kimberley. Not exactly the sort of thing you had in mind perhaps . . . but something on the lines."

Someone had come up to the stall and had picked up a case containing needles and cottons.

"How much is this?"

I turned reluctantly from Roger Lestrange who lifted his eyebrows and smiled. I was afraid he would go away, and I wanted to ask him more about the school. That we might go into a school was a prospect which had not entered our minds.

While I took the money from my customer I was thinking: but wouldn't they want qualified teachers for a school?

The woman had gone.

"Yes," went on Roger Lestrange. "This school in Kimberley had to close down. There was no one to run it. I wonder . . . ?"

"It sounds interesting."

Someone else had come up to the stall.

"Business is getting brisk now," said Roger Lestrange.

He lingered. The newcomer fingered a few things, bought a glass ashtray and departed.

"We ought to have a talk," said Roger Lestrange.

"With Miss Milne," I replied. "Could you come to the vicarage? It's impossible here."

"Tomorrow morning, yes. Ten o'clock?"

"That would be kind of you. Oh dear, someone else is coming. I'll see you tomorrow morning."

I hardly noticed what I was selling. I could not wait to see Lilias and tell her the news.

And when she heard it she shared my excitement.

He arrived at the vicarage precisely on the stroke of ten next morning. We were both eagerly waiting for him and took him into the sitting room which the vicar used for listening to the trials of his parishioners, and we settled down to talk.

"The more I think of it the more suitable it seems," he said. "We need a school, but we had to close this one down. The lady who had run it for some years was getting old. She gave up, and up to the time I left they had not found anyone to replace her. One or two did come but did not stay . . . and then there was no one, so they had to close it. I've written to a man I know who is in charge of these things in the town and I posted the letter last night. I hope you don't think I was precipitous, but I thought there was no harm in finding out what the position was. My opinion is that they'll be delighted at the prospect of finding someone who'll open up the school and run it successfully, as I am sure you two will."

"We'd be working together," said Lilias, her eyes shining.

"That's the idea. The head—I presume that would be you, Miss Milne, your being the senior and the experienced one . . ."

He looked at me apologetically and I said quickly: "But naturally."

"Of course, if you don't like the idea you can always try something else, I suppose, but after I had heard . . . and then our little conversation at the stall yesterday . . . well, it did occur to me that it was a better proposition than going out there and not knowing what you were going to find."

"It is so very good of you, Mr. Lestrange," said Lilias earnestly; and I echoed her words, for it was wonderful to see the anxieties dropping from her and to experience the pleasant feeling that the way was being made easy for us.

"There'll only be a small salary, I believe . . . at the moment, that is. There are not all that many young people seeking education. Some of the inhabitants don't see the need for it alas. So much would depend on how many pupils you could muster. There might be only a few at first, but if you could build it up. There are living quarters, I know, in the schoolhouse, and they would go with the job."

"It sounds like an . . . opportunity," said Lilias.

"Someone will probably be writing to you. I've told them to get in touch."

"We don't know how to thank you," we said in unison.

His eyes held mine for a moment and he smiled.

"I only hope it works out well and I deserve your thanks," he said.

LILIAS was growing enthusiastic. She had naturally been fearful that we might arrive in some foreign place without any hope of employment—and now that fear was gone. And the prospect of a school where we could work together was wonderful.

"It's ideal!" said Lilias, and I began to believe her.

All the same, to leave one's country meant a great upheaval in one's life and now that the time for our departure was growing near I could not contemplate it without some misgivings. I found that I wanted to be alone now and then; I had to practise stopping myself going over that dreadful ordeal; I was trying to instil a peace into my mind, trying to look forward instead of back.

I found a certain peace in sitting in the graveyard which I could see from my bedroom window. It seemed so quiet there.

I was sitting there one day when Roger Lestrange came along.

"Why hello, Miss Grey," he said. "I was just coming to the vicarage to see you and Miss Milne, and I find you sitting here contemplating the scenery. I thought you should have the address of the schoolhouse. I expect to hear before long how delighted they will be to receive you."

"It is kind of you to take so much trouble."

I took the paper he gave me, glanced at the address and put it into my pocket.

"It's peaceful here," he said. "Here, among the dead. Do you often come and sit here?"

"Quite often. I can see it from my bedroom window in the vicarage. I thought it might be morbid, but it is far from that. The quietness and peace is . . . appealing."

"I hope you will like South Africa."

"We have to get used to the idea. We had almost settled on Australia and had been reading quite a bit about it."

"And now you have switched to South Africa. I don't think you'll be disappointed. How soon do you plan to leave . . . when you hear from the school, I mean?"

"As soon as possible."

"Myra and I will be sailing in the not-too-distant future. After the wedding and the honeymoon and I've settled a little business. It may be that we shall sail together."

"I suppose that is a possibility."

"Then I can keep an eye on you."

"That sounds comforting."

"When you sit here, do you wonder about the dead?"

"Yes. I suppose one would, wouldn't one?"

"You read the names on the stones . . . when you can. Many of them are half-obliterated. Just think, some of these people have been lying there for a hundred years!"

"More than that, some of them."

"Do you wonder what their lives were like . . . all their troubles . . . all their joys . . . how they lived and how they died?"

"Yes, I do."

"And think of the people you have known and who are gone . . ."

I was silent. In spite of the fact that he had taken such pains to help us, I was wary of him. I had the feeling that there was an ulterior motive in what he said and did. He knew I came from Edinburgh; he had been present when Kitty had called out my name.

"We have all known people who have died," he went on. "Died . . . before their time."

My heart was beating fast, and I drew away from him, for I had suddenly realised that he was sitting very close to me.

"I suppose it is natural that we should think such thoughts in a place like this," I said briskly.

"I lost someone . . . my wife. She was very young to die."

"I'm sorry."

"It was tragic . . . unexpected. That makes it harder to bear."

"Yes," I said quietly. "Was it long ago?"

"Two years."

I suppressed my astonishment that it was so recent and said: "It must have been very sad for you."

He nodded. "I thought I should never marry again."

"Well, I hope you will be happy now. I am sure Miss Ellington will make you so."

"Thank you," he said. "You see, I have a child . . ."

"Yes, I did hear that."

"Paul. He is named after a very distinguished man whom his mother greatly admired. Of course, she couldn't give the child the name exactly . . . rather too ponderous, one might say. Stephanus Johannes Paulus . . . so she was contented with simply Paul. After Kruger . . . the great man over there. If the child had been a girl I've no doubt it would have been Paula. People do that sometimes . . . turn the male into the female and vice versa."

Why did he say this? I was Davina; my father had been David. It was almost as though he were hinting at something. He was a disturbing man; I was sorry that he was the one from whom we had to take help.

I said quickly: "How old is the boy?"

"Nine, coming up to ten."

"You will be pleased to be home with him."

"I shall be pleased to be back, yes. I shall be starting a new life. It is no use living in the past, is it? We have to realise that."

He gazed at me intently and I rose.

"I must be going," I said. "Lilias . . . Miss Milne . . . will be so glad to have the address. I can't tell you how grateful we are. This has made such a difference."

"It has been my pleasure," he said. "Don't forget, either of you: I shall be there . . . if you need me."

He took my hand and pressed it.

"Well," he said. "You've saved me a journey to the vicarage, and it was so pleasant to have a little chat with you in the graveyard, Miss Grey."

I went back to the vicarage, trying hard to shake off that feeling of uneasiness which he aroused in me.

• • • • •

I THOUGHT I OWED a letter of thanks to Ninian Grainger, after all the trouble he had taken, to tell him of the progress we had made. I wrote:

Dear Mr. Grainger,

Miss Milne and I are so grateful for your help. As I told you, we went to see Mrs. Crown and shall be calling on her again shortly, we hope.

It is our great good fortune that a Mr. Roger Lestrange, who is here on business and staying at the big house in the neighbourhood, comes from South Africa and he is helping us considerably. He knows of a school and it seems that Miss Milne and I may be able to work together there. This is a wonderful piece of luck because, as you can imagine, we were somewhat apprehensive as to how long it would be before we were able to find posts in a foreign country. We feel much happier now and are awaiting confirmation from South Africa. When this comes we shall be very relieved.

I hope all goes well with you and thank you once more for all the help you have given us.

D.

I had, of course, written to Zillah. She wrote back and said how sorry she would be when I had gone, but she quite understood why I wanted to go.

Your Mr. Lestrange sounds an absolute darling and I should love to meet him. Your Mr. Grainger continues to call. I wonder why! South Africa seems a very long way away. I shall come down to see you off. I must do that. I suppose you haven't any dates yet? Still . . . let me know when you have.

I'm going to hate it when you've gone. True, you've been away for some time, but I know you are not far-off.

Keep in touch.

Your loving ZILLAH

The wedding day had arrived. I went to the church and heard Lilias' father pronounce Myra Ellington and Roger Lestrange man and wife.

Afterwards we went to the reception to which Mrs. Ellington had graciously invited us and in due course the couple left for their honeymoon.

Myra looked very happy and I remarked—with fervour—to Lilias that I hoped she would remain so.

"You sound doubtful," said Lilias.

"Do I? Well, they do say that marriage is something of a lottery. You have to draw the right number or whatever it is."

"You've become a cynic."

She was full of hope now, and I understood how frustrating those months at home must have been for her.

The honeymoon was still in progress when we received a letter from South Africa. It was signed by a Jan Van Der Groot. He said he was pleased to hear from Mr. Roger Lestrange that we contemplated coming out to South Africa to teach. There had been only one teacher in the school in the past, for it was very small. But if we liked to come and share the salary, there would be room for us both, for the living quarters which were part of the school would certainly be big enough. The place had been shut up for some months, but it would be made ready for our arrival.

We read it together.

"One salary," said Lilias.

"It's yours. I have my own money. I shall be all right."

"It's a little disappointing . . ."

"It's not, Lilias. We'll be together. It's a chance to make a fresh start."

"But the money . . . and I have to pay back . . ."

"There's nothing to worry about. I don't need to work. I'll be all right. We'll make that school grow, Lilias. It's a challenge . . . a way out."

Her spirits revived. It was not all that we had hoped for, but it was more than we could expect.

Everything moved quickly after that.

We went to see Mrs. Crown once more. We had decided. We were going to South Africa. We already had employment waiting for us.

"Congratulations!" said Mrs. Crown. "You've been lucky. We'll get you a passage as soon as possible."

And this is what she did.

We were to sail on the *Queen of the South* to Cape Town and from there make the journey across the country to Kimberley.

Kimberley

Outward Bound

THE TIME for our departure was approaching. In less than a week we were to sail. Acting on the advice of Mrs. Crown, we had sent the bulk of our luggage to the docks; and after the harassed preparations of the last few days we had come to a lull when there seemed to be nothing to do.

Lilias and I were sitting in the garden going over, for at least the hundredth time, all the things we had to do before we left, asking ourselves if we had packed all we needed in the little luggage we were taking with us. We were to leave the vicarage the day before we sailed, spending a night in a hotel near the docks which Mrs. Crown had arranged for us. Zillah had been helpful and had sent those possessions which I had wanted to take with me straight to the docks; this was a great help and it had meant that I had not had to return to Edinburgh which would have been very painful for me.

Now everything was settled and there was nothing to do but wait.

As we sat there Jane came out.

"There's a young man who has called to see you, Diana," she said. "His name is Mr. Grainger."

I felt myself flush. I was tingling with pleasure. All I could say was: "Oh . . . so he's come . . ."

Lilias, to whom I had talked of him and confessed something of my feelings for him, and who, perhaps, guessed a little more, said: "He'll want to talk to you. I'll go in." Then: "Bring him out, Jane. They can talk in the garden. It's pleasant out here."

Ninian came to me and, taking both my hands in his, held them firmly.

"I felt I had to come and see you before you left," he said.

"That is very good of you."

"It's a big step you are taking."

"Let's sit down. A big step? Yes. But we

have thought a good deal about it and in the circumstances it seems a good thing."

"I'm so glad Miss Milne is going with you."

"Yes, that is a great piece of luck for me."

"Tell me about this Mr. Lestrange."

"He's a friend of the Ellingtons who live in the big house here. He's engaged in big business and I think Mr. Ellington has some connections in it. I don't really know much about it. But I expect it has something to do with diamonds. He lives in Kimberley, you see, and when he came over Myra Ellington and he fell in love and married."

"It sounds like a whirlwind romance."

"It was. He was a widower. I gathered his wife died . . . not long ago. He probably came to England to get away from it all . . . and he met Myra Ellington."

"So it all turned out well for him."

"The fact of the matter is that they are going back to Kimberley. I believe they will actually be sailing on the same ship."

"I'd like to meet Mr. and Mrs. Lestrange."

"I don't suppose you will. Are you going back tomorrow?"

"I thought I'd come and see you off."

"Oh!" I was amazed but inordinately

pleased. I kept thinking how strange it was that he should continue to show such interest. I had told myself many times that it was because I was still smarting from Jamie's rejection . . . but it was something beyond that. I hated to confess it, but one of the reasons why I regretted leaving England was because I should never see him again. That was quite foolish, I knew; I constantly reminded myself that all I meant to him was an interesting case which had brought him quite useful success.

"I've booked in at the Royal Oak," he said. "I thought I could travel down to Tilbury with you and be of some help."

"What a lovely idea! But can you spare the time?"

"Just about," he said.

"Are you comfortable at the Royal Oak?"

"Very comfortable."

"That's good, because it is the only hotel around here."

"I'm glad it's so near. Tell me about the school."

"I don't know much except what I have told you already. I am sure we shall be able to manage all right. Lilias is a wonderful teacher, and I shall try to follow in her footsteps."

"And this has all come about through Mr. Lestrange. What do you know of him?"

"Only what I've told you. He's engaged in the diamond business; he's apparently wealthy; he's a widower with a son named Paul; he is considered to be very attractive and is a good match for Myra Ellington."

"What about Myra herself?"

"I don't know much about her either. She is very pleasant and quiet . . . not like her mother. She's very good at . . . doing what she is told. I could never understand why she has not married long ago. I should not have thought Mrs. Ellington would have been the sort of woman to allow her daughter to remain unmarried. But I suppose most of them want to ensure their daughters' financial security . . . and with Myra, Mrs. Ellington does not have to consider this. It seems that she is quite well off in her own right."

"Perhaps I shall meet them."

"Perhaps. But everyone's very busy. Mrs. Crown has been very good. She has arranged everything for us. We are spending our last night in England in a hotel called Harbour View, which speaks for itself, and we shall be right on the spot for the day we sail."

"I'll book in there."

I must have shown my surprise, for he said: "I feel responsible for you! After all, I introduced you to Mrs. Crown."

"It was the best thing you could have done."

"I do hope so," he said fervently.

Daisy came out with some coffee.

"Miss Jane thought you could do with this," she said.

There was a small table under a tree and she set the tray on this; and we drew up our chairs.

"This is delightful," said Ninian.

I was happier than I had been for a long time—just for a moment; then the thought hit me: I am going right away . . . out of the old life . . . out of his life.

He watched me as I poured out the coffee. I wondered what he was thinking and what had really prompted him to come so far to see me before I left.

He said suddenly: "If this should not work out . . . if you should want to come home for any reason . . . let me know. I'll do what I can to arrange it."

"You are so good. And all because you defended me. There must be so many . . ."

He shook his head. "It was unfair, that verdict. It rankles."

"I see."

"One day perhaps . . ."

I waited and he shrugged his shoulders. "It has happened, you know. The truth comes out, even after years."

Then we talked of those young women who, as Lilias and I were doing, had left their homes to go away and work in foreign countries. I told him about the letters we had read in the Society's offices. He was very interested, but he kept bringing the conversation back to Roger Lestrange.

He stayed to dinner. It was clear to me that he had made a good impression on the vicarage family.

Lilias said, after he had left for the Royal Oak: "What a charming man! It is so kind of him to care about what happens to you."

I was very happy that night. I dreamed that I was sailing away from England, and Ninian Grainger was standing on the dock watching. Then suddenly he lifted his arms and cried loudly: "Don't go! Don't go!"

I knew that I must not go, that it was wrong for me to go. I tried to leap overboard, but someone was restraining me, saying: "You can't go back. None of us can go back. It's too late . . . once you've started."

And that was Roger Lestrange.

THE NEXT DAY my pleasure in Ninian Grainger's care was dampened.

It was in the morning. Daisy came to my room and said: "There's a visitor for you, Miss Grey. In the sitting room."

I went down, expecting to see Ninian. It was Zillah.

She looked even more beautiful than I remembered. She was dressed in a black silk dress with a big green bow at the neck and a black hat with a green feather which tipped down to her eyes, calling attention to their colour.

"My dear!" she cried, embracing me. "How wonderful to see you! I had to come. I'm going to see you off. I'm staying at the Royal Oak."

"Oh," I said blankly.

She laughed almost coyly. "Who do you think is staying there? Your Mr. Grainger. Well, it's the only one, isn't it? And I couldn't expect to be put up at the vicarage. I hope you're pleased to see me. I'm not really very happy about all this, you know. You'll be so far away. I had hoped we could be together. Oh, I do hope this is going to be the right thing for you."

"I had to get away," I said. "And this seems as good a method as any."

"It's so sad. But I mustn't go on about it. We've got to make the best of things, haven't we? How have you been getting on in this place? I'm longing to meet your friend, Lilias. I wonder what she'll feel about me. I took her place, didn't I . . . in the house, I mean."

"You'll like her. She's a wonderful person."

"Oh, I do hope this is going to be all right."

She meant well, and it was good of her to take the trouble to come. But she had shattered an illusion.

I did not realise until then how deeply I had been affected by Ninian's coming here.

I had been very foolish. I had been so stimulated, so happy because I had thought he had been so apprehensive on my account that he had come down to see for himself what was happening. I had had a ridiculous feeling that he was regretting having introduced me to

Mrs. Crown and that he was going to beg me to relinquish the project and go back with him to Edinburgh so that we could fight together to prove I had played no part in my father's murder.

I was naïve. I was reaching out for someone to care for me . . . someone to fill that bitter void left by Jamie.

Face facts, I admonished myself. You are going away . . . right away from the old life, from everyone you ever knew—except Lilias.

He came because *she* was coming. You were misled by Jamie once. Be on your guard that it does not happen again.

I saw a good deal of Ninian during the next day. We talked a good deal. I felt that he knew as much about the place to which I was going as I did. Zillah was there, too.

On the morning before the day we were due to leave for Tilbury, I went down to the village to buy a few oddments which I had found I needed and Ninian had said he would accompany me.

Zillah, who happened to arrive at that moment, said she would join us.

It was on our way back from the village that we met Roger Lestrange. He was riding a big grey horse from the Ellington stables and he lifted his hat as we approached.

"Miss Grey. Ah, the last-minute shopping. All ready to sail?"

I introduced them. I could sense Ninian's interest. He had always wanted to hear all he could about Roger Lestrange.

I noticed that the latter was surveying Zillah with appreciation while she put on that especially seductive air she used for attractive men.

"We are going to see the dear child off on her travels," said Zillah. "It is going to be very sad for me."

"I am sure it will be." He spoke soothingly.

Ninian said: "I understand you are from South Africa."

"Yes, it's my home now. I shall be returning to it on the *Queen of the South*."

"Oh yes. I understood you would be sailing on her."

"Shall you be glad to go home?" asked Zillah.

He looked at her almost slyly. "Well, there are temptations to stay, but alas . . ."

"And you sail . . . the day after tomorrow, is it? So it is hail and farewell. How sad."

"I agree . . . wholeheartedly. Well . . ."
He shrugged his shoulders. "I'll see you on
board, Miss Grey."

"So that is Roger Lestrange," said Ninian
when he had ridden off.

"He seemed to be a most interesting man,"
added Zillah.

Then we rode back to the vicarage and the
next day we left for London, Tilbury and the
Queen of the South.

As SOON as I stepped on board I felt a sense of
irreparable loss. Melancholy took hold of me
and I was sure that no exciting new experience
could dispel it. This was largely due to having
said goodbye to Ninian. I had taken this step
and there was no going back.

Ninian and Zillah had travelled to the ship
with us. So, Zillah had said, that she could
spend every possible moment with me. She
constantly expressed her sorrow at my departure, but I could not get rid of the notion that
she was rather relieved. Perhaps she was
thinking what was best for me and was fully
aware that while I remained in England I
should be constantly on the alert for someone

to recognise me. That was no way to live and a sacrifice was worthwhile to change it.

I had to keep remembering that and then I could be reconciled to leaving everything that was familiar to me and going off into the unknown.

I did have a short time alone with Ninian. I think Lilias helped to arrange this by making sure that she kept Zillah away. My spirits were lifted because I sensed that this was what Ninian wanted, too.

He talked seriously about my future.

"You don't need to look on it as permanent," he stressed. "You will come back. But for a time I believe this is the best thing to do. I want you to promise me something."

"What is that?"

"That you will write to me and tell me everything . . . however seemingly trivial. I want to know."

"But surely . . . ?"

"Please," he said. "It may be important."

"Do you still regard me as 'a case?' "

"A very special case. Please, I am serious. Give me your word. I know you will keep it."

"I will write," I said.

"I shall want to know about the school . . .

and the Lestranges . . . and how everything works out."

I nodded. "And you will let me know what happens at home?"

"I will."

"You sound so serious."

"It is very important to me. And there is one thing more. If you want to come home, let me know. I will arrange it."

"You . . . ?"

"I shall see that you get a passage home at the earliest possible moment. Please remember that."

"It is comforting to know that you are so concerned about me."

"Of course I'm concerned about you . . . . Davina."

I looked at him in alarm.

"I can't get used to that other name," he said. "I always think of you as Davina."

"Well, no one can hear now."

"One day you will come back."

"I wonder."

"You will," he insisted. "You must."

I remembered that conversation for days to come and it brought me comfort.

We were on deck as the ship sailed out. The

hooters were sounding all round us; the quay was crowded with the friends of passengers come to see the last of them. It was a moving scene. Some people were weeping, others laughing, as slowly the ship glided out of her berth and sailed away.

Lilias and I stood there waving until we could no longer see Ninian and Zillah.

I SHALL NEVER FORGET those first days on the *Queen of the South*. I had not dreamed of such discomfort. In the first place we had to share a cabin with two others. The cabin was little more than a large cupboard and there were four berths, two lower and two upper. There was one small cupboard for the use of the four occupants and there were no portholes. We were shut in with many other similar cabins and the noises around us never seemed to cease. We were at the after end of the ship and there were barriers to prevent our leaving that section.

Meals were taken at long tables. I suppose the food was adequate, but eating in such conditions was far from pleasant and neither Lilias nor I had much appetite for it.

Our section of the ship was overcrowded.

Washing was not easy. There were communal quarters for this and little privacy.

I said to Lilias: "Can you endure this till Cape Town?"

"We must," she answered.

When the weather turned rough, as it did very soon, this was an added trial.

The two women who shared our cabin were prostrate in their bunks. Lilias felt queasy, too. She could not decide whether to venture out on deck or withdraw to her bunk.

She decided on the latter and I went on deck. I staggered along as far as the segregating barrier and sat down. I looked at the grey heaving waves and wondered what I had let myself into. The future seemed bleak. What should I find in this country to which we were going? I had been a coward. I should have stayed at home and faced whatever I had to. People would say that if I were innocent I should have nothing to fear. I should have held my head high, faced whatever was coming and not hidden behind an assumed name.

And now here I was, in a condition of acute discomfort, being carried over this turbulent sea to . . . I could not know what.

I was aware of someone on the other side of the barrier.

"Hello," said Roger Lestrange. He was looking down on me over the top of the fencing which separated us. "Facing the elements?"

"Yes . . . and you, too?"

"You find this uncomfortable, do you?"

"Yes, don't you?"

"Mildly. Nothing to what it can do, I assure you."

"Well, I hope it doesn't attempt to show me."

"I didn't see you when you boarded. You had friends to see you off, I believe."

"Yes."

"That was nice. How are you liking the trip . . . apart from the weather?"

I was silent for a while and he said quickly: "Not good, is it?"

"It's hardly luxury."

"I had no idea you would travel in such a way."

"Nor had we. But we did want to do so as cheaply as possible. Miss Milne has a horror of debt. How is Mrs. Lestrange?"

"Laid low. She does not like the weather."

"Who does? I am sorry for her."

"We'll soon be out of this and then we'll all forget about it."

I had been standing up while I was talking to him, and a gust of wind threw me against the deck rail.

"All right?" he asked.

"Yes, thanks."

"I think you should go below," he continued. "The wind can be treacherous and one really shouldn't face the decks when it is like this." He smiled wryly. "I'm sorry I can't conduct you to your quarters."

"You're right," I said. "I'll go down. Goodbye."

"Au revoir," he said.

And I staggered down to the cabin.

LATER THAT DAY the wind abated. Lilias and I were alone in the cabin. The other occupants, feeling better, had gone out, as they said, for a breath of fresh air.

One of the stewards came to our cabin.

He said: "I've got orders to move you."

"Move us?" we cried simultaneously.

"Some mistake, I expect. You shouldn't be in this one. Get your things together."

Bewildered we obeyed. He took our cases and told us to follow him. We did so and he led us through the ship, opening one of the dividing doors. He took us to a cabin which seemed magnificent after the one we had just left. There were two bunks which served as sofas by day, a fair-sized wardrobe, a washbasin and a porthole.

We stared at it in amazement.

"That's it," he said, and left us. We could not believe it. It was such a contrast. Lilias sat down on one of the beds and looked as though she were going to burst into tears, which was extraordinary for her.

"What does it mean?" she demanded.

"It means that they made a mistake. They should never have put us in with the emigrants."

"But we are emigrants."

"Yes . . . but here we are. Isn't it wonderful? I feel dignified. I don't think I could have borne much more of that."

"Yes, you would . . . if you had to."

"Well, don't let's worry about that. Let's rejoice."

"I wonder how it happened," said Lilias.

"Doubtless we shall hear."

We did ask the purser, who told us there had been some mistake and we were so relieved we did not take the matter farther than that. All we knew was that we could now continue the rest of the voyage, weather permitting, in a comfort we had not dared hope for.

EVERYTHING CHANGED after that. We were often in the company of the Lestranges; and it was during that voyage that I began to know Myra.

She was a self-effacing person, rather timid, in contrast to her mother. I often wondered whether having spent so much of her life in close contact with such a woman had made her as she was, for in such a presence even the most confident people must be aware of their shortcomings. I grew to like her. She was rather withdrawn in the presence of her husband, and rarely spoke unless addressed. I noticed that he often finished a sentence with "Is that not so, my dear?" as though trying to draw her into the conversation. "Yes, yes, Roger, indeed it is," she would invariably reply.

"She's completely subservient," said Lilias.

"I think she wants to please him. After all, he is always kind and courteous to her."

"Well, if he likes absolute obedience, she must suit him very well," was Lilias' rather terse rejoinder.

Practical Lilias might dismiss her as a woman of no spirit, content to be dominated by her husband, but I saw some character beneath that attitude, and perhaps because she sensed my feelings she revealed a little more of herself to me than she did to most people.

Our first port of call was Tenerife and as it was not easy for two women to go out alone, Roger Lestrange suggested that we accompany him and his wife. We accepted willingly.

We had a pleasant day, and under the guidance of Roger Lestrange went for a ride through the town and some miles out into the country. We revelled in the balmy air and marvelled at the brilliant flowers and shrubs, the poinsettia trees growing wild by the roadside, the banana plantations and the mountains.

Roger Lestrange was an amusing and knowledgeable companion and when we returned to the ship Lilias said how fortunate we were to be travelling with them; and I agreed.

Myra said: "It is a great pleasure to have

you with us." I was glad she felt that as the thought had crossed my mind during the day that we might be intruding. After all, it was not long since their honeymoon, and that was a time when newly wed people liked to be alone together.

As we came down the west coast of Africa the weather was warm, the sea smooth, and life on board was very pleasant indeed. Neither Lilias nor I wanted the days to pass too quickly. After our change of cabin, which had brought us to another part of the ship, we had found the life very congenial. We were meeting people who interested us.

Roger Lestrange was quite sought after. He was an asset to social gatherings; he was on good terms with the captain whom he had met on a previous voyage; and, as his friends, we were drawn into his circle.

It was delightful to sit on deck, to look over the water which scarcely moved, to watch the dolphins sporting in the distance and the flying fish skimming over the surface of that pellucid sea. It was conducive to confidences.

Myra was reluctant to talk, but eventually she began to give me a glimpse into her childhood.

"It would have been different if I had been brilliant," she said to me one day. "But I wasn't. I was slow . . . slow to walk . . . slow to talk. Right from the beginning I was a disappointment. My mother wanted me to be outstanding . . . not so much clever as beautiful . . . a success socially. You know the sort of thing . . . something she could arrange and then . . . grandchildren whom she could plan for."

"People have to manage their own lives."

"My mother would never accept that. She was so good at managing everything, so naturally she wanted to manage me. I was lucky in one way because there were the grandparents . . . my father's parents. I spent a great deal of my childhood with them. I was happy there. They did not care whether I was clever or beautiful. They liked me just as I was. My mother said they spoiled me. She did not want me to be so much with them, but they were important. They were very rich and she respected that."

"I can well believe it."

"My grandmother died." Her voice trembled a little. "I was fourteen then. After that there was just Grandpa. I was often with him.

He wanted me to live with him. My mother could not allow that. My place was at home with her, she said; but I was with him a great deal. We used to read together; we would sit in the garden and play guessing games. Then he was in a wheelchair and I used to wheel him about the garden. My mother said it was no life for a girl, but I loved to be with him. I had to have a season in London. My mother insisted and my father agreed with her. The season was a failure. Nobody asked me to marry him. Soon after that my mother gave up. I went to stay with Grandpa. He said, 'Don't let them push you. You do what you want. And never marry a man because they tell you you ought to. That's the biggest mistake a girl can make . . . or a man for that matter.' He was wonderful. I was twenty-four when he died."

"How sad for you."

"I was heartbroken. I was very rich. He had left everything to me. It made a difference. My mother changed towards me. I knew she thought I should get a husband now, but when she started managing I said to her, 'Grandpa told me I was never to marry anyone just because people told me to. I was to marry only if I, myself, wanted to.' "

"I think your grandfather was very wise," I said.

"Oh, he was. But I'm talking all about myself. What about you?"

That freezing sensation came over me. I heard myself say: "Oh, there's nothing much to tell. I just had a governess . . . and then . . . I went to stay at the vicarage."

"And your father?"

"He . . . he died."

"And now you have to take this post in South Africa?"

"I don't exactly have to. I just wanted to do something. I have a little income . . . not a great deal . . . but adequate, I suppose."

"Did you ever think of marrying?"

"Well, once. But it didn't work out."

"I'm sorry."

"Don't be. I'm sure now that it was all for the best."

"Are you sure? I think you seem a little sad sometimes."

"Oh no . . . no. It's all in the past. Our families didn't approve and . . . ."

"Oh dear."

"It would hardly have been right for us. If it

had been we should have married, shouldn't we?"

"I rather liked that lawyer . . . the one who came down to see you. It seemed that he was really concerned about you. And your stepmother. She's very beautiful, isn't she? When I look at her . . ." She laughed a little mirthlessly. "Well, I think she is all that I am not."

"You are very nice as you are, Myra. You must not denigrate yourself so much."

"And *you* are nice to say so. But tell me about this lawyer. You knew him in Edinburgh, did you?"

"Yes."

"He was a friend of your family, I suppose."

"You could say that."

I had to stop the trend of this conversation.

I said quickly: "And it all turned out well for you."

She said: "Yes. My grandfather was right. I might have married someone my mother found for me. But I didn't and if I had there wouldn't have been Roger."

"So you are completely happy now?"

"Well . . ."

"You are, aren't you?"

She hesitated, looked at me thoughtfully and then, I believed, decided to confide in me. "Sometimes . . . I'm afraid."

"Afraid of what?"

"He is so distinguished, isn't he? Sometimes I wonder . . ."

"Tell me what you wonder."

"Whether I'm good enough. What does he see in me? If he hadn't been rich himself I should have thought it was the money . . ."

I laughed at her. "Myra, you must stop thinking like that. He married you, didn't he? He loves *you,* not your money."

"It's so hard to believe. He is so wonderful. Of course, if he had needed the money . . ."

"Stop it, Myra!" I laughed again and she laughed with me. I was so relieved. I had thought she was afraid of *him* and all she feared was that she was not attractive enough for him.

I must overcome this ridiculous feeling that there was something rather sinister about Roger Lestrange.

IT WAS NO USE trying to hold back the days. They were passing with alarming rapidity.

Very soon we should arrive at our destination and reality would take the place of this dreamlike idyllic existence which we had been enjoying for the last few weeks.

We should have to face whatever we found —our school. Where should we find the pupils? Lilias had said it was no use planning anything until we saw what we were coming to.

We were due in Cape Town in two days' time.

Roger Lestrange had said we must accompany him and Myra to Kimberley. It was a longish journey, but he had done it more than once and he could help us and take us to our new home.

We accepted his offer with alacrity.

"It really was good fortune for us to be travelling in the same ship," said Lilias. "They have made it all so much more interesting for us than it would otherwise have been."

She did not realise how much we owed to Roger Lestrange, but I was soon to discover.

That night I went out onto the deck as I often did. I loved to sit there underneath the velvety sky with the stars more brilliant than they seemed at home. The air was warm and there was hardly anyone about. It was perfect peace.

It will soon be over, I thought, and what shall we find? Myra and Roger Lestrange would not be far away. It was good to have them as friends—particularly in a foreign country.

And as I sat there I heard a light footstep on the deck and before I looked up I guessed who it was.

He said: "Hello. Revelling in the starry night? May I?" He drew up a chair and sat beside me.

"It is pleasant, isn't it?" I said.

"It's more than pleasant. It's delightful."

"I agree."

"I wonder more people don't take advantage of it. Never mind. It gives us an opportunity to talk in peace. How are you feeling? Nearly there, you know."

"I was just thinking of that when you came up."

"It's a bit of a gamble, isn't it?"

"Rather more than that."

"You'll be all right. We shall not be far away."

"You must be looking forward to getting to your home."

"I've enjoyed the trip."

"Of course. You met Myra."

"Yes, and you . . . and Miss Milne. It has been very illuminating."

"Illuminating?"

"It is always interesting meeting people, don't you think?"

"Oh yes, of course."

"You and Myra seem to get along very well."

"I think we do. I've grown fond of her."

"That's good. She's rather retiring. I like to see you two friendly. I couldn't bear to think of you down there in that steerage . . . or whatever it is."

"Oh . . . yes, at first it really was rather dreadful."

"I'm glad I rescued you from that. Glad for myself as well as you."

"Rescued us?"

"Well, I couldn't leave you down there, could I?"

"You mean . . . you . . ."

"Look, it was nothing. Forget it."

"But . . . they said there was a mistake. We thought . . ."

"I insisted that you were not told."

"Please tell me exactly what happened."

"It's quite clear. You paid for a cabin and you got what you paid for."

"I . . . I see. Lilias wanted to have the cheapest. That Society was lending the money and she could not bear to be in debt."

"Very worthy sentiments."

"So it was you who . . ."

"I had you moved. I paid the extra so that you could enjoy the voyage in comfort."

I felt myself flushing. "But . . . we must pay you back."

"Certainly not."

"Lilias . . ."

"Lilias need know nothing of the transaction. Just imagine her feelings. Besides, she would feel she had to pay me. That would be as bad as paying the Society. And you know how she hates to be in debt."

I was silent for a moment. Then I said: "I can pay you."

"I shall refuse to take it."

"But you must."

"Why? It was a little gift. It was nothing.

And think what a pleasure it has been for me . . . and for Myra . . . to have your company, which we could not have had, you know, if we had had to be separated on different sides of the barriers."

"It was very good of you, but you must allow me to refund the money, my share at least."

"I will not allow it."

"I cannot accept."

"My dear . . . D–Diana, you already have."

"But . . ."

"No buts please. Think of proud Lilias. She must go on believing that there was a misunderstanding in allotting the cabins and when it was realised it was put right."

"Why should you do this?"

"Because I could not bear to think of you two ladies in such conditions. I should not have told you."

"But you have."

"It slipped out. Perhaps I wanted to let you know that I wanted to help you. After all, it is a big step you're taking and I suggested you should come to South Africa. I very much want it to be a success."

"You are very good and I am grateful to you. But I would rather . . ."

"Will you please me in this matter? Say no more about it. I have been delighted to have your company . . . so has Myra. In fact, we have all had a pleasant voyage." He laid his hand on mine. "Please see it this way . . . and not another word about the matter."

I should have guessed. We had paid so little for the voyage. We had been so inexperienced in these matters. It was good of him to be concerned. That was how I must try to see it.

But the discovery did make me feel a little uneasy.

IN TWO MORE DAYS we should reach our destination. One could sense the tension throughout the ship. For myself—and I knew that Lilias felt the same—there was an immense excitement which at times would almost be overcome by a fearful apprehension. There were times when it was brought home forcibly to us that, somewhat blithely, we had decided to leave all that was familiar to start an entirely new life.

We now began to ask ourselves how well equipped we were to do this and we were very preoccupied. We would sit in silence staring out over the sea, each aware that our thoughts were running on similar lines.

Roger Lestrange, I was sure, was fully aware of our feelings; he continually sought to allay our fears. All was going to be well. He would be at hand. We must remember that we had friends.

I remember vividly that sunny day, sitting there on the deck, looking out over an aquamarine sea with scarcely a ripple to disturb its tranquility. Lilias and I had been joined by Roger and Myra. Poor Myra; I guessed her apprehensions about her new life were as deep as mine and Lilias'.

The captain, who was on his daily round of the ship, came into sight.

"Good afternoon," he said. "Lovely day."

We agreed that it was.

"Soon be there," he added.

"On a day like this it seems too soon," said Roger.

"Yes . . . and the weather is set fair for the next few days, it seems. Though the Cape can be tricky."

"Indeed," said Roger. "I've had experience of that."

The captain smiled and his eyes rested on Lilias, Myra and me.

"You young ladies will be visiting South Africa for the first time."

"Yes," said Lilias.

"You could have chosen a better time, wouldn't you say, Mr. Lestrange?"

"It will probably blow over," said Roger.

"This time it seems to be a little more serious."

"Oh, there's been trouble before?" said Lilias.

"Oh yes . . . brewing for years, but I'd say that now it seems to be coming to the boil."

"The captain is referring to Kruger. He's getting rather truculent just now."

"It's been seething for some time, I know," said the captain. "But after the Jameson Raid . . . well, things have gone from bad to worse."

"Why is this?" I asked.

"What would you say?" asked the captain, looking at Roger.

"It's simple. Cecil Rhodes wants a British South Africa. Kruger wants it for the Afrikaners. It will be all right. Kruger wouldn't dare go too far."

"We'll wait and see," said the captain. "Well, I must be getting along. I'll see you later."

After he had gone I turned to Roger. "I should like to know more about these matters."

"Of course. You're going to live there. Naturally enough you want to know."

"The captain seemed quite concerned," said Lilias.

"Well, to put it briefly," said Roger, "this jostling for power has been going on for some time, but when diamonds and gold were found in the country, it meant that people came and settled from elsewhere. They were mostly British subjects. Consequently the population changed and the newcomers, whom the Afrikaners called Uitlanders—Outlanders, of course—wanted to play a dominating role in the administration of the country. Paul Kruger was President of the Transvaal and he could see what was coming."

"He's a very strong leader, I believe," said Lilias.

"Indeed he is. He realised at once that if the Uitlanders were given a vote the Afrikaners would be outnumbered, with disastrous consequences to them. They were suspicious of the British who, right from the first, had maintained a different attitude towards the black population. When the emancipation of slavery had taken place in Britain the British wanted to extend it to South Africa. This was something which the Boers could not tolerate because it robbed them of the labour on their farms. It is a long story of conflict."

"And now the captain seems to think it is 'coming to the boil.' "

"We've been thinking that for some time. The reason that there is a scare now is because Kruger has ordained that no Uitlander may have a vote in the presidential elections, and only those who have lived fourteen years in the country and are forty years old can vote in the Volksraad elections. That is for the parliament, of course."

"It seems hardly fair if these Uitlanders had settled in the country."

"Exactly. Besides, many of them have become wealthy and are contributing considerably to the finances of the country and yet are denied a vote. You could not expect men like Cecil Rhodes and Jameson to stand aside and let such a state of affairs go on."

"Then, of course, there was the Jameson Raid," said Lilias.

"That delayed matters for some time. Especially when the Emperor of Germany sent a telegram congratulating Kruger on his success in the affair; on the other hand, there is no doubt that the British government is more determined than ever to show its strength."

"So it does seem as though there is some danger of big trouble?" said Lilias anxiously.

"As I say, the trouble is not new. It will be sorted out, no doubt. Negotiations are going on now, I believe, between Joseph Chamberlain, who is Secretary of State for the Colonies, and Jan Smuts, Kruger's young State Attorney. Being away all this time, I have only heard what is happening through the British press."

"We did not take very much notice of it," said Lilias. "Since we decided to come to South Africa there has been so much to do."

"I should forget it."

"But if there is this conflict between the Afrikaners and the Uitlanders, of whom we should be regarded as members, might they not be a little hostile towards us?"

"My dear lady, nobody would be hostile to

you, I am sure. No, no. They will be delighted to have you come to give your skills to their children. I am sure you will find a warm welcome awaiting you. Moreover, I shall be nearby. Riebeeck House is not far from the schoolhouse. So I shall be at hand if needed."

I felt he was expecting us to say that we were greatly comforted, but I—and I am sure Lilias felt the same—could not truthfully say that. We were beginning to wonder with a certain trepidation what lay ahead of us.

CAPE TOWN WAS BEAUTIFUL. I wished that we could have stayed to explore. The sun was welcoming; the people seemed friendly. From what I had heard from Roger and the captain, I had been prepared for a hostile reception from some members of the community. We were Uitlanders; and there was a controversy in progress among the people here. But there was no sign of this.

I marvelled at the grandeur of the Table Mountain and Table Bay.

"What a beautiful country!" I cried; and Lilias agreed with me.

We smiled at each other. We both felt that it was going to be all right.

The long train journey through the veldt was of absorbing interest, if somewhat exhausting. It was five hundred and forty miles from Cape Town to Kimberley and Roger had warned us that it would take thirty hours.

"It's fortunate that you do not have to trek," he added.

We had to be grateful to him. Throughout the journey, his air of authority brought him the best and immediate attention; and we shared in that.

"How different it would have been without his help," I said to Lilias, and she agreed.

At last we arrived in Kimberley.

Roger Lestrange insisted on taking us to the schoolhouse before going on with Myra to Riebeeck House.

As we drove through the town, Lilias and I gazed intently from the windows of the carriage.

"It's a prosperous town," Roger told us. "It's growing fast. That is what diamonds have done for it. Besides, it's on the direct route from Cape Town to the Transvaal." With pride he pointed out some of the fine buildings—the Town Hall, the High Court and the botanical gardens.

Lilias and I exchanged gratified glances. We had said when we heard of the troubles of this country that we should have been better in Australia or New Zealand. But this was very agreeable.

The carriage had drawn up before a small white building set back from the road in a kind of courtyard.

"The schoolhouse," announced Roger.

The door opened even as he spoke and a man emerged. He was in his early thirties, I imagined, fresh-complexioned and smiling.

"Mr. John Dale," said Roger. "Let me introduce you to the new schoolmistresses, John."

"This is Miss Milne and Miss Grey?" said the young man, looking from one of us to the other.

"This is Miss Grey," said Lilias. "I am Miss Milne."

He shook her hand and then mine.

"And this," said Roger Lestrange, "is my wife."

John Dale held out his hand and shook Myra's.

"Welcome to Kimberley," he said. "I hope you will be very happy here, Mrs. Lestrange."

Roger stood smiling benignly and said: "Well, we have had a long journey and my wife and I will be off. Can I leave the ladies in your care, John?"

"Certainly." He turned to us. "Do please come in. Let me take your baggage."

"There is much more to come," said Lilias.

"Of course. But now, let's get in."

"So," said Roger, "we'll leave you."

We thanked him sincerely for all he had done.

"We shall be seeing you soon. We shall want to hear what you think of it and how you are settling in, shall we not, Myra?"

"Oh yes . . . yes. Please come and see us soon," said Myra.

"Of course they will, my dear," put in Roger. "We're so close. You're not going to lose them. Well, we shall be getting on. You're safe in John's hands. Au revoir."

We had stepped into a hall and John Dale brought in our bags and set them down.

"Now," he said. "Let me explain who I am. I'm a member of the council which looks after the town. We have been very concerned about the education of our young people. It's a very small school, as you will see. We've never had more than about twenty pupils. The difficulty has been to get teachers who stay. Originally we had a Miss Groot who was here for twenty years. Then she became too old and we had a young woman who stayed for two years, married and went away. Since then we have found it difficult to find someone who would come and feel a real interest in the school. When Mr. Lestrange told us about you, we were delighted. I hope you will like it here."

"And I hope you will find us satisfactory," said Lilias.

"There are two of you . . ."

He hesitated, and Lilias said quickly: "Yes, we know that you only needed one teacher."

"The fact is that we should like to have two teachers . . . but the funds won't run to it. If we had more pupils, well then, we should need more teachers. But the fees we charge are not large and the school is really supported by the town . . . and sometimes it seems that not everyone gives education the respect it deserves."

"We do understand," said Lilias. "That is quite satisfactory. We wanted to be together and we are prepared to come and work here."

He still looked worried. Then he said: "I am

forgetting. You must be tired and hungry. I have brought with me a bottle of wine and some food. Would you like to eat now or would you prefer that I show you the place?"

"Let us see the place and perhaps we could wash some of the grime from the journey from us. Then we could eat and talk in comfort, if that is agreeable to you."

"That's an excellent idea. There is an oil stove on which we can heat water. I'll put that on and while it is heating I can show you round."

We were quite pleased with what we saw. There was a large room with a long table and chairs in it together with a large cupboard. We opened this and found books and slates inside.

"The schoolroom," said Lilias with approval.

In addition to the schoolroom there were two small rooms on the ground floor, and a kitchen with a back door which opened onto a small garden. Shrubs grew in profusion and Lilias gave a cry of pleasure.

John Dale was smiling, evidently delighted by our appreciation.

Lilias said: "We had no idea what we were coming to."

"And feared the worst?" he asked.

"Well, we did not imagine anything so good as this, did we, Diana?"

Upstairs there were four small rooms, simple but quite comfortably furnished.

"Bedrooms and a study and still one room left," said Lilias. She went to the window and looked out on the street. Then she turned to me with shining eyes.

"I want to make this into a flourishing school," she said.

"You will," replied John Dale. "And now that water will be hot and I'll bring it up for you."

"We'll help," said Lilias. I had rarely seen her so excited.

In the room downstairs John Dale had set out the meal. There was cold chicken, crusty bread, a bottle of wine and some luscious pears.

"This is a lovely welcome to our new life," said Lilias.

"I want you to know how glad we are that you have come," John Dale told us. "Let me tell you something about the town and the people."

"We are longing to hear."

"I think you will like the climate, although you may find it a little too hot in summer."

"We are prepared for that," I said.

"Kimberley, as you probably know, owes its prosperity to diamonds. Before '71 it was more or less a village. Then, of course, there were the discoveries . . . and everything changed. Kimberley *is* diamonds. Most of us here are engaged in the business in some form or other . . . if not finding them, preparing them for the market and actually marketing them."

"You, too?" asked Lilias.

"Yes, I work in the offices of one of the biggest companies."

"Would that be Mr. Lestrange's company?"

"Oh no . . . not ours. When he came to Kimberley some years ago, he bought a share in one of the other companies. Shortly afterwards he married and acquired Riebeeck House. It is one of the finest residences in the town. Tell me, when did you propose to open the school?"

"There is no reason for delay," said Lilias. "Let us have a day or so to settle in and find out what pupils we have and what materials there are . . ."

"Of course. What about starting on Monday? That would give you the rest of this week and the weekend."

"And the pupils?"

"There are about ten of them so far. There will be more."

"What ages?"

"Varying." He looked at her anxiously. "Will that make it difficult?"

"It is what one expects and as there are two of us, we can divide into two classes perhaps. However, we shall have to see."

"I'll circulate the news that school will start on Monday."

"How very kind you are."

"Not at all. I am delighted that we are getting the school started again. Education is so necessary. I wish everyone here agreed with me."

"These pears are delicious," I said.

"We grow the finest fruit in the world here."

"What a beautiful country it is!" said Lilias. "To us it is like the Promised Land."

He laughed. "I'll remember that. I am going to drink a toast. May it live up to that."

When he had left and we were alone in our schoolhouse, Lilias and I agreed that it had been a wonderful welcome.

The Kimberley Treasure

THE NEXT WEEK was a busy one and most enjoyable. I had never seen Lilias so excited.

"If I had tried to imagine something I wanted to do, it would have been exactly this," she announced. "It's like starting a new school . . . my school."

She went through the books that were there and made lists of what she would like to have. John Dale, who was quite a frequent visitor, joined in the enthusiasm. He would see the council and discover whether she could have what she wanted.

"He's a great ally," said Lilias. "How lucky we are to have him here!"

On the appointed day the children arrived. There were fourteen of them—not a great number but more than we had dared hope for. Their ages ranged from five to fourteen and Lilias decided that I should take the fives to sevens, of whom there were six, and she would teach the elder ones; I with my pupils would be at one end of the largish room and she at the other.

It was a strange feeling to be confronted by the young children. They stared at me with interest and I felt it was going to be a trying ordeal and I only hoped that I should be able to deal with it satisfactorily. I managed to struggle through and began by teaching the alphabet and nursery rhymes.

When the children had gone to their homes Lilias and I cooked simple meals for ourselves in the little kitchen and discussed what had happened during the day. Lilias was in her element; I was less sure of myself. This was Lilias' vocation, I reminded her. My abilities in the teaching field were yet to be tested.

"You'll come to it," she assured me. "You must remember that you mustn't lose your patience. Never let them see that you are ruffled in any way. You've lost the battle if you do; and there is a certain battle on. They're watching you as closely as you are watching them.

You have to show the right amount of authority. Be kind. Be patient. But make them aware all the time that you are in charge."

"I'll try to remember that. I'll stick to the rules . . . if I can."

For the first week I thought of little but doing the job. The days started to pass quickly. The routine had to be followed rigorously. Lessons all morning. The children came at nine and left at twelve. Then we would cook something light and eat a meal to be ready for when they returned at two o'clock; they stayed till four.

We were becoming known in the town and the shopkeepers were very pleasant to us. We had the impression that the townsfolk were pleased that the school was open again.

Of all the children in my class there was one girl who interested me particularly. I was haunted by her rather sad little face. Her name was Anna Schreiner and she was about five years old. Her mother brought her to school each morning and called to pick her up at the appointed times with most of the parents of the younger children. She was a quiet child and, if addressed, usually replied in monosyllables; she hardly ever smiled. Her mother was young and pretty, fair-haired, blue-eyed and rather plump. It struck me that Anna was brooding on something which she could not get out of her mind.

One day the children were copying the letters I had put on the blackboard; so deep in concentration were they that there was hardly a sound except that of pencils scratching on slates. I wandered round, looking at what they were doing, commenting now and then. "Is that an *O* or a *Q? A Q?* It hasn't got its little tail on, has it?" "The loop on that *P* comes down too far. See?" Then I came to Anna. She was working laboriously and all her letters seemed perfect.

I sat down beside her. "That's very good," I said.

She did not smile. She just went on with the letters.

"Is everything all right, Anna?"

She nodded.

"Do you like school?"

She nodded again.

"You are happy here?"

Again the nod. I was getting nowhere.

She continued to bother me. I thought she was an unnatural child, aloof from the others.

I watched her with her mother. Her face did not brighten when she saw her. She just ran up to her and took her hand; and they went off together.

I told Lilias of my interest in the child.

"Children vary," she said. "She's just a solemn child."

"She has that pretty mother. I wonder if she is an only child?"

"John Dale would probably know. Ask him next time you see him."

That time would not be far off, I guessed. He was a frequent visitor to the schoolhouse. He often brought food and wine as he had on the first day and we would share what he called a "picnic."

When I asked him about Anna Schreiner he said: "Oh yes. Poor child. I understand her living in perpetual fear. She probably imagines Hell's Gates are open wide to receive her if she's five minutes late for school."

"Her mother looks as though she is quite a jolly person."

"Greta, yes. Well, she was . . . once. I don't understand why she married old Schreiner. Although there were rumours . . ."

"Rumours?" I cried.

"It's probably a lot of scandal."

"Mr. Dale," said Lilias. "It helps us to teach our children if we know something of their background."

"Well, I'll tell you what I know. Piet Schreiner is rather a formidable character. Calvinistic . . . puritanical. There are a few like him in this town . . . and all over the country, it seems. There is a strong feeling of puritanism among the Boers. He is even more fanatical than most. One could imagine his going off on the Great Trek. Hard-working . . . strictly honest and . . . godly—so he would say. It seems sad that someone with his virtues should put such an interpretation on his religion as to make life miserable for everyone around him. For such as he is, everything people do seems to have its roots in sin. I suppose he himself is always on guard against it."

"And that's little Anna's father?" I said.

"Well . . . on the surface. There are some who say that is not the case."

"What do you mean?" asked Lilias.

"Schreiner is all of twenty years older than Greta . . . she's the child's mother. A pretty girl who was inclined to be flighty . . . once. Her family were strict with her . . . and I suppose that may have added to the incentive to stray . . . or to do something that shocks. The fact of the matter is that her family were very friendly with Schreiner. He's a lay preacher in the chapel which they attend. Whether or not Greta married him because she was in trouble, I am not sure, but I cannot imagine she could have had any other reason for doing so."

"So Schreiner is not Anna's father . . ."

"He calls himself her father. It's all on the records. The girl is Anna Schreiner all right. The fact is that Schreiner married Greta in a bit of a hurry. No one had thought he would ever marry anyone—let alone a young girl like that. There was a lot of talk about it. However, there it was. They married—that frivolous young girl and the hellfire preacher so much older than herself. It was a nine days' wonder. There was as much talk about it as when Ben Curry found the Blue Diamond and made a millionaire of himself. But that happened more than five years ago. People forget. They only remember now and then."

"So that poor child lives with her flighty mother and this fanatically religious man who may or may not be her father."

"Poor little thing. I don't suppose she has too good a time."

"I must try to help her in some way," I said.

"Don't get into conflict with old Schreiner," warned John. "Holy men can be fiendish when they are fighting the enemies of the righteous . . . which means anyone who doesn't agree with them."

"That's not likely," said Lilias. "But I know Diana will be gentle with the poor little thing."

After that I took an even greater interest in Anna Schreiner, but no matter how I tried, it was impossible to get her to talk. She just worked more diligently than the others and quietly walked away with her pretty mother.

What sort of life did they have with each other? I wondered.

ON OUR SECOND SUNDAY in Kimberley Lilias and I were invited to lunch at Riebeeck House.

Myra had called on us on the previous Wednesday about four-thirty, after school had closed.

She said: "I guessed that I should be interrupting school if I came at any other time. Do tell me how everything is going."

"Very well indeed," Lilias told her enthusiastically. "We have been agreeably surprised."

"That's wonderful. I hear that the school is a great success."

"That's a bit premature," cautioned Lilias, but she was well pleased. "Where did you hear that?"

"From Mrs. Prost, our housekeeper. She is one of those women who know what is going on everywhere."

"Useful to have around," I commented. "And how is everything with you?"

"Oh . . ." There was a brief hesitation. "Everything is very well."

"And you like the house?"

"It's . . . very large and one is apt to get lost. The servants are nearly all Africans. It makes it difficult to . . . be understood."

"But this Mrs. Prost, she looks after everything, I suppose."

"Oh yes. I came to ask you over to lunch on Sunday. It has to be a Sunday for you, doesn't it?"

"Yes," said Lilias. "That is the best day."

"Roger wants to hear all about the school.

He says you will have settled in and formed an opinion by now."

"People have been so good to us," said Lilias. "It was lucky for us that we met you on the ship . . . and since that mistake about our cabin, we were able to be with you. And now that we are here, well, Mr. Dale has been quite invaluable to us, hasn't he, Diana?"

I said that he had, for from the moment we had arrived he had taken us under his wing.

"They're so glad to get the school going again," said Myra. "You will come, won't you?"

"But of course," I said. "We shall be delighted, shall we not, Lilias?"

So it was arranged.

When she had gone, I said to Lilias: "I can't help feeling that all is not quite right with that marriage."

Lilias laughed at me. "You and your fancies! First it's little Anna Schreiner, and now it is the Lestranges. The trouble with you is that you have too much imagination and you let it run wild. You like something dramatic to happen and when it doesn't you set about creating it."

"Perhaps you're right," I said. "But all the same . . ."

Practical Lilias. She could only smile at me.

And as I liked to see her happy I smiled with her.

RIEBEECK HOUSE was something of a mansion. Although it was situated in the town, once one had passed through the gates and entered the grounds which surrounded the house, one might have been miles away from any other dwelling.

The drive in was about a quarter of a mile in length, but the foliage was so lush and abundant that one felt one was in the heart of the country. Flowering shrubs of colourful blossoms were huddled together. Flame trees and poinsettias added a further dash of colour. I shall never forget my first sight of the place as we came through this mass of vegetation to the white house.

It was an imposing place, built in the Dutch style. There were steps leading up to a stoop in front of the house and on this were urns which were almost hidden by the prolific plants.

It was large and there seemed to be many windows. It was one of those houses which had a personality of its own. Lilias laughed at this when, later, I mentioned it to her. Practical Lilias saw everything with absolute clarity for what it was.

Very soon I felt there was something a little repellant about the house. Perhaps it was because I could never feel absolutely at ease in the company of Roger Lestrange. I also had an idea that Myra was not as happy as she should be and that she shared with me that vague lack of ease.

Mrs. Prost came down to greet us.

"You must be Miss Milne and Miss Grey," she said. She had small light eyes which darted everywhere. Her light brown hair was plaited and wound round her head. I had the impression that there was little she would miss. "Do come in," she went on. "I'll tell Mrs. Lestrange that you are here."

"We're glad to meet you, Mrs. Prost," said Lilias.

"Welcome to Kimberley. I hear the school is doing well."

"It's early days yet," said Lilias cautiously. "But all is well . . . at the moment."

"Very pleased to hear it, and so is every-one."

Myra appeared.

"I thought I heard your arrival."

Mrs. Prost stood watching while Myra greeted us.

"Luncheon will be served at one o'clock, Mrs. Lestrange," she said.

"Thank you, Mrs. Prost." Myra turned to us. "Do come up. Roger is in the drawing room. He is so looking forward to hearing your news."

She took my hand and held it lingeringly.

"Are you well?" I asked.

"Oh yes . . . thanks. I am so glad you came. I wanted to call at the school, but I thought you would be so busy just at first."

"We're teaching in the mornings . . . and then again from two till four," said Lilias. "Any time after that we love to receive visitors."

"Roger says that John Dale has been looking after you."

"He is," said Lilias warmly. "We are so grateful to him. He has made everything so easy for us."

We were taken through a large hall with white walls and vivid red curtains, up a staircase to a room on the first floor.

Myra opened a door and said: "They're here."

It was a spacious room with tall windows. My first impression was that of an interior painting by one of the Dutch masters. The floor was of delicately tinted tiles which gave an impression of coolness. Later I noticed the heavy furniture—baroque style—the table with the scrolls and the inlaid ebony, the cabinet on stands, impressive with pilasters and decorative carving.

But there was no time to look round then for Roger Lestrange had risen and was coming towards us, hands outstretched.

"Miss Milne . . . Miss Grey . . . what a pleasure!"

He took our hands and smiled warmly. "How good of you to come. I have been hearing of your success. It is especially gratifying as I shall receive the thanks of the grateful townsfolk for bringing you here."

"We have been here only a short time," began Lilias tentatively.

"And," I added, "we have fourteen pupils, so there has hardly been a stampede to our gate."

Lilias smiled at me. "We are really very

pleased," she said. "We were warned that there would only be a few pupils and Mr. Dale did not really expect so many as there are."

Roger looked at Myra expectantly and she said hastily: "Come and sit down. Luncheon will be served at one."

"What do you think of our house?" asked Roger.

"We are very impressed by what we have seen," said Lilias.

"After luncheon you shall see it all and then you will be able to pass judgement."

"You seem to be isolated, though, of course, you are not really," I said.

"I'm glad you get that impression. And you are right, of course. No one can really be isolated in a town. But it is good to be here for business reasons and I like to create an impression of detachment, even if it is not strictly true. That was one of the reasons why I bought the house."

"Oh? I had the impression that it was a sort of house which had been in your family for years."

"Oh no. I bought the place . . . lock, stock and barrel . . . furniture and everything. It belonged to an old Dutch family who had been here for a hundred years. They decided they did not like the way things were going and they sold up and went back to Holland. It was very convenient for me. We . . . my first wife and I . . . wanted a place and this seemed to suit. So there it was, waiting for us. We just walked in and took on everything that was here . . . furniture, Mrs. Prost, most of the servants, I believe. Mrs. Prost would know how many."

"You didn't mind just walking in and taking over someone else's possessions?"

"We didn't mind in the least. We found it convenient . . . That was Margarete . . . my first wife."

I glanced at Myra. I saw her flinch slightly. I wondered what that meant. Or did it mean anything? Was I imagining again?

We went into luncheon . . . to a similar room. I noticed the tiled floor, the heavy table and chairs.

Roger Lestrange sat at one end of the table, Myra at the other, Lilias and I facing each other.

As we ate Roger said: "There is one thing I wanted to ask you. It's about my son, Paul. He is at present without a tutor. I was wondering whether it would be a good thing to send him away to school in England? It's a big undertaking for him and I am not sure that he is ready. I thought that . . . for a while . . . if you would have him, I might send him along to your school."

Lilias cried: "Of course, we should be delighted."

"You must meet him before you go."

While silent-footed Africans served the food, Roger Lestrange made a few comments about the weather and I could see that Lilias was impatient to hear more about Paul.

"Isn't he rather young to be sent overseas?" asked Lilias.

"Oh no. He's nine years old. Isn't that the time boys go away to school? I should imagine many boys in England would be in boarding schools at that age."

"Yes, but this is sending him overseas . . . right away from his home."

"I don't think he would mind that, do you, my dear?"

Myra agreed that he would not mind.

"He's a strange boy," went on Roger. "He keeps out of our way since we've been back." He was looking at Myra, who seemed embarrassed, as though it were her fault that the boy kept away. Perhaps he resented his step-mother. Very likely. In any case, it appeared that Myra might be accepting the blame.

"Oh well, you'll see for yourselves." He wrinkled his brows and looked at us rather anxiously. "Do you know," he went on, "I'm seriously beginning to wonder whether you were wise to come here."

"Why?" I asked sharply; Lilias was looking at him questioningly.

"I don't much like the way things are going. I haven't liked it for some time . . . but now that I'm back, I see what's happening more clearly."

"What is happening?"

"Kruger is getting very stubborn. Trouble is blowing up fast between him and Chamber-lain."

"Chamberlain?"

"Joseph Chamberlain, Secretary of State for the Colonies. The trouble goes back a long way . . . you might say, right to the beginning of the century . . . ever since the British captured the Cape from Napoleon's Dutch allies. I believe I have mentioned the trouble about the slaves when the British tried to reform conditions for the Khoi servants and made laws to protect them against cruelty. There has been antagonism between the Boers and the English ever since."

"They don't seem to be antagonistic towards us . . . individually."

"Oh no. It's the leaders who are at each other's throats. They don't blame us for what they call the arrogance of our leaders."

"We have become quite friendly with a number of them now," I said. "They have all been . . . well . . . rather especially nice to us."

"It's a quarrel between states. All the same, it can blow up. There would not be another Great Trek. This time they would stand firm and fight for their land."

"What Great Trek was this?" asked Lilias.

"It happened about fifty years ago, but it's still remembered. The conditions imposed by the British had robbed them of their slave labour, and they were unable to exist on the land, so they gathered their families and their goods together and set out across country in their ox-drawn wagons. Life was difficult. They were hard-working people, sternly religious, self-righteous, as such people often are, and they firmly believed that all who were not of their way of thinking were on the road to hell. All they wanted was to be left in peace with their slaves and their dogma, to work and make a living. So, harried by African tribes . . . the Zulus, the Ndebele and the Matabele . . . prevented from making a living by the British laws against slavery, what could they do? Only escape from their rulers to another land. Hence the Great Trek across country. They went as far as Natal and settled in the Transvaal."

"They had a great deal of courage," said Lilias.

"That's something no one could accuse them of lacking. Then, of course, diamonds were discovered . . . and gold. That was to have a marked effect on the country. People came pouring in and Rhodes and Jameson dreamed of a British Africa. They managed to persuade Lobengula, King of the Matabele, to let them have mining concessions, and you know these lands are now Rhodesia . . . a British colony. But the trouble is between Kruger and Chamberlain."

"That," said Lilias, "means trouble between the British and the Boers."

"There was a possibility at one time that Germany might come to the aid of the Boers and it seemed unlikely that the British would want to risk a war with Germany. It was a different matter with South Africa alone. That is what people are afraid of."

"Wouldn't it be better to come to some compromise?" asked Lilias.

"The Boers are not people to accept a compromise . . . unless it were forced on them."

"And would it not be forced upon them by the power of Britain?" I asked.

"That might be, but I believe they are prepared to put it to the test. That is the crux of the matter: the franchise which Kruger is imposing in the Transvaal. The Uitlanders outnumber the Boers, so Kruger can't give them the vote. Oh dear, I am spoiling this luncheon which I wanted to be so pleasant. It makes us very happy to have you here, does it not, Myra?"

"It does indeed," she said fervently.

"Forgive me for bringing up a subject which would have been better left alone."

"If it's happening we would rather know about it," said Lilias.

"Well, don't let's worry about it. There is

peace so far. No one wants war. It is devastating to a country and almost always profits no one."

"Yet there are constantly wars," said Lilias.

He sighed. "That is the nature of man. Now . . . you must see more of this country. You will find it impressive, beautiful . . . often awe-inspiring."

It came out during the course of the conversation that he had only been in South Africa some six or seven years. When I had first met him I had decided that he could not be of Dutch origin as so many of the people in South Africa were; but I had read somewhere that a certain number of French settlers in Africa were Huguenots who had left their own country to escape persecution, and I had assumed from his name that he was one of those. When I told him this, he said that he was indeed of French origin and his family had come to England at the time of the Edict of Nantes. So I was right in thinking that he came from a Huguenot family. He had, though, lived in England most of his life.

"You are very knowledgeable about your adopted country," I said.

"I always believe in finding out all I can."

He looked at me steadily. "About everything," he added.

I felt myself flushing and felt annoyed. Must I always suspect someone was probing my secret?

It was when the meal was over that a messenger arrived at the house asking that Mr. Lestrange go and meet a business colleague without delay as something important had turned up and needed his immediate attention.

"I am desolate," he said. "At such a time as this! It is too bad I have to leave you."

"Perhaps we should be going," I said.

"Oh no!" cried Myra. "You have to meet Paul, and I want to show you the house."

"Please do not run away because I have to go," said Roger. "We will do this again . . . very soon. We must, to make up for my early departure. So . . . au revoir."

It struck me that Myra was rather relieved when he was gone and with his absence she seemed to acquire a certain dignity. She's afraid of him, I thought.

I was looking forward to meeting Paul Lestrange and I knew that Lilias was. We were different, Lilias and I. She would assess him as a pupil; to me he was an actor in what I felt might be some mysterious drama. I could not get rid of the idea that there was something strange about this household and that Myra was aware of it and that was why she appeared to be nervous.

Paul was tall for his age and bore no resemblance whatsoever to Roger. His hair was flaxen, his eyes blue-grey; and there was a cautious air about him.

"Paul," said Myra, "these are the ladies who have opened the school, Miss Milne and Miss Grey."

He came forward rather awkwardly and shook hands with us both.

Lilias said: "We have just heard that you may be joining us."

He said: "I am going away to school."

"Yes, we were told that, too. But it isn't certain yet, is it?"

"Oh, no."

"Do you think you would like to join us while you are waiting for things to be settled?"

"Oh yes, I should, thank you."

"It is such a small school," went on Lilias. "And there are pupils of all ages."

"I know."

"But, of course, we shall be expanding . . . ."

"When shall you start?" I asked.

"I don't know."

"Why not tomorrow?" said Lilias. "The beginning of the week."

"I don't mind."

He was noncommittal . . . cautious still. But at least he did not appear to dislike us.

Myra said: "I am going to show Miss Milne and Miss Grey the house and after that the garden. Would you like to come with us?"

To my surprise he said he would.

I wondered if Lilias was thinking the same about him as I was. Rather shut in on himself. Difficult to know. A little suspicious of us. Lots of children were like that.

The tour of the house began. There were several rooms on the first floor, all similar to the ones we had already seen. The rather ornate spiral staircase descended from the top to the bottom of the house. The heavy furniture was everywhere and I could not help feeling that it had been lovingly collected over the years.

"You haven't lived here all your life, have you?"

"Oh no. We came here . . . just after they were married."

I was puzzled. "Who . . . were married?"

"My mother . . . and him."

"But . . . ?"

Myra said: "Do you like these drapes? Look at the embroidery on them."

Lilias took the material in her hands, but I turned to Paul. He was looking at me as though he wanted to talk.

"You thought he was my father," he said. "He's not. He lets people think it, but he's not. He's not."

Myra said: "It came from Amsterdam, I think. You can tell by the style of the embroidery."

I said to Paul: "You mean Mr. Lestrange is not your father?"

He shook his head vigorously. "My father died. He died in a diamond mine. That was before . . ."

I moved away from Myra and Lilias . . . with him.

"I didn't know," I said. "Mr. Lestrange always speaks of you as though he is your father."

"No, my father died and then my mother

married him. I'm not his son. I have a real father. Only he's dead."

"I'm sorry about that."

He pressed his lips together and held his head high.

I was thinking: I knew there were secrets in this house.

Myra was saying: "Paul is very interested in the house, aren't you, Paul?"

"Yes," said Paul. "Let's show them the staircase."

"We'll come to it in time."

"And the Model House?"

"Of course."

"The staircase is very fine," I said.

"Oh, not that one," said Paul. "The other."

"Oh, there are two, are there?"

"Yes," he said, and I noticed his lips tightened again.

In due course we came to the staircase. It led from the hall to the second floor. It was obviously a back staircase, used by the servants, I supposed; it was covered in a green carpet held in place by brass stair rods.

"That's it," said Paul.

I could see nothing unusual about it. It was certainly not comparable with the spiral one by which we had ascended. It was natural, I supposed, to have two staircases in such a house.

"Interesting," I said perfunctorily; but Paul was looking at it with gleaming eyes and Myra looked decidedly uncomfortable. I had a strange and uncanny feeling that they were seeing something which was not visible to Lilias and me.

A short while later I was inspecting the Model House. It was quite extraordinary. It was like a large dolls' house. It was in a smallish room, the whole of which was needed to accommodate it, and it reached from floor to ceiling.

I suddenly realised that it was an exact replica of the house. The rooms were all there, the two staircases, the heavy furniture, all in miniature.

I couldn't resist saying: "It's like a huge dolls' house—the biggest I have ever seen."

"It's not a dolls' house," said Paul. "It's not for children."

"No," said Myra. "Roger explained it to me. It's an old custom. It started in Germany and was adopted by the Dutch. Their homes mean so much to them so they have models made of them . . . exact copies. When furniture is taken away it is removed from the model house and when new comes in a small copy is made."

"What an extraordinary idea!" said Lilias. "I have never heard of it."

"Yes," said Myra. "They don't follow it now. But the people who lived here before did. They probably thought it was unlucky to dispense with an old custom. People do, don't they? It's a bit of an oddity and amuses people, Roger says."

Paul was apparently very proud of it. He said: "You've seen it with the doors open. It's like taking away the front of a house. It's the only way to see inside, isn't it? You can see it all in this one. In ordinary houses you can't see what's inside. This house hasn't got doors. It's all open. So it doesn't have the inscription which is on the door of this house. You didn't see it when you came in because it was all covered up with creeper. I think some people are glad about that. It says: 'God's Eyes See All.' It's in Dutch. Most people here know what it means. But it's covered with the creeper. But that wouldn't stop God's seeing all, would it?"

He gave me a rare smile.

I said: "No, it wouldn't."

"You liked it, didn't you?" he said. "I mean the Model House?"

"I thought it was fascinating. I have never seen anything like it."

That seemed to please him.

After that we went into the garden. It was extensive and that section near the house was laid out in lawns and flower beds and little paths; but there was a large area which had been allowed to grow wild and I could see that was what would appeal to a boy of Paul's age.

He grew excited as we approached it.

"I think we ought to get back to the house," said Myra. "You can get lost here. It's like the jungle."

"Just as far as the Falls," said Paul. "I won't let you get lost."

"The Falls?" I said.

"Well," Myra explained. "It's a kind of miniature waterfall. There's a stream . . . well, it's more than a stream. It's supposed to be a tributary of some river miles away, I think. It flows down from higher ground and makes this little waterfall. It's quite attractive."

It was, as she had said, although it was little

more than a stream. It was about six feet wide and there was a rickety wooden bridge over it. But it was indeed attractive with the water cascading from a higher level making, as Myra said, a little waterfall.

Paul was pleased when we admired it.

"And now," said Myra, "we must go back to the house."

"Oh, let's go just as far as the rondavels," begged Paul.

He seemed to have attached himself to me, and I said: "What are the rondavels?"

"That's where the servants live," he explained.

"Sort of native huts," said Myra. "They are circular and have thatched roofs."

We had come to a clearing and I saw them. There must have been about twenty of them. It was like a native village. There were some very small children playing on the grass and at the door of one sat an old woman.

Myra had paused and we all stopped with her.

"It's like a little colony," said Myra. "They couldn't all live in the house. There are too many and they wouldn't like it. They like their own way of life."

A young boy of about Paul's age came running towards us. He stood before Paul smiling. Paul put his hand on the boy's shoulder and patted it.

Myra said: "That's Umgala, isn't it?"

"Yes," said Paul.

The boy had put his hand over Paul's. It was a greeting, I guessed. Paul nodded at the boy and the boy nodded back. This was some sort of ritual. Neither of them spoke.

"Come along, Paul," said Myra. And to us: "They don't like us to intrude, I'm sure."

Obediently Paul turned away.

"Poor Umgala," said Myra. "He's a deaf-mute. Both his parents work about the place."

We had started walking back to the house.

"How can you communicate with that little boy?" I asked Paul.

"Like this," said Paul, waving his hands.

"It must be difficult."

He nodded.

"His parents are good workers," said Myra. "Luban, his mother, works in the house, and his father, Njuba, in the garden. That's right, isn't it, Paul?"

"Yes."

"It must be terrible to be born like that," said Lilias.

"Yes, but he seems happy. He was pleased to see Paul."

"Yes, Paul has established quite a friendship with him, haven't you, Paul?"

"Yes," said Paul.

"This has all been so interesting," murmured Lilias.

We walked slowly back to the house and very soon afterwards we left.

Back at the schoolhouse Lilias talked a great deal about what we had seen. She was delighted that we were to have a new pupil.

"I had no idea that Mr. Lestrange was not the boy's father," she said. "I heard what the boy was saying."

"He has always referred to him as his son."

"Well, he's his stepson, of course."

"But he did give the impression that he was the boy's father. He couldn't have been married very long to his first wife. Did you get the impression that Myra was afraid of something?"

"Well, Myra was always afraid of her own shadow."

"I just thought she was especially afraid."

"She seemed afraid of the boy, too. She's just a nervous person."

"I shall be interested to see more of Paul."

"So shall I. I'm sure he'll be an interesting pupil."

"I think he might be difficult to get to know. He seems to have some morbid obsession."

"About what?"

"I'm not sure."

"I am sure of one thing. You'll do your best to find out."

That night I wrote to Ninian Grainger. I told him that Roger Lestrange had paid for a better cabin for us and that I had kept this from Lilias because she would have been so worried about the debt which would have been a great strain on her; so I had let it pass and accepted.

"It was good of him," I wrote, "and he did not let me know about it until right at the end of the voyage."

I also told him about the school and our high hopes for it. We liked Kimberley and were getting on well with our pupils' parents; and the friendship of the Lestranges made us feel we were not so far from home.

"I was surprised to discover that Roger Lestrange was not a native of this place. He apparently came out from England some years ago. He married out here and acquired this really rather fascinating house . . . and then his wife died. She must have been quite young. The son who I thought was his is his stepson. The boy's mother must have died soon after the marriage.

"Well, there have been lots of surprises and I expect there are more to come. Mr. Lestrange, with whom we lunched today, told us that there is a certain unrest in the country, but there is no sign of it here . . ."

What a lot I was telling him! But I had promised I would tell him the details and I think the visit to Riebeeck House had excited me.

I sealed my letter. I would post it tomorrow.

PAUL JOINED THE SCHOOL and Lilias was very pleased. Like all good teachers she was delighted at the prospect of a responsive pupil.

"I wish I had more like him," she said. "I'd like to give more attention to him. But, of course, before long I daresay he will be going away to school."

Lilias was very efficient and my position was

more or less a sinecure and I was afraid I contributed very little.

The school really resembled one of those village schools of which there were many at home. In isolated villages where there were too few pupils to make a large school possible, they were run by one schoolmistress. Everything depended on her. If she were good then so was the school.

Lilias said that in her early days she had attended such a school and she had found that when she went away to a boarding school she was in advance of the other girls who had been brought up by governesses.

"How I should love to have a big school with several teachers working for me and a hundred pupils! But, for the time being, this will suffice."

She had wanted to share the salary, but I impressed on her that this was absurd. She did far more work than I did. I was prepared to take nothing at all. My income sufficed. She would not hear of that, so all I could do was insist that she take the larger share of the money. The truth was that she could have run the place very easily by herself.

She was happy and I was delighted to see

her so. She dreamed of enlarging the school. But, of course, that was for the future. I realised more than ever that teaching was her vocation and how frustrated she must have been, confined to the domestic affairs of the vicarage. John Dale shared her interest in the school. He was a very frequent visitor. He used to call after school with a bottle of wine and some delicacies and we would talk far into the evening.

One afternoon when Greta Schreiner brought Anna to school she lingered behind to have a word with one of us. I saw her and she asked if we would keep Anna for an extra half an hour when school was over as she would be delayed coming to pick her up. This happened now and then with some of the children, for we would not consider letting any of the little ones go off without their parents. I told Greta that that would be all right.

When school was over Lilias went off to see a parent in the town who was thinking of sending her two children to the school, so I stayed behind with Anna.

We sat at the window watching for Greta to arrive. I tried to interest the child in a game in order to pass the time, but I received little response, and I was rather pleased when I saw Greta hurrying towards the schoolhouse.

Anna went quietly to her mother and I led the way to the door.

"Thank you, Miss Grey," said Greta. "It was kind of you. I hope I wasn't too long."

"Oh no. You're earlier than I had expected. Well, goodbye, Anna. Goodbye, Mrs. Schreiner."

I went back into the schoolhouse and as I did so I heard the sound of horse's hoofs. I went to the window. Roger Lestrange was riding into the courtyard. He pulled up, leaped from his horse and approached Greta Schreiner. They seemed to know each other well by the manner in which he was talking and laughing and she was responding. My thoughts flashed back to the house in Edinburgh and Kitty laughing in the kitchen with Hamish Vosper . . . and then Kitty in the stables at Lakemere chatting with the grooms. Some people were like that. They blossomed in masculine society. Zillah was another.

I watched them for what must have been five minutes. Roger had turned his attention to Anna. Suddenly he picked her up and held her in the air above him. He was laughing at her. I wondered what solemn little Anna thought of this familiar behaviour. It was not the sort of treatment she would be accustomed to from her puritanical father.

Roger set her down. He put his hand in his pocket and brought out what must have been a coin which he pressed into the child's hand.

Then a strange thing happened. Piet Schreiner came striding across the courtyard. He must have been lurking close, watching, for he took the coin from Anna's hand and threw it on the ground at Roger's feet.

For a moment it seemed as though Greta, Roger and the child were turned to stone. No one spoke; no one moved; then Piet Schreiner seized Greta's arm and dragged her away, Anna clutching at her hand.

Roger looked at the coin on the ground, shrugged his shoulders and came walking towards the schoolhouse, leading his horse which he tethered to the post there.

He was coming to see us.

When I opened the door he was smiling urbanely and showed no sign that he was in the least ruffled by the little scene in which he had taken part.

I said: "Hello, so you have come to see us?"

"To see *you*, Miss Grey."

"Is everything all right? Paul . . ."

"I think Paul is enjoying his new school."

"I couldn't help seeing what happened just now."

"Oh, that pious old fool! It was because I gave the child money."

"It was so extraordinary."

"He's a little mad, I suppose. Religious maniac. He thinks everyone is destined for Hell Fire—except himself."

"It seemed so amazing . . . when you have merely been generous to the child."

He shrugged his shoulders. "I feel sorry for his poor wife."

"I suppose everyone must be. I thought she seemed very pleased that you were friendly towards her."

"I'm a friendly person. I can't tell you how pleased I am about the way things are working out here. Miss Milne is out, isn't she?"

"How did you know?"

"Ha! I'll tell you. Mrs. Garton, whom I happen to know, was visiting us yesterday and she was talking about sending her girls to England to school. I pointed out that that was something of an undertaking—particularly as things are now—and while she was waiting why didn't she send the girls to the school which was really an excellent one since the new ladies had taken it over. I could vouch for that as I was sending Paul there. I said, 'Why don't you consult Miss Milne, who is the senior teacher?' She said, 'I'll do that tomorrow.' I said, 'I daresay Miss Milne would come and see you when school is over.' So there you are. That is why I knew I should find you alone."

I felt a twinge of uneasiness. In spite of his urbanity and obvious desire to help, I felt vaguely suspicious of his motives.

"I expect you are wondering how Paul is getting on with his studies," I said. "I can tell you that Miss Milne thinks he is very bright. She knows a good deal about children, of course."

"And you, too."

"The fact is I am not really needed here. It's a post for one . . . at the moment."

"And you came out because you wanted to get away from England."

"It seemed an exciting adventure."

"And you were not very excited by life at home?"

He was looking at me quizzically. What

does he know? I was asking myself. I could not quite understand the expression in his eyes. I fancied they were a little mocking. I did not understand this man. In spite of his flattering words and his attitude of gallantry, I felt he was taunting me, and that he knew it had been imperative for me to get away.

I had to turn the conversation away from myself.

"I was surprised to hear that Paul is not your son."

"Oh . . . did you not realise that?"

"But . . . I think you said he was your son. Or that was how I understood it. You spoke of him as though . . ."

"He is my stepson, but I wanted him to regard me as his father. When I married his mother I felt I had a duty to him."

"He remembers his father too well to accept someone else, I imagine. Children are faithful, you know."

"I realise that now." He smiled at me deprecatingly. "But I shall go on trying."

"If he had been a little younger," I said, "it would have been easier. He might have forgotten his father and have been ready to accept you."

"I know."

"How old was he when his father died?"

"About five, I think."

"He's nine now, isn't he? It was only four years ago."

"Yes, it happened rather quickly."

"You must have married his mother soon after."

"Well, it was more than a year . . . eighteen months perhaps."

"I should imagine the speed of it all was too much for him. At seven his mother dies . . . and at nine he has not only a stepfather but a stepmother. Oh, I understand how difficult he must find it to adjust to all the changes."

"I hadn't thought of it like that. It seems that Margarete has been dead for a long time. Margarete . . . oh, she was such a sweet and simple girl! She could not deal with everything that had to be done when her first husband died. I helped her with her affairs. She was lonely and I was sorry for her. We slipped into marriage. And then . . . she died."

"Was she ill?"

"When she lost her husband she was quite, quite bewildered. She felt she couldn't cope with life. She was the sort of woman who needs someone to look after her. I did that as best I could. But it had all been a terrible shock for her. She began . . . well . . . please don't mention this to anyone . . . but she began to drink a little . . . at first. I suppose she found some solace in that. I did not realise what a hold it was getting on her. She did it secretly, you see. But it was undermining her health, and one morning she was found . . ."

"Found?"

He turned away, as though to hide his emotion. He reached for my hand and gripped it hard. Then he said: "Found, at the bottom of the staircase."

I knew which staircase. I understood now Paul's obsession with it.

"She had fallen," he went on. "It was an accident. I was greatly relieved when nothing came out about the secret drinking. They thought she had tripped over the carpet. One of the stair rods was loose. However, she fell from top to bottom. Her neck was broken."

"What an awful thing to happen! And you had only been married for such a short time. Poor Paul."

"He was dreadfully upset. It's changed him. Made him moody. He misses his mother."

"I understand that. And then you married Myra . . . quite soon after."

"Myra is a sweet and gentle person. I think she reminded me of Margarete." He was silent for a while and then he said: "I'm rather worried about Myra. I think she may be a little homesick. Do you think she is happy here?"

I hesitated and he went on: "Please tell me the truth."

"Well . . . I don't think she is entirely happy. I think she is afraid of disappointing you."

"Disappointing me! Why should she be?"

"She is quiet and a little nervous, and you . . ."

"I am the opposite."

"Well, you are, aren't you?"

"I thought she would enjoy a little freedom. Her mother was a bit of a gorgon . . . and in that village . . . well, it was hardly riotously merry!"

"Perhaps she does not want to be riotously merry."

"I thought I could get her away from it . . . make her happy, Diana . . . May I call you Diana? Miss Grey is so formal and we are good friends and we shall see more and more of each other here. I wanted to talk to you about her. I want you to help her."

"In what way can I help?"

"I want you to see more of her. Come to the house. Go out with her . . . shopping . . . and all the things you ladies like to do. Be a friend to her. Come and stay at the house. Miss Milne is so efficient. She can manage without you now and then. I'd be so grateful if you could . . . . get closer to Myra. You're someone from home . . . you're already friends. Try to find out what will make her happy."

I could not understand him. He had always given me the impression that he believed himself capable of dealing with any situation. And here he was, almost humbly pleading for help.

I was intrigued. I had always been interested in people and their motives, the reasons why they acted as they did, the manner in which they often covered up their true intentions with subterfuge. Lilias was so different, so realistic, so practical. I really wanted to know what went on in that house. It fascinated me; Paul, the staircase, the hasty marriages, the strange death of Margarete. I could find life in the schoolhouse a little dull. What suited Lilias did not necessarily suit me, and I was not going to be as dedicated to the school as she was.

"Will you do this for me . . . for Myra?" he asked.

"I should very much like to help if I can."

"Oh, you can. I know you can. Myra needs a friend. She needs you."

I said: "It takes two to make a friendship. It may be that Myra will like to make her own."

"But she is already your friend. She brightens at the thought of your visits. Please . . . Diana . . . come and see us often."

"Of course I will."

"Get her to confide in you. You can help her."

It was then that Lilias returned.

"Two more pupils!" she cried out, then: "Oh . . . Mr. Lestrange."

"And I know who they are," he said, rising and shaking her hand. "It was I who suggested to Mrs. Garton that she should see you."

"Thank you. How kind . . . ."

"I am so pleased it has turned out to your

satisfaction," he said. "As a matter of fact I was just on the point of leaving. I hope you will both come and see us very soon. What about luncheon next Sunday? It has to be a Sunday, does it not?"

"Oh yes, that's the best day because of school," said Lilias. "I should enjoy it . . . . and you, Diana?"

"Yes, thank you very much. It will be a great pleasure."

When he had gone, Lilias said: "Why did he call? Surely not just to ask us to lunch?"

"He's worried about his wife."

"Oh?"

"He thinks she's lonely . . . homesick. He wants us to be friends. He really seems concerned about her."

"Well, he married her, didn't he?"

"I've promised I'll go and see her more often."

Lilias nodded and said it was time we thought about getting supper.

IT WAS AFTER SCHOOL. Lilias was marking essays which she had set for the older children.

She said: "The subject was 'The Most Important Thing That Ever Happened to Me.' I thought that would stretch their imaginations a little. 'The Day My Mother Gave Me Thomas, My Terrier.' 'A Picnic with the Wagons' and such like. But here's one that's different. Paul's. He's got a real touch of the dramatic, that boy. It's interesting. Here, read it."

I took the exercise book from her and studied Paul's clear, round handwriting.

"The Kimberley Treasure," I read.

"The most important thing that ever happened to me was when my father found the Kimberley Treasure. The Kimberley Treasure is a diamond. It weighs eight hundred and fifty carats and that is a lot—almost more than any other diamond has weighed before. We were ever so excited when he found it because we would be rich when he sold it.

"I saw it. It looked like a lump of stone, but my father told me it was a diamond all right. I'd see when they got to polishing and working on it. My mother said, 'Now we're all right.'

"The others were jealous of us because they all wanted to find some big diamond that would make them rich for the rest of their lives. Then somebody said it was unlucky. Big diamonds can bring bad luck, they said. But we didn't believe them. We thought they were just jealous because they had not found the Kimberley Treasure.

"My mother said we should sell it and give up mining. But my father said that there must be more where that came from. He wanted to be not just rich but very rich. He was sure he knew where to find another diamond like the Kimberley Treasure. He went to look for it and he was killed in the mine. So it was right about the Kimberley Treasure. It was unlucky.

"My mother cried a lot. She didn't care about the old diamond. What was the use of it if he was dead? But she would not sell the diamond. She said he wanted to keep it so she would too.

"Then she married my stepfather and he said what was the good of keeping a diamond like that just to look at it? Diamonds were comfort and riches. So he sold the diamond and we came to Riebeeck House. He missed the bad luck because the diamond had never really been his. But my mother had owned it, so she had the bad luck. My stepfather turned the diamond into Riebeeck House, but my mother had the bad luck and so she fell down the staircase and died.

"That is why the day my father found the

Kimberley Treasure was the most important in my life."

I dropped the book and stared at Lilias.

"What an extraordinary essay!"

"I thought so. The boy has imagination and a rather powerful way of expressing it."

"I don't think he's imagining that. That is just how it happened."

"Do you think it's true?"

"I know that his mother married Roger Lestrange soon after her husband's death and that she died by falling down a staircase."

"And soon after he married Myra?"

"Yes. What do you think of it?"

"That that boy has a certain talent for expressing himself."

I SAID: "That was an interesting essay you wrote, Paul."

His eyes lit up. "Did you like it?"

"Very much. That diamond. It must have been exciting when your father found it. You were very young then. Do you remember very much about it?"

"Oh yes. When things like that happen, it's

so important. Everybody . . . however young
. . . gets to know. Everything was different."

"Different from what?"

"From what it was before."

"What was it like then?"

"It was nice . . . nicer really. We were all
together . . . my Daddy, my Mummy and
me. We were there . . . the three of us . . .
and neither of them are there anymore."

"It sometimes happens like that, Paul."

"Did you have a mother?"

"Yes. She died."

"How did she die?"

"She was ill for a long time . . . and then
she died as we knew she would."

"And your father?"

I felt myself shrink. "He . . . he died
also."

He said nothing for a while. Nor did I. Too
many unpleasant reminders were chasing
themselves round in my mind.

"They said it was unlucky," he said at
length.

"What?"

"The diamond. Diamonds can be unlucky if
they're big. I suppose it is because everybody
wants them. They were all right before they

found that. My father ought to have sold it. We ought to have gone away. But he had to go on looking for more just because he'd found that one. He wouldn't have died if he hadn't gone looking for more. He left it to my mother. So it was there and she took the bad luck with it."

"That's pure fancy, you know, Paul. Things like diamonds are not unlucky in themselves."

He looked stubborn. "She had it and she kept it and a lot of people wanted it. There was another man who wanted to marry her. It was all because of the diamond."

"How can you be sure of that?"

"I just know. And then she married him. He had the diamond then. But he sold it. And he bought Riebeeck House. But the diamond had *been* hers . . . so . . . she died."

"Perhaps she was not well before she died."

"She *was* well."

"Tell me, Paul, what it is you have on your mind."

"She died because she fell down the stairs. She was all right. Why did you think she was not well?"

I could not mention to him that she had been drinking.

He went on: "If she hadn't had the diamond, he wouldn't have married her. There wouldn't have been that house. She wouldn't have fallen down the stairs. It was all because of the diamond." I thought he was going to burst into tears. "That's why the most important thing in my life is the Kimberley Treasure."

"Oh, Paul," I said. "You mustn't think like that. Diamonds can't hurt anybody."

"Not by themselves . . . but what they mean."

"How could a diamond have made your mother fall down the stairs?"

"I don't mean that the diamond did it. But because of it, someone might have . . ."

"What?"

"I don't know. I only wish my father had never found it. I wish we could have gone on . . . finding little ones . . . little ones that were enough to keep us happy."

"Paul," I said firmly. "You have to stop brooding on this. It's over. It isn't going to help to go on thinking about it . . . making up what might have been. Try to grow away from the past. There's so much that's good for you. Miss Milne thinks you are going to do well at school."

He looked at me sadly, frustration in his eyes which I knew meant: nobody understands.

I felt I had failed him. It was cowardly, but had I been afraid that he might have said too much?

Figures

on a

Staircase

I WENT TO SEE MYRA as Roger had suggested.

"Go in the afternoon," Lilias had advised. "I can manage for two hours on my own. I'll set the older ones an essay or arithmetic problems which keep them occupied and I can easily look after the others. I'll enjoy it. It will be a challenge."

Myra was delighted to see me and I spent a pleasant afternoon with her. She was a little reticent and I did not probe; we talked lightly, mentioning Lakemere and village affairs. I remembered some amusing incidents and was able to make her smile. When I left she begged me to come again.

When I returned to the schoolhouse Lilias said: "I don't see why you shouldn't go now and then. I managed very well. It's not really difficult."

"The fact is, you could do very well without me here."

"Oh no. I should be desperately lonely. It's wonderful to have you to talk things over with. In any case, I shouldn't have come out here without you and I think it is one of the best things I ever did. John is such a good friend and so interested in the school. I'm happier than I have been for a long time. I felt so frustrated at home after that terrible affair of the necklace. But I do believe I'm getting over it now. How do you feel?"

"Oh . . . . I don't think I shall ever forget."

"Yours was such a terrible ordeal, but you will get over it . . . in time. It's nice that you meet people. How lucky we are that John is here to help us."

"Yes, we are."

"And your seeing Myra will be good for her and you. You must go again soon."

I did and it was on my third visit that Myra

began to talk a little more freely, and I felt I could ask her if she were worried about anything.

She hesitated for a while and then she said: "It's this house. There's something about it. Do you feel it?"

"What do you mean?"

"It's as though it has two parts. One just an ordinary, normal sort of house . . . and the other that's . . . haunted. Sometimes, Diana, I feel that she is still here."

"Who?"

"Margarete . . . Roger's first wife."

"She's dead, Myra."

"But some people think the dead can return. Sometimes I feel . . . that she can't rest. She was his wife . . . just as I am. I think she must have been rather like me. Quiet . . . not very attractive."

"That's being foolish. Roger must have found you attractive. He married you."

"I feel she and I are like one person."

"Really, Myra, you're getting fancies. He married her and she died soon after. It was a tragic accident. These things happen."

"I know. That's what I tell myself. I am beginning to believe she can't rest. When people die violent deaths, it is said that they can't rest. They sometimes come back. Just imagine it! You are alive one moment and then . . . without warning . . . you're dead. You've left everything unfinished." She looked at me fearfully. "I should hate to go like that."

"Why do you think of such things? You're here. You're healthy. And you're by no means old. Your whole life is before you."

"Sometimes I wonder."

I looked at her intently. "What do you mean?"

"Oh . . . nothing. I suppose I'm just nervous. My mother was always telling me to pull myself together." She laughed. "You're reasonable, Diana."

"Am I? Lilias thinks I am very unpractical. I've got a wild imagination, she says. I don't know what she would think of you and your fancies."

"Even my mother admired Lilias. I can't tell you how much better I feel now you are here. And it is lovely to have our afternoons together. I look forward to them. I expect I'm like this because I haven't been very well. Roger got a tonic for me from the doctor."

"So the doctor has been to see you?"

"He came to dinner . . . he and his wife. Roger told him that I wasn't as well as he would like me to be. I was listless and homesick. It was all natural, of course, but he wondered if the doctor could give me something to 'buck me up.' Well, the result was he sent round this stuff. It's something mixed with wine . . . and something else, I suppose. It's not very pleasant to take."

"Is it doing you any good?"

"I haven't felt much different. Your visits do me more good than the doctor's tonic, I think."

"Then we must continue with that medicine."

"I'm so pleased Roger asked you to come."

"Yes, he was really concerned about you."

"He's always so good to me." She hesitated and I waited for her to go on. She bit her lips slightly and said: "He wants me to settle down, I know. I try to. You like it here, don't you?"

"Yes. Lilias is delighted with it. It's such a change from the village. She always wanted to teach."

"We wondered why she gave it up."

I thought then how difficult it was to throw

off a part of your life which you wanted to forget. It kept coming back to hurt you.

"Perhaps she needed a rest," she went on. "She had just come to the end of one post and maybe did not like the prospect of facing another—though I should have thought Lilias would always be ready to face what she had to. Oh well, I'm glad it is turning out so well for her." She paused and went on: "What were we saying about the house? Do you know I avoid going to the part where it happened?"

"You mean . . .?"

"The staircase. I always feel there is something . . . haunted . . . about it."

"That's your imagination."

"Maybe, but I want you to come there with me. I want to make you understand what I feel."

"Now, you mean?"

"Why not?"

She rose and led the way, looking over her shoulder, as though to reassure herself that I was with her.

We reached that part of the house and stood at the top of the staircase. I could see what she meant. In the first place it was dark and shadowy. There was only one small window which gave little light, even in the afternoon. It might have been due to that that one felt it was gloomy, plus the knowledge that someone, not so very long ago, had plunged to her death down that staircase.

"There," said Myra. "I see you can feel it."

"I was just thinking that there was so little light here."

"It's more than that."

"It's because you are thinking of what happened here."

She moved away and said: "Come and look at the Model House. I always do when I'm in this part of the house. I find it fascinating to see the house . . . just as it is . . . though on this small scale."

As we came up to the house she stopped short and gave a gasp of dismay. "Oh . . . look!" she said.

I looked. A small carved figure, which was clearly meant to represent a woman, was lying at the foot of the staircase. I thought she was going to faint . . . and I caught her.

"It's only a piece of wood," I said.

"Who put it there?"

I said: "Would you like to go to your room? You really look shaken."

She allowed me to take her there. She was trembling visibly. I suggested she lie down and when she did so I sat beside her. She held my hand and I was sure there was something she wanted to say to me but could not bring herself to do so.

"Stay with me," she said. "Don't go back to the schoolhouse tonight. There's plenty of room here. Stay."

I was astonished. "But . . . ." I began.

"Please . . . *please*. I want you to. It's important to me."

"Myra . . . why?"

"I just feel . . . ." She looked so earnest, her eyes pleading more than her words. I thought: she is afraid of something. I have to help her. If I did not and something happened . . .

I was romancing again. What was it about this house . . . the staircase . . . the Model House? She was making me feel, as she probably did, that there were evil forces at work.

I could not leave her.

I said: "I'll send a note to Lilias. I'll tell her I'm staying the night."

"Oh, thank you. Will you really? Ring the bell . . . please ring the bell."

I did so and a woman arrived.

"Luban," she said. "Will you prepare a room? On this floor please. Miss Grey is staying the night."

Luban was a lithe youngish woman; her skin was black as ebony and her large dark eyes seemed to hold some tragedy. I remembered that she was the mother of the deaf-mute I had seen on my previous visit, and I guessed that her air of sadness might have something to do with that poor boy.

"I must send a note to Lilias at once," I said.

Myra found a pen and paper and I sat down and wrote:

Dear Lilias,

Myra wants me to stay the night. She is not very well and I think it is rather important to her. I hope that will be all right.

DIANA

Luban took the note and said it would be sent at once.

I was still in a state of amazement that I had fallen into this situation. It was only when I received Lilias' note that I realised that it was not so extraordinary, after all.

Of course, it is all right, [she had written]. I'm sorry Myra is not well. Give her my best wishes.

LILIAS

As usual she brought calm common sense into the matter.

Nevertheless that night I spent at Riebeeck House was an uneasy one. I had dinner in Myra's room as she said she did not feel well enough to leave it. Roger joined us. He seemed very pleased to see me there.

"This is delightful," he said. "It was so good of you to stay with Myra. I am sure you are very grateful to . . . er . . . Diana, Myra."

Why did he stumble over my name? I wondered. It was almost as though he knew it was not my true one.

Myra said that she was grateful and it was delightful to have me there.

"And this faintness?" he went on in deep concern.

"It was nothing. Just the heat, I suppose. I'm not accustomed to it yet."

"Do you think we ought to consult the doctor?"

"Oh no . . . no."

"Have you been taking your tonic?"

"Yes."

"Well, we shall see. If you have any more attacks like this I am going to insist on your seeing the doctor." He smiled at me. "You and I will take care of her, won't we, Diana?"

"She will soon be well, I am sure."

When I was alone in my room that night I found myself going over what had been said that evening. Roger Lestrange did seem to be a devoted husband, but, as always, I could not be sure of him. I wondered why he hesitated over my name. It really did seem as though he knew it were not mine.

I must talk to Lilias. She would soon drive away my misgivings. But Lilias was not here, and I was in a strange bed in a house which Myra thought was haunted.

There were times during that restless night when I had an idea that I was being caught up in something mysterious, perhaps sinister, which I could not understand.

WHEN I AWOKE next morning I could not for the moment recall where I was. I sat up in bed startled: and then when I looked at the unfamiliar Dutch-style furniture I realised I was in

Riebeeck House and I recalled the events of last night.

After a while Luban came in with hot water.

"Mrs. Lestrange was ill in the night," she told me, in her melancholy sounding singsongy voice. "She very sick. Mr. Lestrange . . . he very worried."

"Oh dear! She is better now?"

"Yes. Yes . . . better now."

After she had gone I washed and dressed. Poor Myra! She was rather delicate, I supposed. It was not easy to uproot oneself and live in another country; and she had been terribly upset by that little figure in the Model House. I wondered who had put it there and why. Was it meant to represent Margarete? I supposed so, as it was lying at the foot of the staircase. It was a mischievous thing to do. I wondered if Paul had had a hand in it.

I went downstairs. The breakfast things were set out on the table, but there was no one there. I stepped out onto the stoop and walked down the steps to the garden. I was struck afresh by the lush beauty of the place. It seemed particularly delightful in the early morning. The sun was not yet too hot; everything seemed fresh; the scent of the flowers was almost overpowering and there was a murmur of insects in the air.

As I stood there Roger Lestrange came out. "Good morning," he said. "It was good of you to stay last night."

"I felt a little guilty about leaving Lilias."

"Lilias is quite capable of looking after herself."

"I know. How is Myra? I heard from one of the servants that she was not well during the night."

"She is better this morning, thanks. Who told you she had been ill?"

"It was the one who brought my hot water. Luban, I think."

"She must have heard from Mrs. Prost. Luban doesn't live in the house. She is with her husband and family in one of the rondavels."

"Yes, I know. I did go out there and saw them once."

"Yes, I had to call Mrs. Prost in the night. I was worried about Myra."

"So it was as bad as that?"

"I wasn't sure. I don't know much about

illness. I'm worried about her . . . Myra, I mean. What do you think?"

"I think she's taking a little time to adjust to this new life. After all, she lived so long in that village and this is all very different. In time she will settle down."

"Do you think so?" He sounded relieved. "She has never been ill like that before. She's had her headaches, but she was sick . . . really ill. I was really alarmed. I thought of sending for a doctor . . . but she begged me not to. And then she began to recover a little. She probably ate something which did not agree with her."

"Oh, maybe that was it. I know the heat can be very trying to people who are not used to it. I daresay she will soon be all right."

"I was just wondering if I should get the doctor to have a look at her."

"I should see how she feels."

"You are a comfort, D–Diana."

"I'm glad. I think she was rather upset by that figure in the Model House."

"Figure? What figure?"

"A carved figure. It was supposed to be a woman, I think."

"In the Model House?"

"Yes. I was with her. She was showing me one or two things about the house and there it was . . ."

"What was it like?"

"Oh, rather crudely carved."

"Native work?"

"I suppose it could be. It was there at the foot of the staircase . . . not the spiral one, the other."

His face had darkened. He muttered: "Who, in God's name, could have put it there?"

"Myra had no idea. It was . . . just there."

"Show me," he said rather fiercely. "Show me exactly where it is."

He went hurriedly into the house and I followed him. Swiftly we passed through to the other end of the house.

The figure was no longer in the Model House.

"Where is it?" he cried. "Show me."

"It's gone. It was lying there . . . just there, at the bottom of the staircase."

For a few moments he did not speak. I had never before seen him at a loss for words. Then he said slowly: "It was that spot where we found her. Someone . . . is playing some silly joke. We must find out who."

"Well," I said, "it upset her. I thought she was going to faint. That was when I took her back to her room."

He had recovered, but the colour had faded from his face and he looked rather pale.

"Thank you, Diana," he said; and I noticed he used my name without the usual hesitation. "Thank you for looking after her."

We walked to the other side of the house and descended the spiral staircase. "Don't mention the figure to anyone. It might upset people."

I said I wouldn't.

Myra joined us for breakfast. She told us she was feeling considerably better.

"I thought I was going to die in the night," she said.

"Oh come, my dear," replied Roger. "You know I wouldn't allow that."

She laughed. She seemed quite happy.

"Thank you so much for staying, Diana. I did feel comforted to have you there. You will come and . . . and . . . stay again, won't you?"

"*I* am going to insist that she does," added Roger.

WHEN I RETURNED to the schoolhouse it was to find that two letters had arrived. One of them was from Ninian, the other from Zillah.

Ninian began by saying that we should come home without delay.

Things are getting worse and I can see no solution to the problem but war. Chamberlain and Milner are going to reject this five years' franchise suggested by Kruger and Smuts. It is only to be expected. Those who contribute so largely to the wealth of the country cannot be denied a say in its affairs. The British foray into South Africa some years ago was something of a humiliation for us. We cannot allow that to happen again. There is a rumour that Chamberlain is sending ten thousand troops to augment the army already there. You must realise what a dangerous situation is brewing. There is time. You cannot have settled in very firmly yet. You and Miss Milne should get the next ship back to England while there is time.

He had clearly not received my letter as he had made no mention of it.

I reread his letter. It contained little else but the need for us to come home.

I turned to Zillah's. Hers was more light-hearted.

I hope you are getting on all right. Ninian Grainger goes on and on about the trouble out there. He is certain you ought to come home. He asks me to write and add my persuasion to his. So I will. I miss you. Life is rather dull here. I think I shall travel a bit. I've been to London several times, but I mean go abroad. I think that would be fun. Wouldn't it be nice if you were here? We could go together. I hope you will soon be home. We could have fun.

I showed Lilias Ninian's letter. She read it and frowned.

"Go home!" she said. "Of course we won't. Just as the school is beginning to expand. It's doing us so much good here. The people are nice to us. They don't want to make war on *us*. This insistence of his is almost hysterical."

"People in Kimberley are mainly British."

"But the Boers and the natives . . . they are all very friendly."

"Well, it wouldn't be our war . . . yours and mine, Lilias."

"You're not hankering after going back, are you?"

I hesitated. I was thinking how kind and thoughtful Ninian was. I liked what Lilias called his hysterical insistence. It surprised and comforted me that after all this time I was still more than an ordinary case to him. I should love to talk to him and it saddened me that we were so far apart. So perhaps the answer was yes, I was hankering after going home.

I believe that if I had not suffered such bitter disillusionment over Jamie, if Ninian had not shown such an interest in Zillah, I might have faced my true feelings towards him. But having been so deceived, how could I be judge . . . even of myself? Perhaps I had been in a bewildered state since the trial.

"Are you?" Lilias was demanding.

"Well . . . we do seem to be settling in here, I suppose."

"And you are so much better. I know you are. You don't jump every time someone mentions something from the past."

"No, I suppose I don't."

"What are you going to do? Write to him?"

"I suppose so . . . . in due course."

She nodded. "Tell him that these matters

are exaggerated. Everything is just the same out here as when we came."

"Yes, I will." Lilias was right. We could not pack up and go home at a moment's notice just because Ninian . . . miles away . . . had heard rumours of war.

I WAS BECOMING a frequent visitor to Riebeeck House. Sometimes I stayed the night. Lilias did not mind that; I felt she rather enjoyed dealing with all the pupils; and I was realising more and more that my presence in the school could be easily dispensed with. Lilias was delighted to have paid off the first instalment to the Emigration Society. I said that as I was taking more and more time off to be with Myra I did not deserve what I was paid and it should be hers. But she was adamant. "That matter is closed," she said.

Meanwhile I was becoming well acquainted with the Lestrange household. Paul and I were good friends. He liked school and was doing very well; and although I sensed that he still bore a grudge against his stepfather for marrying his mother, he seemed to be accepting it. Roger was always charming to me, as he was with everyone. The servants all liked him; and

I gathered that the house was a more pleasant place than it had been under the Riebeecks.

Mrs. Prost, the housekeeper, appeared to take quite an interest in me. She was a woman who liked to gossip; and I must confess, so did I.

A strong friendship was growing between Myra and me and I fancied that she was less nervous. Mrs. Prost said my visits did her a power of good. I stayed a night or two occasionally. We played chess together. Lilias had taught me and I taught Myra. She was becoming quite an enthusiast.

There was one day when Roger went to Johannesburg on business and he asked me if I would spend the night at the house to keep Myra company. I said I would and we spent a pleasant evening chatting and playing chess.

In the night Mrs. Prost came to my room to tell me that Mrs. Lestrange was ill and she needed my help with her. I went with her to Myra who was very sick.

After a while she recovered and I said I would stay with her, which I did. I was very relieved when, in the morning, she was considerably better.

She took great pains to make light of her disorder.

"Don't tell Roger," she said. "I'm glad it happened when he was away. He doesn't like illness . . . and he worries about it too much."

"Perhaps he ought to know," I said. "Perhaps we ought to call the doctor."

"Oh no . . . no. That's the last thing. I tell you I'm perfectly all right. It was just something I ate . . . something that didn't agree with me. I'm going to be all right now."

She did admit to feeling a little tired and said she would spend the morning in bed.

While she was resting I went down to Mrs. Prost's sitting room.

"Do you think it was something she had eaten?" I asked the housekeeper.

Mrs. Prost was a little shocked.

"Cook wouldn't be very pleased to hear that, Miss Grey."

"Well, certain things upset some people. It may be something that she just can't take."

"I don't know, I'm sure. But I reckon we ought to be watchful. She was really bad. She frightened me. I was glad you were here . . . Mr. Lestrange being away."

She told me it was a different household from what it used to be. "When the Riebeecks were here . . . my goodness. You had to be all right and proper then, I can tell you."

"You must know this house very well, Mrs. Prost."

"I was here before I was married. Then my husband and I . . . we were both here together. He was a butler and I was a housemaid when we met . . . and I stayed on when we were married. It worked well, the pair of us . . . and then he died . . . a heart attack. Very sudden. And I stayed on."

"That all happened when the Riebeecks were here, of course."

"We never thought there'd be change. The house had been in the Riebeeck family for years . . . about two hundred, I think. Very strict they are . . . Boers . . . I know because Mr. Prost was one of them. My family came out when I was a little girl. And once you're English, you're always English, and though I married Mr. Prost I was never one of them . . . if you know what I mean."

"It must have been a great shock when the Riebeecks decided to sell the house."

"You can say that again! It was all this trouble that's been going on for ten years or more. The British and the Boers. It went badly for the British, but old Mr. Riebeeck said it wouldn't end there. There'd be more trouble and he didn't like the look of things. The British would never let things stay as they were, so he thought he'd get out while the going was good. He'd always been back and forth to Holland . . . something to do with business. He was more Dutch than anything else . . . and I suppose, getting old, he had this hankering for going home. So he just sold Riebeeck House, lock, stock and barrel."

"All the furniture and everything . . . and the Model House."

"Yes, that and all. The lot. So it's all just as it used to be as far as that goes. Well, Mr. Lestrange, he'd just got married to Margarete Van Der Vroon."

"So you were here when all that happened!"

"Of course I was. I can tell you there was quite a stir in the town when Jacob Van Der Vroon found that diamond. They reckoned it was one of the biggest finds, not only in Kimberley but in the whole of South Africa."

"Did you know the Van Der Vroons?"

"No . . . not really. I didn't know any of

the miners. They lived in one of those places near the mine . . . more like huts than houses. No, I can't say I knew them. What a find, though! The whole town was buzzing with it. They were nothing and then overnight . . ."

"Paul was quite a child then. I was surprised to hear he was not Mr. Lestrange's son."

"Oh, Mr. Lestrange is such a *good* man. He tries to be a father to that boy. He's put up with quite a lot from him. When I think of all he's done for that boy . . ."

"Poor Paul. He remembers his father and a child can't be expected to switch fathers just when he is told to."

"All the same, I think young Paul ought to be a little more grateful. But Mr. Lestrange makes the best of it. It was a bit of luck for Margarete Van Der Vroon that she got such a man."

"I didn't think she was very lucky. Didn't she die soon after?"

"Oh, a tragic accident, that was. Poor Mr. Lestrange. He was heartbroken. They'd only been married a year. I used to think how lucky she was. To come to a lovely house like this

with a man like Mr. Lestrange as her husband.
She'd never had much before, I can tell you.
They bought this house soon after they married. It fitted in nicely. The Riebeecks leaving
everything like . . . the house and all the furniture that went with it. A ready-made home
for them, all waiting."

"I heard that."

"And Mr. Lestrange was here with his
bride. It must have been an eye-opener for her
. . . after living in one of those little places
. . . and Paul a little boy who'd lost his father, now to have another who'd look after
him. There she was . . . a frightened little
thing when she found herself left a widow
. . . but a widow with something worthwhile
. . . this Kimberley Treasure as they call it.
There were one or two after her . . . or shall
I say after the diamond. Mr. Lestrange was
different. He had money of his own. He just
fell in love with her. I think it was because she
was a poor helpless little thing. It touched him
somehow . . . and that sort of thing can lead
to love. The present Mrs. Lestrange is rather
like that. He's a tender-hearted man, is Mr.
Lestrange."

"You admire him very much."

"Anyone would who'd worked for the Riebeecks. They are as different as chalk from cheese."

"The marriage didn't last long. There was that dreadful accident."

Her voice sank to a whisper. "I think she drank . . . too much."

"Oh?"

"Mr. Lestrange was upset about that. He didn't want a slur on her memory. But I think what happened that night was that she had been drinking too much . . . she didn't see the top step . . . and down she went and killed herself."

She paused, clearly upset at the memory.

I said: "Who found her?"

"I did. I was the one. It was early morning. I just went down to see her. I'd just gone to see that everything was all right, as I did most mornings, and there she was . . . lying on the floor. All twisted up. It was a terrible shock."

"It must have been. How long had she been there?"

"Since the early hours of the morning, they said."

"And Mr. Lestrange?"

"When he woke she wasn't there. He thought she'd got up early as she sometimes did. She'd get up without him being aware. She'd go down to the garden. She loved the garden . . . then they'd meet for breakfast."

"What did you do?"

"I ran up to their room and knocked on the door. Mr. Lestrange was asleep. I went in. I couldn't stop myself. I cried out, 'It's Mrs. Lestrange. She's lying at the foot of the stairs and she looks . . . she looks . . .' He stumbled out in his dressing gown and we went together. It was just terrible. We knew she was dead. He was so shocked. All he could say was 'Margarete . . . Margarete' just like that. I've never seen a man so shocked. He was very upset he was . . . heartbroken."

"He soon married again."

"Well, there's some men who have to have a wife . . . lost without one. And the present Mrs. Lestrange . . . well, she reminds me of the first. She's gentle. Not very sure of herself . . . and very much in love with her husband. Of course, Mrs. Myra has been brought up as a lady. You couldn't really say that of the other . . . dead though she is. She wasn't exactly a lady . . . but there's something similar about them . . ."

"I think I understand what you mean."

I came away from that conversation feeling that Roger Lestrange must be a very good master to arouse such admiration and loyalty in his servants.

THERE WAS A CERTAIN TENSION in the streets. Trouble was coming. Everyone was talking of it and speculating what the outcome would be. Negotiations were ensuing between Paul Kruger and Jan Smuts on one side and Joseph Chamberlain and the High Commissioner Sir Alfred Milner on the other. There was deadlock while we all waited for the result.

There were changes in the town. The garrison was being strengthened and one saw more and more soldiers in the streets. There were other new faces. The Afrikaners were coming into the town. I heard their voices, saw their faces . . . stern, weather-beaten, determined.

I had discovered during my brief spell in South Africa that most of the Boers were farmers, whereas the Uitlanders had settled in the towns. The latter were the people who had come to find diamonds and gold and had set up the banks and official buildings, changing the entire aspect of the place.

"It is small wonder," said Lilias, "that they will not tolerate being deprived of taking part in government."

It was in October of that year 1899—the last of the century—when the storm broke and South Africa was at war with Britain.

When school was over John Dale came to see us.

He was very concerned. "I don't know what this is going to mean," he said.

"Surely these people will not be able to stand out," replied Lilias. "They will be subdued in a week."

John was not so sure. "It's difficult terrain and the Boers are familiar with it. Moreover it is not easy to fight so far away from home."

"We shall have the men."

"There are not so many British forces here now."

"More will surely be sent. Why, ten thousand came not so long ago."

"We shall have superior arms, of course, and well trained men. The Boers are only farmers . . . part-time soldiers, but remember they are fighting on territory they know, and which they regard as theirs. I have an uneasy feeling that it is not going to be as easy as some seem to think." He looked from Lilias to me, the anxiety in his eyes obvious. "It was all going so well," he said ruefully. "But perhaps you should not have come."

Lilias smiled at him. "I don't regret it," she said. "I never shall."

He returned her smile rather sadly, I thought. Then he said: "The town is already different. It's full of strangers. They are getting ready to take it over when the time comes."

"It would not be for long," said Lilias.

"What difference will it make to us?" I asked.

"I don't know. We shall be regarded as the enemy, perhaps."

"Most of the people in the town are what they call Uitlanders."

John lifted his shoulders. "We shall have to see," he said.

We attempted to go on with our lives as we normally did. But we were all so uncertain and when news began to filter through of the Boers' triumphs over the British our hopes for an early end of the war deserted us.

Roger Lestrange, John Dale and most able-bodied men joined the garrison, for it looked as though it might be necessary to defend the town. The Boers might be farmers, unaccustomed to urban life, but they were shrewd and would recognise the importance of a prosperous town such as Kimberley. They would surely attempt to capture it.

It was early November, approaching the height of summer in South Africa, and the weather was almost unbearably hot.

Myra seemed to be growing weaker. She admitted to me that she had periodic bouts of illness.

"I feel quite weak," she said. "I don't feel any desire to eat. Of course, if there is a siege we shall all have to go short of things, I suppose."

"I expect so," I replied. "But in the meantime we are trying to keep everything normal. The children are coming to school and life goes on."

One afternoon I went to Riebeeck House and I found Myra in a state verging on hysteria.

I went to her bedroom. She and Roger had separate rooms now. She had told me that she preferred it because she was worried about being restless in the night.

"What is it, Myra? Would you rather tell me . . . or . . ."

"I want to tell you," she said. "I'm being foolish, I think. But it really frightened me. It's uncanny."

"Yes?" I prompted.

"It was in the Model House. I know I shouldn't go there. It upsets me after I saw that other figure. But this . . . it was there. It looked so real . . . I just stared at it. What does it mean?"

"But tell me what you saw."

"It was those carved figures. It was so like . . . something that happened. You could imagine it."

"But what actually did you see?"

"It was the figure of a man cut out of wood . . . and in his hands he was holding . . ."

She shivered and buried her face in her hands.

"What was he carrying, Myra? You must tell me."

"He was carrying a woman. Holding her up. Just as though he were going to throw her down the stairs."

"Oh no," I murmured.

She looked at me fearfully. "It was awful. Because she . . . Margarete had fallen down the stairs . . . I just ran away . . . screaming. I couldn't help it. It was because . . . it seemed to mean something. Roger was there. He tried to comfort me. It was some time before I could tell him what I had seen. He went there then . . . I followed him. I was afraid that the figures might not be there and it would seem that I had imagined the whole thing."

"And were they there?"

"Yes . . . he saw them."

"What . . . did he do?"

"He picked it up and broke it. He was so angry because it had upset me so much. He held it in his hand, just looking at it for a moment. Then he put it back, but it wouldn't stand up. He laid it on the top of the staircase; then he put his arm round me and took me back to my bedroom. He said some person was playing silly tricks and he was going to find out who . . . and whoever it was would no longer be a member of his household."

"And he did not find out?"

She shook her head. "Oh, he is so kind to me, Diana. He made me lie down. He said it was all nonsense . . . nothing to worry about. It was just silly and the only reason why he was so angry was because it had upset me."

"Who, do you think, would do such a thing?"

"We don't know. Roger tried to find out. He summoned all the servants to the library and he asked the one who had done it to own up. Who was it who had thought it was amusing to put figures in the Model House? That house was not to be touched by any of them . . . except those who were to dust it under the supervision of Mrs. Prost."

"Did anyone own up?"

"No one. But Roger is going to find out. He is determined to."

"Myra, why should anyone do such a thing?"

"I don't know."

"They would have to go to the trouble of carving the figures in the first place and getting up there . . ."

"I think it was someone trying to frighten me."

"With little figures like that?"

"I don't understand."

"Tell me what's in your mind, Myra. Why are you so frightened?"

"It's because of that staircase. I think someone is saying that Margarete did not fall down the stairs because she had been drinking too much . . . I think they are saying it was not an accident."

"And you wonder whether . . ."

"I sometimes feel the figures in the Model House are meant to be a warning . . ."

"Oh, Myra!"

"I'm afraid to go near that staircase. But there is a sort of compulsion to go there. It is as though someone . . . is luring me there."

"Someone?"

"It sounds silly, but strange things do happen. Roger is a very attractive man, isn't he, and I . . . well, I'm rather insignificant. It is rather miraculous that a man such as he is should want to marry me."

"He did marry you, Myra. He must have wanted to."

"I thought that Margarete might be a little . . . jealous."

"But she's dead!"

"They say that sometimes the dead return.

And we are in the same house. Just imagine! She was happy here with him. She had never been happy like that before."

"Paul says they were a very happy family when his father was alive."

"But he wouldn't understand the sort of love she had for Roger. In this house I can believe the past lives on, and I think that she is there waiting to separate us . . . to lure me to my death . . ."

"Really, Myra, that's nonsense."

"I know. But I am just telling you my feelings."

"Well, she couldn't make carvings and put them in the Model House to frighten you, could she? And how is that going to lure you to fall down the stairs?"

"I go there sometimes. I stand at the top and think of her plunging down."

"Look here, Myra, you're not yourself. These attacks have been weakening you. They've given you odd dreams and fancies . . . hallucinations perhaps. You've got to get back to normal. No ghost can make you do what you don't want to, nor can it put figures in certain places. Promise me you won't go wandering round this part of the house alone."

"I promise," she said.

I was very worried about her. I talked of it to Lilias. It was a change from the perpetual topic of the war, but, to me, it was almost as alarming.

"She must be losing her mind," said Lilias in her practical way. "They used to say in the village that Myra was a little simple."

"She's not simple . . . just nervous. She has never been confident in herself. That's quite different."

"You don't think she is secretly drinking, do you?"

"I did wonder that. It could give her fancies."

"It might well. It looks to me as though that's the answer."

"But there is no doubt that the figures were there. Roger saw them."

"I must admit this is an odd business."

"You see, first there was a figure lying at the bottom of the staircase, and now these more intricate ones of a man holding a woman and preparing to throw her down."

"I can only suggest one thing."

I nodded.

"That he pushed her down the stairs."

"Or someone did."

"Well, she did have that diamond which was worth a fortune. And he had married her rather promptly. Someone may have a grudge against him."

"I wonder who?"

"Well, there are more important things to occupy us at the moment. I was wondering how long we can go on like this. They are all around us. Oh yes, we certainly have other things to think about than little carved figures."

THE NEWS which filtered in to us continued to be disquieting. The quick and easy victory expected by the British was not forthcoming.

There was an old music hall song which I remembered from my youth and at the start of the conflict it had been revived again. I had heard people singing it in Kimberley when there was talk of war.

> *We don't want to fight*
> *But by Jingo if we do*
> *We've got the men, we've got the ships*
> *We've got the money, too.*

Somehow now it had a hollow ring. The stark realities of war were different from the dreams of glory.

Depression was descending upon us. The war had started in October and December had come; so far there had been no news of any success. Rather it had been the other way.

I sensed an air of triumph among the Boers in Kimberley. We did not communicate with them; there was suspicion between us, for how did we know who among us were not spies?

Those were difficult weeks. Several people were leaving the towns—young men who wanted to go and fight.

One day when I went to Riebeeck House I saw Njuba in the gardens.

I said to him: "Is anything wrong?" for there was a look of abject misery on his face.

"My boy . . . he gone," he said.

"Umgala!" I cried. "Where has he gone?"

"I do not know, Missee. He just gone. He not home all night."

"He can't have gone far. What could a boy like Umgala want to leave home for?"

"He good boy. No speak . . . no hear . . . but good boy."

"I know," I said. "How long has he been gone?"

"Only one night . . . one day."

"Has anyone tried to find him?"

"I ask Massa. He say we try find. But many go now . . . say Massa. Perhaps Umgala, too."

"I am sure he will come back, Njuba."

"I know . . ." He tapped his chest. "I feel here, Missee. He gone. He no come back."

I left the poor man shaking his head.

When I saw Paul he was very upset. He said: "Umgala's run away."

"His father told me he'd gone."

"Where could he go to? He can't speak. Besides, who would he fight for? Whose side would he be on?"

"He's a strange boy, Paul. He may have had some reason for going."

"I know him. He didn't want to run away."

"Well, it seems he has. There are lots of people slipping out of this town, Paul. We live in strange times."

"I wish they'd stop this silly old war."

"I am sure most people feel the same," I said.

It was the next day when Roger talked to

me. I was coming to the house to see Myra when he intercepted me in the garden.

"I wanted to talk to you, D–Diana," he said. "Things're coming to a climax. The Boers are doing well. They'll be taking over the town soon."

"Surely it can't go on? There must be change soon."

"In time perhaps . . . but not yet. I wanted to tell you that I am leaving tonight."

"Leaving? For where?"

"I can't tell you that."

"You mean . . . some secret mission . . . ?"

"We need more reinforcements. The Boer commandos are getting close. We've got to get help. I'm going to see what can be done."

"So . . . you leave tonight?"

He nodded. "I want you to look after Myra. I'm so worried about her. She is really in a nervous state."

"I know."

"I wonder if you would mind staying with her some nights. You know . . . when she is not so well. With things as they are . . ."

"Of course, I will do what I can."

"I've spoken to the doctor. He thinks it's

largely in the mind. She's finding it difficult to adjust. He's given her that tonic."

"It doesn't seem to be doing her much good."

"Dr. Middleburg said it would take time. This . . . er . . . upheaval has been too much for her."

"You mean . . . marriage?"

He smiled at me. "Oh no. I didn't mean that. God knows, I've done my best to make her happy. It's the strange country . . . leaving home . . . and just as we were settling down, all this blows up. Will you persuade her to go on with the tonic? I think she hasn't been taking it regularly and that is why it hasn't been as effective as we hoped. Would you see that she takes it as prescribed?"

"I'll do what I can."

"Good. I am sure this will soon be over, and we can get back to normal."

"Do you really think so?"

"Before long we shall have them on their knees. It's inevitable. It's just at first that there are difficulties to overcome. The Boers are a stubborn race; and they think they have God on their side."

"Don't they all think that?"

"I suppose so, but there is a fervency about these commandos."

"Perhaps that is because it is their home and this is where they live. They don't want anyone to take it from them."

"As they took it from others?"

"Oh yes, of course. Well, that was a long time ago and the place where people have lived for generations means something special to them. To us it is a gold mine . . . a country worthy of development . . . another jewel in the Crown of Empire."

"You are very eloquent, but we all agree on one thing: we want this war over so that we can return to our normal way of life. Please . . . look after Myra for me."

"I will do everything in my power."

"Thank you. Now I can feel more at peace."

He left Kimberley that night, and two days later we were a town under siege.

Siege

CHAOS REIGNED for the next few days. Rumours flew round the town. The Boer commandos were a mile away and advancing on us. They had decided not to take Kimberley and were surrounding the place. We did not know what to believe.

People came out into the streets and stood in little groups huddled together . . . watchful, fearful. They went into their houses . . . gathering their families together. Then the streets were deserted. It changed from hour to hour, and nobody knew what was really happening.

Then the refugees from the outlying districts came straggling into the town . . . exhausted . . . . some needing medical attention as they stumbled in with more tales to tell. Soldiers from the garrison patrolled the streets. Everyone was alert for the approach of the Boers.

The town was well defended, said some.

It would never stand up to an onslaught, said others.

Under the cover of darkness several men who had managed to break through the commando forces arrived. Some of them were wounded and the hospitals were full and all the doctors of the town were working there.

Life had changed completely.

It was during those first days that, in spite of what was happening in the town, my mind was completely diverted from the uncertainty which hung over us all by the events at Riebeeck House.

A messenger came from Mrs. Prost. She was sorry to bother me at such a time when we were all so worried, but Mrs. Lestrange was very ill and she was asking for me. Could I come to the house?

I went at once.

Mrs. Prost greeted me eagerly. "She's in a terrible way," she said. "I've sent for the doctor, but he's not there. I expect he's at the hospital. I thought I'd better wait a bit . . .

things being as they are. I don't know . . .
she seems to me to have lost her senses."

"Take me up to her."

"Yes . . . of course. I thought I'd better
warn you."

In spite of the warning I was deeply
shocked. I hardly recognised Myra. Her eyes
were wild, her pupils dilated. She stared up
when she saw me.

"Who are you?" she said. And then: "Oh
yes . . . yes. It's Diana. Diana, send her
away . . . send her away."

I looked at Mrs. Prost who nodded her head
towards the window. Myra was staring
straight at it.

"She sees something there," whispered Mrs.
Prost.

I said: "It's all right, Myra. There is no one
here except Mrs. Prost and me."

"Stay," she begged. "Don't go. Or . . .
she'll come back."

I went to the bed and put my arm round
her.

"You'll stay with me?" she pleaded.

"I will. Of course I'll stay."

She lay back against me and closed her eyes.

She was murmuring something which I could not hear.

Mrs. Prost looked at me. "I'll leave you with her. I'll send for the doctor again. Let me know if you want me."

She went out.

Myra lay still, her eyes closed. She was breathing heavily.

She opened her eyes suddenly. "Diana," she said.

"I'm here. I'm going to stay, Myra. As long as you want me, I'll stay."

That seemed to please her. She took my hand and gripped it.

"She was there," she murmured. "She kept looking at me. She beckoned."

"Who was there?"

"Margarete," she said.

"She's dead."

"I know. She came back."

"It must have been someone else you saw."

"No. It was Margarete. She was jealous, you see. She had lost him. He was mine now. She couldn't bear it. She wanted me to die."

"Margarete is dead, Myra. And you are here."

"But I am going to die."

"Of course you are not."

"Who'll stop me?"

"I shall," I said. "I'm going to look after you."

"Roger looked after me. He was so good . . . so kind. I wasn't good enough for him, but he never showed it. I was always afraid . . ."

I said: "I know."

"He wanted me to be well. He said: 'Take your tonic. Make sure you take it. It'll do you good.' And I did. I didn't miss . . ."

Her eyes went to the little table at the side of the bed. The bottle was there. It was about half full.

"So you have been taking it regularly?"

"I promised him I would."

"He asked me to impress on you the need to take it regularly while he was away."

"He cares for me. He really does. It shows . . ."

"Well then, Myra, you are a lucky woman. And you must get better."

"I try. I do take my tonic . . . just the same as though he were here."

"I'm sure you do. Myra, suppose you try to sleep a little."

"If I sleep you'll go away . . . and if you go away she'll come back."

"I shall not go away and she will not come back. Myra, she isn't here. She's something you've dreamed about and she doesn't exist except in your imagination."

She shook her head and I saw a tear seep out of her closed eyes.

"Try to sleep," I said.

"Promise to stay."

"I will. I shall be here when you wake."

She smiled and I was surprised that she was soon asleep.

I studied her face. It was pale and drawn. She was very different from the young woman I had first seen in Lakemere. True, she had been reserved, uncertain, overawed by her authoritative mother, but how different from the poor haunted creature in this bed.

She was gripping my hand and I was getting a pins and needles sensation in it; I managed to release it without waking her.

I went to the window and looked out. How peaceful it seemed. It looked just as it had when I had first seen it. It was hard to believe there was so much change all around us.

What would happen to us within the next

few months? I wondered. I thought of the great sieges of the past which I had heard of. The Siege of Orleans, when Joan of Arc had taken the city and brought it back to the French, putting new heart into them; the Siege of Paris which was not so very long ago. What was it like living under siege? Food grew short, of course. There would be no means of getting new supplies. People died of hunger. I had heard that some of them had been reduced to eating dogs and rats. The thought was nauseating. This was different. We were being besieged by a handful of commandos . . . guerrilla troops, not trained for fighting . . . farmers, most of them. They could not last long against the trained British Army. We should be relieved very soon.

And Myra. Poor Myra. She had been happy. She had married a most attractive man; she had come to a new country; and now she was in this state. She had not believed that such happiness as she envisaged with Roger Lestrange could ever have been hers. She had not thought herself worthy of him. Her mother had made her feel her inferiority. Poor Myra, who was accepted because she was an

Ellington . . . and because she had a fortune of her own.

I went back to the bed and looked down on her sleeping face.

A light tap on the door startled me. I moved too quickly and in doing so overturned the small bedside table. I tried to grasp the bottle, but it was too late. Myra's tonic was running over the carpet surrounded by specks of glass.

Mrs. Prost came into the room.

"Look what's happened," I said.

"Oh dear. I'll send someone to clear it up. It's Mrs. Lestrange's tonic, isn't it?"

"Yes, I'm afraid so. We shall have to get some more. I thought perhaps you'd brought the doctor."

"There's no hope of getting him just yet. The doctors are so busy at the hospital. A little party of men managed to get through last night and some of them are badly wounded. We'll try again later. How is she?"

"She's sleeping."

"Poor lady." Mrs. Prost shook her head.

"I'm terribly sorry about the mess," I said. "It was careless of me. And then there's the tonic . . . ."

"Never mind. It's just the tonic. The doctor

will give her some more though . . . when we get hold of him."

"I hope she'll be all right without it for a little while."

"Oh, it won't be for long. I daresay we'll be able to get that. Even if he can't come . . . he can give her that. These are terrible times. You'll be staying here for a while, I expect, Miss Grey."

"I promised I would. Could you send someone over to the schoolhouse to explain to Miss Milne that I may be here for a few days?"

"I'll certainly do that and I'll send someone up to clear that mess. I don't like broken glass lying about."

"I do hope she'll be able to get some more soon."

"That'll be all right, I'm sure. We'll do our best anyway. Can't do more than that."

I stayed with Myra all through the day. She slept a great deal of the time, and as soon as she opened her eyes she looked for me. I saw the relief when she was assured that I was still there.

"I feel safe," she said. "She can't do anything when you're there . . . because you can't see her and you don't believe she's there, do you? She's only there in my mind. That's it, isn't it?"

"Yes," I said. "That's it."

"Then please stay."

"I have promised I will."

"All night?"

"Yes. I shall be here. I have sent a note to Lilias."

That comforted her.

I spent the night in her room, sitting in a chair by the bed, dozing fitfully. Her looks had alarmed me so much that I wondered whether she would live through the night.

I was relieved when the dawn came and I looked at her in the clear morning light.

She was breathing more easily and she seemed more peaceful.

Mrs. Prost brought me coffee and bread and butter.

"Not very much," she apologised. "But we have to go carefully. I don't know what things are coming to. How is she?"

"She's had a quiet night."

"She's better when you're here. I'll send something up for her if she wants it. She's been turning away from food. A nice bit of porridge would be good for her. There are some oats left. Goodness knows when we'll get the next."

"I'll let you know when she wakes and we'll see if we can get her to eat something."

"And I'll send someone to see if we can get hold of that doctor. She'll need her medicine."

"Oh yes. It was careless of me."

"Accidents will happen. Well, let me know when she wakes."

She left me. The coffee and food tasted good. I thought: we are beginning to appreciate food now that we realise we may not have it for much longer.

It was about ten o'clock when Myra awoke. I had determined to be there when she did and I was glad, for her eyes alighted on me immediately, and she said: "Oh, Diana. I'm so glad you are here."

"How are you? You've had a good night's sleep."

"Is it morning then?"

"Yes, ten o'clock."

"I've slept all through the night!"

"That's rare, is it?"

"I usually wake and see things . . ."

"Well, you didn't last night. I've been here all the time."

"What? Sitting there?"

"It was nothing. The armchair is very comfortable. I dozed for hours. I just wanted to be here if you awakened."

"Oh, Diana, I am lucky to have such a friend."

"I have a confession to make. I knocked over your tonic. I'm afraid I've spilt the lot. It made such a mess on the floor. Be careful where you tread. They've taken it up, but little splinters of glass can be dangerous."

"The tonic!" she said. "I was supposed to take it last night."

"I hope we shall be able to get hold of the doctor today. We have tried already, but apparently the doctors are all in the hospital. I hope you aren't going to miss the tonic too much."

"Roger made me promise to take it."

"I know. He had great faith in it. But don't worry. I daresay the doctor will be here today and then we shall get some more."

During the day she seemed a little better. She was talking quite reasonably and there were no more hallucinations.

I stayed with her all during the day and the doctor did not come. Mrs. Prost suggested that on the following night I should use the room immediately next to hers so that if she needed me in the night all she had to do was knock.

"You can't have two nights sitting in a chair," she added.

To my surprise Myra agreed with this.

The room I slept in, I realised, was the one Roger used. It was not quite so large as the one he had shared with Myra and which she now occupied alone. The bed was comfortable and there was a bureau by the window. I did not sleep very well. I was waiting for a tap on the wall.

I was glad when the morning came. I went immediately to Myra's room. She was sleeping peacefully; the stick with which she was going to tap on the wall was in the same position as I had left it last night.

During the morning she seemed almost like her old self; I was delighted. And in the afternoon the doctor called. Mrs. Prost and I were with Myra while he examined her.

Afterwards he sat in the drawing room and talked to us both.

He was full of apologies for not having come earlier.

"There is chaos in the hospital," he said. "People are still creeping through the enemy's lines . . . if you can call them lines. It can't be much longer, I'm sure. Now, for the time being, there is nothing to worry about with Mrs. Lestrange. I don't know what happened to her. But she is going to be all right. She's weak . . . but her heart's all right and so are her lungs. Well, everything is. Might have been poisoned by some insect or other. There are some venomous ones here, as you know, Mrs. Prost . . . and they like a bit of new blood. They go for the newcomer. And I think some of the old-timers become immune. She needs building up."

"She has had hallucinations," I said.

"That could well be. I haven't been out here all that time myself. I am sure newcomers react more rapidly to these poisonous things. She needs some good red meat. It's a pity things are as they are."

"By the way, Dr. Middleburg, I had an accident and knocked over the tonic you gave her. She needs more."

"She shall have it."

"We were worried about her missing it."

"Oh no. It was only a mild pick-me-up. I

think she might go on with it. If you could send someone round, I'll give you some more."

I felt very relieved when he left us, and so did Mrs. Prost.

That afternoon one of the servants collected the tonic and I said we should not leave it on the side table again. There was a little cupboard in the room and I put it in that.

I spent another night at Riebeeck House and in the morning was delighted to see that Myra's improvement had continued.

I went back to the schoolhouse and promised I would call the following day.

That was a grim time. No food could be brought in and stores had to be guarded. Military law prevailed and we did not know what our fate would be from one day to the next.

Lilias made an effort to carry on as normal at the school, but not all the pupils came. John Dale continued to be a frequent visitor.

"He's a wonderful friend to us," said Lilias more than once. He was very eager to protect and often smuggled special items of food into the schoolhouse.

Soldiers now and then broke through the commandos who were surrounding the town.

That usually happened after dark. They brought us news and we learned that we were not the only town under siege. Ladysmith and Mafeking were in a similar plight.

The situation was growing more and more alarming. The easy victory expected by the British was even longer delayed. They were learning something of the difficulties of fighting in a strange land far away from home in a terrain unknown to them, while the enemy were fully aware of all its hazards.

"Ninian was right," I said. "We should have gone home."

"I shouldn't have wanted that," replied Lilias, and John Dale, who happened to be there at the time, smiled at her; it occurred to me that the feeling between them was strong and growing stronger, as such feelings will in a situation such as we were in.

Of course *she* wanted to be here. But what of myself? I wished I had gone home, no matter what I should have to face there, because then I could have seen Ninian. When one is close to death—and how could we know at that time what would happen to us?—one faces up to the truth. I had been halfway to falling in love with Ninian. It was only my affair with Jamie which had made me cautious.

Yes, I should have liked to be home with Ninian.

And here I was in a besieged city, only half aware of what was going on around me, never knowing from one moment to another when violent conflict was going to break out.

It was no use denying it. I did wish I had gone home. It was not because I was afraid of this war, but simply because I should be near Ninian.

I WAS GLAD that the schoolhouse was close to Riebeeck House. One could not walk short distances without being stopped by soldiers. They were everywhere. A watchful eye was kept on the commandos who encircled the town and every now and then one heard the sound of gunfire. Soldiers patrolled the town and no one ventured out after dark.

Christmas was with us. How nostalgic I felt, and so, I am sure, did countless others, for the Christmasses at home: the Yule logs in the grate, perhaps the snow falling outside . . . the security. How different was this!

And here we were in a strange land, so different from our own, in a city besieged by an enemy who could at any time come in and force our garrison to surrender.

Lilias and I would sit on the little stoop and talk. Dragonflies and insects whose names we did not know flew around us. Even the evenings, when the sun had dropped out of sight, were hot. I was homesick for the rain and Ninian. I dreamed of a life wherein I had met Ninian at some other time and place than at my trial; I dreamed that everything was as it had been when my mother was alive. I imagined Ninian had been brought to the house by one of our Edinburgh friends and love had grown between us. Zillah was not in that dream, of course. She belonged to the nightmare life which I was trying to pretend had never existed.

Foolish dreams! But Ninian had cared about me. His last letter had been urgent. "Come home." Would he have written so if he had not cared a little?

Then reality would creep in. I remembered how he had turned his attention to Zillah.

"We ought to try to do something for Christmas," Lilias said.

"Such as?" I asked.

"Give the children some sort of party. Say on Christmas Eve."

"Give them a feast? Goose? Turkey? Delicate chestnut stuffing? Plum pudding to follow? I do not think, Lilias, that those items are on the rations this week."

"I wish we could give them a party, though. Play games . . . that sort of thing."

"We could play the games, I suppose. And that is about all. We're in the wrong place for feasting."

"Nevertheless, I think we should try something. Perhaps they could all bring their own food."

"Surely not! Where would they get it?"

"From their allowance."

"I don't think it would amount to much. Has it occurred to you, Lilias, that food is getting more and more scarce?"

"Well, I suppose that is the way with sieges."

Lilias was determined. A few children still came to school, though the numbers were dwindling. Paul was one of those who came. Lilias was determined to act as though there was nothing to worry about. She told the children we should soon be relieved. The Queen and her soldiers would never allow us to remain in this state. One of the glories of being under the protection of the British flag was that it flew over almost the whole of the world. She pointed out the red sections on the map. "It is the Empire on which the sun never sets," she told them, "for when it is nighttime in England it is daytime in some part of the world which belongs to our great Empire."

She spoke with such fervour and passion that every child believed that we should be rescued before long, and some, I am sure, expected the Queen herself to appear at the head of her soldiers.

Paul was very enthusiastic about the Christmas party. He suggested some games we might play. Lilias told all the children who still came to school that they must let the others know there was to be a party on Christmas Eve and they must all come if they could.

On the twenty-third of December, Paul came to school in a state of great excitement. He was carrying a large can and when he took off the lid he revealed four fair-sized fish.

"It's for the party," he said. "We can give them a feast after all."

"Where did you get them?" asked Lilias.

"In the Falls," he said. "In our grounds."

"I didn't know there were fish there," said Lilias.

"I was walking past and I saw the fish leap over the Falls and I thought, that would be good to eat. So I went back and got a rod and things . . . and I caught these."

"What a find!" cried Lilias. "It's Providence. Paul, you are going to make our Christmas feast possible!"

"We can make some bread. We have a little flour," I suggested.

"The loaves and fishes," said Lilias. "This is truly a miracle."

The party was a great success. Most of the children came. Anna Schreiner was absent. Her father said that Christmas was not a time for feasting and making merry but for prayer. Poor little Anna! I did not think she would have much to rejoice about this Christmas.

However, we cooked the fish. There was not a great deal of it. But it was different. We were able to make lemonade and, if the children were not overfed, at least they were able to play games.

The story of the fishes spread through the town. Food! And discovered in the stream which ran through the grounds of Riebeeck House! People took their rods and went down to the stream.

I do not think there were any great catches, but even a little was welcome.

WE HAD MOVED INTO JANUARY. Little had changed except that food had become more scarce and there were no means of getting fresh supplies. Hopes for early relief were fading.

Myra had made a surprise recovery. She was still weak and nervous, but there were no more hallucinations. She was even surprised that she could ever have believed in them.

I made a point of being there when the doctor visited her again, because I was anxious to hear what he had to say.

I sensed that he thought she was a rather hysterical woman who had found it difficult to adjust to a new country, especially in the prevailing circumstances. He was growing more and more certain that she had been poisoned by some insect. Her symptoms could have been due to a form of poisoning; and she had reacted badly in view of her state of health. However, the trouble was over now and she was getting better every day. All she needed was to eat good food—not very easy in the circumstances—but the main thing was to stop worrying about herself. Then all would be well.

"You must make sure that your mosquito net is secure at night. Avoid those places where you know there are insects. I really don't think there will be any need for me to visit you again."

It was good news.

It must have been about a week after the doctor's visit. I was on my way to her and, as I approached the house, I knew that something disastrous had happened. There was a great deal of shouting from the servants who seemed everywhere. They were gabbling together. I could not understand their language, although I had picked up a word or two.

When I discovered what had happened I felt sick with shock.

Mrs. Prost, who was in the garden, saw me and came up. She told me what had happened. It seemed that one of the boys, fishing near the Falls that afternoon, had discovered the body of the little deaf-mute in the water. The boy had immediately gone to tell Njuba.

"He's been there ever since . . . just kneeling, staring into the water. It's terrible. That poor child."

"How could it have happened?" I asked.

"We wondered at the time," said Mrs. Prost. "You remember how he disappeared. We thought he'd run away . . . and to think all that time he was lying there . . . dead."

That afternoon stands out clearly in my mind. Whenever I smell the frangipani blossom I remember it vividly. I can see Njuba kneeling there on the bank. I have never witnessed such abject misery. When the men came to take the body away he was still there. Then he stood up, his hands clenched. He cried out: "This my boy. Someone kill him I will not forget."

Luban took his hand and led him back to their rondavel and we heard lamentations all through that day.

It was true that the boy had been murdered. There was sufficient evidence to prove that he had been strangled even though he had been so long in the water.

"Who could have done this to a little boy?" demanded Myra.

"And why?" I asked.

"What terrible times we live in. Do you think it has anything to do with the war?"

"I don't know. What harm could he do to either side?"

It was a mystery and for a few days people talked of little else. It was all, who did it? and why? That was a question no one could answer.

But when there was so much about which to be concerned, the mysterious death of a little native boy did not seem so very significant.

LIFE MUST NECESSARILY become more difficult as time passed. We knew we were all in acute danger. With the arrival of each day we wondered whether this would be the one when the Boers attacked the town. But the garrison had been strengthened just before the siege began; there were soldiers everywhere; it would be no light task and the battle would be fierce.

Lilias was as strong and practical as ever; and because of her growing friendship with John Dale, I did not feel that I was deserting her because I was so frequently at Riebeeck House. Myra needed my company more than she did.

I was getting to know Paul better. He was a

pleasant boy and I sensed he rather enjoyed the dangers of living in a besieged town. Danger to him meant excitement, which was preferable to dull ordinary living. He was learning to shoot, as many boys of his age were, but, of course, they lacked live ammunition, which was hoarded in case it should be needed for real battle.

I seemed to have become part of the household at Riebeeck House because I was so often there.

Mrs. Prost's attitude towards me puzzled me a little. I was never quite certain of how she regarded me. There were times when I thought I was welcome and she was quite fond of me. At others she seemed to be regarding me with something like suspicion. This surprised me a little, for I should have said she was a predictable woman, with fixed ideas from which she would find it difficult to swerve.

She had an affectionate contempt for Myra. Nobody could dislike Myra. She was always thoughtful to the servants and never behaved with the slightest arrogance. She was as different from her mother as one person could be from another. She was gentle, inoffensive and likable.

I understood Mrs. Prost's feelings towards her, but in my case her attitude seemed to sway between confiding friendship and a strange aloofness.

I discovered the reason for this one day and it was a great shock to me.

Myra was lying down, as she did most days, for she still tired easily, and Mrs. Prost asked me if I would go along to her sitting room.

I did so and when I was seated there I thought her manner decidedly strange. It was almost as though she were forcing herself to perform some unpleasant duty.

At length it came.

"I've been meaning to talk to you for some time, Miss Grey," she said. "It's been on my mind and I couldn't decide what to do for the best."

"Is it about Mrs. Lestrange?"

She pursed her lips and frowned.

"Well, it's not really . . . although I suppose you could say she might be concerned."

"Please tell me."

She rose and went to a little chest in the

corner of the room. She opened a drawer and
took a handkerchief which she handed to me.

To my amazement I recognised it as one of
mine. It had been given to me by my mother
with six others. They all had my initials embroidered in a corner. I looked down at the *D*
and *G* attractively entwined. Davina Glentyre.
I flushed slightly, for into my mind had
flashed a picture of Zillah. "It's safe to use the
same initials." How right she was.

"It's yours, isn't it, Miss Grey?"

"Oh yes, it is. Where did you find it?"

"Well, that's what upset me a bit. I've been
meaning to talk to you for some time. You see,
you've been so good to Mrs. Lestrange and I
know she's really fond of you. But when I
found that . . ."

"I don't know what you mean?"

"I think you do, Miss Grey. Cast your mind
back. It was the day . . . right back, you
know. It was one of the times when you spent
the night in this house. I found the handkerchief under the master's bed."

"What? How did it get there?"

I was flushing hotly while she looked at me,
gently shaking her head.

"Now," she went on, "I'm not one of these

people who thinks everybody ought to live like monks and nuns when they're not. I know these things can happen . . . men being men. But it's different somehow with a woman."

I stood up indignantly. "What are you implying, Mrs. Prost?"

"Now sit down, Miss Grey. I'm not exactly blaming you. The master is a very attractive man. He's a kind man, but even kind men find their fancy straying, and it's not in men's nature to control that sort of thing. It's different with a woman. She's got to be a bit more careful."

"What you are saying is absurd."

She nodded her head. "I know, I know. The temptation comes and I must say he is a very good-looking man and he's got all the charm you could wish for. And I know things are not . . . well, what they might be with him and Mrs. Lestrange. Separate rooms and all that. But I just thought you ought to be careful. I just happened to glance under the bed to see if it had been swept. It hadn't . . . and there was this handkerchief."

"I have no idea how it came to be there."

"Well, I thought I'd better warn you. When he comes back . . . and you being in and out of the house . . . and all that . . . just like family."

"You have no need to worry about that, Mrs. Prost. There has never been anything of an intimate nature between Mr. Lestrange and me."

"I guessed you'd take it like this. That's why I didn't say anything before. I'm not what you might call a prude. I thought it might have been just a slipup. These things happen. I'm not saying it's very nice . . . but there it is."

"I must insist . . ." I began.

"Well, I've said my say. It's not my affair, but I think it could lead to trouble."

"I keep telling you there's nothing . . . . nothing . . ."

"Oh, I suppose it got in there somehow. You never know, do you? But there it was . . . and I wouldn't have liked anyone else to have found it."

I stood up, still clutching the handkerchief. "Mrs. Prost," I said, "I assure you that I had never been in that room until the night I slept there when Mrs. Lestrange was so ill and Mr. Lestrange had gone away."

"Then if you say so, dear, that's all right

with me. I just thought I ought to mention it
. . . because when he comes back . . . well,
it wouldn't be very nice, would it, for you or
him or Mrs. Lestrange?"

"I see," I said, "that you do not believe
me."

"Look. We're good friends. That's why I
told you . . . warning you like. These things
can cause a lot of trouble."

"But I keep telling you . . ."

"All right," she said. "I've said my say and
that's an end of the matter."

But was it an end of the matter? Mrs. Prost
believed that I visited Roger Lestrange in his
bedroom. I felt as though I wanted to run out
of that house and never come back again.

As soon as I entered the schoolroom Lilias
knew that something had happened.

"What's wrong?" she said.

I was silent for a few seconds, then I burst
out: "I never want to go to that house again."

"Riebeeck? What's happened?"

"Mrs. Prost . . . she believes I have had
a . . . relationship . . . with Roger Lestrange."

"A relationship?"

"She found a handkerchief under his bed. It was the morning after I had stayed in the house when he was there, too. She drew conclusions."

Lilias stared at me.

I said: "You don't think . . . ?"

"Of course not."

"It's horrible, Lilias. She seems to think he is irresistible. It was awful. She kept saying she understood. I think that was the worst thing. And I think when she showed me the handkerchief I looked . . . guilty. It was one my mother had given me. It had my initials on it. And for the moment it took me right back. I had thought it best not to change my initials . . . whereas if I had changed them, she wouldn't have known the handkerchief was mine."

"Wait a minute," said Lilias calmly. "There's not much tea left, but this is the occasion to use it."

Sitting talking to Lilias was a comfort.

"Do you think," she said, "that someone put the handkerchief there?"

"Who? and why?"

"Someone who wanted to suggest that you had spent a night there."

"Not Mrs. Prost."

"No. There doesn't seem much point in that. But suppose someone put it there for her to find."

"It might have been someone else who found it."

"Perhaps that wouldn't have mattered."

"What are you thinking, Lilias?"

"I don't quite know. But someone in that house might have wanted to suggest that you and Roger Lestrange were lovers."

"But why?"

"That's all part of the mystery. How could your handkerchief have got into a room in which you had never been at that time, unless someone had taken it there?"

She was frowning and I said: "What are you thinking, Lilias?"

"I am not sure. Myra was there . . ."

"She was not well. That was the reason why I stayed."

"She was a little strange, wasn't she? Imagining things? Perhaps she wanted to prove something against her husband and you."

"She is devoted to him and I think he is to her."

"But she was seeing visions. Or did that

come later? I'm just letting my thoughts run on. The fact remains that the handkerchief was there. It had to be put there. Then who . . . and more to the point . . . why?"

"I feel I never want to go into that house again."

"If you don't it might look as though you are guilty."

"How could I tell Myra?"

"Stay away for a while and see how you feel. Something may occur to you. A handkerchief! It's strange what trouble such insignificant objects can cause. Think of Desdemona. But try not to brood too much on it. I think there's enough for another cup in the pot. We mustn't waste the precious stuff."

We had come to no conclusion, but it was, as always, a comfort talking to Lilias.

THERE WAS A FEELING of desperation in the town. We knew that something had to happen soon. There was no actual talk of surrender, but the thought was in the air. No matter how strong the spirit, people could not live without food.

Nothing was coming in now. All through that stiflingly hot January we waited for news.

We would hear the sound of sporadic gunfire which seemed to be getting closer. Occasionally a shell hit the town and there were casualties. We lived with the thought that at any time we could be among them. All through those hot days death hovered over us. Familiarity made it easier to live with. I suppose we accepted it and it ceased to be uppermost in our minds.

All the same it seemed almost incongruous at such a time to be upset because a suggestion had been made about me; but it was constantly in my mind. Images suggested by Mrs. Prost's conclusions kept recurring and there was always the mystery as to who could have put my handkerchief in such a place. It could only be that someone wanted to prove something against me.

Lilias, with whom I talked again of the matter, said I was making too much of it.

"You've suffered a great shock," she said, "and you must be on guard against allowing yourself to imagine some evil fate is working against you."

I knew that she was right when she said I was haunted by the past. I had hoped to escape it by leaving England. I knew as well as she did that there was no hope of a peaceful life for me until I had cut myself away from what had happened.

"Innocence should be your shield against all that," said Lilias. "You know you were innocent. I knew I was innocent when I was accused. It helps. I've told John about the affair of the necklace and he agrees with me."

She was right, of course. I had to be reasonable. The handkerchief must have been caught up in something and got carried into that room. It seemed implausible, but strange things did happen.

After a few days I began to feel a little better about the affair, but I had no desire to go back to Riebeeck House.

Myra came to the schoolhouse. She was looking much better now. Her cure had been quite miraculous and she had lost most of her nervousness.

She looked at me in some consternation.

"You haven't been to see me."

"Well . . . there's been a lot to do here."

She looked surprised, but did not ask what.

"We missed you," she went on. "Mrs. Prost was quite upset."

And so she should be, I thought. It is because of her that I've stayed away. All the same I was glad she had mentioned what was in her mind. I would rather know than have her continue with her speculations.

"She thought you might have been offended about something. I told her that was nonsense. But I thought I'd come to see you. Is everything all right?"

"Hardly all right, Myra. Things are getting worse. We shall all be starving soon."

"Yes, I know. And someone was killed last night . . . near the church."

"It's unsafe to be in the streets."

"It's unsafe to be anywhere, so one might as well be in one place as another. I wonder when it is all going to end. Oh, Diana, I wonder about Roger. Where can he be?"

"He didn't say, did he? Well, he couldn't, of course. It was some mission from the garrison . . . to let people know what was happening in the town, I suppose, and get help if possible."

"I pray he is all right. It's awful that he's not here now that I am so much better. He couldn't understand what was wrong with me. He used to worry so much. And to think it was that wretched insect. Who would have thought little things like that could do so much harm? We've had rather an upset at Riebeeck. It's poor old Njuba."

"It was so terrible about the boy."

"If it had been an accident it would have been different . . . though that would have been terrible enough. But to think he was strangled and someone had deliberately killed him . . ."

"Who could have done that, Myra, to a helpless little boy?"

"It's a mystery. If it wasn't for the siege there would have been an enquiry, I suppose. But now nobody thinks of anything but how long we can hold out."

"That is understandable."

"What I was going to tell you was that poor Njuba is acting strangely. He just wanders about, muttering to himself. He got into the house and was found going in and out of the rooms . . . as though he were looking for something. Mrs. Prost found him turning out cupboards. She asked what he wanted and he wouldn't tell her. She didn't know what to do. She sent for Luban to take him home. It's very sad. Poor Luban. She's lost her son and her husband seems as though he is losing his wits. What terrible things happen, Diana!"

"Yes," I replied. "That's true."

"Please come and see me."

"It is just as easy for you to come here."

"Yes, but there is more room at the house and the gardens are nice."

"All right. I'll come."

Lilias was pleased when I told her. "It's the best thing. Mrs. Prost would think she had been right if you stayed away. You can convince her how wrong she was, I'm sure."

"But *I* am not sure about that," I replied. "I think she has made up her mind that her beloved master is irresistible, and she exonerates him absolutely; and she doesn't take too stern a view of me because he is the man in the case."

FEBRUARY HAD COME. We were living on small rations. When we awoke in the mornings we wondered what the day would bring. This state of affairs could not continue. Something had to happen soon.

There were constant outbreaks of gunfire; it had ceased to be sporadic and was normal now. One night a party of three men arrived in the town, having broken through the forces surrounding us; one of them was wounded.

There was jubilation in the streets next morning. People stood about talking with an animation which I had not seen for some time. We should not give up hope yet. The British were advancing. They had suffered a major defeat at Spion Kop, but after that things had changed. Ammunition had been pouring into the country. Two names were mentioned with awe: Major General Horatio Herbert Kitchener and Field Marshal Sir Frederick Sleigh Roberts. They were marching on and were coming to our relief.

New hope was springing up everywhere. People were saying that it was not possible for the great British Empire to be beaten by a handful of farmers. The British now had the measure of the land. "We've got the men, we've got the ships and we've got the money, too."

Hope was a great reviver. People were smiling in the streets. "It won't be long. Kitchener and Roberts are on the way."

I went to Riebeeck House. Lilias was right. To stay away could imply that Mrs. Prost's suspicions were correct. All the same I did not like staying in the house. I often suggested to Myra that we sit in the gardens. In any case, they were beautiful. The scent of the flowers, the murmur of insects suggested peace . . . even in these troubled times. Sometimes we walked.

We went along past the waterfall where poor Umgala's body had been found and on as far as the rondavels.

I do not know what impulse led me to that particular rondavel. It was a little apart from the others and it looked as though it were falling into decay. The grass grew tall about it. There was a hole in the thatched roof.

"That would have been repaired, I daresay, if all this hadn't happened," said Myra.

"Who is supposed to keep them in order?"

"The natives. They are their homes. They look after them themselves."

Something urged me to go forward and as I did so a small boy darted up to us. He smiled, his teeth dazzlingly white against his dark skin.

"Whose home is this?" Myra asked him.

His smile disappeared. He looked furtively over his shoulder. "No one live here, Missee. Devil man there."

"Devil man?" I said.

"Bad place. Missee no go."

"It's only one of the rondavels that has been left to decay. That's what's wrong with it."

"Old man live there. He die. No one want place. It bad. Umgala . . . he not know. He go . . . he like. He always there. He die . . ."

The mention of Umgala startled me. I wanted to go into the rondavel.

"Let's just take a look," I said, and started forward.

"No . . . no, Missee." The boy was really alarmed. "Bad place. Big snakes in grass. Devil's snakes. They wait . . . to catch . . ."

"We'll be careful," I said, and I went forward.

Myra said: "Perhaps we'd better not . . ."

But I was already making my cautious way through the long grass.

I reached the door, lifted the latch and went in. There was a buzzing noise and a huge insect, which looked like an enormous dragonfly, cruised across the rondavel and settled on a small bench.

"Let's go!" said Myra. "We don't want to get stung."

But something held me there. Under the bench was a rough drawer and below it on the earth floor I noticed wood shavings and splinters of wood.

I went across the room. The insect was still perched on the bench. Keeping my eyes on it I opened the drawer. I had to shake it to get it open and when I did so I saw several carved figures, among them that one which I had seen lying at the bottom of the staircase in the Model House.

I turned to Myra who was standing in the doorway.

"Come away!" she cried. "I don't like this."

I said slowly: "That boy . . . he said Umgala came here . . . no one else did. He was often here . . . before he was murdered."

Myra said: "I'm going. It's horrible here . . ."

I followed her. She was already pushing her way through the long grass.

"Myra," I said. "Myra, it was Umgala . . ."

At that moment we saw the snake. It had risen and was close to us. It hissed ominously. It had been lurking in the grass.

Evading it, I ran after Myra. I think we were lucky in seeing it in time.

We had reached the clearing. We stopped, panting. I turned to look behind us. There was no sign of the snake.

Myra was trembling. I put an arm round her. "It's all right now," I said. "It's back there in the grass." And all I could think of was: Umgala made the figures . . . and Umgala was murdered. This was a momentous discovery. I was bemused, bewildered. Ideas were jostling each other in my mind. I felt I must not mention my discovery to Myra. I wanted to talk it over with Lilias first.

Myra was clinging to me.

"It was awful . . . that horrible thing in the grass. It was waiting there for us . . . while we were in that place . . . it was there in the grass . . . waiting for us. I didn't want to go there. I knew there was something dreadful about it. I hate these places. Diana, I want to go home."

I knew that by "home" she did not mean Riebeeck. She wanted to be in Lakemere.

"You'll feel better after a rest," I said, calming her and myself at the same time. But I was not really thinking of her but of that boy who was the carver of the figures and who had died because of them.

Mrs. Prost was coming across the lawn.

"Oh, good afternoon, Miss Grey. Mrs. Lestrange, you look as if you've seen a ghost."

"We've seen a snake," I said.

"Nasty beggars."

"It was close to us," said Myra. "It was lurking in the grass. It hissed at us."

"What sort of snake?"

"I don't know. It was big. We just thought of getting away."

"Quite right, too."

She came with us into the house.

"A nice cup of tea's what's wanted now," she said. "There's none left. It's come to a pretty pass when you can't have a cup of tea when you want one."

I wanted to get away. I desperately wanted to talk to Lilias.

"You ought to have a lie down, Mrs. Lestrange," said Mrs. Prost. "You look all shaken up."

"I think that's a good idea, Myra."

She agreed. So I said goodbye to her and prepared to leave. But as I came out of her room Mrs. Prost was waiting for me.

"There is something I ought to say to you, Miss Grey," she said.

I hesitated. Was she going to apologise for what she had suggested on our last meeting?

"Come into my room," she said.

So I went.

Mrs. Prost looked embarrassed and I began to feel uneasy, suddenly fearful of what she would reveal next.

She said: "I ought to have told you before. I couldn't bring myself to. But I've got fond of you . . . and I couldn't believe it and yet there it was."

"Yes?" I said faintly.

"I . . . er . . . know who you really are."

"What . . . do you mean?"

"You're Miss Davina Glentyre."

I gripped the sides of my chair. I felt sick and dizzy. That which I had never ceased to dread had come to pass.

She was looking at me steadily.

"How . . . did you know?" I asked.

She rose and went to a drawer—the same one from which, on that other occasion, she had taken the handkerchief. She brought out two newspaper cuttings and gave them to me. The headlines stared back at me.

"Guilty or Not Guilty? Miss Davina Glentyre in Court. Dean of Faculty Addresses Jury."

I could not read the print. It danced before my eyes. All I could see was those damning headlines.

"How long have you known?" I asked, and I thought at once: what does it matter how long? She knows now.

"Oh . . . for some time."

"How?"

"Well, it came about in a funny way. I was dusting Mr. Lestrange's room and he came in. He was one to have a little chat . . . always the gentleman . . . never making you feel small like. I said, 'I won't be a minute, sir. I always like to do your room myself, to make sure everything's all right.' He said, 'You're very good, Mrs. Prost. I've just come in to get some papers. Don't let me stop you.' He went to his desk there and took out some papers, and as he did so these fluttered to the floor. I picked them up. I couldn't help seeing them."

"He had them in his drawer? Then . . ."

She nodded, and went on: "He said, 'You've seen these cuttings now, Mrs. Prost. So I think you and I should have a little chat. Sit down.'

So I sat and he said: 'You recognise the young lady?' I said, 'Yes, it's her that calls herself Miss Grey.' He said, 'She was most unfortunate. I believe in her innocence. She was definitely not guilty of killing her father. You couldn't believe that of her, could you, Mrs. Prost? Not a nice charming young lady like Miss Grey.' I said: 'No, I couldn't, sir, but . . .' Then he said: 'She's come out here to start a new life. I want to help her, Mrs. Prost. Will you, too?' I said, 'Well, I'm ready to do what you say, sir.' 'Take these papers,' he said. 'Put them away somewhere. Just hide them. I shouldn't leave them about. The servants . . . you know . . . one of them might find them. Just take them and make sure no one sees them. I want you to help me rehabilitate Miss Grey. I like her. I like her very much. She is a young lady who deserves another chance.' Then he gave me these cuttings."

"Why did he give them to you? Why did he want you to keep them?"

"He didn't say. And I thought I'd better, since he'd said."

She took them from me and put them back in the drawer.

"Nobody comes in here," she said, "unless I invite them. I do my own room. He's quite right. They're safer here with me than they are with him."

"But why should you want to keep them?"

"I don't know. I just feel I ought to . . . as he said. He might want them back. But what I wanted to say to you was that I knew. I suppose Mrs. Lestrange doesn't?"

I shook my head.

"Well, it's only the master and me."

I was feeling ill. I just wanted to get away. First the shock of what I had discovered in the rondavel and now, immediately afterwards, this which had temporarily driven all else from my mind.

I said: "What are you going to do?"

"I'm not going to do anything. But I thought you'd understand me better if I told you I knew. I could see Mr. Lestrange was very fond of you. After all, he's gone out of his way to help you, hasn't he? Didn't he let you know about the school? That's why you're here. Your secret's safe with me. It's some time since I knew. It was just before Mr. Lestrange left, of course. When he comes back I shall tell him I've told you. I shall say it was only right and proper that I should. Now look, don't you worry. Mr. Lestrange doesn't believe you did that terrible thing . . . and nor do I. Nice girls don't go round murdering people . . . especially their own fathers. He took it himself. Men are like that . . . and him with a young wife. It's easy to see . . . and that's what they thought it was, didn't they, because they let you off. So don't you worry. I'll go on calling you Miss Grey though you're not. But you couldn't very well use the other, could you?"

I wished that she would stop. I stood up.

I said: "I'm going now, Mrs. Prost."

"All right. But don't worry. I just thought that you ought to know that I know and I didn't hold it against you. You just have to be careful, that's all. I understand. I'm the sort of person who can put myself in other people's place. I was young myself once. But you don't want trouble."

"If you don't mind, I'll go."

"Get a nice rest. I know this has been a bit of a shock . . . but it's safe with me. So don't you fret."

I hurried back to the schoolhouse. At the sight of me Lilias knew something was wrong.

"What news?" she said. "There's been a lot of activity out there. Something's going to break soon."

"Lilias, I've had a terrible shock. Mrs. Prost . . ."

"Oh, not on again about that handkerchief!"

"No. She knows who I am. She has cuttings . . . newspaper cuttings of the case. She knows what happened in Edinburgh."

"No! How?"

"Roger Lestrange had them. He gave them to her. So he knew . . . and now she knows. You see, there was no escape. You can't run away from a thing like that."

"Let's get this straight. She told you, did she, that *he* gave her these cuttings?"

"She was dusting the room. He went to get something out of a drawer and they fell out. She picked them up for him . . . and saw."

"Rather fortuitous, wasn't it?"

"It sounded accidental, the way she told it. She rushed to pick them up. She couldn't help seeing. There was a picture of me. He realised that she had seen. He said he believed in my innocence and wanted to help me."

"So he kept the cuttings and dropped them at her feet?"

"He gave her the cuttings, he said, because he thought they might fall into the hands of one of the servants."

"What's wrong with a nice bit of fire?"

"I don't know why they had to be kept. But she has them. She *knows*, Lilias. She says she believes in my innocence and wants to help me as he does. Oh, Lilias, I wish I had never seen Roger Lestrange. I wish I'd never come here."

"I am wondering what this means. Why should he have let her see those cuttings? Why should he have given them to her . . . to keep? What does it mean?"

"I don't know."

"I don't like it."

"Oh . . . and something else has happened. I'd forgotten in all this. I've found out who did those carvings and put them in the Model House. It was Umgala . . . the little deaf-mute who was murdered."

"What?"

"There is one of the rondavels which is empty. Someone died there, and you know how superstitious these people can be? It's a little apart from the others and quite dilapidated. One of the boys warned us about going there and told us that Umgala used to go there often . . . and he was unlucky. He was murdered. The boy seemed to think it was because he had gone to that place. I went in and saw the wood shavings on the floor. I opened a drawer and there was one of the figures. The one I'd seen in the Model House."

She was looking at me incredulously.

"And you think he was murdered because he did those figures and put them in that place?"

"Oh, Lilias, I'm beginning to think all sorts of things."

"The figures were significant."

"Oh yes. There was one lying at the bottom of the stairs. I didn't see the others . . . the ones which upset Myra so much. It was a man holding a woman and it was set at the top of the staircase. Myra said it was placed so that it looked as though the male figure was throwing the female down."

"It would seem that Umgala saw this happen. He couldn't speak . . . so he tried to explain in some other way."

"Yes, he was trying to convey something . . . that it was no accident. Margarete Lestrange had not fallen down the stairs accidentally. She had been deliberately pushed . . . murdered, in fact."

"And that was why the boy died. Someone did not like those figures."

"Roger Lestrange did not like them. He was furious when he found them. Though he gave the impression that it was because it had upset Myra."

"And soon after that the boy disappeared."

"Do you think that he . . . murdered his first wife . . . and would have murdered Myra? She has been so much better since he has gone. She is almost recovered. She began to get better after I broke the bottle by her bedside. Was she being poisoned . . . not by an unspecified insect . . . but by her husband through the tonic? It's a terrible situation. Did he murder his first wife and was he trying to remove his second?"

"That's a theory," said Lilias slowly. "He had reasons, didn't he?"

"His first wife had the big diamond . . . the Kimberley Treasure. He bought Riebeeck with her money . . . and then she died. He came to England looking for a wife . . . one with money . . . one who was docile and unassuming. You see, Myra fitted exactly what he wanted."

"Are we running on too fast? Was it as simple as that? And following on those lines, I see another aspect of the case. Why was he interested in you?"

"Was he?"

"Certainly he was. That was obvious."

"True, he paid for the cabin."

"What?"

"I never told you. I knew you'd hate it. The cabin we had at first was the one we had paid for. There was no mistake. He paid the difference. That was why we went to a better one."

"What a fool I was!" said Lilias. "I might have known. Why didn't you tell me?"

"I didn't know until we were almost at Cape Town, and then it was too late. We couldn't have gone back. I thought you would be upset about the money . . . so I decided to accept graciously."

"I shall pay him back," said Lilias. "But that is not the point now. That's for later. I am trying to make sense of this. That handkerchief story. Found under his bed the day after the night you spent in the house. What if he put it there? And the newspaper cuttings . . .

fluttering onto the floor. A likely story! He *wanted* her to see them. And why should he give them to her? She was to keep them. Why? Oh, Davina, I don't like this. I think you could be in danger."

"How?"

"Don't you see? His first wife died in mysterious circumstances."

"Did she? She fell down the stairs . . . after she had been drinking."

"There may have been suspicions. She had inherited this diamond and she had died soon after their marriage. Then he married again— an acquiescent woman, rather like the first; she also has money. She is being slowly poisoned. Now he may be clever and get away with the second, as he did with the first . . . but suppose he doesn't? He'd want an escape route. And there is a woman who has been accused of poisoning her own father who was threatening to cut her out of his will. She is tried for his murder and suspicion still hangs over her as the verdict is Not Proven. She comes to the house; the housekeeper finds her handkerchief under the bed. A little indiscretion perhaps . . . but indiscretion is not murder. She is interested in the handsome master of the house, but he has a wife already. Once she was on trial for the murder of someone who stood in her way. Suppose she were really guilty? Might she not try the same method again? I know this is a wild supposition. He could hope to succeed and then you would not be necessary. But if he did not . . . well then, he has his scapegoat. Oh, Davina, I may be romancing . . . but this could just be the truth!"

"How can you think of such terrible things!"

"Because I'm being practical. I'm being hard-headed. I'm trying to get a clear picture. I am asking myself why this, why that? And I'm putting the worst construction on every thing just to see whether it fits . . . and it could, Davina. It could."

"I'm frightened, Lilias. I couldn't go through all that again. So much of it fits. He has always made me feel a little uneasy. And now . . . now I feel he was there right from the first . . . like that snake in the grass . . . waiting for the moment to strike . . . lurking there . . . laying the snare . . . because of what had happened to me. Thank God he went away. I can even thank God for the siege.

If he had stayed . . . oh, I can't bear to think of it! Lilias, if this is true, when he comes back he will expect to find Myra dead."

"Perhaps he won't come back . . . perhaps we shall never know. How do we know what is happening all over the country? People die in wars. Where did he go? We do not know. He was on some secret business, he implied, did he not? How could one know with a man like that? But if he comes back . . . perhaps we shall know more."

"He can hardly come back while we are in siege."

"Then we shall never know the truth."

"What shall we do, Lilias?"

"We can only wait and see. But I tell you one thing. When he comes . . . if he comes . . . we shall be prepared."

We sat up late that night, talking, for we knew neither of us would sleep. We went over and over everything that seemed significant.

I could not really believe that he had helped to bring me out here because he planned to murder his wife and wanted a scapegoat, should the need arise.

Lilias said: "It might not have been deliberately planned. Such things often are not. Perhaps in the first place he really wanted to help you. He must have discovered early on that you were Davina Glentyre."

"I remember there was an occasion . . . you were there. We had been visiting Mrs. Ellington and I fell while mounting my horse. Kitty was there. She called out my name."

"I remember. That would have been enough."

"It's an unusual name. It might have started a train of thought in him. He has certainly been very friendly. He was so anxious that I should go to the house to be with Myra. Then there are the handkerchief and the cuttings . . ."

"We can go over and over it, Davina, and still we shall not be sure. Let's wait and see what happens when he returns. Perhaps we shall learn more."

And so we talked.

WE DID NOT HAVE TO WAIT very long. We knew the Army was closing in. Between it and the town were the Boer commandos, and what hope had a group of wartime fighters, fresh from their farms, in conflict with trained soldiers?

How could Kruger and Smuts stand up to Kitchener and Roberts . . . and the British Army? The breakthrough was inevitable. It would be any day now. We were waiting for them. And at last they came.

It seemed that every man, woman and child was in the streets. We were out there to greet them as they came in and their welcome was tumultuous. People were embracing and kissing each other.

"It's over. They're here. We always knew they'd come . . ."

It seemed as though it was worth living through a siege because it was so wonderful when it was over.

Mafeking. Ladysmith. They were now free.

"Good old Bobs. Good old Kitchener," cried the people.

We were all carried along on the wings of victory during those days.

THE RELIEF OF KIMBERLEY was such an exhilarating experience that, in spite of all that had so recently happened to me, I was caught up in the rejoicing. But the terrible realisation of what evil might have been hovering over me was never far from my mind.

After the first days had passed, after we had grown accustomed to having the Army in town, to food arriving, to feasting, to singing "God Save the Queen," I became haunted by the thought that now Roger Lestrange would come back. And then . . . what? What could I say to him? I could not accuse him of attempting to poison his wife and devising a devious plot to implicate me. I could not say to him, "Myra started to recover as soon as she stopped taking the tonic which you insisted on her having." What could I say of the handkerchief and the cuttings? It was, as Lilias had pointed out, nothing but theory even though it did seem a plausible one.

But I did not have to speak to Roger Lestrange again.

Four days after the relief of the town he returned.

I never knew what he said or thought when he came back and saw Myra alive and well, for on the night of his return he was shot dead by someone who was waiting for him in the gardens of Riebeeck House.

The news travelled quickly and John Dale came to the schoolhouse to tell us about it.

"Who killed him?" I asked.

"Nobody knows as yet. They suspect one of the servants who has been acting strangely for a long time."

Lilias and I were certain that Njuba had shot him because he had discovered that Roger Lestrange was the murderer of his son.

I said: "Poor Myra. She will be distraught. I must go to see her."

"I'll come with you," said Lilias.

There was chaos at Riebeeck House. Roger Lestrange's body had been laid in one of the rooms. Myra was weeping bitterly.

Mrs. Prost was present. When she saw me she looked relieved.

"I'm glad you're here," she said. "There's no comforting her. To think he came home for this."

They found Njuba in the gardens. He seemed bewildered and his eyes were wild.

"He's mad," said Lilias. "Poor man. It's turned his brain."

"What will happen to him?" I whispered.

"It's murder," said Lilias, "whichever way you look at it. It may be rough justice, but it's murder."

Njuba kept murmuring: "He killed my son." He held up a button. "This . . . in my son's hand. It from his coat. I find. He killed my son. Held fast . . . in my son's hand. Still there . . . when I find him."

They took him away.

So there was proof that Roger Lestrange had killed the poor little deaf-mute. It could only have been because he knew the secret of Margarete's death and, because he could not explain in words, was doing so by using the figures he carved. If Roger Lestrange could kill his wife . . . if he could kill a small boy . . . the theory of his idea of shifting the blame to me did not seem so implausible, particularly as we were now certain that he had paved the way with the handkerchief and the cuttings. He had meant to snare me . . . so that I should be there if the need arose. Serpent-like he had waited for the moment to strike.

Poor Luban was half crazy with grief. We all tried to comfort her. Myra helped with this. Luban had lost a son and was about to lose her husband; but Myra had also lost a husband. It seemed ironical that she had so loved a man who was callously plotting to kill her while at the same time he set out to enchant her. But I think that by helping Luban she found some solace for her own grief.

The sequel to the story amazed everyone when, the following day, Piet Schreiner made an announcement in the chapel.

He stood in the pulpit facing the congregation. The chapel was full of those who were there to give thanks to God for the relief of the town.

"This is the justice of the Lord," cried Piet Schreiner. "I killed Roger Lestrange. He deserved to die. He was a sinner. He seduced the woman I married and deserted her. I married her to save her family from shame and to give the child a name. God directed me to do such and I will always obey the Lord. Now He has directed me to destroy this despoiler of virgins, this fornicator, this evil liver, who now stands before his Maker. He will be judged for what he is, and the fires of Hell await him. The man Njuba has been wrongly accused. He had murder in his heart. He had his reasons. I and I alone destroyed this wicked sinner. I am the messenger of the Lord, and now that my work is done, I take my leave of this world and go to that place of glory which awaits me."

The congregation listened spellbound to this

peroration. And when it was over, Piet Schreiner took up a gun and shot himself.

THE RELIEF OF KIMBERLEY did not mean that the war was over, and the euphoria began to evaporate fairly soon. The comfort of being able to walk about the streets without fear of sudden death and the fact that food was not growing more and more scarce had ceased to be such a great delight to us. The country was still in the throes of war, and a victory here and there was not going to deter the Boers. They were a persistent people. Not unaccustomed to hardship, they believed they were fighting for their homeland and were determined to hold out.

They were fully aware that their army was inferior to that of the British, but that did not prevent their forming into guerrilla bands which attacked the British Army quarters and the lines of communication which were essential to bringing the war to a conclusion.

So the expected peace was delayed.

However, our siege was over; we tried to return to normal life as far as possible and the pupils came back to school.

I went to Riebeeck House frequently, in

spite of the fact that I had to meet Mrs. Prost which was an embarrassment to me. She had been deeply distressed by the death of Roger Lestrange. The revelation that the dead boy had been clutching a button from one of his coats had shocked everyone profoundly. Njuba had taken the coat and it was unmistakable evidence. Then there was the accusation that he was the father of Greta Schreiner's child. Roger Lestrange had been a hero in Mrs. Prost's eyes and no doubt she would want to think that another man had been the father of Greta's child. But she could hardly condone the murder of a helpless child.

As for Myra, she was prostrate for some days after the death of her husband, but gradually she began to rouse herself. She took Njuba and Luban under her care. Njuba was very ill and in danger of losing his mind. I was amazed at the manner in which she and Luban helped each other at that time. Paul was with her a great deal. He had been fond of Umgala. He told me afterwards that the boy had been trying to tell him something, but he could not discover what, and Umgala must have tried to do so through the figures. If he had been quicker to comprehend there would not have been any need for Umgala to make the figures and, presumably, be caught putting them in the Model House, and so meet his death.

Both he and Myra had need of each other at that time.

I used to lie in bed at night going over the dramatic events of the last months, and I would brood on our conjecture that Roger Lestrange had planned to use me. There was little doubt in my mind that he had planned to murder Myra and he would have succeeded but for the turn of events, for if the town had not been besieged he would have been able to come back and complete his work.

I would let my mind run on and imagine Mrs. Prost perhaps going into Myra's room and finding her dead . . . poisoned by some insect. But would there have been an enquiry? Would they have discovered that the tonic was poisoned? And if her husband was suspected . . . he would produce his trump card . . . all ready to play. Diana Grey was in fact Davina Glentyre. She had been with the deceased a great deal during that time when she was taking the tonic. She had stayed in the house. A handkerchief was found under Mr. Lestrange's bed which suggested that she was a visitor to his room. Mr. Lestrange had helped her a great deal. Did she have hopes of marriage? In which case there was a motive and Davina Glentyre had stood trial for the murder of her father who had once stood in her way.

I would sweat with fear . . . imagining the courtroom. The only difference would be that this one would be in Kimberley instead of Edinburgh. But it did not happen, I kept telling myself. You were saved from that . . . by the war. But I could not stop thinking of what might have been.

I said to myself, you were in danger . . . because of what happened before. There is no escape from the past. It has followed you here. He brought you here because of it. He planned to murder her and if necessary shift the blame to you, but now he cannot harm you. But people know of the past. There is no escape from it.

We had news now of what was going on. Johannesburg and Pretoria were now in the hands of the British, but de Wet and de la Rey, with their bands of commandos, were harrying the Army everywhere. Kitchener was growing impatient with the Boers who would not accept defeat. He was following a scorched earth policy, setting fire to those farms which he believed harboured guerrillas; he was setting up concentration camps in which he imprisoned any suspects. But resistance continued; the Boers were as determined as ever; and the war went on.

It was afternoon. The children were leaving after their lessons and Lilias and I were putting the books away when there was a knock on the door.

I went to open it. A man was standing there. I stared at him. I thought I must be dreaming.

He said: "This must be something of a surprise."

"Ninian!" I cried.

Lilias had come out. She was as dumbfounded as I was.

"Is it really . . . ?" she stammered.

As he stepped into the hall, I felt an overwhelming joy take possession of me.

HE SAT IN THE LITTLE ROOM near the schoolroom and told us how difficult it had been to get here.

"All the formalities . . . all the ships carrying troops. I managed, though . . . pleading an important case for a very special client."

"A client? Then . . ."

"*You* are the client," he said.

Lilias made us a meal. She would not allow me to help.

She guessed, as I did, that Ninian wanted to be alone with me. But I was still bewildered, marvelling at the fact that he was here.

I sensed that he had important things to say to me but was waiting for the appropriate moment, and Lilias announced the food was ready. She apologised for its simplicity.

"We are no longer in siege, but things are still a little difficult."

We talked about the siege and the news of the war. Ninian thought it could not last much longer. The Boers were outnumbered. If it had not been for the difficulties of the terrain they would not have had a chance in the first place . . . and so on.

I was aware of his impatience . . . which I shared. I wanted to know what it was which had made him undertake such a journey in wartime.

Lilias was very perceptive and as soon as the

meal was over she said she had to go and see John Dale. Would we forgive her if she went?

As soon as she had gone, Ninian said: "I know she is in your confidence and that you are great friends, but I did feel that what I have to say is for you alone."

"I want so much to hear," I told him.

"You know I was very uneasy about your coming out here, and when I heard that Lestrange had paid for the cabin and befriended you . . . and that you were seeing a great deal of his wife who was very ill . . . I began to get more and more disturbed."

"You know that he is dead?"

"Dead?" He looked at me blankly and I explained.

He put his hand to his head. "Then you are safe," he said. "That explains so much. I was right. Oh, what a lucky escape you have had!"

"Tell me what you know."

"It's damning against him. I thought I recognised his face, but it didn't come to me until after you'd sailed. I just could not remember where I had seen that face before. The fact of the matter is that the man was a murderer . . . the worst sort. Not the man who kills in the heat of passion . . . or from sense of injustice . . . but in cold blood . . . for the lust for money. He killed two women whom he married for their money, and was planning this third crime . . . Myra Ellington. How is she?"

"She is well now. She has been very ill. But Roger Lestrange went away before the siege and was unable to get back." I explained about the tonic.

He breathed deeply. "Thank God that you broke the bottle, or it might have been too late. Let me tell you more of this man. The reason I was suspicious about him was that there was a case in Australia. It came to my notice because there was a lawsuit about money. It brought out one of the finer points of law, and as you know, we keep records of that sort of thing. A man named George Manton went out to Australia from England. There he married a wealthy young heiress and within nine months of the marriage she was dead through drowning. Her fortune passed to her husband of a few months: George Manton. It appeared that some years after his wife's death, the heiress's father had travelled to England. His daughter was then four years old. While he was in England he married again; the marriage was unsuccessful and the couple agreed to part—the husband returning to Australia, the wife remaining in England. But there was a son of that marriage and this son in due course claimed his share of his father's fortune. The case was tried out in both the English and Australian courts; and during it a picture of George Manton was published. That is when I saw it. But it was not until after you had left that I remembered the case and looked up the relevant papers. When I heard that Myra was ill I was very alarmed. You remember, I wrote to you, telling you you must come home."

"I thought that was because war was imminent."

"It was . . . but there was this as well . . . and there was another reason."

"What was that?"

"A personal one. I will talk to you about that later. I had a strong feeling that you might be in acute danger."

"Lilias and I have thought that I might have been. But tell me first about this wife in Australia."

"In your letter you mentioned that he had had a wife who died through falling down stairs. It was too much of a coincidence. One wife drowned in Australia shortly after marriage, another falling down the stairs, and the third . . . very ill . . . doubtless being poisoned. He was varying in his methods. And then . . . he had taken great pains to get you out here."

I told him about the handkerchief and Mrs. Prost.

He was shocked. "I don't think there can be any doubt," he said. "What an escape!"

"I believe he killed a little native boy who must have seen him push his wife down the stairs. The child was both deaf and dumb. He was often in the house. Nobody took much notice of him. His mother worked there. He made carved figures which he put in the Model House. I must tell you about that. I discovered it in one of the dilapidated rondavels where I saw wood chippings. Roger Lestrange must have found out the boy did them. Perhaps he caught him in the house . . . putting that figure there. Then he would have guessed that the boy knew something. It is all falling into place and it is horrible."

"You should never have come here, Davina."

"I know now."

"I cannot forgive myself for introducing you to that Society."

"It seemed a good idea at the time and we might have gone to Australia or America which was what we planned in the beginning."

"As soon as I had suggested it I was furious with myself. But you wanted to get away."

"I thought it was the answer. I now know that there is no safe escape. As you see . . ."

He nodded.

"I tried to get out here before."

"You have come all this way . . . ?"

He smiled at me. "Yes, I have come all this way. It is miraculous that everything turned out as it did. It could have been so different."

"I am sure he was going to suggest that I hoped to marry him and therefore removed his wife."

"He was probably hoping that he would get away with it, as he had on two other occasions. Perhaps he thought that the second time in the same house might have aroused suspicions . . . even though he had used different methods. It seems reasonable to suppose it was a good idea to have you standing by, as an escape route for him, if anything went wrong.

He would, of course, have hoped that it would not have been necessary to use you in that way, as the less fuss the better. But he wanted you at hand just in case you should be necessary."

"It is so cold-bloodedly calculated."

"He *was* calculating . . . cold-bloodedly so. How thankful I am that he was not able to carry out his diabolical schemes. He lived violently. It was rough justice that he should die so."

"Two people had marked him down for death: the father of the murdered boy was so upset because someone killed him before he could."

"But we should be rejoicing, Davina. I could have come too late to save you."

"I don't think I could have gone through all that again. The court . . . the dock. It is the terrible stigma that I find so hard to bear."

He stood up and came to me. He drew me to my feet and put his arms about me. On impulse I clung to him.

"Thank you, Ninian," I said. "Thank you for coming."

"I could not forget you," he told me. "You haunted me. That verdict. Not Proven. They should have known you could not have done it."

"The evidence was there against me."

"That woman, Ellen Farley. They never found her, you know. She just disappeared. Why should she have disappeared? She could have come forward. Heaven knows, we tried hard enough to find her. Her evidence would have been so important."

"I can't forget that you came all this way."

"I felt a letter was not enough. I asked you to come home before. I knew it would be difficult to come, because of the war. But here I am."

"And that personal reason you were going to tell me?"

"I realised after you'd gone what it meant for me not to see you again. I knew then that I was in love with you."

"You . . . in love with me?"

"Couldn't you guess?"

"I knew you had taken a special interest in my case . . . but advocates have to be interested in their cases. I thought you were rather taken with my stepmother."

He smiled. "The enchanting Zillah!" he murmured. "I had a feeling that she knew more than she let us know. It was due to her that we got the verdict we did. She was a vital witness. But I still felt there was more. I wanted to find out what. That was why I cultivated her acquaintance. What I wanted more than anything was to get to the truth. I know what it feels like to come out of the courts Not Proven."

"Well, thank you, Ninian. You have been wonderful to me. You have helped me so much."

He shook his head.

"I have not done enough," he said. "I should have shown my devotion to you. I want you to know exactly how I feel. I love you and want you to come back to Scotland with me."

I stared at him in amazement.

"I want you to marry me," he added.

I thought I must have misunderstood.

"I have been hoping that you might care for me," he went on.

I was silent. I was too deeply moved for speech. I had longed to be with him. I remembered how his interest in Zillah had hurt me. When I had seen him standing at the door I could not believe my eyes. I could not get used to the idea that he had come all this way to see me.

Did I care for him? I had always cared for him. He it was who had drawn me from the slough of despond, who had sustained me with his determination to defend me. When I had left England, as I thought never to see him again, my desolation had been so deep that I had forced myself not to admit it. I had insisted to myself that my depression was due to the fact that I was leaving my native land. But it was not that so much as leaving Ninian.

I said: "I have never forgotten you."

He took my hands and kissed them. "In time," he said, "you could care for me."

"I don't need time," I told him. "I care for you now. The moment when I opened the door and saw you there was the happiest in my life."

He looked suddenly radiant. "Then you will come back . . . now. You will marry me . . . ?"

"Go back with you . . . to Edinburgh? You can't mean that!"

"But I do. It is the reason why I came here . . . to take you back with me. I intend that we shall never be parted again."

"You haven't thought of this seriously."

"Davina, for weeks I have thought of little else."

"But have you considered what this would mean?"

"I have considered it."

"You, a rising figure in law, married to someone who has been tried for murder . . . the case Not Proven . . ."

"Believe me, I have considered all that."

"It would be very bad for your career."

"To be with you will be the best thing that ever happened to me."

"I should have expected you to show more calm common sense."

"I am doing so. I know what I want and I am doing my best to get it."

"Oh, Ninian, how foolish you are, and how I love you for your folly! But it could not be. I should go back to Edinburgh . . . the place where it all happened. How could I? Everyone knows me there. It is bad enough here to be aware that Mrs. Prost knows who I am. But back there . . . they would all know. And if you married me . . . it would all be brought back. They would suspect me, Ninian. We have to face the truth. There will always be those who believe that I killed my father. It would ruin your career."

"If I couldn't stand up to that I don't deserve much of a career."

"I should prevent your rising. I could not do it, Ninian. But I shall never forget that you asked me."

He took me by the shoulders and shook me gently.

"Stop talking nonsense. We're going to do it. We're going to defy them all. I know that you love me . . . and I love you. That is at the root of the matter. The rest . . . well, we'll deal with that when the time comes."

"I couldn't let you. It's wonderful . . . it's quixotic . . . it's noble . . ."

He laughed. "It indulges my own wishes. I want to marry you. I shall never be happy again if you refuse me. Listen, Davina, there will be difficulties. I know that. There may be unpleasantness now and then. But we shall be together. We'll face it together . . . whatever it is. I want that, Davina, more than anything in the world. I cannot explain to you what these last months have been like for me. All the time I have been thinking of you in this place . . . here . . . under siege. It was more than I could endure. And then I learned about Roger Lestrange . . . I thought of his efforts to get you here. I could not imagine what his motives were. I had to come out here . . . I had to see you . . . I had to explain my feelings . . . and now I am not letting you go again. I am going to be with you for the rest of my life."

"It is wonderful to contemplate," I said sadly. "But it cannot be . . . I know . . ."

"You do not know. Whatever there is to face, it is better for us to face it together."

"But there is no need for you to face it at all. You should go back to Edinburgh . . . carry on your successful career . . . become Lord Justice . . ."

"Without you? Certainly not. I am going to sweep away all your excuses."

"But you know they are . . . sensible."

"Maybe, in some respects. But we are talking about love. Now, Davina, will you marry me?"

"I want to say yes . . . more than anything I want to."

"Then that is enough."

So I gave myself up to dreaming.

Lilias returned with John Dale. There had

to be introductions and explanations. There was a great deal of talk about the war and the feeling about it home in Britain.

Ninian said there were some enthusiastic and some dissenting voices. But there was always great rejoicing at the victories; and Kitchener and Roberts were the heroes of the day. He explained the difficulties of travel in wartime and how he had been trying some time to get a passage.

The men left together—John Dale to his home and Ninian to his hotel. He said he would see me tomorrow morning. There was a great deal to discuss.

When they had gone Lilias looked at me questioningly.

"That was a surprise," she said. "He's come out here to see a client. What does that mean? He's come out here to see you, hasn't he?"

"Yes," I said. "He has confirmed a great deal of what we thought about Roger Lestrange. He had another wife in Australia who died by drowning."

Lilias stared at me.

"And," I went on, "I think our theory about what my role was to be in his scheme was the correct one."

She closed her eyes and clenched her hands together.

"What an escape!" she murmured. "So Ninian found this out."

"Yes, there was some court case over his first wife's money and Ninian had some records."

"So he thought you might be in danger. It was a long way to come. I suppose he thought he'd defend you . . . if necessary."

"He has asked me to marry him."

"I see. And . . . ?"

"How could I accept? How could I go back to Edinburgh . . . his wife? It would ruin his career."

"Well?"

"Lilias, how could I accept?"

"He's asked you. My goodness, he's come right here to tell you this. That gives you some idea of the depth of his feelings, doesn't it?"

"Yes," I said happily. "It does. But all the same, I can't accept."

"Yes, you can," she said. "And you will."

How could I help this feeling of intense happiness which had gripped me? I could not suppress my true feelings. I was happy. Ninian loved me. He had come all this way at this most difficult time because he feared I was in danger.

What could I do? I could never escape from my past . . . nor would Ninian, if he shared it. He knew this. None could know it better. And yet he chose it . . . it was what he wanted.

So I was going home.

Ninian was making plans. We were to be married in Kimberley. Then we would travel home together as husband and wife.

There was no point in delay. The journey home might be long and difficult. We should have to get to Cape Town and wait for a ship. But we knew where we were going and it did not matter as long as we were together.

I had wondered about leaving Lilias, but everything seemed to be working out neatly. With one wedding in view it seemed only natural that there should be another. I had known for a long time that there had been a special relationship between Lilias and John Dale. He asked her to marry him—and how delighted I was when I heard the news.

There would be two marriages on the same

day which would be appropriate as we had come out together.

Myra was sad at the prospect of my going. She did not know everything about her husband. We did not speak of him. The murder of the deaf-mute was revealing, for there was the indisputable evidence of the button from one of Roger Lestrange's coats to prove the case against him. Umgala had obviously witnessed the crime and was attempting to reveal what he knew—so he had had to die. And now Roger himself was dead and Myra was no longer a wife. She had been fascinated completely by her husband—but at the same time she had been fearful of him. She could not be aware that she had come close to death herself.

But we did not speak of it. She had been bemused and bewildered, but gradually she seemed to realise that she must start a new life. Strangely enough she turned to Paul. Together they made Njuba their concern. They looked after him and Luban and it brought them close together.

I had thought she might want to come back with me and for a time I think she considered doing so. But as her new relationship with

Paul began to ripen they both decided that he would be better if he stayed in his native land; and she decided to stay with him.

So Ninian and I were married, and in due course we were able to set sail for England.

Edinburgh

Proven

I HAD NEVER BEEN SO HAPPY in my life as I was during those first months after I became Davina Grainger. There was a tacit agreement between us that we should not think beyond the immediate future.

Ninian knew as well as I did that when we reached Edinburgh there would be certain difficulties to be faced; but for the time being we must forget about them.

This we did very successfully. We were close companions by day and passionate lovers by night. It was an idyllic existence, if one did not look ahead.

But, of course, it was impossible not to and there were moments when I thought with apprehension of what it would be like when we returned home. People would remember and, even if they had the good manners not to speak of it, it would be in their minds. We must be prepared for the little moments of unpleasantness . . . the moments of distress.

All the difficulties of travel at such a time became amusing to us because we were together. We laughed at them.

We managed to get down to Cape Town where we spent a week waiting for a ship; and when it did come, we had a wonderful voyage home. The storms at sea were fun to us; and we revelled in the long hot days when we sat on deck and talked of our good fortune in being together. But as we came nearer to home, I felt I wanted to hold back the days to make them last longer. I knew that Ninian felt the same. But there was no holding back time, but I kept reminding myself that I was going back with Ninian and that made all the difference.

We arrived in due course at Southampton, said goodbye to the friends we had made on board and spent a night in London before making the long journey to Edinburgh.

The city looked cold and unwelcoming. Ninian had lived with his parents, but now that we were married he would buy our own house. It would be near the courts for convenience. But at first we must go to his home where we should stay until we found our house.

I felt uneasy about meeting his parents, and as soon as I did I realised they did not approve of the marriage.

Mrs. Grainger was a gentle lady with greying hair and bright dark eyes. His father was not unlike Ninian himself, tall, of rather commanding appearance, with an aquiline nose and bright shrewd blue eyes.

"Ninian, how wonderful that you are back," said Mrs. Grainger. "And this is Davina . . ."

She had taken my hands and was kissing me on the cheek, then looking at me, trying to hide the fact that she was assessing me. But of course she would, I told myself. I was her new daughter-in-law. Naturally she would sum me up. I must stop thinking that when people met me they immediately asked themselves: did she or did she not kill her father?

Mr. Grainger was less inclined, or less able, to hide his feelings. His attitude towards me was cool. It was clear to me that he thought his son was foolish in marrying me.

I tried to be reasonable. Their reaction was natural. Of course, they were disappointed.

Mr. Grainger, Senior, had risen high in his profession and he would wish his son to do the same; and none could realise more than I that I should be a hindrance rather than a help in his career.

Ninian assured me again and again that his parents would grow accustomed to the marriage. People always regarded their offspring as children throughout their lives. The fact was they objected to his marriage . . . not to me.

I could not expect them to be pleased that their son had married a woman who had been on trial for murder and was only free because the case had not been proved against her. What parents would? I understood them thoroughly, and I knew that the halcyon days were over.

Ninian said: "We'll soon find our house."

And I thought, we must.

Ninian's parents entertained frequently and most of their guests were connected with the law. They were all extremely well-bred and, although they would have been well acquainted with my case, they took pains not to mention anything that might lead to it. Indeed, there were times when they seemed to make studied efforts to avoid it, for they often discussed cases which were of particular interest to their profession.

But there was one occasion when an old friend and his wife, whose daughter and her husband had recently come home from India, came to dine and brought the daughter and her husband with them.

The conversation was mainly about some new statute which had recently come into force and the company was expressing views for and against it.

The young woman said: "All these laws about stuffy old cases which no one is interested in . . ."

"My dear," interrupted her father. "This matter has engendered tremendous interest throughout the profession."

She replied: "Well, *I* think it's boring. You ought to tell us about some of your more interesting cases. Murder, for instance. You must have had some of those."

Silence across the table. I found myself staring at my plate.

"I was very interested in what the Lord Chief Justice was saying," began Ninian's father.

"Like Madeleine Smith," went on the young woman. "Do you remember that case? Oh, it was ages ago. She got off . . . though I'm sure she did it. Not Proven, they said. Is it true that they have that verdict only in the Scottish courts? They say she went to the United States of America to start a new life. It's the only thing she could have done really . . ."

I felt the embarrassment round the table. The girl who had spoken was, I supposed, the only one who did not know who I was.

The subject was immediately changed. She looked bewildered. It must have been clear to her that she had said something indiscreet. I was sure that afterwards she would be told who was present.

I felt very upset about that. When we were alone, Ninian tried to comfort me. But it was not easy.

"You should never have married me," I said. "This sort of thing should never have happened to you. You have been drawn into it. And it will go on for ever. It will be there all our lives."

"No . . . no . . . people will forget."

"She didn't forget Madeleine Smith and that must be nearly fifty years ago."

"That was a notorious case."

"So was mine, Ninian."

"We'll get our own house."

"People will still talk."

"If only we were not here . . . in the city."

"It would be the same wherever I was. I couldn't escape in Kimberley."

Ninian tried to shrug it off, but I could see that he was as upset as I was.

I suppose that was why he decided on the house the very next day.

It was a pleasant house in one of the squares of grey stone houses. We were close to Princes Street and, in spite of everything there to remind me, I could still find pleasure in it. I passed the garden and thought of Jamie, and Zillah who had found us there.

When we told Ninian's parents that we had found a house which would suit us, they could not hide their relief; and I felt that the shadow which was overhanging my life was spoiling Ninian's, too.

The house was not very far from my father's, where I had spent my childhood, where the terrible tragedy had happened. I could not bring myself to call on Zillah, which would have meant going back there. I wondered if the Kirkwells and the Vospers were still there; and I asked myself if Zillah would have heard that I was in Edinburgh.

We moved into the house and I felt a little better. Shortly afterwards I discovered that I was pregnant.

That made a great deal of difference. I stopped brooding and ceased to think that everyone was remembering. My joy was intense; so was Ninian's. Even his parents softened towards me. They were delighted at the prospect of a grandchild.

One day I received a note. It came by hand. It looked like Zillah's handwriting, but it was slightly less bold than it used to be; and when I opened it I found that it was from her.

My dear Davina,

I believe that you have reverted to your true name now, and I hear that you are in Edinburgh. My dear child, why did you not come to see me?

Things have not gone very well with me. I am wretchedly ill. It smote me suddenly and here I am . . . more or less an invalid. I don't know how these things happen. I was hale and hearty one day and ill the next. It is very annoying. I just had a horrid cough at first, which I could not shake off. It's consumption, they tell me. It's a bore. I sometimes feel quite ill and at others my jaunty self. I make plans and then can't act on them.

Do come if you can bear with a poor invalid.

My love as always,

ZILLAH

After receiving such a note there was nothing I could do but call immediately, though I had to steel myself to do it.

Mrs. Kirkwell opened the door. I guessed she had been warned that I was coming.

"Oh, good afternoon, Mrs. Grainger," she said. "It's nice to see you again."

"Good afternoon, Mrs. Kirkwell. How are you?"

"As well as can be expected, thank you."

"And Mr. Kirkwell?"

"He's all right. And you look just the same. My word, you did get caught up in that awful place. Siege, don't they call it? You should have seen the people in the streets when we heard it was relieved. Mafeking and Ladysmith, too. Mr. Kirkwell knows all about it. He was watching for news all the time and telling us what was going on. And of course

. . . you being there . . . well, we wanted to know. I couldn't get it out of my mind, our Miss Davina out there with all them savages."

"They weren't savages, Mrs. Kirkwell."

"Well, near enough . . . foreigners. And you shut up in that place . . . And I remember you when you was a little thing no higher than my knee . . . and then to be stuck in that place. Mrs. Glentyre is waiting for you."

"Is she very ill, Mrs. Kirkwell?"

"Up and down. She's right as a trivet one day. You'd never guess. Of course, she passes it off. Last person you'd have thought would get caught like that. She's that pleased you're coming to see her. I'll take you right up. That was her orders."

I went up the familiar stairs to the familiar room.

She was sitting in a chair by the window. I was amazed at the sight of her. She was so much thinner, but her hair was as bright as ever, but somehow it did not match her rather gaunt face.

I went to her and took her hands in mine.

"Oh, Davina . . . my sweet Davina. It was wonderful of you to come."

"I'd have come before if I had known."

"Just because I'm a poor old thing?"

I said: "It was difficult for me to come back here. I'm afraid I put it off."

She nodded. "So you married your Mr. Grainger. How is that going?"

"Very well."

"He was always asking questions. And then he went out and brought you home. News travels in a town like this. My word! That was something! Shows how keen he was to get you. And at one time I thought he was interested in me! But I realised it was just because he wanted to probe. He's a real old prober. I soon got his measure. But it *is* good to see you. Tell me about the awful time you must have had. Shut in like that . . . not much to eat, I suppose . . . living on what you could get." She shivered. "We heard a lot about it here, you know. I'll not forget Mafeking night in a hurry. The noise in the streets! It went on all night. And I thought of you out there. It is good to see you."

"Tell me about yourself, Zillah."

"Oh, things didn't turn out as I thought they would. I had plans. I was going to have a house in London. I was going abroad. I was going to enjoy life. All planned, it was, and then, suddenly, I got this cough. Just a nuisance at first. Then I couldn't get rid of it. The doctor shook his head and wanted examinations. So I had them and they found this. I reckon I picked it up in those draughty old digs when I was with the Jolly Red Heads."

"I'm so sorry, Zillah. It is the last thing I would have expected of you. So you have to stay quiet, do you?"

"Don't only have to, want to sometimes. I have my down days and my up days. Sometimes I feel . . . almost well. I make the most of that."

"Everything else seems more or less the same here. Mrs. Kirkwell is just as ever."

"She's like an old monument . . . she and her old man. I never forget them when I first came here. What a long time ago that seems, Davina!"

"I remember it well. I thought I had never seen anyone less like a governess than you."

"You always paid nice compliments, dear. And to think that you once thought of becoming one! What happened about that old school?"

I told her and that Lilias was now married.

"You both found husbands. It can't be such a boring old profession, after all."

"So did you," I said.

For a moment we were both sober.

"And the servants here?" I asked.

"The girls left. There are new ones now. Only the Kirkwells stayed."

"And the Vospers?"

"They're not here. I've got Baines now. Baines and Mrs. In the mews, of course. She helps in the house; he's a good steady man. Not that I use the carriage so much nowadays."

"What happened to the Vospers?"

"Oh, they shot up in the world. Hamish did anyway. He's in the horse racing business . . . or something like that. Making money, so I hear."

"He always had such a good opinion of himself!"

"Apparently he has made other people have one, too."

"Do you ever see him?"

"Now and then. He comes to see the Kirkwells. I think he likes to show off his affluence to them and remember the old days."

"Did you ever hear any more of Ellen Farley?"

"Ellen Farley? Oh . . ."

"You remember, she used to work here. She was the one they tried to find at the time . . . of the trial."

"That's right. Ellen Farley, the one who disappeared into the blue."

"Ninian used to say that if we could have found her she could have corroborated my story . . . you know . . . that she asked me to buy that stuff."

She leaned forward and laid a thin white hand over mine.

"Don't think about it, dear," she said. "It's all over and done with. That's what I tell myself. Doesn't do any good to go over it."

"It's not all over for me, Zillah. It never will be. All through my life, I shall be waiting for someone to remind me and to wonder whether I was really guilty."

"Oh no. It's all done with. People forget."

"I wish they did."

"What a morbid subject! Your Ninian is charming, isn't he? I thought so. He truly loves you, doesn't he? Be thankful for that, and you wouldn't have known him if . . .

that hadn't happened. That's a consolation, isn't it? He must love you a lot, mustn't he, or he wouldn't have gone all the way out to South Africa to find you, would he?"

"No, he would not."

"Well, that's nice. Think of that and not the other."

"I try. And there is something I want to tell you, Zillah. I'm going to have a baby."

"Really? Isn't that the most wonderful news! You must bring the baby to see me."

"It's not due just yet."

"I can't wait. I'm going to live long enough to see it."

"What do you mean?"

"Nothing. Just talking nonsense. It's this old cough. It gets at me sometimes. I'm ever so pleased to see you happy, and I'm pleased you're going to have this baby. Won't Ninian be pleased!"

"He's very pleased."

"And so am I. I'm glad it all turned out right for you."

Being with her was exhilarating, and talking to her I forgot, temporarily, that physically at least she was just a shadow of what she had once been.

. . .

I RECEIVED A LETTER from Lilias' sister Jane. She hoped that I would come and stay with them for a few days. She was longing to hear firsthand news of Lilias and to see me, of course. Perhaps I could come with my husband? We should be very welcome.

I could understand their anxiety to get news of Lilias from someone who had been with her during the siege, and I decided that I must go before I was too advanced in pregnancy.

An opportunity came. Ninian had to go to London on business. He would have taken me with him, but I thought it would be a good idea if I spent a few days at the vicarage while he was in London. We could travel down together and I could go on to Devon.

I had to tell Jane every detail I could remember, beginning with the voyage out and right through to the siege and our marriages. She and her father listened intently, now and then asking a question.

They were very interested in John Dale naturally, and I told them what an admirable young man he was and how he and Lilias were devoted to each other. The vicar's eyes were bright with unshed tears and Jane unashamedly allowed one or two of hers to escape.

"When things have quietened down," I said, "she will want you to go and pay her a visit. Perhaps she will come to see you."

"We will manage to go and see her," said Jane firmly to her father.

I had to tell them more of the siege, more of our first impressions. The talk flowed on until it was time to retire for the night.

The next day there was a message from Mrs. Ellington. She had heard that I was at the vicarage and begged me to come and see her before I left. She wanted to hear news of Myra.

So I went.

"She was so distressed," she said, "at the death of dear Roger. Shot by some madman." I guessed she did not know all the full story and it was not my place to enlighten her.

Poor Myra. She wondered she did not come home.

I said: "Myra is making a home for herself over there. She seemed to be settling. You see, there is Paul."

"Dear Roger's son. He did tell us of him."

Still I did not explain. There was no need for her to have even a glimmer of the truth.

"He's not very old," I said. "He needs someone to care for him."

"I understand. But it would be better for Myra to bring him back. I would look after Roger's son. He could be brought up here . . . so much better for him."

"You see, that is his home. He was born there."

"But it would be so much better for him to be here."

It was not much use contesting Mrs. Ellington's opinions, but I persevered.

"It is quite a large house to run and Myra enjoys doing that. She has adjusted herself to it and her main concern at this time is the boy. He is helping her to grow away from her tragedy. She has had a terrible shock."

"And all those people daring to rebel . . . and her being in the middle of it."

"You mean the Boers."

"I should have thought that war should be over by now. People are saying it cannot be long now."

She asked a great many questions and I was able to satisfy her curiosity to some extent,

and I think when I left she was a little reconciled to Myra's absence.

She thanked me for coming and hoped I
would find time to do so again before I left.
She added that she would insist on Myra's
coming home for a visit and they would go on
from there.

As I went out I saw Kitty. I fancied she had
been waiting for me.

"Hello, Kitty," I said. "How are you?"

"Married now, Miss. I married Charlie who
works in the stables. We live over the stables.
I've got a little baby."

"Oh, Kitty, that's wonderful."

"Miss Davina . . . there's something I
ought to tell you. It's been on my mind ever
since."

"What is it, Kitty?"

She bit her lips and looked over her shoulder.

I said: "Could you come over to the vicarage and see me? I shall be there for another
two days."

"Yes, Miss. When?"

"Tomorrow afternoon?"

"Oh yes, Miss. I could come then."

"It's very nice to see you, Kitty. I'm glad about the baby. That must be wonderful."

"She's a lovely little girl."

"I must see her before I go."

The next afternoon, she came to the vicarage. I told Jane that she was coming and wished to tell me something, so Jane left us to ourselves in the little room where the vicar saw his parishioners.

Kitty began by saying: "It's been on my mind because Miss Lilias did say not to mention it . . . and I promised I wouldn't . . ."

"What?"

She bit her lips and continued to hesitate. Then she said: "It was when you fell off your horse that time . . ."

"I remember. You called out my name."

"That was it. 'Miss Davina,' I said. I could have killed myself as soon as I said it, but it sort of slipped out. I thought that horse was going to drag you along. That would have been terrible."

"I understand how it happened."

"Well, Mr. Lestrange was there . . . and he heard."

"Yes. I had thought he might have done."

"He was a lovely gentleman . . . ever so

kind, he was. Always a word and a smile. Mind you, since Charlie I've never . . . you know what I mean. I wouldn't want anything to go wrong between Charlie and me. I've never looked at nobody since."

"But you . . . looked at Mr. Lestrange?"

My mind switched back to the courtyard before the schoolhouse and Greta Schreiner smiling up at him. I had been reminded then of Kitty. I thought: so he had beguiled Kitty, too . . . beguiled her so that he might get information from her about me. Kitty was physically attractive, with that attraction, as Lilias had once remarked, of a girl who can't say no. What was it? A sort of promise, an assurance of a speedy seduction?

"He asked a lot of questions about you and it just sort of slipped out . . . all about how your father died and they'd accused you."

"I see."

"I did tell him that I'd seen your picture in the paper . . . twice, I did. I cut it out and got one of the men who could read to read it to me. I kept the papers . . . and . . . well, him being so interested . . . I showed them to him. He took them and said he'd like to read them sometime. He never gave them back to me. I'm ever so sorry. As soon as I'd done it I knew I shouldn't have. But he was such a nice gentleman, I knew it wouldn't do no harm with him knowing . . . It didn't, did it? He was always ever so nice to you."

I said nothing. I just sat there listening.

"I knew it was all right, but you see I'd said I wouldn't say anything and I just did. He was the sort who could get anything from a girl if he wanted to. And you and Miss Lilias had been so good to me . . ."

I said: "It's all right, Kitty. It's over now. He's dead."

"Yes, I heard. I was ever so shocked. A lovely man like that."

"You don't want to think of lovely men anymore, Kitty . . . except, of course, Charlie."

She hunched her shoulders like a child and smiled.

"Oh, I'm glad it's all right," she said. "I've had it on my mind ever since."

I asked about the baby and Charlie and I walked back with her to the stable quarters to see the child. I told her I was expecting one. Her eyes lit up with pleasure. Kitty was a good girl at heart, and I knew it was as though a great burden had dropped from her shoulders.

She had really been very upset because she had betrayed a confidence. But now she had confessed and had been forgiven.

I RETURNED to Edinburgh and was happy during the months that followed. I could think of little but the coming of the baby. While I was able, I visited Zillah frequently. I was surprised at her interest in the coming child.

Once, when I was coming away from the house, I met Hamish Vosper. He was flashily dressed in a brown check suit and wore a carnation in his buttonhole. With an exaggerated gesture he swept off his hat to greet me and I noticed his black hair glistening with pomade.

"Why, if it isn't Miss Davina! My word, you look in the pink of health!" His eyes assessed me with something like amusement, I thought.

"Thank you," I said.

"All going well?" he went on.

"Very well."

"That makes two of us." He winked.

"I see you are very prosperous."

He slapped his thigh with an exaggerated gesture. "Can't deny it. Can't deny it."

"Well, good day."

I was glad to escape. I found him as repulsive as when he had sat in the kitchen watching the maids slyly while he pulled at the long black hair on his arms.

MY SON WAS BORN in the May of that year 1902—in the same month that the war with South Africa was finally over and the Peace of Vereeniging was signed, depriving the Boers of their independence.

I wondered how Lilias was getting on. There would be tremendous relief out there, I was sure.

My days were taken up with my son. We called him Stephen after Ninian's father who, with his wife, was so delighted with this grandson that I was sure they almost forgave me for being who I was.

As for myself, I could forget, at this time, all that had gone before.

I took the child to see Zillah. She was delighted. It had never occurred to me that she would have much time to spare for children. Her illness had changed her. In the past she had seemed to be straining for excitement, looking for adventure; now she seemed almost reconciled at times.

I was happier than I had thought possible,

for I could not regret anything which had brought me to this state. I remembered Zillah's saying that if that nightmare had not come to pass, I should not have met Ninian. Stephen would not have existed.

I wrote to Lilias telling her about the wonder child and, now that the war was over, I heard from her. She was expecting a child. The bond between us seemed stronger than ever. We had both come through tragic times together and both found happiness.

Happiness was sometimes fragile; but now I had Ninian and my baby, I felt secure.

The months passed. Stephen was beginning to smile, then to crawl, and then to take notice. He liked Zillah. He would sit on her lap and gaze at her. He was quite fascinated by her red hair. She still took a great deal of pains with her appearance. Her skin was delicately tinted, her eyes bright under her darkened brows. Sometimes I thought she could not be so very ill—except that she was thin.

One day there was news which startled us. Hamish Vosper had been killed in a fight by a rival. There was a hint of something called the Edinburgh Mafia.

It was revealed that for some time there had

been trouble between two rival gangs, both engaged in nefarious practices, and that Hamish Vosper, who was the leader of one, had been killed by the other. Such men, said the press, were a disgrace to the fair city of Edinburgh.

They were suspected not only of deciding which horses were allowed to win races, by the use of drugs so that they could back the outsider winners, but many other crimes.

"We want no such gang rule in Edinburgh," wrote one commentator. "The death of Hamish Vosper is rough justice on one of our ignoble citizens."

I went to see Zillah when I heard the news. Mrs. Kirkwell received me in a mood of subdued triumph.

"I always knew that Hamish Vosper would come to a bad end," she said. "I don't want to speak ill of the dead, but the master ought to have got rid of him years ago when he was caught with that maid. Well, I've seen something like this coming. I said to Kirkwell, 'He's up to no good, mark my words. There he was in his fancy clothes, throwing his weight about. Ah,' I said to Kirkwell. 'He's up to no good, mark my words.' It's terrible to think that he was here . . . one of us, you might say . . . though never really that. And then after you'd gone . . . he used to come here . . . even going up to see Mrs. Glentyre. I never could understand why she allowed it."

I went up to Zillah. She was looking better. I thought, something has happened.

She said: "I feel fine today. Just like my old self."

"You certainly look it. Have you read the newspapers today?"

"Why yes. You're thinking about Hamish."

"It's rather shocking . . . particularly as he was here and we knew him."

"Yes."

"I never liked him . . . but to think of him . . . dead . . ."

"These things happen. It seemed he was living dangerously, and when you do that you can't be surprised if you come to a bad end."

"Had you any idea . . . ?"

"Well . . . yes . . . I guessed he was up to no good. He was that sort. He was dabbling in all sorts of things . . . playing with fire, you might say. Well, he got burned."

"You must have seen him quite recently. I met him here not long ago."

"He used to come to the house. He wanted

the Kirkwells to see how he'd got on. Foolish man. A lesson to us all, Davina."

I was surprised at her attitude. But then Zillah had always surprised me.

Ninian's comment was: "Gang warfare. This sort of thing has been going on in some places for years. It's not what one would expect in Edinburgh. But it is an indication that it can happen anywhere. Let's hope that will be the end of it . . . here at least."

ZILLAH CONTINUED TO IMPROVE. She was quite lighthearted. I was seeing more of her, for she so enjoyed having Stephen with her.

I vividly remember one conversation I had with her at that time. Stephen was playing in a corner and we were both watching him.

Zillah said suddenly: "He's the most adorable child. I never thought I should want children. But, do you know, when I see him I think of what I have missed."

"Perhaps you'll marry again."

She smiled at me ironically. "It's a bit late in the day to think about that."

"One never knows. You are so much better. You could be cured. You're not old and you are very beautiful."

She laughed quite lightheartedly.

Then I said: "I worry about Stephen sometimes."

"Worry? There's nothing wrong with him, is there?"

"Oh no. He's in perfect health. I just think that someone might say something."

"Say what?"

"Someone might remember. It might come out that his mother stood trial for murder . . . and what the verdict was."

"That's all over and done with."

"Not as far as I am concerned, Zillah. It will always be there. How would one feel to learn that one's mother might have been a murderess?"

"Stephen would never think that."

"How could he help it? The question is there and always will be."

"It's a morbid thought."

"But it is the truth, Zillah."

"People are going to forget . . . by the time he grows up."

"There could be some to remember. Not long ago someone referred to Madeleine Smith, and that happened fifty years ago."

"It was a very famous case."

"Mine was very well-known."

"You must stop worrying about it. Stephen is going to be all right."

She spoke with conviction, but I could see that my words had made her very thoughtful. She knew that what I had said was true.

I told her the truth about Roger Lestrange then; how, through Kitty, he had discovered who I was; how he had the newspaper cuttings of my trial; how he was going to use me, if need be, to indicate that I was an unconvicted murderess who might be ready to try the same methods again.

She was deeply shocked. "It's hard to believe . . ." she whispered.

"Nevertheless it's true. Now you see what I mean? It will be there as long as I live."

She was silent for a few moments, staring blankly before her. Then she reached for my hand and pressed it firmly.

She said slowly: "You must stop worrying about it. You're going to be all right. Stephen is going to be all right."

I CALLED ON ZILLAH and, to my surprise, Mrs. Kirkwell said she had gone out.

Mrs. Kirkwell's lips were pursed disapprovingly.

"She's not fit," she went on. "I told her so. 'You must be mad to think of going out, Mrs. Glentyre,' I said. She was well wrapped up, but she looked far from well . . . and she's so thin. You notice it in her outdoor clothes."

"Why should she go out? She hasn't been out for some weeks, has she?"

"Only when she gets this letter. That's the only time she goes out."

"She had a letter then?"

"Yes. It comes now and then. And then she always insists on going out."

"I hope she'll be all right. Of course, she's seemed better these last days."

"That's true. But I'm worried about her. I wished you'd come earlier, Mrs. Grainger, then you might have gone with her."

"You've no idea where she's gone?"

"Well, as a matter of fact I have. I happened to hear her give orders to the cabby. That's another thing. I said, 'Why shouldn't Baines take you?' and she said she wouldn't bother him. And there he is, hardly ever taking the carriage out."

"That's strange. Perhaps she wasn't going far."

"It's to a place called the Coven."

"The Coven? Isn't that the little tea shop in Walter Street?"

"That's it. Little place not been open long. I'm really worried about her. She seemed a bit shaky."

"I see," I said.

I came out of the house and walked to Princes Street.

She must be going to have tea, since the Coven was a tea shop. I thought, she wants to get out, that's what it is. It must be boring for her to be always indoors. That would be a real trial for someone who had always liked gaiety. I pictured her taking a cab to the tea shop, having tea and cakes . . . and then going home. It was just a little outing.

She was really very frail. Suppose I went to the Coven, just to see if she was all right. I might have a cup of tea with her. I would suggest that we make these little excursions now and then when she was feeling well enough. That would get her out of the house.

I came to the Coven. It was small. In the

window were homemade cakes and a sign which said "Lunches. Teas."

I looked through the window between the cakes and I saw her at once. She was not alone. There was a woman with her.

I stared—first at her and then at her companion. There was something familiar about the latter. Then she turned and I saw her face clearly.

It was Ellen Farley.

I could not take my eyes from her, and just at that moment Zillah turned her head and gazed towards the window. We were looking straight at each other.

Her eyes dilated slightly and I saw the colour rush into her cheeks.

I turned and walked away.

I went straight home and up to my room.

Zillah going out to meet Ellen Farley—the key witness who could not be found!

What did it mean? What could it mean?

I COULD NOT REST. I wanted to tell Ninian. I thought of the pains he had taken to find Ellen Farley without success. It would have meant so much if she could have told the court that she had asked me to buy arsenic. It would have explained that entry in the book which was so damning against me.

I could hear Ninian's voice: "If only we could find that woman!"

It so happened that he was working late that night on a specially demanding case. He had brought some books home with him on the previous night in the hope of finding a similar example which could be of use to him. It was a point of law which he wanted to verify.

I must tell him that I had seen her! Could I have been mistaken? It might have been someone who looked like her. I should have confronted them. Why had I been so foolish as to go away? I had been so shocked . . . so shaken . . . so bewildered.

But Zillah had seen me. She had looked horrified. It must have been Ellen Farley. But even now doubts kept coming into my mind. Could I trust myself?

I was in bed when Ninian came home. He looked very tired. He would be in court the next day. I thought, I will speak to him tomorrow evening . . . after I have seen Zillah.

The next morning I went to see Zillah. Mrs. Kirkwell met me in the hall.

"She's very bad," she said. "I've sent for the

doctor. He should be here at any minute. It was going out yesterday. She came back in a state."

"Was she alone?"

"Oh yes. The cabby knocked at the door and helped me in with her. He said he didn't think she was well. I got her to bed right away and said I'd get the doctor. But she said no, she'd be better in the morning."

"And she wasn't?"

Mrs. Kirkwell shook her head. "So I sent for him without asking her. I thought I'd better."

"I'm sure you're right. I'll go up and see her."

She was lying propped up with pillows and seemed to be finding difficulty in getting her breath.

"Hello, Davina," she said. "Can't talk very much. It's my breathing."

I went to the bed and sat close.

"Zillah," I said. "Tell me . . ."

She pointed to the table on which lay a large, rather bulky envelope.

"For you," she said. "There's another, too."

I saw that beside the large envelope was a smaller one. They both had my name on them.

"You . . . . can read them when I've gone."

"Gone? Gone where?"

She smiled at me. "The big one, I mean. The little one you can read when you get home."

"This is mysterious."

She lifted her hand in a feeble gesture. "You'll understand. You'll see . . ."

"Something's happened," I said. "You shouldn't have gone out yesterday."

"Had to," she said. "You saw . . ."

"Was it really? I couldn't believe it."

"You'll understand. I had to. You'll see."

I heard someone coming up the stairs. There was a tap on the door and Mrs. Kirkwell came in with the doctor.

"Ah, Mrs. Glentyre . . . . not so well today, I hear," he said.

Mrs. Kirkwell looked at me meaningfully. I was to leave, she was implying.

I went downstairs, wondering what had happened. I had not been mistaken. She had been with Ellen Farley. What could it mean?

I was clutching both envelopes. The large one and the small one. She had said she wanted me to open the small one when I arrived home. I went into the drawing room to wait for the doctor's visit to be over, and I opened the small envelope.

I read:

Dear Davina,

I have been thinking so much about you, particularly since you have come back. There is so much you ought to know and you shall. I have been on the point of confiding in you many times but I could not. I just hadn't the courage. But you shall know and it won't be long now.

I know I haven't much time left. The doctor has more or less told me so. I begged him to tell me the truth. I didn't want to be kept in the dark. There's no cure for what I have. It may be a day . . . a week . . . or a month. But it is not far-off. Who should know that better than I?

I want you to read what I have written. It's taken me a long time to get it all down. I did it some time ago as soon as I knew how ill I was. But I can't tell you yet. You'll have to wait. And when you do know, you'll understand.

I didn't think I was going to get so fond of you. I am so happy you married your Ninian. He's a good man and he truly loves you. He's proved his devotion and any woman would be grateful for that.

So be happy. There isn't going to be anything to stop you and Ninian and little Stephen having a wonderful life. That's what I want for you. But please . . . . please don't open the other until I am dead. I know you ought to, but I'm selfish . . . and I want you to wait.

One who loves you,

ZILLAH

I reread the letter. I had a burning desire to open the other, but I restrained myself.

I had not been able to ask her the question I had come to ask. Why had Ellen Farley been at the tea shop with Zillah? She had been upset when she received the letter which must have come from Ellen. She always went out when she received such notes. Why should she be seeing Ellen Farley?

The door opened and Mrs. Kirkwell came in with the doctor.

I stood up uncertainly. He was looking very grave.

"She's very ill," he said. "It's a turn for the worse, I fear. She's resting now. She'll rest all day. Her breathing's bad. I'll send a nurse tomorrow. She'll be all right today because she'll be sleeping most of the time. I think you should be prepared."

Mrs. Kirkwell said: "We've known, of course, doctor, that she was getting worse."

He nodded. "I'll look in tomorrow. Let her sleep. It's the best thing for her."

Mrs. Kirkwell took him to the door and when she came back she said: "It was silly of her to go out like that. If I've told her once I've told her twenty times."

"Well, there's no point in my staying, Mrs. Kirkwell. I'll just take a look at her before I go."

"Just peep in. Don't wake her."

I went up the stairs . . . very much aware of the envelope I carried. I looked in at her. She was still propped up by pillows. I supposed that made it easier for her to breathe. She was very still and her white hands lay inert on the bed coverlet.

She was in a deep sleep.

I was not able to talk to her again.

Three days later she died.

I was very sad indeed to realise I should never see her again . . . never be able to talk to her.

I had called at the house as I did every morning.

I had looked in on her on those occasions, but she was very tired and always half asleep.

I was not really surprised when I approached the house and saw that the blinds had been drawn at the windows.

It was a house of death.

I OPENED THE ENVELOPE and read:

My dear Davina,

I am going to tell you all that happened. I am going to, as they say, tell you the truth, the whole truth and nothing but the truth. And I am going to tell it my way, because it is important to me that you should understand how it all came about, and I hope you won't judge me too harshly.

I want you to imagine a girl who hadn't had very much. I won't go into details about my origins, but they were sordid. I was a sad bewildered child. I had my mother, it was true. I was an only child. My father seemed to be always drunk. I can hardly remember him anything else. Every penny he earned went into the local ginshop. It was a struggle. There was not always enough to eat. I was fourteen years old when my mother died. Then I ran away.

I won't bore you with all that happened but I did finally work in a rather sleazy boarding house near the Tottenham Court Road. All I had was my red hair and the sort of appearance that made people notice me. I had long before learned that this was something I could use to my advantage, and I did.

In the hotel I caught the attention of a minor theatrical agent and it was through him that I got one or two little parts. I wasn't much good. All I had was my looks.

All the little things that happened to me at that time don't really come into this, so I'll skip them. Finally I joined the Jolly Red Heads and we toured the music halls when we could get engagements.

And then we came to Edinburgh. That's where it all began. Men used to come to the theatre to look out for the girls. They'd be at the stage door. You know the sort of thing. And one night Hamish Vosper was there.

I know how you dislike him. You always did. But there was something about him which appealed to some women. He was arrogant and selfish, but he was virile . . . he was a man. He thought he was irresistible to women and somehow he made them feel he was—and for a time, I was one of those who did. He used to come to the theatre every night we were there and after the show we'd be together.

He told me about his employer—a gentleman who was strict and the glory-be-to-God type, but underneath all that he liked to indulge in a little fun now and then. Hamish said he had a hold over him because he'd discovered what he was up to. He had this invalid wife, said Hamish, and of course there had not been much between them for some years, which was more than the old fellow could take. So he had his little jaunts. He knew that Hamish knew and Hamish only had to give him what he called "the eye" and the old fellow would turn a blind one to whatever Hamish wanted to do.

It was an intriguing situation . . . . and one night Hamish brought me to the notice of your father.

He took me to supper and we liked each other from the start. He was a courtly gentleman and I hadn't seen many of that sort. And I can say he was very taken with me, which made me like him all the more. It wasn't long before we were going to hotels together. It was all very discreet because of his position. I thought it wouldn't last but he got more and more fond of me in a sentimental sort of way.

Hamish was tickled to death and he had an idea. "You ought to come to the house," he said. "I know . . . you could be a governess. There is a girl." That made me laugh. Me . . . a governess? Well, the Red Heads were on the way out. We had the occasional boo when we came on. We'd known for a long time that we simply weren't good enough for the West End. That was why we were touring the provinces. I thought it would be nice to have a comfortable home and not have to do all this travelling, so I said I was interested in this governessing business.

I swear I did not know how Hamish arranged it. I had no idea that there was already a governess and she had to be got rid of. I wouldn't have agreed to that . . . or I don't think I would. I want to be absolutely honest, you see. And I was rather desperate at that time.

Well, your Lilias went and Hamish suggested to your father that he brought me in. It shows how besotted your father was about me . . . for he agreed.

I took to you from the start. I knew, of course, I couldn't teach you anything. You were far better educated already than I ever could be, but I thought it was a bit of fun . . . and much better than doing the Jolly Red Heads to audiences who were growing more and more critical.

Then your father asked me to marry him. I couldn't believe my luck. I would leave the old life behind me. It was the chance of a lifetime. I could be comfortable for the rest of my days, the darling of a doting old man. It seemed too good to be true.

I was more contented than I ever hoped to be. I had forgotten Hamish. I would have a secure home and a promise of comfort for the rest of my life. I would be the mistress of the house. But Hamish was still the coachman.

He was dissatisfied. Whose idea had it been? And who was getting everything out of it while he was getting nothing? Then he had a plan. He wanted to marry me . . . and be master of the house. I was horrified at what this implied. I was fond of my new life, fond of my husband, fond of my new stepdaughter. I liked it all. But Hamish wouldn't have it. He had started it and he was going to see it carried through as he wanted it.

You can guess the rest. I was weak. Hamish still had some power over me. I knew what was

in his mind. I should have exposed him. I
should have confessed to my relationship with
him. Oh, there were lots of things I should have
done!

Davina, you don't know what the comfort of
that house meant to me . . . the easy way of
life and all that. No one could understand
unless they had been through what I had. I am
not making excuses. There are no excuses. It
just seemed that I had started on this and I had
no choice but to go on.

Hamish had planned it. We would get rid of
the old man. I would mourn for a year. Hamish
would comfort me. I would, after a respectable
period, marry him. I would, of course, have to
make sure that the old man's fortune was left to
me. We wouldn't want to stay in Edinburgh.
People would raise their eyebrows when the ex-
governess married the coachman. We'd sell the
house and go abroad. He had it all worked out.

Ellen Farley—that's not her real name, of
course—was a friend of Hamish. He
recommended her to your father and he
brought her into the house. He thought it
would be a good idea to have one of the
servants working with us.

Well, he bought the arsenic for the rats.
There were some near the mews so he made

sure others had seen them and it was the fact that they were there which gave him the idea to do it that way. Hamish said he knew something about arsenic. Hamish said he knew something about everything. His idea was to poison your father slowly. He thought through the port wine.

Then there was all that fuss about you and Jamie and the whole house knew that your father had threatened to disinherit you. We knew too that he had chosen Alastair McCrae for you. If you had married Alastair McCrae you wouldn't have come into Hamish's plan, but you didn't and Hamish wanted to have a way out, as he called it, if things shouldn't turn out as he planned. Just like Roger Lestrange, he thought it would be a good idea to have a scapegoat . . . . if anything should go wrong. I suppose these calculating murderers think alike. And like Roger Lestrange, he laid the snare to entrap you . . . . to have someone at hand in case he should need to shift the blame to someone else. He set you up to be that scapegoat because Fate had given him a reason —your father's objection to the young man you wanted to marry.

Hamish arranged for you to buy the poison. Ellen was to ask you to. Please believe me when

I say I did not know of this at the time. Hamish did not tell me. He thought me squeamish—soft and sentimental—and he knew I was getting fond of you. Do you remember the night I was late back? I was with Hamish. We went to a place outside Edinburgh. It's true we were lovers then. I know how dreadful it must sound . . . and it is no use my offering excuses because there really aren't any. Hamish was anxious not to be caught because that would have spoilt the whole plan . . . so we always went some little way out of the town.

Do you remember that inquisitive old woman who came to the house? It was when we were late back and made that excuse about the carriage breaking down. She was going to tell your father that she had seen the carriage outside that rather disreputable hotel. She had even waited and seen us come out together. She was going to tell your father. That was when Hamish decided it would have to be done that night.

Ellen took fright at her part in it and made her excuses to get away.

Then it happened. Your father died.

It hadn't worked out as Hamish planned. First I want to tell you that I did not know that Ellen had asked you to buy the arsenic.

Hamish had not told me that. I suppose I must not make excuses for myself. I was in the plot. I played my part in it. I am guilty of murder. But I would not have used you. And when you were on trial I suffered . . . I really did. You might ask why did I not then confess to everything? I hadn't the courage for that. I want to say that I was dominated by Hamish . . . but I am not sure of that either. I felt I was caught up in it and there was no way out for me but to do exactly what I did. You see, Hamish really thought we should get away with it. He did not plan that you should be accused. You were only there in case things turned against us. He didn't want to take chances. He really thought we'd get away with it. Your father had already had one or two attacks. The doctor had seen him and not suspected. At the back of Hamish's mind was the thought that he was so clever that everything must go as he had planned.

Well, you know what happened. You were arrested and charged with murder. It was terrible for you. But please believe me when I tell you it was terrible for me, too. I wanted to tell everything . . . confess. Hamish threatened me. He was in a rare panic. All his swagger deserted him then. We were all in a state of terror.

What hurt me most was what they were doing to you. I really thought your father's death would be accepted as natural. I couldn't sleep. I had to do something.

In the shed near the stables I found a little of the arsenic which Hamish had bought. Just a few grains still on the paper it had been wrapped in. Hamish hadn't bothered to get rid of it because he had a perfect alibi about the rats. I had this idea then. I knew arsenic had certain powers. I remembered a man I had known in my Jolly Red Heads days who had taken it. He had told me he took it to make him feel younger.

I took the paper. I put the grains into another piece and I said I had found it in the drawer and that your father had confessed to me that he had once taken arsenic acquired on the Continent.

I provided the doubt. I knew I should never have had another moment's peace as long as I lived if you had been condemned as a murderess.

When I heard that verdict I was furious. I had wanted you free of all doubt. I've wanted to make up to you ever since. I wanted to put it all behind us and start again. And those idiots had made it Not Proven.

But you were free. I could rejoice in that. I wanted you free but I did not realise that you would have to go through life under that shadow of doubt.

I was wicked. I agreed to the plan. It is no use my saying I was under Hamish's spell, that I suffered from an unhappy youth. I am guilty and I shall never forgive myself.

I don't enjoy what I have gained. There is not a great deal left of your father's fortune which seemed such riches to me in the beginning. Hamish had a large part of it . . . and kept wanting more. It set him up in the business which finally brought him to his end . . . I was blackmailed all the time. I would not marry him. I think he realised that that might have been dangerous. The murder of your father was Not Proven; there might be some who wanted to discover the truth. He ceased to press for that but he wanted the lion's share of the spoils.

Then there was Ellen. She used to come back regularly claiming her dues. Ellen is not a bad sort, though. She, too, has found life hard. She is planning to go abroad. I told her of that place which helped you and Lilias Milne. But she wanted a little behind her before she went. She made her regular demands and I think she may well be on her way to Australia or New Zealand. I think she learned a lesson. She was a frightened woman . . . always afraid that someone would find her. Hamish should never have brought her into it. She was almost as upset as I was every time she came to make her claim. She wasn't a *natural* criminal . . . no more than I think I am. Impulsive we both were . . . trying hard to get a place in the sun . . . not realising how much we should have to pay for it.

Well, Hamish will not be able to do more mischief . . . and I am on my way.

You will find enclosed an account of what happened. I do not want the sordid details of my life made public. That is for you alone. The letter enclosed you will give to your Ninian. He will know what to do with it. It is my confession. It explains everything that is necessary. It is all people need to know and you will be completely exonerated from all guilt. No more Not Proven.

God bless you, Davina. In spite of my wickedness I did love you. You became like a daughter to me. I love little Stephen and I want everything to be perfect for you. I want to rub out that stigma forever.

No one can say now that the case against you was Not Proven.

Be happy. You have a chance now.

Goodbye, Davina,

ZILLAH

I could scarcely read the note she had prepared because of the tears in my eyes.

And later I showed it to Ninian.

He read it through and when he lifted his face to mine I saw the joy there.

He stood up and took my hands in his. Then he held me tightly against him.

"She's right," he said. "We're free. It's over, Davina. I knew we were right to come back and face it. It happened here and here was the solution."

"It is strange," I said. "She did that . . . and I really loved her. She was truly . . . lovable . . . and yet . . . she could do that."

"Life is strange. People are strange. And she is right when she says we can be happy now. The case is proven, Davina, my dearest, proven without a doubt."

He was radiant with joy; I suppose we both

were. Life was good and seemed the brighter because of the darkness. I could now look ahead without fear. I had my husband; I had my child; and Zillah had cleared for me the way to contentment.

LP   Holt, Victoria
         Snare of serpents

4/19   LP